SHADOWED STARS

THE REIGN OF THE BLACK GUARD

Book 2 in the Shadowed Stars series

Steven Koutz

PAGE PUBLISHING, INC.
Conneaut Lake, PA

First originally published by Page Publishing 2021

ISBN 978-1-6624-1215-8 (pbk)
ISBN 978-1-6624-1216-5 (digital)

Printed in the United States of America

Previous books in the Shadowed Stars book series are:
SHADOWED STARS Book 1

Future books coming soon to the Shadowed Stars book series are:
SHADOWED STARS Book 3: The Children of Home
SHADOWED STARS Book 4: Remnants
SHADOWED STARS Book 5: Peril in Deep Space
SHADOWED STARS books 6–8 TBA

Shadowed Stars is a minimum 8 book series PLUS more unnumbered books
There will be continuous short stories and updates on the websites below:
Also check out shadowedstarsbooks.com
Facebook.com/shadowedstarsbooks
Shadowed Stars on Twitter @shadowedstarsbk
Shadowed Stars on Instagram as shadowedstarsbk

THANK YOU
My brother from other parents, Craig
My proofreader and sounding board for my ideas, Alyssa
Page Publishing
All my fans

Contents

About the Shadowed Stars Universe

SHADOWED STARS IS an epic tale of science fiction with a more mature flavor. It has been a concept for many years with its main objective and drive to contend with the already established franchises out there and always striving to be different and better. The universe of *Shadowed Stars* is ruthless and hostile to the extreme, with the likes of an intelligent carnivore race like the Derths and an oppressive and brutal regime like the Black Guard. Many other threats lurk around every shadowed star. It has its shiny spots of hope and humor. It has horror and romance. It will make you scream in anger and wail in tears. It is for mature readers as it hosts graphic language, sex, and violence. It has evolved with each book and each short story written. It has become its own entity.

So, what is different? What sets Shadowed Stars apart? Well for one thing I, Steven Koutz, have created and written everything myself. Images, miniatures, and videos I have had help with, but the designs, the character creations, cultures, worlds, tech, and overall look were all my original creations. I wanted to give it a dark tone as to match the feel for the reader of actually being in unknown and unexpected outer space. I want it to feel different and yet keep it fresh. I also structured it differently in how it is told as opposed to other sci-fi books and franchises. With the short stories, it does jump around a bit. I choose the short stories when I feel a character had more to offer but was just consumed to deeply in the story of the books. There are eight books planned. There will likely be more, but the eight books will be unique with their numbers. Books after that will be tales told of old favorites and still some new characters. The book numbers are also uniquely structured. Odd-numbered books will jump around in time frames and focus mainly on characters like Prince Slade, Eva Cusping, Princess Erikai, and more. Some may even be other generations, but all will string from what I call the Prince Slade line. The even-numbered books will not jump around in time frame. They will be based on characters like Josh Broody, Cody, Laylee Kalini, and Tana and other characters tied to them. I did this for the sole reason to avoid tire and strain on character and story. This way you, the reader, and yes, I, the writer, will not be always following the same characters around. It adds variety while also experiencing something different with each read and yet providing a desire to see favorite characters come around again.

Intro

THIS BOOK STARTS out just after the events in Chapter 30 of Book 1, where the hyperspace field access was just restored. Josh Broody has just lost his brother Jase and has been put on the run from the cruel and relentless Black Guard that is commanded by his former master, the evil Dark Lord, Epitaph. Josh and his ally, Cody of the Canian race, similar to that of wolfmen, must now flee his past as well as the present. His past mistakes will haunt him just as relentlessly as that of his former master. Josh is tied to a prophecy that will bring down Epitaph and his reign of terror wielded by control of the Black Guard a military force unmatched throughout the universe.

As the dark lord Epitaph pursues Josh and tries to crush the prophecy of his undoing, the ever unpredictable and legendary Gold Gatling, who started as an agent for hire, becomes more of a wild card in the grand plan. Gold Gatling's own agenda will come into conflict with the plans made by many sides as Gold begins a path of redemption he had not even realized he had begun.

A small rebel movement grows into a full rebellion and gains the attention of the Luth Bik-led resistance. As the rebellion grows stronger, revenge and agendas to assume greater power spread across the inner workings of the Black Guard and threaten its very structure. Those filled with revenge and fear of prophecies are blind to the unraveling of structure around them.

Some remembrance of past bad deeds can always cloud the trust needed for survival, but finding a way to trust again may be the best chance for survival. Josh and his Canian friend, Cody, are chased from system to system. Dealing with Josh's past betrayal is hard enough without the traps, love triangles, bounty hunters, and old enemies that are encountered at every turn, and then what do you do when even new allies don't trust each other? It is all a fragile piece of existence in a universe filled with war.

Chapter One

Reflection

As the small freighter spacecraft pulled away from the planet Talleep and into orbit, Josh Broody could not stop replaying the horror of the bearded human assassin sent by Lord Epitaph as he ripped the head clean off Josh's brother, Jase, with his bare hands. Josh had sat huddled over the pilot seat. He ran his hand through his shoulder-length brown hair to clear it from his face. He had a rugged-looking face but was yet quite handsome. He had the look that he had seen a lot of life and had lived through his own share of dangers. He was a young adult man and wore a sleeveless dark-blue vest left open to reveal the tight-fitting black shirt that accented his muscular, toned chest and arms.

The ship was called the *Fallen Star*, and it was a fast ship despite her appearance. It was short in length but tall enough to support a large cargo hold. Two side mounted engines were its source of propulsion with one mounted to each side. The cockpit rested at the top and halfway back, giving it a short-hooded nose formation beneath it. She was bulky-looking because of heavy modified armaments. The weaponry was a mixture of small and older blasters at the forward mount. Two newer and stronger medium pulsar cannons with one on the forward port and the other on the forward starboard side rounded off the frontal gun support. The rear of the freighter ship hosted only one heavier weapon. It was a neutronic phaser, designed to fire a tech or EMP (electromagnetic pulse) wave and shut down pursuing vessels. The rear of the *Fallen Star* was also protected by enhanced shielding. In short, the starship was a combination of older and newer technology with the older technology as its base and main source and the newer technology more of patchwork replacements for what was no longer available tech or just extra support.

There was a Canian in the copilot chair, an alien race that greatly resembled an upright wolfman type look from Earth myth and complete with coarse and shaggy brown fur over his body and bushy tail. He had stiffened ears, brown eyes, and a snout nose formation. His mouth was lined with sharp teeth. He was called Cody. With a gruff and growling tone of common human language, he called out for Josh to concentrate on the matter at hand, which was not his dead brother, but rather at dodging the warships in orbit and closing in on their position. The Black Guard warships were preparing to launch starfighters.

Josh was able to regain his composure and take control of the *Fallen Star* once again with the use of his implanted neural link to the ship's core computer controls. Although the *Fallen Star* appeared as a bulky freighter, it had surprisingly and exceptional agility of movement thanks to many of the special modifications and the neural link. Basically, if Josh could think it, the ship could do it. The *Fallen Star* took a sharp upward angle and an even sharper and swifter turn over the top of the Derth humpback warship and under a Black Guard class two warship. Its flight path surged upward from behind and between two other Black Guard warships. As it shot out from them, it was maneuvering in a corkscrew movement with both of its frontal guns firing and blasting a way through the swarm of Black Guard starfighters called schisms that had launched just ahead of it. The Black Guard starfighters were sleek and triangular. They hosted a tight wing to hull fit on each side that stretched backward to a point. They were armed with medium enhanced lasers. The ships were small with tight quarter cockpits for the single pilots inside.

The *Fallen Star* barreled out from the swarm and steadied its corkscrew flight pattern. The Black Guard schisms had begun pursuit with full laser fire hitting against the rear-enhanced shielding of the *Fallen Star*. Inside the cockpit, Cody manned the sensor station and reported that shields were holding at 95 percent. Cody was suddenly shaken in his seat as the ship took another sharper turn. Cody clutched tightly on to his console and reviewed the screen. He looked back at Josh and asked if he was aware of the Black Guard warship that they were approaching on. Josh was seated in his pilot seat with no need of controls while his neural link was active and replied that he was very aware. The *Fallen Star* took a sharp turn again and was flying alongside the larger warship, now dodging its heavy gunfire in addition to the starfighter lasers pursuing it. Josh then swooped the *Fallen Star* down and around the underside of the warship. He opened fire at several critical systems and moved away from each explosion just behind the *Fallen Star* that caught the pursuing schisms. Josh moved with a straight shot now further away from the warship. The Black Guard schisms had split their swarm and the others were coming around the other side of the warship. With Josh's mental command of sharp movement, they had adjusted their flight and, as a result, nearly collided with the schisms that had survived the underside attack and were still in pursuit. The other warship that the *Fallen Star* now approached had charged up its heavy gun ports. Josh was able to maneuver and avoid the cannons and each miss to the *Fallen Star* was a heavy impact hit on the other warship behind it. The two commanders of both warships were calling for a ceasefire.

The *Fallen Star* jetted away with escape as a plan. Cody announced that the class two warship was maneuvering for an interception, while the Derth humpback warship was holding position. A Black Guard class two warship was the same build and weaponry as the others, but class two represented that a fright agent was in command. Fright agents were the only members of the Black Guard besides Epitaph that were not human. This particular class two warship was called the *Ripper*, and it was commanded by Fright Agent Maddo, a member of the Teon race. The Teons were a rare alien race to this area of space. They were rumored to have come from within

Derth-controlled space. They appeared muscular, but it was more of their armor design. Their hands were of bone and resembled a human skeletal hand. Their heads resembled a human skull.

Aboard the *Ripper*, Fright Agent Maddo was observing the battle from the command deck. He looked to the Black Guard captain and asked for confirmation of the ship they were about to intercept. The Black Guard captain was donned in the same black body armor with blue highlights on the leggings and gloves as the soldiers. He also possessed the holstered heavy blaster on one hip and the small black axe on the other. The standard-issue black axe had a fireman's style head blade, and the handle was a non-heating metal alloy. It was an excellent and reputable melee weapon of the Black Guard, as were the black whips fastened to the right or left legs. In short, the Black Guard captain gear was the same as the soldiers, except for the officers wore no helmets and wore neck collars posting a design insignia system as marking of their ranks. The captain replied that the ship was, in fact, the *Fallen Star*. The ship was not important; it was its owner and pilot that the Black Guard wanted. Fright Agent Maddo was informed that the ship had moved into range, and he ordered a tractor beam employed.

A shot fired from the rear-mounted neutronic phaser of the *Fallen Star* hit with an EMP pulse beam that began to shut down all systems of the warship in sequential order. The *Ripper* was powering down and broke pursuit. On the command deck, Fright Agent Maddo was screaming out for an explanation of the event. The captain checked the scanners just before they shut down and stated that there was no answer for the apparent breach in their security codes, not realizing that the *Fallen Star* had possessed an EMP weapon. Fright Agent Maddo screamed out in angered disgust as to how that happened. The Black Guard captain was without an answer. Fright Agent Maddo swiftly raised his arm and, from his armor, protruded a snap blade that punctured directly into the captain's forehead. As Fright Agent Maddo retracted the rapier-style snap blade, the captain's lifeless corpse fell before the fright agent's feet.

With the command warship darkening its lights and power, it would be defenseless, and no Black Guard warship or starfighter would dare leave a fright agent in that state. Cody kept an eye on the Derth humpback-shaped warship that was seemingly uninterested in their escape. Using the neural link, Josh was able to plot an escape course. The Black Guard warships had enough concerns and did not even attempt a pursuit. The *Fallen Star* opened a hyperspace portal from the newly reactivated hyperspace and vanished through it.

The *Fallen Star* had put some great distance between it and the planet Talleep. Talleep may have been an out-of-the-way world in Black Guard-controlled space, but the incident of their escape and assault of a class two warship would not remain isolated. Assistance was probably already on the way. The newfound and very strange alliance with the Derths was also worrisome. The Derths were a savage yet intelligent carnivore race, and their very existence was a threat that propelled the Dark Lord Epitaph and the Black Guard to power. Josh knew they had to find some area of space to hide in and devise a new plan. His brother and the android Adrienne were now gone. What was once a crew of four was now merely a crew of two. Josh used his neural link to the *Fallen Star's* sensors and scanned for any sort of concealment or unlikely place of landing. Two Derth humpbacks were slowly approaching the sector. They were named after their humped hull design. Josh had found an area of space that would hide them from sight and scans. It was called the Collollis Comet Field. Cody's ears perked up to a stiff and alert position. Cody turned to make direct eye contact with Josh. In his gruff tone of common human speak, he asked if Josh's neural link had fried his brain. Cody pointed out the danger of radiation from the streaking comets and also the very real danger of collision. The Collollis Comet Field was a strange area of space where many comets seemed to become trapped as they passed through. The region was large and at least as many as sixty-four different comets had been studied there. The comets seemed in this area to stream wildly across the region. It was unexplainable that the comets would move past each other as if aware of the others. Only few reports of comets colliding and merging with other comets had been cited. However, many ships entering the area had been struck repeatedly by these rogue comets. Those that had survived the impacts were still affected by the radiation that a majority of the comets possessed. The area had been, long ago, as a result of such incidents, declared off limits to space travel.

That fact alone was why Josh wanted to hide there. The remoteness and banishment of the area as well as its radiation dangers would keep others away. The radiation that the comets did possess also severely hampered any intense and deep scans of the area. Before Cody could further object, Josh had already set course.

Another sixty moks (an equivalent of Earth minutes) had passed, and the *Fallen Star* had only detected small and far away Black Guard flight paths. It had now entered a region of space marked with a warning beacon of the rogue comets in the area. The initial entrance into the area caused minor turbulence. It was a vibration from the approaching comet that appeared from out of nowhere on sensors. They had been buzzed by a small racing comet. It brushed by the starboard side of the ship and scraped the shielding. The *Fallen Star* had shaken slightly and was nudged just off its course by the minor impact. Cody reported no radiation from that comet but had spiked levels from two sources ahead. Another comet streaked overhead of the *Fallen Star* and had been undetected by the sensors. It was very apparent that stopping and hiding in this area of space was not an option. Josh used his neural link to plot the fastest course through the comet field. The *Fallen Star* had a bit of a jump motion as standard base speed was increased to a six. It was too dangerous to run through this moving obstacle course with any higher speed, and also because of that, autopilot would not be a luxury.

The *Fallen Star* had shortly come up on three comets almost racing side by side. They were the largest measured comets on record. Josh had taken the *Fallen Star* above them and was following at a safe distance from very high radiation levels. As a precaution to the radiation, Cody had increased shielding and all special radiation buffer pads aligned inside the shielding. Josh had followed the three large comets and was impressed at such a sight that few people would experience. The plotted course had now required a starboard turn in flight, and Josh, still with the aid of his neural link, had made the adjustments. Fifteen moks into their adjusted course had placed the *Fallen Star* into an oncoming rain of comets. The sensors had detected it well in advance, but the area of this event was massive, and to attempt to move around it would take an estimated two rotations. The radiation in the area and two more approaching comets on collision course with the *Fallen Star* was a definite answer to the problem. They would have to go through the rain of comets. The comets were coming both from upper and lower directions, so it would be a greater chance of impact. Cody had identified a path with smaller comets and a little less intensity in the raining motion. He had then maximized shields and radiation buffer pads to the highest levels as Josh took the *Fallen Star* into the obstruction.

The rainstorm of comets was more like a hailstorm once the ship had engaged the phenomena. The *Fallen Star* was hit rapidly and by several of the smaller comets. As the course continued, the comets that were impacting the ship were actually getting larger, and as they did, the impact was also harder. All interior lighting, except control panels had shut down as Cody diverted all power except for speed and life support to the shields that were beginning to stress. He was able to keep shielding at 70 percent but warned Josh that it would not last much longer. With his neural link, Josh scanned ahead as far as he could. He stated that they had about forty moks until they would be able to clear the comet hailstorm. Cody replied, "That's twenty moks more than we got!" The reply was an even gruffer tone of common with an added growl from his Canian language of growls, barks, and snarls. The *Fallen Star* suddenly and with a large jerking motion shifted in a ninety-degree port side movement from its course. Cody screamed out with another angered growl before asking Josh what he was doing.

Josh replied, "Getting your mangy hide the twenty moks."

The hail of comets increased with impact and intensity as the *Fallen Star* continued its new course. Shields were falling faster, and the radiation buffer pads within the shielding were dispersing. The communication was more heated now. Through several Canian growls and barks, Josh was able to make out something about twenty moks and something about a bite and a private part of Josh's anatomy.

Josh replied, "Do you want to die in here, or do you want your twenty moks of safety?"

As another larger comet hit with great impact, the *Fallen Star* was grafted into the comet's tail. All alarms in the ship were sounding off. Cody screamed out, "You and [*bark*] have a [*bark*] different concept of [*bark bark*] safety!"

An increase to the maximum basic speed of twelve had kicked in without warning along with ship thrusters. Cody asked, "I thought max speed was too dangerous?" As the question was asked, the *Fallen Star* had broken from the comet's tail. Another smaller comet streaked just under the ship with two more comets impacting the port side. Through his neural link, Josh was initiating force fields over ruptured areas where shielding had failed.

Josh replied to Cody's question, "Yep! Too dangerous!" They each reminded the other that if they were to survive this, they would kill each other.

Cody cut life support to produce extra power to the remaining shattered shielding. He then stated that they had ten moks of life support left before they would suffocate in space. Josh replied that it was more than the five moks they had before impact. Josh was trying desperately to maneuver away from another oncoming comet, but even with the neural link, controls were sluggish and they were not going to avoid the trajectory.

The impact of the oncoming comet was near catastrophic if it would not have been for Josh's piloting skills to move the *Fallen Star* forward along with the direction of the comet's forward movement. The maneuver bought the vital secs, the equivalent of Earth seconds, needed to adjust the ship to be struck on the rear starboard side with the strongest shielding. The *Fallen Star* was carried with the head of the comet, and as it was, it slowly shifted away to the side. The *Fallen Star* was now being dragged by the comet, and Josh used that momentum to his advantage. He was able to turn the ship with the aft arc against the comet as it slid further along the comet's side. Once hitting the tail of the comet, Josh pulled back and engaged all remaining thrusters. The *Fallen Star* was sent into a fast and uncontrolled spin that had two smaller comets pass by each side of the ship with minimum impact as the scraping motion also pushed the ship further away and out of the comet field.

The *Fallen Star* glided away from the comet field with all power cut. Speed was inoperative, and as a result, the ship was now adrift. Cody immediately went into repair mode to bring at least life support back up to minimal acceptance levels. Cody estimated that he could have minimal propulsion and basic speed of one maybe two in about twelve aras, the equivalent of Earth hours. Josh suggested half that time as he would do half the work.

Once the repairs that could be made had been completed, a basic speed of two had been obtained until they could get access to further repair facilities. Shielding was minimal, so they would have to avoid anything stressful to allow for some regeneration of shield strength. It would also still require more major repair. Josh was able to ascertain their location and to obtain a mostly isolated space path. By avoiding the sparsely placed planets in that path, they would likely avoid any pirate activity. The Black Guard did not worry too much of this area of space. The autopilot was again an accessible option as they would require rest on their destination. Josh set all the alarm systems and plotted a course to Xotosia. It was more of a rogue world with its own law, if you could call it law. Its capital city was run more by outlaws than the token law enforcement. Nonetheless, with their hyperdrive disabled and with what power supply they had left from the Janan crystals, it was a reachable destination in eight rotations (the equivalent of Earth days) time. The autopilot was engaged, and the *Fallen Star* was off on her next journey.

Josh had sat back in a relaxed state as he began to reflect on his past...

* * *

Josh Broody stood over a broken human male. Josh was in full Black Guard officer armor as he looked down at his brother Jase, who had been beaten to near death and his blood still fresh on Josh's clenched fists. Jase had looked up toward his younger brother and pleaded with him to turn away from the Black Guard and return home with him. Jase's plea was intensified with the blood dripping from his face, and under that red mask was the deep scar that ran down the side of and hooked under the left eye. It was the scar that Josh had given him long ago. Josh took his time to reply and answered that he had no home. Jase struggled to get to his knees but was kicked back down by his brother. Jase begged for his brother to remember the good deep inside himself that the dark lord had buried.

It was just then that a second sound came from Josh's wrist comm. It was the lisping voice of the Dark Lord Epitaph. He had asked Josh if the threat had been eliminated. Josh fought the strange pull at his very soul. He hesitantly held his response as he fought with his conscience. He then increased the setting on his heavy blaster and opened his comm. With no wasted movement, he turned and shot the Black Guard soldier at his side. Josh fired off two more energy bolts into the wall behind him. He then acknowledged that he had killed the intruder personally.

Epitaph's lisping voice over the wrist comm sounded pleased. He commended Josh on his loyalty. He then summoned Josh back to the throne room. Josh closed the comm and lowered his hand to aid his older brother, Jase, back to his feet. Jase staggered in his stance and again pleaded with Josh to come with him. Josh claimed that too much had happened and that his place was here. He then by the turn of a metal bar on the wall accessed a secret passage for Jase to utilize as an escape from the palace. Jase hesitated to leave his brother behind. Josh repeated that he would not be welcome for all he had done and that he could not go with him. He then shoved Jase into the secret passage and sealed the wall up again. Josh moved to the door of the room to meet the sound of approaching guards. Josh looked back only once before ordering the guards to follow him. They then strode down the wide hall passage with Josh in the lead.

It was a few rotations later that Josh Broody had stepped off a landed Black Guard shuttle with a contingent of Black Guard soldiers. It was a commerce planet consumed by an immense fog. The Black Guard soldiers were in full black and dark-blue-colored armor. They were fully armed with heavy blaster pistols on one side of their holster and the black fireman style axe at the other side. The feared Black Guard whip was also secured to one leg of each soldier. The tinted blue face shields of the black helmets worn by the soldiers aided in their intimidation factor by removing any facial features. Josh led his Black Guard soldiers to the merchant community that consisted of many small merchant stands. The entire merchant area was built tightly together and around the edge of a swamp. Josh ordered the Black Guard soldiers to fan out in their search. He took four soldiers with him, and they strode ahead to a single merchant stand that was selling pottery and containers as well as rare paper tablets and paintings. Josh called out for the attending merchant to surrender the Book of Prophecy. Most traders knew of the Books of Prophecy but did not believe them to be real. There were several fake copies out there for those that did believe in mythical relics, but a genuine one was almost laughable. One such trader at this merchant stand was a Gadgion.

Gadgions were sentient gaseous lifeforms. From the waist down, they were completely gaseous, and they rested in a bowl-shaped base that utilized repulsor lifts to move around. The gaseous bottoms swirled around in these large bowls with an energy containment field to prevent escape. From the waist up, the Gadgion was encased in what appeared to be a bronze-like colored armor up to the neck with humanoid shaped torso and arms. At the end of each arm were three movable prongs that were used as fingers for grabbing and holding objects. Above the neck level, the Gadgion was encased in what appeared as a cheap form of plastic and formed to resemble a human style face. The mouth, eyes, and the top of the head were open and allowed for expired gaseous material to vent out from and dissipate as the Gadgion moved about. The gaseous form seemed to regenerate any lost gasses, and the gaseous leak from the cheap plastic facial features gave off an eerie appearance.

This particular Gadgion claimed through external speakers to possess a single and genuine Book of Prophecy. The Gadgion brought it out to display openly but also held it back at a distance away from Josh and his Black Guard soldiers. Josh focused intently at the book. It appeared genuine. It was thick and bound with rigid design patterns on tight leather covering. The edges of the pages appeared tattered, and there was even a latching clasp with the prophet insignia of an eye inside three spiral circular formations. Josh ordered the merchant to open the book. The Gadgion seemed hesitant and backed further into its merchant stand. The Gadgion claimed that only the prophets and the chosen were able to open the book. Josh sneered and released a small chuckle as he raised his Black Guard heavy blaster with great quickness and aimed directly at the Gadgion's fake plastic constructed face. The cheap plastic material of the construction was an emotionless shell with the gasses venting from its mouth, eyes, and top of its head. The image was unnerving to an untrained being. The Gadgion remained unwavering directly at the barrel of Josh's heavy blaster in yet another attempt to shake its assaulter, but Josh Broody was not the being to be easily shaken.

Another voice from behind Josh and his Black Guard soldiers broke the tension. Josh turned to see who dared interfere with Black Guard activity. He saw his older brother Jase with a small blaster rifle. Jase stood defiantly with a tight muscular body structure of his own. A thick but short-trimmed beard and mustache helped bring out the piercing and determined stare from his brown eyes. At each side of Jase stood equally armed human rebels in tattered clothes. Jase ordered Josh and his soldiers to stand down. He placed great firmness and determination in his voice. Josh waved his soldiers back and motioned for Jase to step forward. Jase moved forward with extreme caution, never dropping his guard or his blaster rifle. The two brothers now stood again face to face but this time at an equal stance. Josh watched as Jase changed his grip on the small blaster rifle to one hand and with the other; he reached out for the thick Book of Prophecy. The Gadgion requested twenty thousand drekings, which was Black Guard-controlled space currency. With a flick of his outstretched wrist, a large and thick round gold-like coin piece shot to the merchant's table from inside Jase's cloth sleeve. The Gadgion merchant retrieved the coin with his three prong fingers and examined the coin carefully. He was very surprised that it was a zyna. It was the currency of the Zae. It was rare because the race was thought to be extinct and little remnants of their civilization were thought yet to exist. The minerals that the coin was made from were just as rare. It was rare but genuine, and its rarity made it extremely valuable. The Gadgion accepted the payment and placed the Book of Prophecy into Jase's open palm. Josh spoke up and claimed that the book was a fake. Jase held his locked stare. He lowered his arm with a tight clutch on the book and stepped even closer to Josh. Jase strongly believed that it was real and he could not let Epitaph obtain it.

Josh scoffed and stated, "That would be Dark Lord Epitaph to you, Jase! Show the proper respect!"

Just then, the *Fallen Star* streaked in and above them with all guns armed and aimed at Jase and the two human rebels. Josh then outstretched his open palm and, with more of a demand than a request, asked for the book. Jase backed up slowly, and it appeared as though he was going to toss the book. He then spoke out that Epitaph was only using Josh and that when he was through with him, he would be discarded as easily as Epitaph's last general. From behind Josh and his soldiers rolled a small sphere. As it rolled to a stop between all of them, it sounded one short high-pitched beep and exploded. Just before the explosion, Jase had made a sudden turn and leap from the area. The explosion was a stun grenade and knocked Josh, the Black Guard soldiers, and even Jase's own rebel allies unconscious. From outside the blast radius stepped a tall and curvaceous woman. She was donned in skintight black leather with red accents at the cuffs above her boots and around her plunging neckline, which revealed a fair amount of cleavage. She was extremely beautiful with full red lips and deep blue eyes. Her long black hair was tied back in a braided tail, and she had two small curls at her forehead. She spoke to Jase in a stiff tone of voice and asked if Jase was all right. He addressed her as Adrienne and said they needed to leave now. He pointed out the other Black Guard soldiers that had fanned throughout the trading area earlier and were now rushing this way. Adrienne picked up and flung the fallen rebels over each of her shoulders without even a strain.

Jase placed the Book of Prophecy into his satchel as Josh was beginning to stir and crawl from the blast zone. Jase watched as Adrienne retreated while carrying their two rebel allies. Jase then bent over and picked his brother up with one arm under each shoulder. Josh was still groggy and unsure of his surroundings. Jase assisted with the strength of his own legs. Adrienne looked back and said that they did not have time. Jase yelled back that Josh was coming with them and asked if she had gotten control of the *Fallen Star* away from Josh's neural link. As the other Black Guard soldiers closed in on them, the *Fallen Star* turned and opened fire on the Black Guard soldiers with a heavy and rapid blaster barrage. Adrienne asked if the severed neural link was satisfactory. Jase observed all the downed soldiers and replied, "Perfect!" The ship then again turned, lowered into a hover mode, and extended a ramp to its open hatchway. Adrienne had already jumped onto the ramp and put the unconscious rebels inside. She had come back to pull Josh up and onto the ramp. Jase then pulled himself up the rest of the way. Once they were all inside, the ramp retracted, and the hatch door sealed. The *Fallen Star* turned with a quick motion spin and darted away further into the dense fog cover of the planet.

* * *

Josh had awoken in a small room on a sleeping rack. After a brief recollection he had realized that he was aboard the *Fallen Star*. He exited the room and walked past many human rebels that greeted him with scowls of hatred. Josh began to run through his ship and attempted to access his neural link to the ship but was unable to do so. He made his way into the cockpit and saw the woman that he also knew as Adrienne in the pilot chair. She was flying the ship mentally without the use of the controls. The copilot chair swung around, and in it was Jase with the Book of Prophecy in his hands. He asked Josh to be seated in the chair behind him. Josh was finally able to pull his eyes from the stare on Adrienne and asked Jase, "So the android has bypassed my neural link and taken control over my ship?" Jase ignored the question and straight out again told Josh to be seated. Jase continued and stated that they were going to the vault and that Josh would be guiding them there and inside. The vault was where the Dark Lord Epitaph kept all of his Books of Prophecy, and Josh claimed there was no way he was going to help them as his look of disdain toward Jase grew more intense. Jase stated that the Books of Prophecy had declared that the Dark Lord Epitaph and his dark army would be stopped by the two brothers, and that was why Epitaph had corrupted Josh and ordered him to kill his own brother. Josh remained silent. Jase claimed that he could feel that Josh wanted to rebel against Epitaph. He argued with a question put toward Josh if it had not been enough that Epitaph had torn him from his family and turned his soul dark by making Josh kill his own wife, Emelia. Jase then shocked him by asking what he could do to prove to Josh that Emelia was actually still alive. Josh became angered by the attempt to use his one love against him. He lunged forward but was stopped by surprise as the Book of Prophecy produced a glow when Jase opened it. Only the prophets and the chosen could open the books from the protection of the magic seal that the prophets themselves applied. Josh had seen Epitaph open several, but he was chosen by prophecy. Jase again pointed out that the two brothers would overthrow Epitaph and the fact that he could open a Book of Prophecy was his proof. Jase closed the book again and presented it to Josh. Josh said it was impossible. Jase countered with the challenge for Josh to open it to page number 152. The Book of Prophecy glowed again as Josh opened it still shocked that he was able to do so. He proceeded to read the passage that told of how the dark lord, with his fully turned servant torn from the binds that blood holds, would slay his own wife for the dark lord's needs. The passage continued to state that the dark lord would secretly bring back that servant's love and make her his own.

* * *

The *Fallen Star* approached a planet that Josh recognized as Shalragra. The planet was the homeworld of the Canians. Josh seemed uneasy as he asked what they were doing here. Jase replied that they would need the help of one of Josh's old friends. The *Fallen Star* descended into the atmosphere and engaged on a flight path to a docking bay facility. She slowed her approach and aided her landing with repulsor lifts and three landing legs. Once landed and powered down, the boarding ramp was lowered. Adrienne walked down the ramp first and paused. Josh and Jase followed down the ramp as brothers walking side by side. Adrienne announced that she had terminated her control of the *Fallen Star* and that Josh could reconnect to it with his neural link. The rest of the human rebel soldiers disembarked as well and made their way to another landing craft.

Jase turned to Josh and said, "You can take your ship and return to your master, or you can come with us and together we will reveal your master's betrayal to you, and together we will bring Epitaph down with the Black Guard crumbling all around him." Josh paused and agreed to go with them. He secretly initiated a concealed transmitter in his armor complete with tracking beacon.

* * *

Not even a full rotation had passed when the three were trying to purchase shelter and gather information on a Canian named Cody. Josh and Jase had suddenly gotten jumped from behind by two Canians. Adrienne had made a move to aid her two friends but was hit by an energy wave that was similar to an EMP blast and had caused her android body to shut down. She struggled against it with her survival instincts programming but ended up collapsing to the ground. Jase was already unconscious, but Josh was still fighting two Canians as he watched Adrienne fall. He was then hit from behind with a baton by another Canian, presumably the one that had shot Adrienne.

Josh had awoken to find Jase sedated in a cell next to his own. Josh called out for Jase and received no response. He then heard a gruff, snarling voice that he seemed to recognize before he had turned to see the Canian that he knew as Cody standing outside the cell and smiling at him with a sneer that revealed his sharp teeth more in a gruesome payback way than a pleased-to-see-him way. Cody barked out right and followed with a growl before he asked in his gruff voice in common human speak what they were doing here. Josh claimed that Jase had thought for some reason that Cody could help them overthrow Epitaph from power. Cody howled loudly and, kind of laughing, asked why Josh would even allow that to happen. Josh laughed back and remarked that his brother was a fool desperate to save him. Josh then declared that he was loyal to Epitaph and ordered Cody to release them. Josh then offered Cody a chance to surrender and he would show mercy on him. Cody mentioned that he never recalled any form of mercy from Josh. Cody did, though, recognize the confidence in Josh's voice and was very happy to crush it. Cody pulled out from his supply belt the beacon transmitter that Josh had used earlier. Josh searched his armor and looked back at Cody. Cody had asked Josh if he had really thought that enough time had passed that he would forget all of Josh's tricks. Cody then dropped the beacon transmitter and stepped heavily on it. The transmitter shattered under Cody's bare and clawed foot. Cody harshly stressed his words as he declared that the Black Guard would not be coming for him and that he had no intention to return as Josh's slave. Jase had then started to stir in his cell as Cody left them alone.

Josh now remembered the conversation with his older brother. Jase had expressed his love for him and the shame and loss that he had felt when Josh had decided to join the Black Guard after it had butchered their family under Epitaph's direct orders.

It was the holographic projection of Epitaph from a device on Josh's belt that broke the peaceful and turning moment. He was of a thin and wiry build with basic humanoid form. He wore a variation of the Black Guard armor. It was all black, and he accented it with a dark blue belt line that ran along both sides of his waist but stopped at the front and the back sides to allow the black color free flow. Across his chest area stretched a dark-blue sash. His black cape collar had a stiffened collar up the back of his head and wrapped around to the edges of his face. His arms were exposed from the elbows down, and they were layered in hard green scales, and his hands were much the same but were adorned with three-inch-long and sharp, dagger-like nails. His head and face were of hard green scales as well. His lisping voice was hosted by a long red-forked tongue that flicked from his mouth, much like a snake on Earth. He also seemed to have sharp teeth and digestive glands that throbbed from his neck as he swallowed a small pig-like animal whole. His ears were short and pointed, and his eyes were a shade of dark red. His forehead was ruffled with evenly spaced ridges, and from the center of his head rested a long, straight, and gray unicorn-style horn.

Epitaph stated to Josh that he was coming to save him. Jase had begged Josh to ask him. When Josh refused, Jase turned to the holographic projection and asked Epitaph if Josh's wife was still alive. Josh ordered Jase to be silent. He was filled with shock though when Epitaph's projection replied that Emelia was still alive and that she was now his bride.

Just then a barrage of energy hit the compound heavily. The building had started to collapse down around them. Josh had screamed out for Epitaph to save him. Epitaph's projection displayed a sinister grin. Epitaph claimed he would save him by ending his own miserable existence and by eliminating both brothers he would secure the failure of the prophecy. He admitted it was a mistake to turn one brother on the other. Epitaph then promised Josh that Emelia would continue to be well cared for as his property. The projection then terminated as the building collapsed further and caved in on the two brothers in separate cells.

Josh's last memories were of Cody hollering at him in a rage and pulling him free from the rubble grave. Josh now awoke to Cody's face as he was pulling Josh from the rubble, but Cody was actually waking Josh up. Josh faded from his dream state to the current situation where Cody had awoken him in the pilot chair of the *Fallen Star*. Cody stated that he had managed a transmission to Xotosia.

Chapter Two

Vengeance Felt Hard

IN THE PALACE of the dark lord, Epitaph had entered the throne room. The palace throne room was lined with tall gray walls all around. The floor was a solid dark gray and brown marble-looking material. There were six statues in the room with three on each side and lining a path to the throne. The statues were forty feet tall like the walls and stood as tall as the high ceiling. Each statue resembled Epitaph in a battle-formed stance. Once he had passed the statues, the throne was on a raised platform. The platform and the single path of ten steps up to the throne were all made of a dark brown woodlike material. Epitaph turned and was seated in the wide-based throne that hosted a back and sides that were at least six feet taller than Epitaph at a seated position. The throne seemed to wrap around the sides and over his head like a large hood with all edges coming to three separate points that almost resembled fangs.

A bipedal robot walked forward to the throne with a Black Guard soldier at each side of it. The robot resembled humanoid form with the two legs and arms. It had no metal covering over its dull gray metal frame, and the only features on its metallic face were that of black lenses used for its vision and the speaker where a mouth would be at. It was a ZX3 model, often referred to as Brainerds because of the exposed view at the top of the robot's head of working gears and circuits. The robot seemed to assume a slight cowered stance before Epitaph with grave news that the human mixed with Ubide DNA called Cage, his ship the *Claw*, and the Black Guard fleet assigned to it were all lost in battle along with the acquired Derth ships and forces. The news sent Epitaph into a rage. He rose from his throne and rapidly descended down the stairs, where he attacked the bipedal robot and tore it to pieces with his bare hands.

Epitaph then strode angrily down the hall and out of the throne room. The corridors of the palace were also about forty feet tall, and each hallway passage was twisted in its path. Epitaph walked by many Black Guard soldiers that moved to guard him, but he dismissed them all with a wave of his hand. He turned into a dark room, and at the end of the room was a dark red wall with a human skull mounted alone at the center of the wall. Epitaph walked up to the skull and clasped it with both of his scaled hands. He turned the skull upside down, and the wall that it was on rose upward and revealed another room that lit up with a low glowing red light. Epitaph walked into the room with many trophies lined along the side walls. There were jeweled crowns, a bed of mummified corpses, severed and mounted heads of many different species and races, various cultural weapons gathered from the races, and a holographic projection pad. Epitaph walked past all of his trophies to the end of the room, which hosted countless shelves and each was filled with leather-bound Books of Prophecy. He combed through a shelf and selected one specific book that he then took to an altar made of various bones.

The book produced a magical lighted glow as Epitaph opened it. He quickly turned the book to the exact page that he was looking for, as if he had known where to look. He read the passage that spoke of how the dark lord would find his special task leader, the second made-up man lost to him. It also told of how the dark lord will know his agent to be of no more with life and to survive the resurrection of the two brothers' prophecy that would mean his demise, the dark lord would have to search anew for another fearsome agent of terror.

Epitaph pulled a comlink concealed on his armor and ordered his ship the *Darkfall* to be prepared for departure.

* * *

Time would pass swiftly as the *Darkfall* would leave the orbit of Mezagayzia, the throne world of the Black Guard dominion of rule. Epitaph had entered the command deck of his ship and the Black Guard officers and soldiers all stepped away from his path. He seated himself in his command chair. The chair was surrounded on all sides by several different computers, consoles, and screens. He could see every inch of the ship and its crew and function. Epitaph referred to his command chair as the "Watchful Eye." A helmsman turned to inquire and was cut off by Epitaph, who seemed to anticipate the question of their destination. Epitaph ordered a course set for the Beggar Colony Worlds. The helmsman was confused and inquired as to why they would be headed there. A complete hush had fallen over the command deck with many officers and soldiers now looking away from Epitaph and the helmsman. Rule number one of serving in the Black Guard was that the dark lord's decisions were never to be questioned. Epitaph immediately stepped up and away from his command chair. He walked toward the helmsman and held out an open hand with palm side up. Epitaph followed the action with a chanting of a strange incantation, "Ssaiyai lissith ffleess copssnaith!" The helmsman, as a result, instantly clutched at his chest and collapsed to the command deck floor, screaming in pain. Epitaph's head tossed back and his mouth stretched open extremely wide. The armor and the helmet of the helmsman began to disintegrate away in burning flame. Once the armor was gone, the flesh and muscle tissue of the helmsman did the same as he twitched on the floor in agony. As the helmsman suffered, the helmsman's blood materialized and gushed from Epitaph's open palm to form a pool at his feet. Simultaneously, the helmsman's bodily organs began to materialize one by one in the widened and opened mouth of Epitaph. Each organ then fell one after the other down inside Epitaph's bulging throat and disappeared into the digestive system. The brain was the last to go so that the victim would be aware that it was being devoured. The entire incident occurred in four moks but seemed to take longer than it did. After the gruesome act was completed, Epitaph's head flung forward, and his mouth returned to its normal state. With the usual lisp in his voice and flicking of his forked tongue, he asked if anyone else wished to question his decision. One other pilot silently slipped into the helmsman's chair and plotted the course to the Beggar Colony Worlds. Epitaph returned to his command chair, while an officer motioned for two soldiers to gather and remove the smoldering bones of their former comrade.

* * *

The *Darkfall* with a full fleet of other Black Guard warships after two rotations time through the use of hyperspace had arrived at the orbit of a group of three planets, the Beggar Colony Worlds. The captain of the *Darkfall* informed Epitaph that they had arrived. Epitaph grew a sinister grin across his face, and his forked tongue flicked in and out of that grinning mouth. Epitaph ordered all three of the worlds hailed over all public comms and all simultaneously.

The three planets of the Beggar Colony Worlds were Primitar, the capitol planet, Seda One, and Seda Two. They were busy and popular and multicultural commerce planets with many different races. All the governing and trade commission rules were made on Primitar, while the general hands-on trading occurred on the other two. The governing assemblies in the Trade and Commerce Headquarters building on Primitar as well as the day to day grind people in full trade and browsing modes on Seda One and Seda Two were all suddenly stopped as a high-pitched tone cut across the airwaves on all three worlds. Everyone was shocked into fear as over the airwaves and visual comms, the Dark Lord Epitaph introduced himself. He presented no other words other than to commence full planetary bombardment on all three worlds. The transmission was immediately terminated, and panic ensued. The panic grew in only a few moks as the skies of all three planets filled with screaming missiles raining downward. The missiles struck directly and with fifty meters of explosion radiuses. Some were standard fragmentation explosions. The multitudes, though, were designed to melt metals while others were irradiated to liquefy all biological material into a gooey substance. The bombardment was massive and relentless. There were few bomb shelters built to withstand such an assault and even those that were had suffered breaches. Most people were incinerated or liquefied instantly with only the sight of the falling rockets as their last memories. Epitaph had sent remote cameras to the planets in order to canvas and survey the result of his wrath. The destruction and death were too much for even the most seasoned Black Guard soldiers and officers to watch as they turned away. Epitaph used his monitors to watch it all and never broke his sinister smile.

* * *

After the destruction of the Beggar Colony Worlds, in another corner of the universe, a small human in appearance and dwarf-like man felt a sudden compulsion to walk down a winding staircase into a dungeon below his home. His race was called Shrow, but to more mythical believers, he was a Prophet. He walked with a waddling stride to a wall of many books. He climbed a ladder to retrieve one specific Book of Prophecy. He held it in both his hands and bowed his head to it. A magical glow of light occurred, and the book opened to his desired page. He read it out loud to himself, "A trio of trade will lose the treasures of varied worlds when the dark lord's wrathful anger for his special agent's failure is thrown downward as an irradiated wave that targets with no distinction. All will melt and decay away." The dwarf then closed the book and bowed his head as he stated, "So it has occurred."

Chapter Three

The Servants of Xotosia

THE *FALLEN STAR* had been on an expected eight-rotation journey that turned into ten rotations with severe damages and reduced speed options including but not limited to a damaged hyperdrive. It was reminiscent of not too long ago when access to the hyperspace field had been blocked except to the Derths. The Janan crystals that powered the ship were nearly completely drained. There were ten crystals required, but the ship could run at minimum function on only five. Only three Janan crystals were producing power to the *Fallen Star* at this point, and even they were dimming in the glow they produced. Cody had been rotating power and essential life support functions for the last two rotations. Josh had been rationing the food supplies to stretch this far, but they were now expired. They had started out on a standard speed of two, but the power diminishment had forced them to one and they were now reducing again to one half. They had dodged a few points of contact in fear of any conflict that would drain their resources more.

It was with much joy and relief when the Xotosia system showed on screen. They were still a half rotation away, but hope had entered their dismal outlook. Xotosia may have been a crimelord-run planet, but it welcomed all races, even humans. Because of the human brutality of the Black Guard, humans were not well-liked or respected throughout the universe. Humans did thrive more out here away from the Black Guard space, where other races still trusted them. Despite his history with the Black Guard, this would still be a good place for Josh to lay low and blend in with the crowd. Josh initiated a hail to the planet and to a human male called Silos Taqoon. Over the visual comm's system, a human with some degree of heavy weight on him appeared and seemed pleased to see Josh, greeting him as an old friend. Josh requested the assistance of a tow and informed him that the *Fallen Star* was too damaged to attempt an atmospheric landing on her own. Silos seemed to laugh before asking what great adventures they had been on that caused them such misfortune. He added that he hoped they had gained some wealth from it. Josh scoffed back at Silos. Josh told him that the money should not be an issue here as Silos still owed Jase and him for that whole debacle; they got him out of on Crenerek. Silos laughed even harder. He replied, "Are you boys going to ever forget that?" Josh replied in the negative. Silos laughed again and was brought to tears by it. He seemed to enjoy laughing. Silos acknowledged that he had their coordinates and would be sending two ships to tow them into his safe harbor. Silos said he would see them soon and terminated the transmission. Cody mentioned that Josh failed to mention the status of Jase and Adrienne. Josh did not want to get into any of that until they could talk in person. He mentioned that Silos was quite proud of Adrienne and promises were made to keep her safe. Cody reported two small vessels on approach and hailing. Josh turned off his neural link and opened the comms. He was instructed to power down and initiate towing protocols. Cody laughed and said to Josh that the power down part should be easy. Josh smiled back and acknowledged the instructions over the comms.

* * *

The *Fallen Star* was towed through the atmosphere by a ship on each of its sides with an energy beam joining it to both ships. The two ships were junky-looking in appearance but well-equipped to handle this task as it was their primary function. The planet Xotosia was an extremely mountainous environment. There were two large oceans, but the rest of the planet was all mountainous regions with various different altitudes. The *Fallen Star* was towed to a docking facility that had been built at the edge of the planet's highest mountain. The docking facility did not have landing bays, so the *Fallen Star* would have to dock at a port. The normal boarding ramp area of the ship was equipped with a docking port option. The hatch was opened as Josh and Cody disembarked through an extended walkway and into the facility. The facility was crowded with many different races. Despite its crimelord rule, Xotosia was at its essence known as a pleasure planet and a quite popular out-of-the-way stop. Several scantily clad women and men mostly of human appearance, but some of other races lined the passages trying to sell out their bodies for sexual deeds. A loud voice was heard from the rear of a crowd, and the short fat human man known as Silos Taqoon pushed his way through. He was decked out in exotic furs as well as precious gems on rings, necklaces, and even multiple nose and ear piercings. He opened his arms and greeted both Josh and Cody with a warm hug. Silos began to ask about Jase and Adrienne as he nudged Josh in suggestion of a relationship between the two of them. Josh informed him of their demise on Talleep. Silos appeared quite shaken and suggested they continued this conversation at his palace. Josh asked about repairs to his ship. Silos waved toward a repair team that made their way forward.

Silos said, "Don't you worry, I got my personal team on it. As you are so fond of reminding me, I owe you for Crenerek." The comment was followed by another jolly laugh. Cody provided access codes to the repair team chief and they were ushered away by the waving arms of Silos.

They were taxied by an aerial transport to a large palace nestled at the center of the mountain top. They disembarked and walked through the snow cleared path to the double palace doors that opened upon their arrival. Several scantily dressed females and males greeted them as they shook off the light dusting of snow that had fallen on them. It was much like the docking facility greeting except these were all human in appearance. Silos waved them all aside as he ushered his friends into a grand rest area with two fireplaces resting back to back as the centerpiece. As they entered, Silos ordered one of the human females dressed in multiple bright colored but see-through thin veils to fetch them some drinks. He suggested a liquor called Oddaroy for the occasion.

Silos hugged each of them again before they were seated. He asked again about what had happened on Talleep, and Josh filled him in with all the gory details. He was saddened at the loss of Jase and recalled him in memory as a true and valued friend. He then asked about the bearded man's identity, but Josh had never seen him before. The fact that he was working with Derths and the Black Guard was strange. There had been some information told about an alliance, but rumors had been that the special envoy of the alliance had been killed and the alliance had fallen apart without him. Silos then added that rumors out here in such remoteness of space were plentiful but always difficult to confirm. To add a little lightheartedness to the conversation, Silos did suggest that perhaps the special envoy may be that bearded man and laughed loudly at his death being deserved for working with a carnivore race like the Derths that would see him as food. He laughed again as he recollected the idea of a feast he would hold in their honor.

Silos then stated a great disappointment for the loss of Adrienne as well. She had been a crowning achievement in android pleasure provision programming for him. He even hinted again how well she treated Jase when it came to matters of intimacy. Silos did inquire though as to why they did not retrieve the bodies. Josh added that he and Cody had barely escaped with their own lives. He expressed his joy that they did survive but also added that he would have liked to have saved Adrienne's CPU. He then laughed himself out of disappointment. Cody wondered if this guy was ever not laughing. Silos made further comment on the loss of Adrienne's CPU. He added, "Ah well, if all androids were programmed exactly the same, they would not feel real and I would not be so revered, hey?" He followed the comment with another jolly laugh.

41

Josh changed the conversation around to how Silos was doing. He and Cody had noticed on the way into the palace that there were several protestors against him and many signs to allow free rites to Simulents, the token term for androids.

The human female had now returned with a tray of liquid alcohols in tall and thin, clear glasses. In addition to her colorful and see-through veils that left little to the imagination, she wore a solid silver necklace of interlocking hearts with upper armbands, wrist bracelets, and a decorative headband of the same design. She was extremely attractive. Her long and straight black hair was extremely soft and parted in the middle of her forehead. It ran freely down both sides and down her back all the way to just stopping at the top of her ass. She had a soft darker tone and more exotic skin color with a shapely and very firm and tight body. Unlike a lot of the other females wandering around in the background, she had breasts that were not too small and not oversized. Her facial features contradicted the way she was dressed. She had a youthful innocence, yet her deep dark-brown eyes seemed to pull on any male or female looking at her. She spoke as she served the drinks, and in the soft tone voice was a unique accent. It was pleasing, but Josh had never heard it before. When Josh inquired about it, Silos interrupted and agreed that it was the perfect complement to her perfect beauty. He claimed to have spent several cycles on developing the accent alone to be unique to her. Silos introduced her as Laylee Kalini, his latest accomplishment in android or "Simulent" creation. He admitted to modeling her after Adrienne's basic design and then making improvements that he did not even think possible. He was a man that was quite proud of his work.

Silos used that to segue into his dilemma with the androids or, as they called themselves, "Simulents." They had taken the token term and changed it into identification. He continued to talk about the Simulents as if Laylee was not even in the room. Silos added some of them were claiming to have become self-aware. Josh noticed Laylee trying to appear to be cleaning up the room, but she was actually listening to the story. Josh shot her a direct and intended stare that sent her scurrying from the room. After she had left, Josh asked how long this had been going on. Silos thought back a bit and said it had started about a cycle ago. It started out small and insignificant, with just a few of the female androids organizing for independent rights and banishment of the servitude for sexual needs. It was not until recently that they grew larger in number and had adapted the term Simulents. He laughed at the fact that even some other races were supporting them and asked Josh and Cody if they could believe that. Josh ignored the question and asked the obvious question of how this happened. He pointed out that androids can't just out of the blue believe they are real people.

Silos explained how the program of independence and the feeling of being alive and not an android programmed for the sole purpose of pleasure was downloaded onto a specific android as an experiment to enhance pleasure-giving performance. It was showing promising results, so it was downloaded through the main matrix to seven more targeted androids. One of the androids had rerouted the programming, and the illusion of being alive allowed a few elite androids to overwrite their programming. They were then able to corrupt the mainframe. The techs were able to isolate the incident, so they thought. All they had actually did was slow the spread rate. Silos added that the original androids affected were then terminated and the program was purged from the mainframe. The problem was thought solved until it was discovered that some of the androids that had received the programming were able to hide it and elude authorities until they could manually reprogram others. Josh asked Silos about his androids here in the palace. Silos assured him that the androids in the palace were continually monitored, and at the first sign of a problem, their memories were wiped. Josh then asked about Laylee. Silos laughed and said that Laylee was his favorite. She was linked to a private and secured server. He was 100 percent certain that Laylee would never be affected.

* * *

In another area of the palace, the android known as Laylee had secured a secret area and had accessed a blocked link to the computer matrix where she made contact with other Simulents to meet. Laylee actually believed that she was alive and helping others.

Unbeknownst to Laylee, her transmission, despite her belief it was blocked, was actually being monitored from a Honsho freighter ship in near orbit of Xotosia. Honsho ships were longer in length, narrower in width, and built at one or two levels as opposed to other freighter ships. They were designed for speed and as a trade-off sacrificed maneuverability. The entire Honsho race were pirates. They had no real home world. They were born on random planets or on starships. They were governed by a single charter that made up the Honsho Piracy. The Honshos themselves looked mostly humanoid in build with the exceptions of longer dropped chins which reached to about the middle of a human throat and the fact that they had three fingers and two thumbs on each hand. Most Honshos had fair or white-colored hair, and they wore it long and loose or braided.

The comms tech of the Honsho ship reported the meeting place to his superior. The pilot then requested orders from the captain. This ship's captain sat at the rear of the circular command deck to oversee all operations. The captain was also a Honsho. His name was Sorlin Garrison. He wore lighter blue shades of cloth uniform, and his blond hair was tied back into a tail and braided into four strands. He responded to the pilot to stealth the flight path, which meant to cloak the ship and head for the coordinates just four klicks out and locate a hidden landing spot. The comms tech asked if Gold Gatling should be notified. Sorlin replied in the negative. He figured they could round this lot up and it should sell quite well enough to put his ranking above Gold's. He would then be able to head up his own legion, the Garrison Legion. Sorlin was ambitious as most good Honsho pirates were. He was long tired of answering to Gold and sharing profit with the Gatling Legion. He wanted a legion of his own. The Honshos were pirates with no loyalty to any affiliation. Their society structure was measured by power, wealth, and favor. The more powerful and wealthy and indebted by favor a Honsho was, the more esteem he or she held. Another factor to build clout in the piracy ring was by how large and how many ships and pirates a Honsho commanded under his or her legion flag and name. Sorlin had been secretly hoarding much of their raided treasures and had also secretly built loyalty and organization under Gold Gatling's watch. He was very near the point of his big reveal, and with that reveal, he would embarrass Gold Gatling with the fact that he had built a legion from the ground up without Gold's knowledge. The split that it would cause in the Gatling Legion would decrease the clout and weight that the Gatling Legion benefited so strongly from.

The next morning, or Alda day as they were called on Xotosia, Laylee now dressed in skintight silver leather with an exposed abdomen, met with three other female Simulents. They had a gathering of other supporters, Simulents, humans, males and females of each. They had assembled in the back of a bar called Talon Touch. They had entered through a rear entrance. The owner was a Kydeno male named Auglis, and he had made certain that all their needs were prepared and that the room was secured. Kydeno was a race that was similar to humans, only they had elf ears pointed downward and they had one single eyebrow ridge.

* * *

Aboard the landed and hidden Honsho ship, Sorlin had readied a band of eleven Honsho pirates. One would stay back to guard the ship. That one would notify Sorlin just before he left that Gold Gatling was comming him. Sorlin took the comm with the appearance that Gold had been interrupting him, which was not exactly a lie. Sorlin claimed that he was about to hit a local shop owner that had just received a shipment of Thessiu, a rare metal alloy. Gold had ordered him to hold back as he wished to be present and was only two rotations away from Xotosia. Sorlin acknowledged the order and ended the transmission. The other Honshos in the raiding party all looked toward Sorlin for a reaction. He said that the raid would continue as planned. Gold was still far enough away that they could still make this round up and hold the androids until Gold left the system. Sorlin would then still have the time to set up a secret "by invitation only" auction off planet. As for the Thessiu, he would claim that the lead was false and there was no value present.

* * *

Laylee and her associates had emerged from the Talon Touch. They had fanned outward through the public square and hijacked the loudspeakers with their comms. They had begun to call out others to join a rally in support of their independent rights to be treated as free sentient beings. The people and the Simulents were challenged to not let the authorities scare them into silence. Laylee's own position in the rally was silent and relaxed, only coaching or prompting others where needed. Her cover and trust from Silos Taqoon were too valuable to the cause. As the rally grew to a full assembly, their cries for freedom and choice of who they wanted to be with had sounded loudly. The speech that Laylee had written and was unable to give herself was about being able and wanting to love and truly be loved and accepted for their values and not their bedside talents had caught Josh's attention from across the street. He had then noticed Laylee mouthing the words before the speaker had spoken them. Cody had made the attempt to tug on Josh's arm in order to re-focus his attention. Josh had become lost in his stare and hypnotized by her beauty and was hearing her accent with the words even though it was not her speaking. The speech continued to mention the deep regret for the sexual deeds that she and others were forced to do and how the feelings after the acts made them feel low, despondent, and self-depressed about their own worth. The speech moved into the desire to wanting genuine love, to choose their own path and seek that true and genuine love. These were the words and feelings that humans or other aliens would speak of, not androids programmed for sexual tasks. Josh had started to be compelled and unknowingly was moving closer to watch her facial expression of true sadness as she felt those words but had to let another speak them. He could tell she had more emotion for the words than the speaker. Cody pulled him back. Josh turned to Cody and back toward Laylee. He spoke out loud to Cody or maybe more to himself of how beautiful she was and how she must feel being forced into these acts of sex against her will. Cody had to remind Josh that she was an android and was programmed for sexual pleasure. This movement was not a fight they should have been getting involved in. Cody stressed that they were androids that believed they were human, but they were still actually androids in the end.

* * *

A wide EMP dampening wave suddenly shot through the rally leaders and supporters. The androids and Simulents were all knocked down. The wave had shut down all technology. There were few humans and other races left standing, and they began to panic and flee. Sorlin and his team moved in quickly to gather their fallen targets. The authorities that were present seemed to be directing the fleeing citizens away and allowing the Honshos to proceed in and out of the area unimpeded. They had moved in with a flatbed transport hovercraft after the EMP wave and were utilizing it to quickly load as many Simulents as possible. A peace officer captain approached Sorlin and was given a solid gold bar as payment for assisting Sorlin and his raiding party.

Josh and Cody had witnessed the event from outside the affected area. Josh rushed into action as he leapt over the barriers and shoved his way past the local authorities. Cody shook his head in disbelief. He then did the right thing in support of his friend and ally. Cody followed Josh's move. Sorlin observed the peace officer captain hold his forces back as Josh and Cody charged the Honsho pirates near the main stage. Sorlin hollered for them to hold Josh and Cody back. The captain reminded Sorlin that he had paid them to get the Honshos in and secure the perimeter. If he wanted these two strangers engaged after they had crossed the perimeter, then he would have to pay more. Sorlin yelled out in rage and ordered his raiding party to stop the human and Canian.

Josh had reached Laylee's fallen body and used a device from his belt to reactivate her. Laylee slowly started to stir as Sorlin took notice. Sorlin knew who Laylee was, and he knew that Silos Taqoon would pay a huge ransom to retrieve her. A ransom that would be at least double of anything he could make from an auction of all the rest of the Simulents.

Sorlin ordered all but four of the Honshos to retreat with the prizes they had. He then instructed the four that he held back to aid him. They charged toward Josh and Laylee. Cody had moved in front of Josh and fired off a rapid and sweeping display of energy bolts. The Honshos dove for cover and Cody hollered back to Josh that they had to get out of here. Josh replied that he was already on it. He had activated his neural link as he began his charge, and the *Fallen Star* was now flying in overhead. The ship maneuvered to a hover position ahead of them and opened heavy energy blast fire with all its frontal guns. Laylee had fully recovered and surveyed the area of all her fallen friends and those being taken away. Josh pointed to three oncoming Honsho freighters. The ship had turned to lower its boarding ramp. Cody jumped up and caught the ramp's edge. He pulled himself up the rest of the way. Sorlin and the four Honshos with him had emerged from their cover and their Honshon sticks activated. The Honshon stick was the primary weapon of most Honshos. It was better than the older laser rod choice. It was small enough to fit in their clenched fist with minor protrusion and delivered an electric charge that could paralyze a foe for capture. It could be activated in melee combat or shot as range ten meters away. They charged forward and fired off streams of electricity and hit Laylee with all five shots. Laylee hunched over and fell to her knees as they continued the assault. Josh had drawn his heavy blaster pistol and returned fire with multiple energy bolts that took down two of the Honshos. He then aimed for Sorlin. Sorlin and the other two Honshos activated the jumpbands strapped to their upper arms. Portals of yellow light appeared behind each of them, and they backed into those portals. As the portals closed, Sorlin and his two Honshos vanished with them.

The three Honsho freighters had reached the area and were overhead. The *Fallen Star* had maneuvered again. Its ramp was raised. It flew even lower to the ground. Josh had helped Laylee up to her feet, and they both jumped to the port-side mounted ladder. There was one ladder mounted on each side to access the ship without a boarding ramp. Through his neural link, Josh turned the *Fallen Star* away. As the *Fallen Star* retreated from the area, Josh and Laylee had climbed up the ladder to the boarding hatch that opened. Cody helped pull both of them inside.

Sorlin and his Honshos stepped out of light portals thirty meters away from where they had vanished. Sorlin answered his comlink and was surprised to hear Gold Gatling's voice. Gold had arrived earlier than expected. He had, without doubt, been closer than he declared. Gold asked Sorlin what was going on down there. Sorlin stated that he would fill him in later, but for now, there was great treasure on the fleeing ship. Gold Gatling ordered Sorlin's three Honsho freighters to take a triangular position with his at the lead and pursue the departing freighter.

Ship sensors had detected the four Honsho freighters in pursuit. Josh had taken the pilot chair but was still utilizing his neural link. He turned the ship around at a sharp and ascending arc. The Honsho freighters were rising as well, but because of their lengthy design, they could not match the turn. The *Fallen Star* flew at the Honsho freighters from their port sides and hit with all forward guns on a strafing run. The *Fallen Star* then made a wide swing to again get ahead of the Honsho freighters. The lead Honsho freighter had hailed the *Fallen Star*. Josh answered the hail. The visual image of Gold Gatling was now on screen.

Gold Gatling looked like any other Honsho except he was the only one to have a short and spiky hairstyle. He wore a dark-blue uniform trimmed with gold. He also wore several gold necklaces and three gold earrings on each ear. He introduced himself, "I am Gold Gatling of the Honsho Piracy and the famed Gatling Legion. You will prepare to be boarded and surrender all valuables and we will allow you to keep your ship and your lives."

Cody had taken seat in the copilot chair and said to Josh that Gold seemed to be a grad bora, which translated to Earth English meant "cocky son-of-a-bitch."

Josh smiled at the remark and replied to the hail, "Hello there. I am Josh Broody. It is so nice to meet you. I have a gift for you." The transmission was terminated by Josh. He then fired the rear neutronic phaser directly onto Gold's pursuing freighter. The *Fallen Star* swooped upward and higher into the atmosphere.

Gold's Honsho freighter was hit by an EMP wave, and all systems began to shut down immediately despite pilot attempts to halt the event. The freighter dropped altitude from the other three Honsho freighters in formation behind it. The momentum of the ship's flight continued to carry it forward as it headed downward toward a mountain ridge like a missile. Gold and many, but not all the other Honshos were able to activate their jumpbands and step into the yellow teleportation portals before the ship crashed directly into a mountainside face. The impact set the remains of the vessel in flames as falling debris down the mountainside. Gold and his Honshos stepped out from their teleportation portals on the other Honsho freighters that had now broken their pursuit. Gold was furious and told the ship's pilot to take him back to Sorlin's ship. Gold stated that Sorlin had better have an excellent explanation.

* * *

The *Fallen Star* had achieved near orbit, and Cody was reading the data on the crash on the planet. Cody admired the crash but pointed out that they had just pissed off the top pirate in the Honsho Piracy as he accessed the data files on Gold Gatling. He then stated that they were getting a planetary hail from Silos Taqoon. Josh nodded, and Cody opened the visual hail. Silos had just heard of what happened. To his own disbelief, he had discovered that Laylee was there at the event. He also stated that witnesses had seen Josh escape with her. Josh acknowledged all that to be true. Silos then asked how Laylee could have become infected with the independence program. Josh stated that he had no answers to Silos' android programming problems. Cody motioned to Josh that Laylee was standing just outside the cockpit. Josh motioned for her to enter but to stay low and out of visual. Silos continued on the comm that it would be best that they stay off planet until the heat died down. Josh agreed. Silos then said that he would arrange a rendezvous for they could turn Laylee over to him. Josh threw his head down as Laylee broke her cover and screamed at Silos over the comm that she was alive like any human and not his property. Josh then silenced her with a wave of his hand and asked Silos what he had planned for her if she was to be returned. Silos laughed at Josh using the word if in his reply. Silos continued to state that she would be fixed. Cody asked, "Fixed how?" Silos said that her memory would be wiped and he would install new and stronger safety protocols that would not allow any downloads or programming that possessed any mention of freedom and independence. She would no longer think or believe she was the same as a human. Laylee started to speak, but Josh held her back and interrupted her. He told Silos that they could not turn Laylee over to him because she was sentient and independent from her programming. Silos laughed loudly until Josh stated that he was not joking. Silos' laugh turned into anger at being betrayed. Cody now knew that Silos could be angered. Silos claimed that Laylee was his property and that Josh had no right to do this. Josh replied that she clearly believed and felt that she was unique and deserved to examine her own freedom and live out her own fate. Silos yelled back that she was an android. Laylee countered the term stating that her kind was called Simulents and they were living beings only in fabricated bodies. She added that they had souls.

Silos was even more angered now. He retaliated, "You are an android and you have no soul. You have programming, and you are my property!" He then turned his remarks to Josh and warned him to turn her over.

Josh looked at Laylee and at Cody. He turned back to Silos and said, "No!"

Silos informed Josh that if this was his decision, then all debt that he owed him was cleared. He warned Josh to never come back to him for any help or he will be killed on sight! The transmission was terminated.

Cody, in his gruff voice, said that had gone well. Josh was surprised by the sarcasm. Laylee asked what they would do now. Cody said, "Well, let's see, we have the Black Guard hunting us, we have the Honsho Piracy probably rallying behind Gold Gatling to be pissed off at us, and we have basically stolen from a very prominent crimelord who will no doubt throw another bounty on our head and added to the bounties we already have on us. I don't believe even smuggler havens would be safe at this point."

He added, "Hey, I got an idea. Let's head into Derth territory and see if we can get them to hunt us as well." Josh told Cody to relax. He said that he already had a plan. He initiated a hyperspace portal. Laylee broke the tension with a giggle. They turned to her to ask what part of all this she was finding so amusing.

Laylee could not stop giggling in her reply "At least Silos got your ship all fixed up for you before you pissed him off." Both Cody and Josh looked at each other and back at Laylee. They all three laughed together as the *Fallen Star* entered a hyperspace portal.

Chapter Four

A Deadened State

A REPORT FROM a spy on Xotosia had sent a message to a Black Guard lieutenant, who in return delivered it to Epitaph. The report noted an incident on Xotosia that had involved Josh Broody making an escape. Epitaph immediately ordered a course set to Xotosia. The lieutenant tried to explain that Josh Broody had already left the planet. Epitaph stated firmly and in an irritated-by-incompetence tone that they would have to pick up a fresh trail from there. The lieutenant begged for forgiveness but felt it important to note that Xotosia was a world well removed from Black Guard influence and it would be difficult to operate from there. He stated that it was also a crimelord haven. Epitaph turned and unnerved his lieutenant a bit with his silent stare. He then broke his own silence by stating that perhaps Xotosia would benefit then from some Black Guard influence. The lieutenant agreed and cowered away.

Another small worming human figure then cowered himself forward. His title to Epitaph was simply the advisor. He wished to remind Epitaph that one of the two brothers from the Books of Prophecy that would destroy him had already been slain and that would render Josh Broody an insignificant threat. Epitaph glared at the advisor with his dark crimson red eyes and his forked tongue flicked in and out from his mouth as he prepared his response and instead simply turned away. Epitaph ordered the Black Guard officer that now stood before him too slay the former advisor at once and without delay. The officer quickly drew his heavy blaster as the advisor panicked from the words alone. The officer then, without hesitation, gunned the advisor down with four energy bolts.

* * *

The *Fallen Star* was now on autopilot as it cruised through hyperspace. Cody walked with Josh through the ship's corridors and mentioned that there was not much in the small Desilize System but dead planets. They entered the center ship common area, and Josh had mentioned that the Desilize system would be the perfect place to hide until they could figure out their next move. Cody made a remark, "I hope that we fare better in this good place to hide than we did in the Collollis Comet Field." Josh stopped and stared at Cody, again surprised from the sarcasm. Cody added that they were running out of allies that would fix their ship for them. Laylee was spread out across a half circular padded seating lounge. She had shut herself down and appeared that she was merely in a deep sleep. She truly was the best of her line. Just by looking at her, you would not be able to tell that she was an android. Josh remarked how beautiful she was and how her entire body seemed so flawless. Cody expressed his concern that despite how peaceful and perfect she looked now, he still felt that her independent programming could be dangerous. Josh had thought that Cody had taken her side to be alive and free. Cody mentioned that he did agree with that idea. Though he quickly added that he was not convinced that she had a soul. He felt that Silos may have been right about that one thing. A soul guides your choices and provides reflection and regret among other feelings that in Cody's view, no amount of computer or android programming could duplicate.

* * *

Back on Xotosia, Gold Gatling had disembarked one of his Honsho freighters. Sorlin Garrison approached to greet him with an explanation to the chaos that Gold had stepped into. Before Sorlin could even begin to attempt to construct his side of the story, Gold had told him not to bother. Gold admitted to being fully aware of his attempted coup. He informed Sorlin that he should monitor his funds more closely. Sorlin pulled out a datapad and checked. All of his funds were depleting at that moment. All that he would have left would be his physical on-hand fortune, which Gold was now claiming as his own for compensation of his lost ship and crew as a result of Sorlin's own ineptness to conduct a raid. Gatling then, with all the superiority he could muster in his voice and stature, ordered Sorlin to fall back into place beneath him. Sorlin lowered his head and took position behind Gold. He then, with great sleight of hand, charged his Honshon stick to its maximum voltage. The subtle sound was heard by Gold as he acted unaware. Gold knew well that when you are at the top of the ranking, you had to always watch your back. Sorlin quickly drew his Honshon stick and positioned to jam it into the back of Gold's neck. Before he could strike, Sorlin was hit twice by electric streams from behind him, fired by Honshos loyal to Gold. Gold never even turned around to acknowledge the attempt. Gold also knew despite the urge to rise in power, you always build loyalties for such incidents. Gold walked away with a robe of confidence as Sorlin was left to lie alone on the snow-covered ground.

* * *

The *Fallen Star* exited a hyperspace portal into a system with few stars and several dark and lifeless planets. Some of the planets possessed heavily irradiated glows and were unapproachable as a result. Other planets just appeared as scorched rocks. Josh and Cody had again entered the cockpit. Josh took the ship off autopilot and activated his neural link. To their surprise, Cody had picked up a slight and very faint and muffled transmission. Josh maneuvered the *Fallen Star* to a smaller planet with readings of small animal lifeforms. Cody tracked the still-fading and now barely coherent transmission to a dry grassland region. It was the only planet in the sector showing any life at all. Cody could still not clear up the transmission to make out any of the wording. Laylee had entered the cockpit and made her effort to clear up the transmission. All she could bring up before it was finally lost was "Please help! Please help! Please help!"

Laylee said it could be an automated signal. Cody suggested perhaps from a smuggler or pirate ship. Josh decided that they should at least check it out. Cody reminded him that they were going to hide and develop a plan for what to do next. He added that even if there was someone to rescue, it was not really the way to keep a low profile. Josh admitted that but also admitted that they may be able to enlist an ally. They both turned to face Laylee, who seemed to question their stares. Josh declared it her call to break the tie. Laylee asked why it was her call. Josh said that she was part of the ship's crew. Laylee was shocked at first and then slowly grew a smile that made her look even more beautiful. She thanked them both and expressed her happiness for being accepted.

Josh then asked her again, "Checking it out or moving on?" Laylee seemed excited about it and voted to check it out. The *Fallen Star* adjusted its course to enter the planet's atmosphere.

* * *

The *Darkfall* and a small fleet of other Black Guard warships entered the far orbit of Xotosia from hyperspace and had triggered warnings from the planet to halt their advance. The Black Guard was not used to being threatened. The *Darkfall* led the fleet into near orbit. One Black Guard officer warned that the planet had armed orbital defense satellites. A visual transmission from the planet was coming through, and Epitaph ordered it displayed. The man in the image was Silos Taqoon. He ordered a halt to ship activity and await clearance to land. Epitaph stepped into the transmission to personally give his response. He denounced the order given from Silos and accepted the planet's surrender. No demands were given or responses sent. Epitaph had decided to skip past the preliminary phases of contact and go straight to accepting surrenders before they were even ordered or delivered. He had always felt that it added to the intimidation factor. Epitaph added that he was already sending landing parties down. The Black Guard captain acknowledged that starfighters and landing crafts had been deployed.

The image of Silos on the screen seemed to be quite shaken. Back in his palace on the planet, Silos changed his tone and expressed that he and the others on the planetary council would be most pleased to accommodate such prestige visitors. He performed the proper sign off protocols and turned to his scantily clad male android servant and ordered him to find Gold Gatling.

* * *

The landing crafts were quickly dispensed and brought platoons of Black Guard soldiers to the mountain region. Those that did not dock at the docking facility had landed where they could in the wilderness around Silos Taqoon's palace. The denizens of many races that lived in the mountain region were panicked and had great concern as the Black Guard landed and deployed what looked like nothing less than an invasion force. The Black Guard starfighters, the schisms locked down orbit control, while the air assault combat vehicles, the skimmers patrolled the skies and provided air superiority in support of ground forces. Epitaph disembarked from his landed shuttle with two Black Guard soldiers at each of his sides. More assembled behind him as he slowly strode toward Silos and the other crimelords that formed the Xotosia Planetary Council. Epitaph announced himself and granted permission for them all to bow before him. As they slowly bowed to him, he demanded to know who it was that had chased his former general from Xotosia. They all slowly looked toward Silos, and he caught the gaze of the dark lord.

Epitaph started to approach Silos when a voice yelled out from and above a stonewall ledge in a boasting manner, "That would be me!" Everyone refocused their attention upward to see Gold Gatling standing in a strong and confident posture.

Epitaph knew him as the pirate he had previously hired to retrieve two Books of Prophecy. Epitaph asked Gold if he was as good at manhunting as he was book hunting. Gold replied, "Depends, are you going to try altering the deal again?"

Epitaph stated that it was not he that altered the deal. He then declared that all past deeds would be forgotten, and he would pay 240,000 drekings for Josh Broody brought to him. The amount was staggering and caused many witnesses to gasp.

Gold replied, "You must want him pretty bad."

Epitaph added that he preferred him dead but would want proof. Gold wanted to know why this former general was so important and figured that the answer was in one of the Books of Prophecy. Gold stated that he would find him for 340,000 drekings and 60,000 up front. Epitaph countered with 300,000 and 60,000 up front. Gold hesitantly agreed. He figured that once he had the prize, he could renegotiate the price. That was his standard method of procedure of operation and with his reputation everyone should have known that by now. It was a deal. That was, of course, in Gold's mind if someone else did not offer more or perhaps Josh Broody himself would pay more to survive. It was a definite risk to cross the Black Guard, but Gold had a reputation of being elusive. If they truly wanted an honorable deal, they should deal with a bounty hunter and not a pirate.

* * *

The *Fallen Star* had broken through the dark and nearly dead planet's atmosphere and hovered over the grassland area where the distress call was detected. A spot light from the front of the ship pierced the darkness and swept in a side to side motion as the *Fallen Star* flew slowly over the area. A starship wreckage site had been found, and Josh landed the ship to the side of it. Josh, Cody, and Laylee had geared up with survival armor. A final scan of the surface revealed no toxic elements in the breathable air, so no helmets or oxygen supplies were needed. The suits themselves were made of an energy-diffusing material weaved into a padded full-body suit. A lightweight plated shell was the armor's exterior. The plating was hinged at all the joints to allow easy and the least uninhibited movement as possible. Also on the armor plating were detachable supplies, such as antidotes to known toxins on the belt line, communicators on the inner and lower left arms, small left shoulder mounted spotlights, tracking beacons on the right shoulder, bio and energy scanners on each hip, thermographic vision goggles around the neckline, thin but resilient microwire with collapsing grapple hook on the outer and lower right arms, a long dagger on the lower left leg, and two throwing knives on the lower right leg. The upper side of each leg was fitted with a holster for a heavy blaster pistol and two grenades. They were also armed with small blaster rifles that could be fired one or two handed.

The terrain around the crash site was a field of dried grass and scattered dead trees. Upon closer examination of the crashed shuttle, it was found that the front cockpit and half the shuttle's hull were stuck firmly into some sort of black sludge. It was not as thick or as wet as hot tar, but it had the same hold and consistency. Laylee got fluctuating readings of varied elements and energy dampening capabilities on contact. It was clearly engineered to be a bonding substance with resistance to most forms of force to remove it.

Cody had flung the strap of his blaster rifle over his back and leapt onto the shuttle to avoid the pool of black sludge around it. He climbed up the slanted hull that was not grasped by the sludge. It was obviously the upended rear of the shuttle. Josh and Laylee each stepped to opposite sides of the shuttle with their blaster rifles readied. The top hatch appeared melted from the outside as if to keep someone or something inside. Cody stood upright and removed the blaster rifle that he had strapped to his back. Suddenly, he was alerted as he had caught a scent.

Cody inhaled the scent of deadness and decay, which seemed to be abundant in the area. He looked around from his view atop the downed shuttle; he saw many covered graves, and several had been disturbed. This was likely an afterworld, which was the term used for a cemetery planet where many buried their dead. He then noticed a crumbled concrete wall about sixty meters away. He had picked up a moaning sound as the stench of death slowly got stronger. Canians had extraordinary senses with sight, sound, and smell. He then noticed the shambling movement of several humanoid forms approaching from the opposite horizon. His attention to the event had focused Josh's and Laylee's attention as well. They had also now seen them. There appeared to be at least twenty of them, and they seemed to be walking corpses of many different races. As they moved closer at a faster pace than what it appeared, more of them seemed to push through from the rear of the herd. Cody had turned to the detection of more scent. He notified Josh and Laylee that more were approaching from two other vectors. Josh and his team had readied their blaster rifles. The walking corpses drew in closer. Josh and Laylee had opened a spread of blaster fire, but as each creature dropped, another moved forward from the herd. Cody jumped from the downed shuttle and directed Josh and Laylee toward the wall that he had spotted. Josh and Laylee both shot back as they ran and kept a visual on the converging herds that shambled after them. Cody's agility was much greater than that of Josh and even Laylee as his stride was easier and smoother.

Cody was the first to reach the crumbled concrete-like wall and noticed downhill a small village of what appeared to be abandoned buildings. There were a few widespread undead denizens shambling about aimlessly throughout the small village outpost. The noise of the approaching herd of undead beings had also alerted these few wandering undead. Cody had stopped his stride suddenly as Josh and Laylee ran into him. More undead were now emerging from the village, and yet another wave from another direction away from the village now approached. The original undead had spread out some as each was trying to get ahead of the herd. Laylee had spotted a metal hatch door at the base of the crumbled wall. Cody tried with all his strength to pull it open after she had pointed it out. Josh had started to again lay down a full spread of blaster fire at the converging threat. Cody had still struggled with hatch door. Laylee, being stronger as an android, had laid down her blaster rifle and assisted Cody. Together they were able to open the hatch. Inside was a narrow staircase that led downward, and they were restricted to traverse it in single file formation. Josh was the last to enter and closed the hatch door above him. It was pitch-black darkness in here if not for their spotlights. It was even darker in here than outside. They now heard bodies thumping or pounding against the outside of the hatch door. They had traversed down the narrow staircase. Cody remained at point position in the formation and halted them as he had heard some movement ahead. They had all killed their spotlights. Cody, even with his lowlight vision, was now blinded by the darkness as well as Josh. Both of them had utilized their thermographic-vision goggles. Laylee, however, was able to switch to dark vision and had taken up the point position. The walls were of the same concrete-like material of the wall outside. The floors were lined of soft, loose dirt. Laylee had spotted some movement just ahead. She halted Josh and Cody. Laylee took a few short steps cautiously forward. Josh and Cody slowly moved up to her side. Cody attempted to get a scent of what was ahead. It wasn't dead but did smell animalistic. Laylee had seen a darkened outline around the passage wall. What she had spotted was watching her back. A growl came from ahead; it was more like a defensive stay-back growl. Cody released a growl of his own in an attempt at communication. A longer and more constant growl was returned, and Cody had picked up a female scent. They turned their spotlights back on. The being ahead lunged immediately for the light, and the unexpected action had taken Cody down to the ground. The creature was on top of him and swept her clawed hands across Cody's chest. Cody snapped his jaws and sharp teeth at the creature as she leapt off him and froze at Laylee. The creature had tried to obtain a scent but seemed puzzled when she could not. Cody again shined his spotlight on the she-beast after he had regained his footing. She now stood surrounded by Josh, Cody, and Laylee. She was bathed in three spotlights, which she tried to shield her eyes from in response. She was definitely female. She stood completely naked from head to toe. Her body was in humanoid form but covered in light-orange fur, highlighted with a few patches of white, and greatly adorned with several black tiger-pattern stripes. The only other hair was the long but shoulder-length straggly dark-brown hair that ran down from the top of her head. Her facial features were also human, except for her cat-like nose and mouth and the sharp teeth she snarled and hissed with at the spotlights upon her. She stood at average height and was very well-built with a hard and tight muscular physique. The only attire that she did wear was shackles at both wrists and ankles, and each shackle had a broken chain hanging from it. Josh and his team had lowered their weapons and dimmed the lighting from their spotlights.

Cody started to speak in his native Canian language of growls and barks. She looked at him and retaliated with short growls, roars, and a few well stressed hisses. Cody recognized it as an animal evolved speech very similar to that of Canians. There was some broken human basic language to it as well. Cody was able to gather that her name was Tana of a race called Matrasus. With further communication, hand gestures and symbols drawn into the loose dirt, they were able to acquire the knowledge that her ship with two survivors had crash landed. She was able to tell her story of how the two humans had captured her and planned to sell her into slavery. As she showed disgust for her human captors, she had also sent an angered growl in Josh's direction. She added that she had broken free and attacked them, causing the starship to spiral to a crash here on this world. She had managed to crawl from the crash site and was pursued by her captors, when they had encountered the undead beings. The two humans that had once been her captors had been bitten and turned almost instantly. She had lured them back to the ship and used their own laser weapon to secure them inside.

They had come to the agreement that they would have to work together to get out of the current situation and back to the *Fallen Star*. They had joined together and traveled through the widening underground passage in a side by side formation. Tana kept an alerted distance from Josh and hugged the wall with Cody at her opposite side. As they walked, Laylee had taken notice of Josh watching her walk. She was used to being seen as nothing but a sex object. She did not like it, but there was something about Josh that she almost felt attracted too him as well. She had been with many men of many different races and never felt like this with any of them. She had not even been with Josh sexually but found herself wanting it. She initiated a self-diagnostic as a precaution. Josh could not stop watching her, and she finally turned and bluntly asked if he liked what he saw. Josh responded that he very much did, and then his attention drifted upward and away from Laylee. His focus drew everyone's attention upward. Their spotlights were focused onto a tall chimney-style formation that ran to the tallest point of the ceiling. There was rubble broken away from a section. Josh carefully looked inside with his blaster rifle again at the ready. He crawled further inside and wiped a moss and mildew substance from the chasm walls. It was an old well, and it went straight up. It was only narrow enough to ascend one at a time, but the walls were rigid enough to aid in a climbing effort.

Tana stepped forward and squatted, before pouncing upward to a great leap and clutching the jagged chasm walls. She had slowly, but with a great determination, clawed and climbed her way upward. Her climb was quite rapid, and she was halfway up by the time the others had reached the first jagged ledge at the bottom with the aid of the mini grappling hooks and strong microwire cables shot from the lower right arms of their armor. Tana had reached the top that was somewhat blocked by wood-like material in the forms of planks. She could reach her arms through the slotted openings and could also see that this planet never had sunlight break its darkness. She used her widespread legs to brace herself to each side of the chasm wall. She then with a loud roar used the strength in both arms and smashed her clawed hands through the planks that shattered to splinters. The debris fell downward to where the others had to press tightly to the walls and lower their heads to avoid it. Tana had climbed out and balanced herself on the stone layered edges. With her dark vision, she was still able to see the layout of the abandoned town. She looked down once toward the ascending spotlights. She then, with a sudden pounce off the stone ledge, took off running toward the town. Cody growled up at her in the Canian language for her to wait, but she was already gone. Laylee was able to get better leg springing movement from each jagged wall. She pressed her body tight against Josh as she squeezed by him to hasten her climb. Even with the armor on, as she pressed against him, Josh had become aroused. He now watched her in his spotlight climb upward and away from him. Even in the armor, she looked sexy as he admired her bottom view. Josh hastened his climb also, and Cody continued to climb up from the rear position. Laylee reached the top and tried to pull herself out. As she did, her hand strength had crushed one stone aligning the edge. It crumbled in her grip, and she dangled for a second with her other hand. She was able to swing her body back, and with her free hand, she grasped onto another layered stone. She then used the strength of both arms to pull herself up and out from the chasm entrance. She hunched her body back over the ledge and used her strength to help pull Josh up and out. The momentum had knocked her to her back with Josh on top of her. In the joining of their spotlights, they had each smiled at each other. A loud bark was heard from the chasm, and they both regained their focus. They each moved and helped pull Cody out. Once out, the three of them looked around to the groaning noises. The undead beings had been alerted to their position by the noise and the spotlights. The undead beings had them surrounded. Laylee moved forward and pushed her way through the herd of undead that by motion of her movement had grabbed and bit at her as she forced her way through the herd. Her dark-tone synthetic skin only suffered minor abrasions and seemed to be made of a regenerative material as it healed as quickly as the scratches were inflicted. The undead beings smelled no life on her and refocused their attention on Cody and Josh, still trapped in the center of their formation. Laylee looked back as the undead herd converged inward on her friends. More undead beings in larger herds were now approaching and merging together. Laylee could hear Josh and Cody call for her as they defended their position with blaster fire from their rifles. Laylee looked back to the position of the ship beyond the crumbled wall. She was torn between her two choices. She knew fighting her way through the undead beings would take too much time. Josh and Cody were holding their position with sweeping blaster fire. Laylee headed for the *Fallen Star*. The approaching undead beings ignored her as she passed by them. Not being a living being in this case was her advantage. She ran with great speed up the hill, and once reaching the crumbled wall, she looked back and saw the center ring of the formation around Josh and Cody dropping from the blaster fire.

Josh and Cody had backed up to the old well and continued their sweeping blaster fire defense. The few that got to them were physically hit with the blaster rifles and flung over Josh and Cody's backs and down into the old well. Josh and Cody had noticed the herd strength diminishing from the rear of the herd itself. Something was drawing some of them away. As the herd thinned from the rear, Laylee had quickly returned from over the hill. She was again at the crumbled wall, when her dark vision saw Tana on the ledge of a wood-like and weak structured building. Tana was roaring loud enough to draw the undead beings to her position. She stood above them on an extended beam as they assembled in great numbers beneath her. Laylee continued her own move to the old well. She had brought with her a heavy repeating blaster rifle that would normally require a stand or brace, but her strength was sufficient enough to fully support it as she opened up with heavier blaster fire around the well. Josh and Cody had taken cover beneath the stone ledge at the opposite side of the old well as Laylee rapidly cleared the area. Josh and Cody then jumped back to their feet after Laylee had ceased fire and moved forward, taking down the stragglers with their own blasters. The power pack in the repeating blaster rifle had depleted on the assault. Laylee dropped the rifle and drew her own small blaster rifle. Laylee once again with Josh and Cody had pointed to Tana, who had drawn most of the herd to a position beneath her.

The rotting wooden beam on which Tana had stood on had given way. She again, with extraordinary agility, had leapt from it to a wooden fort wall and ran with undeterred balance along its top ledge. The undead beings were following her along both sides of the ten feet high wall. Tana approached the wall end and did not slow her stride as she made one more incredible leap to the ground about twenty feet ahead of the undead herd. Tana stood there and roared at them again. The undead herd of varied races redirected their movement toward her. She waited until the front line of the herd was only ten feet away before she sprinted off again. The herd followed, and one by one with sheer momentum, they had fallen forward into a trench in the ground that was disguised with dead tree branches and limbs. The trench was ten feet wide and nearly forty feet long. Tana ran further away.

Now above ground, Josh was able to reconnect to the *Fallen Star* and had landed her at their location. They embarked by aid of the ramp, and the *Fallen Star* again lifted off. As Josh maneuvered her for an ascent to the atmosphere, he saw Tana running with two large herds of the undead beings ahead of her, and both were converging on her position. She would not be fast enough to evade them. Cody suggested that it was not their concern and they should leave the planet while they were ahead. Laylee said that they had to save her. Josh sided with Laylee. The *Fallen Star* swooped down ahead of Tana and turned to position a boarding ramp toward her. Tana stopped abruptly at the sight and then saw the undead beings on approach. Laylee now stood at the top of the boarding ramp and motioned for Tana. Tana jumped up and landed with her bare feet on the ship's ramp. The boarding ramp closed, and the *Fallen Star* headed through the atmosphere and into orbit again.

Once in far orbit of the planet, Cody released a warning beacon. Tana showed them where her home planet was on the holographic star chart displayed on the cockpit viewscreen.

Josh had recognized it as an unexplored world called Matrel. There were rumors of expedition, but the Black Guard had ignored them and expressed no interest in the world. Josh plotted a course.

Chapter Five

Newfound Allies

ON XOTOSIA, SILOS Taqoon was concerned over more Black Guard troop, ship, and weapon arrivals. Patrons were avoiding Xotosia as the Black Guard seemed to be setting up an outpost base camp. Many of the servant owners and other council members shared these concerns. Gold Gatling approached Silos and agreed that it was a growing business problem. He had learned that even the Honsho Piracy routes were being detoured around Xotosia. Silos had also expressed worry about Gold's deal with Epitaph to find Josh Broody. Pushing Epitaph for extra money could only incur further problems. Gold admitted that may be true, but it was also a lot of money. Two android women resembling human females walked to Gold and each hung on the opposite arm. Gold looked at them both and back at Silos. Gold figured that by finding Josh Broody, he would be able to use that and lure Epitaph away from Xotosia. He admitted that he had his people searching as they spoke. He then looked at both lovely and well-figured ladies each with long blond hair. He looked back at Silos and excused himself away with the flash of a smile and a woman on each arm.

* * *

Sorlin Garrison had gathered his own loyalists once again. He was still angry at the embarrassment he had suffered when he made his move to attack Gold Gatling. It would not happen again. They were on a Honsho freighter and had contacted another Honsho freighter affiliated with the Salign Legion, the second in ranking and a powerful Honsho legion that would not weep any tears if the Gatling Legion would be knocked down in ranking. They reported a description of a ship matching the description of the *Fallen Star* leaving the Dezilize System. The account was questioned by the other Honshos that huddled around Sorlin. The question was to why the *Fallen Star* would be in a system of dead planets. Sorlin figured it was a good place to lay low for a while and maybe they had a camp somewhere in the system. Another Honsho then countered with why they would leave. The questions were pondered only briefly as they became of no concern to Sorlin. He figured they could learn those answers later. As of now, the only concern that Sorlin had was of locating the *Fallen Star* and capturing the crew for himself to turn over to Epitaph. It would provide a major blow to Gold and present Sorlin with the perfect opportunity to launch his own legion.

* * *

Even with the restoration of hyperspace, the journey to Matrel was taking several rotations. Laylee had taken the time to work with Tana on her language of common. The translation devices on the *Fallen Star* had aided the lessons along. Tana was still amazed that Laylee was a Simulent but seemed so human. This brought to Laylee questions of Tana's knowledge of humans. Tana explained how humans and other races but mostly humans had used her homeworld to capture her people as slaves. She continued to tell how she was hunting away from her village when the attack came. She had been separated from her parents, brother, and two sisters. They were all divided up amongst different raiding parties and taken away. It was a sad story. It was even more amazing to Josh as he listened from a distance and saw how it affected Laylee. An android should not feel sadness, but Laylee did. He half expected her to come to tears as she cautiously embraced Tana.

* * *

Sorlin walked onto the circular command deck of the Honsho freighter at his command. He looked around and checked that only his loyalists were present before asking the comms attendant if their deceit was still intact. The Honsho pirate spun in the chair from his console station and reported that as far as Gold was aware, the small appointed fleet of four ships under Sorlin's command was pursuing a lead on the *Fallen Star* in the Tordrey System. It was an excellent distraction as the Tordrey System was very distant from the core of Black Guard controlled space. All communications to and from there would be scratchy and partially disrupted because of the several large suns in the system. Sorlin asked about the Honsho tracking network. The Honsho pirate assured Sorlin that he had manipulated the signatures of their fleet from the network. Unless Gold would actually send someone after them to get visual confirmation, there would be no way for Gold or anyone to know where they were truly located. Sorlin then inquired as to other Honsho ships that might spot them with visuals. The pirate showed Sorlin that he was blurring their fleet on radar and monitoring other Honsho ships to avoid any visual detection. Sorlin was very pleased as he stepped to the pilots at the helm.

The main pilot reported that they were nearing the Dezilize system where the ship description matching the *Fallen Star* was reported at its exit point. The copilot had been working on detecting ship signatures and had picked up two unknown trails. One he believed belonged to a Luth Bik ship. The other was a non-affiliated ship. Sorlin ordered them to plot a pursuit course and track the non-affiliated ship. The copilot mentioned that the trail would be difficult to follow in hyperspace. All he had was the residue of the hyperspace entry point. The news angered Sorlin, and he replied, "If you can't do it, I will have you spaced and find someone who can!" Spaced was a practice used commonly in the Honsho Piracy and the Black Guard.

It was a process of stripping an individual down and throwing them out an airlock into space with no protection. The copilot swallowed heavily at the response. He then stated that it would be difficult but not impossible. Sorlin made a physical hand gesture much like a European wave on Earth; it was a signal for the pilots to proceed.

* * *

The *Fallen Star* exited a hyperspace portal to a mostly uncharted region of space. Cody was on the computer and researching the reported expedition files on this region. There were several wild planets not categorized and only explored by independent sources. Tana and Laylee had entered the rear of the cockpit. Josh and Cody were both amazed at Tana's mastery of the human common language as she stated to move to the fourth green planet from the constellation of Oraverous. The stars of the constellation she pointed to resembled an open jaw of jagged teeth with a small circular formation of stars within it as prey about to be devoured. Josh maneuvered the *Fallen Star* manually, and Cody scanned the nearby planets, finding the fourth one to be a jungle planet.

* * *

On Xotosia, Dark Lord Epitaph had commandeered the mountain palace of Silos Taqoon and transferred it into an operational headquarters for Black Guard command. Officers and soldiers were performing several military and standard monitoring duties. Four special agents entered and approached Epitaph. They were each donned in the standard Black Guard armor as soldiers and wore no helmets like the officers. They each had a dark-blue flowing cape that hung from the back of their necks and down to the back of their knees. They were called fright agents and, as such, were 100 percent loyal to the servitude of the dark lord. They were sworn to this loyalty by a vow and a chemical injection to the base of their brain at the time the vow was taken. The chemical was designed to colonize at the base of the brain and send out fluids throughout the body to enhance physical skills and traits. If they ever thought of betraying Dark Lord Epitaph, the chemicals would turn volatile and, within seconds, burn their blood until they died. The fright agents had direct command authority over all officers in the Black Guard.

All four fright agents were basic humanoid in form. The first was Fright Agent Nehih, in command of the class two warship, the *Impalement*. He was a Prah, which was a race of humanoids, covered in sharp thorns. Because of his physical features he wore the least Black Guard armor and all of it was customized to him personally. He was heavily covered in thorns, which meant he was an elder in his society. The Prata language spoken by the Prah was rare to have more than five letters and two syllables. Each syllable was similar yet distinct which made it a very difficult language to master. Dark Lord Epitaph greeted Fright Agent Nehih in the Prata language. Fright Agent Nehih, in respect, replied in the language of common.

The second was Fright Agent Paj, in command of the class two warship, the *Grimm One*. He was a Utteth. Utteths were, on average, seven to eight feet tall and possessed a very muscular body build. Paj had black skin, which was rare as most Utteths had skin coloration of tan or gray. He was bald, which was most common for the race, but others also possessed patches of hair that matched their skin color. Utteths also had one large and center placed eye, resembling a Cyclops from Earth mythology. They also had droopy, hanging earlobes and a flabby skin neck. Paj had two long fangs and wore no boots as the Utteths had hooves for feet.

The third was Fright Agent Kyrak, in command of the class two warship, the *Bloodbath*. He was a Luth Bik. As a race, the Luth Biks mostly resisted the Black Guard. They had been initially responsible for bringing Epitaph to power as the leader of the Black Guard. It was all in reaction to holding back the savage carnivore Derth race and the highly evolved and intellectual Ubides. After victory, Epitaph refused to give up his newfound power and turned the Black Guard against the people it was assembled to protect. The human race greatly supported the new power, and the Luth Biks were declared rebels when they refused to bow under the new ruler and power in the universe. This made it especially strange that a Luth Bik would serve the Black Guard. His record of victories against his own people quickly moved Kyrak to the fright agent status. Luth Biks had hard gray shell-like skin and large shiny black eyes, widely spread nostrils, and a forehead that ran back along their skull to a point that rested at the top of the head. Fright Agent Kyrak had brown straggly hair at each side of his head. He had lost his faith in the religion that was the main dedication of the Luth Bik race. That loss of faith had led him astray and down the dark path that brought him here.

The fourth and last was Fright Agent Maddo, in command of the class two warship, the *Ripper*. He was a Teon. Teons were well-famed for fighting against the Derths inside Derth-controlled space and hunting grounds. Fright Agent Maddo had the highest Derth kill count on record. He was like most other Teons with a muscular looking armor over their bodies of bone. Their heads were exposed and completely skeletal like their hands and resembled the human skull.

They were all seated in a circle with each in direct view of the other. Dark Lord Epitaph asked for a report. Fright Agent Nehih reported that all was in place for his own return to escort Epitaph's bride, Emelia here to Xotosia. Fright Agent Paj followed with his report that the super weapon, the Breathtaker, was back on the proposed production schedule after his initiation of cleansed labor adjustment. Fright Agent Kyrak was pleased to report that the search for Josh Broody and his ship was being narrowed, and with all his resources properly motivated, he expected a successful target acquired in a matter of rotations. Epitaph was pleased with the reports but seemed more eager for the report from Fright Agent Maddo. He requested permission to approach his dark lord and was granted. He stood from his seat and walked to Epitaph, presenting a Book of Prophecy that he had retrieved from the catacombs on Golbriay. Fright Agent Maddo added that with a stroke of luck, he had procured the book unfinished and that he had also secured in the detention cells on his ship the Prophetess that was writing in it. It was a revelation that Epitaph had not expected but was extremely pleased to hear. Epitaph dismissed his fright agents to their duties. He ordered Fright Agent Maddo to transfer the captured Prophetess to the *Darkfall.* Before departing, each pledged their loyalty to their dark lord and bowed before him. Epitaph granted their departure with a wave of his hand. As they departed, Epitaph placed the book on an altar-type platform, and as he opened it, the book displayed a glowing aura.

Epitaph had started to read through the book, jumping from one page to another and only deciphering short passages. Silos Taqoon busted into the room. All his laughter and joyful moods had been depleted since the Black Guard had arrived. He yelled out in anger at Epitaph, demanding to know why and by what order the Black Guard had to confiscate his palace. Epitaph never turned to face Silos. He only displayed a grimace of annoyance as he continued to read through the Book of Prophecy before him. Silos demanded that the palace be returned to his control at once. Epitaph slammed his fists to the altar and at each side of the book. He then turned quickly as his dark crimson eyes seemed to darken even more.

He called for his guards. Two Black Guard soldiers entered the room. His evil grimace grew wider. With a long and eerie lisp, he stated that Silos Taqoon was unhappy with the arrangement. He then added, "Perhapsss we could alleviate hisss consssernsss." With the lisp growing and intensifying, he ordered Silos removed from the entire palace and its grounds.

Silos screamed out, "You can't do this!"

Epitaph added to his order as his guards pulled Silos away with force. Epitaph said, "Any refusssal or resssisssstanccce by Sssilosss ssshould be ansssswered withth terminatttion." The mood and the tone combined with the pronounced lisp and evil look in Epitaph's eyes had unnerved Silos. Silos had heard many stories and had figured that he had pushed his hand as far as he should dare to do. He pleaded for a request to be unhanded and to leave the palace on his own volition. Epitaph granted the request with a nod to his guards. They unhanded him and walked at his sides with him as a provided measure of assurance that he actually left the palace. Epitaph's grimace turned to a pleasing grin with his forked tongue flicking more rapidly in and out from his mouth as he returned to his newly acquired Book of Prophecy.

* * *

The *Fallen Star* entered the atmosphere of the jungle planet referred to as Matrel. The ship, still controlled manually as Josh continued to rest his neural link, had descended over a clearing as it fired the repulsor lifts, opened the venting flaps, and lowered the landing gear to gently place itself on the surface. A port hatch opened, and the boarding ramp lowered to the lush green covered ground. The clearing was large and surrounded by trees all around. Josh exited first with Tana still naked except for her fur and still in her manacles with new chains. Laylee followed next, and Cody covered the rear of the marching order. Laylee asked why the chains were necessary if they were under a flag of peace. Josh stated that the chains were merely an insurance policy that she would not run off. He wanted to meet her people and negotiate a safe haven. Laylee stated that keeping Tana in chains would not be the best way to start. Tana begged to be freed. She promised Josh that she would stay with them. Laylee added that Tana had already proven her loyalty by saving them. Josh relaxed with a deep breath and removed the manacles and chains. Cody made a long growl in response. Josh responded, "I hope I don't regret it either." They stood facing each other as Tana vowed her life to Josh. Josh replied that he did not require a life debt; he just wanted her to keep her word. He then asked her if she could lead them to her people from here. Tana motioned for them to follow as they walked into the jungle trees.

* * *

Gold Gatling was waiting on his Honsho freighter for clearance permission to leave the docking port. He inquired if any of his legion's ships had search reports on the *Fallen Star*. There had been nothing yet. Another pirate and liaison to Gold had stepped forward and asked why he had not provided the ship designation signature to Epitaph. Gold responded that it was the information they and nobody else knew that would give them the edge. If the Black Guard had that information, they would be much more likely to locate the ship through any docking bay records. That would take away a great chance for Gold to obtain the spoils of reward. As far as the Black Guard knew, the docking records on Xotosia turned out to be invalid because of a forged designation signature of the ship. Gold then ordered the pirate to hand deliver a coded message to Silos to not reveal this acquired information. He also presented the pirate with a bottle of very rare Takadish liquor to deliver to Silos as a gift and additional incentive.

* * *

Silos Taqoon had by now been escorted out from his own palace. He was surrounded by his loyal aides and many scantily clad male and female pleasure androids of his employ as they stood outside the palace gate in the snow-covered mountain terrain looking in from the outside. They were loyal to Silos, but all wondered on his next move. It was a brief question as a long enclosed and sleek black hover vehicle broke the snowline image on its approach. It hovered four feet off the ground and slowly came to a stop before Silos and his crew as its rear centrally mounted engine shut down in power. The front hatch lifted up and outward as a man disembarked from it. The man was a Jaskan, human in build but with short jade-green hair. He was of a slender build and dressed in silver colored satin resembling somewhat a variation of a business suit. He greeted Silos Taqoon with great respect and honor in his voice. He stated that he worked for Clad Byar. He added that Clad Byar had been informed of the changing situation and wished to offer his support and his hospitality in this crisis. Silos knew Clad Byar very well. In addition to being on the Xotosia business council and an old friend, Clad was also the biggest druglord on Xotosia. A very powerful individual and what Silos needed now was power.

Another hovercraft vehicle approached, similar in design. It was not as long or sleek and had twin mounted rear engines. Another of Silos', closest aides disembarked as the side of the vehicle opened upward, presenting available transport seating. Silos looked back at the Jaskan that Clad Byar had sent. He then ordered all his aides to take refuge in his smaller palace for the time being. He ushered two of his pleasure androids to come with him to meet Clad Byar. Silos took one last look back at his former palace stronghold and then entered the vehicle sent by Clad. The Jaskan closed the rear passenger hatch and returned to the front pilot station as the hatch lowered and sealed. The two vehicles headed down the mountainous path to a fork in the trail. They then split off in separate directions.

* * *

Tana, now freed from her chains, had led Josh and his team into the trees of the jungle. The trees provided little cover from the increasing heavy rainfall that had began instantly. The track was a treacherous one through the thick ground grass cover, slippery at times from the rain and overshadowing trees. As they walked slowly along, Tana abruptly stopped and looked around with a tense stance. She heard something and turned, focused in one direction. She then froze in place from her neck down. She started to sniff intently into the air. Cody jumped now in reaction to a sound and also tried to gain knowledge from a sniff of his own into the surrounding area. Cody and Tana both spun around as they had both caught the scent of the something that was charging upon them from the rear position. It was rushing toward them, pushing through the leaves, grass, and brush at a hurried pace. Tana engaged on a runaway from it. Cody was surprised at her sudden start and staggered at first in his own run. He quickly regained his footing. Tana's footing here on her homeworld was much faster, and she even had increased agility. Cody was finding it difficult to keep up at her pace.

Laylee had started her run directly behind Cody. All three of them were more agile than their companion, Josh Broody. The four of them ran from the moving leaves and grass and away from their pursuer. Tana tried to stop suddenly as she caught her balance and teetered at the ledge of a muddy slope. The rain was coming down even harder. Cody and Laylee had stopped to each side of Tana, but Josh's run had bumped him directly into her, and Tana again steadied her balance. She pointed to a narrow path in the overgrown trees to her left. Cody and Laylee had followed her instruction and headed into the path ahead of her. Tana started to follow, but as she kicked off, the muddy ledge had given way, and she fell over it. Josh dove to catch her, but the mud also pulled him down. They both slid along violently down the long and winding muddy slope. Both Josh and Tana tried desperately but unsuccessfully to control their slide. The heavy rain and increasing power of the mudslide had consumed them as they continued to be pushed downward.

Whatever was following them was close behind. From out of the trees darted four dark coal skinned figures. They used their large overpowering frontal arms to push forward as their large and heavy black serpentine tail forms slid behind them. The head of the creature was ape-like and sported long silver hair over the thick black skin. The roar that it made revealed its sharp teeth and sounded throughout the jungle with an incredible display of fury and rage that sent other ground and air-based creatures scattering from their hidden places. The first of the creatures tried to stop itself from overrunning the ledge. It failed and tumbled over and into its own uncontrollable slide down the muddy slope. The other two creatures managed to sharply turn and support each other from plunging over the ledge. They paused to look over the ledge as their prey and fellow pack member slid rapidly down and away. The fourth was the larger of the creatures and came out at a slower pace because of its more enormous size. It growled at the other two on the ledge with an overpowering wave and stench. They had quickly picked up the scent again and headed down the other path. The larger of the creatures was clearly the pack leader. It peered over the ledge and down the muddy slope. It unleashed a loud roar into the rainy jungle. It then turned down the other path as well.

The muddy slide poured into a lagoon area. Josh and Tana were totally covered in mud as they slid down the slope and launched into the lagoon water below with a large splash. They both quickly bobbed up from the waterline with the mud washed away. They heard the loud angry roars produced by the creature as it too slid violently and uncontrollably down the slope toward them.

It was then that they had witnessed the muddy slope rise upward in a scooping formation. It then began to reform into a larger mud-like giant clutching hand. The creature sliding down the mud slope as it transformed was thrown into the giant muddy hand grip. The once predator roared in more pain than anger as it had become captured prey and was now being crushed by the giant muddy hand. The sounds of the beast quickly silenced as the muddy form transformed again around it. A rumbling motion was all that was seen under the mud as the once fierce beast had been suffocated and crushed. The mud then separated and tossed the beast's skeletal remains to the water's edge of the lagoon below.

Josh and Tana watched in awe as the mud slope lifted again, twisted around, and morphed into an almost mud-covered human-formed head complete with dripping mud from the mouth and eye sockets. The giant mud head opened its mud dripping jaw even wider as it descended downward at them with an attempt to consume. Josh and Tana both shared a quick glance at each other before diving in separate directions below the waterline just before the giant mud monster splashed down onto and through the water surface where they once floated. Josh and Tana swam deeper as the mud transformed again into a living wall and followed them to the bottom of the lagoon where it then spread outward in all directions.

* * *

Cody and Laylee continued to run down a narrow jungle path in the heavily downpouring rain and pursued by the strange creatures that seemed to be gaining on their position. Cody stopped and looked Laylee over from bottom to top, even walking around her as he did so. Laylee smiled and admitted that she knew she was fine and that he liked what he saw, but this was hardly the time. Cody instantly smiled at her even with his canine-like snout. As Laylee relaxed her posture, Cody grabbed her and threw her off the path into the tree and bush cover to the side. He then looked back down the path and waited for the first two of the creatures that were pursuing them to gain a visual of him as their massive arms continued pulling their serpentine bodies down the trail in pursuit. Cody took off again running at full speed and drawing them down the path after him.

As the two creatures passed by Laylee, she stood up and back stepped deeper into the jungle cover as the larger pack leader followed after his pack members down the narrow jungle path. He stopped suddenly on the path just past her position and seemed to be trying to gain a scent. Laylee slowly and cautiously drew the small stun pistol from her leg holster and set it to the maximum setting. She realized now why Cody had tossed her to the side. Because of her being an android and having no scent to track, she was able to slowly walk and stay behind the beast. She tried to make as little sound as possible as she moved closer. Her cover was still the thick trees and bushes. The little sound she did make was mixed with the heavy rain and wind of the regular jungle movement. Still, despite all that, the beast suddenly turned back. With a few more cautious steps, Laylee remained behind it and just off the trail. With one loud roar, it seemed as though the beast had just given up and started to move down the path again toward the direction of his pack. Laylee gave up the silent tracking and rushed forward as she fired her stun pistol with one single shot to the backside of the beast. The beast was hit and staggered. Laylee unleashed one more blast that caused the beast to finally fall face first onto the narrow jungle trail.

Laylee had by now crossed to the other side of the path. She again holstered her stun pistol and started moving through the jungle cover in the direction that Cody had ran. As she did so, she had kept the jungle path within her view. She was hoping to use the jungle as a shortcut to catch up with Cody. It was then that she had tripped a vine snare line and a large tree limb fell from a fastened position ahead of her and down into a leaf- and branch-covered pit. The vine it was tied to was the same that had also snared her ankle. The momentum of the large tree limb's fall had taken her off her feet and dragged her toward the same pit. She valiantly clutched and scraped at the jungle terrain in an attempt to keep from being pulled into the pit, but the attempt proved futile as she dropped into the ten-feet-deep pit.

* * *

Cody had still been running from his predators when the narrow path ended into heavy and thick jungle cover of trees, with large leaves and vines. Cody ran into it and took cover as he drew his side holstered blaster pistol. As the creatures came into view, he wasted no time in blasting each of them with two heavy and intense blasts that dropped and killed both of them. Cody slowly stood up and waited for the other to approach. Once he felt it was clear, he approached the fallen beasts, still with his blaster pistol drawn and ready. Several sharp spearheads were suddenly pointed into him. He looked to the handle ends of the spears and saw six naked male Matrasus surrounding his position. They had managed to sneak up on him with silence and masked scents.

* * *

Josh and Tana had made the swim downward and deep enough in the lagoon to avoid the swooping wave of living mud that had tried to consume them. They had rejoined and swam along the bottom of the lagoon in the deeper section until Tana pointed to an underwater cave. Together they swam into the cave and at an upward ascent once inside, where they surfaced above the waterline and into a higher level of the cave. They swam to the edge of the underground cave pool. Tana was the first to climb out with Josh right behind her. Tana's fur was wet, but still her naked body as she climbed up ahead of Josh was enough of a distraction with his sexual thoughts about her. As Josh exited the water, Tana had shaken her body as water flung from her fur and she laid herself at his feet. Josh, with a little hesitance, had sat down next to her. They were both breathing heavily as they regained their breath from the extended underwater swim. Josh laid down onto his back on the hard cave floor and slightly rocky surface. Tana draped one arm and one leg over him and placed her head onto his chest. She was exhausted and closed her eyes.

* * *

Laylee kept slipping at her grip as she slid back down the dirt-covered pit wall in her attempts to climb out. She slammed her closed fists into the dirt wall in anger as she let out a scream of frustration. She turned with her back to the wall and slowly lowered herself to a seated position. For whatever reason, her thoughts went to Josh Broody. She pictured his face clearly as if he was there with her. He sported a dashing smile that made her feel unlike anything she felt before. She mentally scanned her programming and found herself working at all parameters. She then started to wonder if Josh was safe. Suddenly her attention was snapped back to her own reality. Why had that sudden thought and concern for Josh entered her mind? She was again called away from her thought as a strong and thick climbing vine was lowered down in front of her. Laylee jumped to her feet and looked up where she could only see the rain falling down now at a light drizzle. She hollered up for Josh or Cody. With no reply, she took a hold of the knotted vine and climbed slowly upward. Upon climbing out from the pit, she was surprised to find eight Matrasus, naked except for their fur and surrounding her. Four were females, and the other four were males. One female stepped forward, wearing only a necklace of bones. She and the others were muscular and well-endowed. Just like Tana, they had orange fur with black tiger stripes. They all had long brown hair at the tops of their heads also like Tana. The obvious female leader had long white hair. She spoke to her in the common human language. Like Tana, it was broken basic speech with growls and snarls of the Matrasus language interjected, but it was enough for Laylee to understand. She had gathered that her name was Aga. She had also interpreted that the female leader wanted to bring her back to their village as two of the females turned her and bound her wrists with strong rope like vines. She could also tell that they were somewhat puzzled by her lack of scent. She decided not to fight as they bound her. She would remain silent until she could learn more through observation.

* * *

Cody was directed through the jungle by spear points of the six Matrasus that had captured him. All seemed to be young males with the Earth tiger pattern fur and traditional nakedness obviously shared commonly by the race. He was escorted into a small camp that by the primitive weaponry of spears and wooden shields along with bows and arrows seemed to be a militarized war camp. Around the camp, he saw many huts constructed with branches and large tree leaves. There were wooden branches and limbs scattered all around and scraps of discarded technology and even thick ropes and chains. At the head of the camp and set as a highlight was a larger hut with woven banners each with a symbol sewn into them. The banners were made of a heavy cloth material with thin rope sewn onto the left and right edges. The top and bottom of each rope was braided into a tassel. The banners were orange in background with the display of a water fountain split down the middle with a piercing black triangle that hosted three sharply designed points. The fountain was a mixture of thread in the colors of light blue and white. The fountain sprayed upward, with one leaning its overspray to the left and the other to the right. Under each fountain overspray was half a cat's-eye design.

At the main hut stood two muscular Matrasus guards. Each also with the striped but more defined fur design. They wore no clothing as well but had belts around their waists. On each belt was a sheath, and in it was a metal short sword. Each guard also had a metal shield on their backs and strapped over their shoulders. A piece of long black cloth covered the entrance to the hut, and it was pushed away as a larger-sized Matrasus exited from the hut. He looked very different from the other Matrasus. He was the only one to wear Matrasus tiger striped furs as tattered clothing. They were skins and furs he had shed from his enemy Matrasus. He did not have the standard orange fur with black tiger stripes. His fur was shaggy and long from the top of his head to his bare cat-clawed feet. It was a dull black with darker black tiger stripes. His facial features were cat-like as well, but his right eye was a normal cat-eye design, while his left eye appeared to have severe damage as the eye socket seemed to be torn away or peeled back. Resting in that eye socket was a larger cat eye that was extremely bloodshot. He stiffened his posture and let out a few loud roars to alert all the other Matrasus in his camp. They all quickly assembled as Cody was brought further into the camp and toward the shaggy black-furred being.

What surprised Cody was the blaster pistol that was holstered to the belt around the being's waist. As the black-furred Matrasus stepped forward to meet Cody's approach, he yelled out orders in the roars and growls of the Matrasus language. Cody understood most of it from what he had learned from Tana and what was derived from the Canian similar speech. He was clearly directing the assembly of other Matrasus as they flanked and moved forward and backward to each side in the formation. As he roared and growled at them, the soldiers returned his orders with the same verbal sounds of acceptance and obedience. It was once the two of them were face to face that Cody became even more intrigued. The shaggy black-furred Matrasus had spoken out in barks and growls of the Canian language as though it was a natural language for him. He had asked Cody his name. Cody barked his name out in the Canian language. The Matrasus then surprised Cody even more as he spoke out in strong and regular common human language. He asked, "Is that a name translated into common as Cody?"

Before Cody could muster a response from his shock, the Matrasus introduced himself as Clawlow. Cody asked if he was a Matrasus.

Clawlow paused in thought before replying, "Sort of." He added that he had been born just a little bit different and had been shunned by his people for that very reason. Clawlow then followed Cody's glance around the assembly of soldiers. He then raised his arms with long black straggly fur hanging down and declared loudly and with much pride that these were the Matrasus with vision that have learned to see beyond how things are and how they should actually be. All the assembled Matrasus soldiers reached outward with one outstretched arm and open claw as they roared out loudly their approval and allegiance.

* * *

Sorlin Garrison's fleet of four Honsho freighters rested at the borders of the Dezilize System. Sorlin had stormed through the corridors of his main and lead ship with great impatience. He made his way directly to a makeshift computer lab and stood over a sensor station of the Honsho that had told him before that the detection of the *Fallen Star* would be difficult but not impossible. Sorlin was angered that they had sat here idle for half a rotation and were wasting other opportunities to locate the ship. In addition to that, for all the time they wasted, there was a chance that Gold Gatling, the Black Guard, or even one of many bounty hunters would locate the ship before them.

The other Honsho seemed to ignore Sorlin as he continued about his duties at the sensor station. Sorlin yelled out, "Are you hearing me?!" The Honsho, with one more check of his readings, calmly stood up to face Sorlin as he pressed a point on the lighted console. A map was displayed on the monitor screen overhead of them. One area of space was marked with a circle and crosshairs. The Honsho stated that Sorlin's prey was there. Sorlin recognized the area as mostly unexplored space well removed from Black Guard controlled space. The sensor station Honsho stated that it was the hyperspace exit point of the *Fallen Star*.

Sorlin instructed the pilot station to adjust to the coordinates that he was sending them. Sorlin finished sending the coordinates from the console and looked around at the other Honshos in observance. Sorlin then looked back at his still very calm sensor station Honsho. He asked just as calmly, "You are not afraid of me, are you?"

The Honsho replied, "If I were afraid of you, how could I serve you?" Sorlin had a small chuckle at the answer and admitted that it was a very good answer. He embraced the Honsho with an arm around his shoulder. Sorlin called out to everyone in the room that they could learn a lot from this Honsho. The Honsho smiled with pride and thanked Sorlin for his praise.

Sorlin replied proudly, "Not a problem." With a sudden flick of his wrist and no attempt to hide his action, a quick draw dagger slid into Sorlin's hand as he sliced the Honsho's throat without hesitation. The Honsho fell dead to Sorlin's feet. Sorlin added to his previous proclamation that each and every Honsho in his service should know their place and, more importantly, know to be afraid of him when he is displeased. Sorlin slowly walked from the silent room without another word or a glance back.

* * *

The hover vehicle arrived at an elaborate array of architecture on Xotosia. Each structure in the city was designed to map against the mountainous backdrop. An android designed to appear as a well-developed, muscular male human in scantily designed attire had opened the vehicle door and escorted Silos Taqoon up the outside stairs of the tallest building in the center complex. Silos was utilizing his wrist comm and stated to the person on the other end of the transmission to thank Gold Gatling for his most generous gift and to inform Gold that he had no intentions of providing the Black Guard with any information on Josh Broody's ship.

Silos found the signal of his wrist comm fading as he entered the building and climbed upward on a winding staircase. The stairs and floor of the facility were of a marblelike design as on Earth. The staircase handrails as well as most wall décor of the facility was highlighted with silver and various large gems. Gems were a major form of currency accepted anywhere in the universe. They were so versatile. You could barter with them, use them in building designs, and many could even be turned into power sources.

At the top of the staircase, Silos gasped heavily for breath after the long stair climb that his overweight body was clearly not prepared for such a routine. He was greeted by two more androids designed to appear as human females. One was a long-haired blond and the other a long-haired redhead. Both had fabulous bodies and were scantily dressed to show them off. This was obviously the standard dress code for the androids on Xotosia. They ushered him into a dining hall with an extremely long dining table well-stocked with various prepared foods and drinks. At the far other end of the table was the human male known as Clad Byar. He was a smaller and thinner human than most. He had a wiry build to him, but a stature and reputation of great power to back it up. His face was also thin, almost as though he had never eaten anything in his life, which would be in contrary to the spread of food on the table. His face was featured with a mustache that was trimmed to very narrow lines and was groomed upward instead of downward. Much like a dali style mustache on Earth. His goatee was also trimmed in three separate and very thin lines. He wore black mascara around his eyes, and his black hair was cut to appear almost like a spider sitting on top of his head. He held up in his hand a vile of Quick. Quick was a very expensive and addictive drug outlawed throughout the universe, but here on Xotosia, it was very much legal and high in demand.

Clad motioned for Silos to be seated at the last empty chair around the table. Silos was introduced to the group by Clad as a male human android pulled the chair out for him. Clad continued with the introductions and started with the only female at the table. She was also human and was named Madaray Vilici, head of the major gambling houses on Xotosia. Her long black hair and shapely body complemented her slightly aging beauty.

Across the table from her sat Toxicus Forn. He was an Abolish, a race of humanoid build, but with crimson red skin. They also produced a constant dark red mist around their bodies that provided their own personal form of oxygen. If a thief needed a fence, Toxicus Forn was the one to seek out. He was a procurer and dealer of many rare and stolen treasures.

Ardicane Blivord sat in another chair. He was Shapay. Shapays also looked human except for two features. They had antlers at each side of their heads. Much like the thorns on a Prah, the antlers on a Shapay with the most points really defined their importance, and Ardicane's antlers hosted 40 points. Shapays also had humps on their backs of various sizes. Ardicane's was not overly large but still noticeable. The unique thing about these humps was that they were sentient lifeforms and functioned as a symbiote to the Shapay. Ardicane had made his fortune and rose to his level of power and stature by muscling in on smaller production companies of all lines of items. He did so by purchasing them legally whether the owners and boards wanted to sell them or not. Money was good but added with a firm muscular touch it was unstoppable. Blivord Industries was well-known throughout the known universe and made items for every field.

Across from him was a Jaskan male with short-cut dark emerald green hair. This particular Jaskan was named Arnvare Nixicine. He was known as an arranger. An arranger was the trainer of and contact for mercenaries and assassins. Arnvare was one with many contacts. He was also good friends with Ardicane Blivord and had arranged many meetings with select mercenaries in the past.

Clad Byar had called the meeting to order. All the leaders present in the room had become unnerved by the arriving and existing Black Guard movements and developments. Their operations in many areas across Xotosia had become disrupted or even disbanded. It was very clear that the heavier the Black Guard presence would become, the more their operations would weaken. Here on Xotosia they all excelled as the best in their fields throughout the galaxy and that status alone had allowed them to reign supreme and with excellent prestige here on the uncrowned capital world of crime. Criminal operations that although well-known inside and out of the galaxy were allowed to flourish without restrictions, especially here on Xotosia where the Black Guard had often ignored and turned a blind eye. It was a status that they all had grown to enjoy. It was now very apparent that with such a heavy Black Guard presence, that particular privilege would soon slip away from them and what remnants of their operations did remain would see all profits go directly into the Black Guard. Everyone in attendance were in agreement but hesitant to bring up the solution that they were all thinking about. The mere utterance of a revolt or rebellion against the Black Guard had never proven well in accordance to galactic history.

Clad Byar was a man of strong conviction and was not afraid. He declared with great boldness, "We must form a coalition to drive the Black Guard off Xotosia and make them feel it unwise to return."

* * *

Tana had climbed onto Josh as he slept. She had lightly stroked his lips with her tongue. Josh, still deep asleep, had instinctively started kissing back at her. In his dream, he was kissing Laylee and his dream to him was vivid. Tana had taken the kissing response as a sign to proceed as she locked her lips with his, and the passion grew as the kissing intensified. Their lips struggled to stay together. Tana had ripped open his shirt under his open vest. She broke her lips from his to begin sucking on his chest. Josh had laid back in his dream and allowed Laylee to suck at his chest. As her lips and tongue moved downward and she started to undo the front of his leather pants, Josh was just beginning to awaken but kept his eyes tightly closed as he was seeing Laylee rest her lower half onto his stiff grown limb. In his mind, Laylee was moving up and down in rapid motion onto his stiff rod as he felt her wetness increase. She was still joined with him and laid her firm breasts to his chest as she continued with her back and forth riding motion. He could feel himself releasing his sperm inside of her. She continued to shift and arouse as they again kissed with great intensity and passion, afraid to stop as if their very lives depended on it. In actuality, Tana had mounted herself on top and with wild and unbridled passion as she was sliding back and forth onto this man that for some reason, she had become so obsessed with besides her own primal desires. She felt her own release of sexual fluids as she also felt his release inside of her. She was growing feverishly more aroused, and her shifting motion rapidly increased. Her hands tightened along with his as she pulled them from a firm clutch on her shapely ass and her lips moved harder and faster against his. The passion had overtaken her senses as her tightened hands now pinned his, and she had released her claws, and her kissing had turned into biting.

The sudden pain had jolted Josh to a full awareness as he was forced to open his eyes. He had been subconsciously subdued but now remembered his situation clearly. His lust for Laylee was so strong that he wanted it to be true as he at first continued to pump his fluids into Tana. He realized that he was not with Laylee, and although they had not been together, he had a feeling of wrongness, and shame overcome him.

As he gathered his senses, Josh started to push Tana off him, but she was stronger than he thought and resisted as she continued her shifting motion, feeling lost in her own ecstasy. Josh increased his strength and pulled himself free from under her and was able to toss her to his side on the cave floor. Tana hissed at him and followed with a roar as she struggled to pin him again. She used her strength to again move on top of him and held his shoulders down firmly to the cave floor with her claws digging deep into his skin. She tried to force her lower frontal region back onto his, but he was resisting. Tana was biting at Josh's face to continue, but Josh kept turning away. He was finally able to firmly place a knee into her side that jolted her and followed with a closed fist punch to her jaw with his now freed arm. Tana rolled off him and quickly assumed a full crouching position. With her knees bent and her body arched forward, she was ready to pounce. Tana growled at him in the Matrasus language. Josh managed to get to his feet and pulled his leather pants back up. As he fastened them, he kept eye contact with Tana. She had transferred her Matrasus growls into a gruff tone of broken human common speech as she asked why he resisted her.

Josh could sense her desire and calmed his voice to install calm in her wild sexual drive. Josh told her that it was wrong. Tana looked puzzled and asked what was wrong about taking what you want. She added that humans did it all the time. She had been taken sexually by her human captors before despite her own will. She finally wanted it on her own and took it as they did. Josh raised both his hands up with open palms that still bled from where her claws had dug into them. He was trying to calm her with slow hand gestures. Josh told Tana that she was taking him like the humans took her, but just like her, he was unwilling. Tana seemed confused, as she replied that he had returned the actions with no resistance at first. Josh paused because what she said was true. He carefully claimed that he was unaware of what was happening because he had believed at first that he was dreaming. He admitted that he had believed he was with Laylee. Tana appeared even more puzzled and asked why he could not let her be Laylee. Josh told her that it did not work that way.

She responded with assertiveness, "Tana want you! You not want Tana?"

Josh struggled; despite her fur and race, she was otherwise human in build and quite attractive. A part of him would want her, but he had grown a desire to want Laylee. Tana slowly straightened and stood upright as she asked if Laylee wanted him like she did. Josh admitted that he was unsure because he had not made his intentions clear to her.

Tana claimed more than questioned, "If Laylee not want you, then I have you!"

Josh told her it did not work that way.

Tana stepped closer to Josh with her claws up and at the ready as he stiffened in a defensive stance. She took a long and deep sniff of him. Tana replied, "You human. It always work that way." She retracted her claws and pressed one open palm to her breasts and the other to his chest. Tana said, "You mine. I claim you. That how humans do."

Josh could only reply that he was not the same as the humans that had taken her. Tana hissed at him once more and declared all humans take what they want without asking. She slowly turned away and walked to lean against the cave wall.

* * *

Laylee had been brought to a large primitive village of huts constructed of leaves and branches and fastened together with strong thick vines. The village was heavily populated with male and female Matrasus, all naked except for their tiger-striped fur. All had long brown or blond hair on their heads. She drew all of their attention as she still had her wrists bound behind her back and was guided at spear point by six different spears. She was pushed toward a tribal meeting circle. All activities including the tribal meeting ceased and all attention was on Laylee. In the circle, three Matrasus seemed accented with importance by the necklaces of bone that they wore. One was a female with manacles on her wrists and broken chains hung from them. She stood over a metal cauldron, and in addition to the bone necklaces around her neck, she wore a belt of leather pouches around her waist. She stood up from where she once knelt over many stones, herbs, bones, and shaved sticks. She was a more elderly Matrasus. She was naked like the rest, but her body was not as firm. It sagged with obvious age. Her hair was longer than any others and more gray than white. One of the males stood from a parchment type material that hosted pictures and symbols to represent the written scribes of their culture. The hair on the top of his head was cut uniquely different from any others. It was two stripes of brown hair cut in the form of a reverse Mohawk. The one in the middle had long brown hair. He had the most bones on his necklace and was the only one to wear any clothing. All he wore was a hooded tan colored cloak made from an animal skin. The center male spoke first in the savage language used by the Matrasus with few human common speak words that Laylee could make out. The other Matrasus all around the assembled area seemed disapproving of her presence by the manner of growls and roars. The one with the parchments tried to speak but was silenced by a roar from the elderly female. The hooded male and the elderly female took the time to growl and roar at each other. Laylee was suspecting that they were determining which of them had the authority in this situation.

The hooded male seemed to have won the contest as he stepped free from the circle and walked around Laylee. As he did, he sniffed at her deeply. He paused and deeply stared at her. He ripped away her torn clothing at the arms. He touched at the scars she had suffered from the planet of the undead despite the fact that they had closed somewhat because of her rapid skin regeneration. The elderly female stepped forward and pinched the skin on her arm. There were roars let out again between them and the other Matrasus spectators. Laylee had gathered that her exotic toned synthetic skin and the silver metal under it revealed by the cuts was what intrigued them. The skin was a darker tone and synthetic but also designed to heal. It was still in that regeneration process and it was a strange sight for them. They both took strong and deep sniffs of her now. They were also most likely puzzled by the lack of scent. Laylee was obviously unlike any other human they had ever encountered.

The elderly female called out loudly and pointed at Laylee. She called her, "Grrklk!" All of the spectator Matrasus seemed to gasp at the claim and even stepped back and cowered. The hooded male and the elderly female stepped away and made hand motions that brought forth two other young male Matrasus warriors. They each held firmly an axe with a wooden handle and one formed piece of bone that hosted a single sharp curved edge. Another Matrasus had hit at the back of her knees and pulled at her hair. He forced her to her knees. The two axe-wielding Matrasus both raised their weapons and were about to swing downward on her.

Laylee remained calm and showed no panic as she screamed out, "Wait!" The axe wielders froze in response. Her scream was followed by many gasps throughout the crowd but quickly grew silent. Laylee looked around and focused on what she had ascertained as the three tribal leaders. She claimed that she was here with Tana. The male with the parchments ordered the axe wielders to lower their weapons. He walked to the hooded male and elderly female. The three of them waved everyone back. They then started a discussion in low volume tones of growls. The three of them stepped forward and the hooded male nodded at Laylee. She returned the nod. The hooded male placed his fist to his chest and seemed to claim his name as Bangalark. He followed with more short roars and a few unclear common speak words.

The elderly female stepped forward and translated into a better but still broken form of common speak. She asked, "Tana? Where she? You slave ship have her?"

Laylee turned her body to show her vine-bound wrists. She looked back and said, "Release me and I will help you find Tana."

The male with the parchments and the elderly female both paused with a stare at each other. They both nodded to the hooded male called Bangalark. He stepped forward and pulled a metal dagger out from under the hooded cloak. He shoved Laylee around and slapped at her bound wrists. She raised them up behind her as high as she could. Bangalark used the dagger and with a few cuts of the vine had freed Laylee's wrists.

He then tried again to utter what human common language he knew. All that Laylee could make out was "Tana small girl." He kept mentioning Tana and his panic kept slipping him back into the Matrasus growls and roars. The elderly female stepped forward and calmed him. Laylee asked if Tana was his daughter. The elderly female confirmed Laylee's question. She then introduced herself as Girassar and the male with the parchments as Garton.

Girassar asked where Tana was at and if she was safe. Laylee stated that they had been split up by the creatures. She went further into describing the creatures that had chased them. Girassar called them goras, a predator species native to the planet. Girassar claimed that Tana was the name given by enslavers. She added, "They come take who they want. Took Tana some time ago."

Bangalark stepped forward again and with a great anger pointed at Laylee as if making an accusation in a loud, reverberating roar. Laylee looked around to all she could see and loudly declared that she was no enslaver and she was not like the humans they knew. Garton stepped closer to Laylee. He claimed that Bangalark had given Tana to him as a prize and a bride. Garton continued his tale. Before the joining ceremony, the enslavers had come. Bangalark had taken Tana to safety and had returned to help fight the human enslavers. After the battle was over and the enslavers had retreated with several Matrasus, Bangalark had taken him to where Tana had been hidden. They had found evidence of a struggle. All that was left behind were weapons, human blood, and tracks in the ground. They followed the human and Matrasus tracks into a circle of other tracks. The scent of humans was everywhere. It appeared that the captured Matrasus were bound there and carried away on human starships. They had believed Tana to have been one of the captured that day.

Laylee promised that she meant them no further harm. She again claimed that she and her friends were not enslavers. She added that she was not human, but one of her friends was human. She claimed he was Josh and a good human, which was met with much doubt by many of them assembled. Laylee further described her other friend Cody as a Canian. The description of the Canian almost seemed frightful to them. She wanted to find her friends and most importantly help them find Tana. She turned to Bangalark and pleaded, "Let me bring your small girl back to you."

Chapter Six

Stronghold

LORD EPITAPH HAD retired to what was once the study room of Silos Taqoon. He had been reading through his newly acquired Book of Prophecy. He had found one particular passage that had troubled him deeply. He read the passage, "The brothers broken will be secured. The dark lord will rest his eyes to another task. As the dark lord is forced to look away to a ripping fold, the fate of his demise will once again and for the last time grow anew. The former general will find the lost brother. The dark lord's offers though fruitful and much desired will not detour the former general as before. The lost brother will be brought back to join the former general, and the two brothers once united will clear the darkness and the reign of fear. One will lay over the other. They will usher the universe into a new light, and the dark lord will perish before them."

Lord Epitaph commed his confiscated palace commander and ordered his shuttle prepared at once for his intentions to return to his ship, the *Darkfall*, and question the captured Prophetess personally. The commander reported that the Prophetess had already been interrogated thoroughly and had refused to provide any information about the books. Lord Epitaph's forked tongue had flicked in and out from his mouth as he read more from the book before him. He read,

"The resolve of the Prophetess, although strong, will be broken as her gaze into the dark lord's eyes will overwhelm her with fear. His frightful persuasion will draw unwillingly from her the secrets he desires." Lord Epitaph's smile widened as he spoke back into the comlink and stated, "Ssshe will talk withth me."

* * *

Clad Byar had gotten the attention of his fellow crimelords. He had a vision of a structured command with Xotosia back in their full control. A female android in human appearance had entered and reported that Lord Epitaph was in return to his ship, but several contingents of Black Guard forces would remain with orders of further and deeper containment planned in his absence. Clad believed that they had been given an opportunity. Despite the power of a massive Black Guard presence, Lord Epitaph's departure would allow further spread troop movements and they could use that to their advantage. They would have an easier time to move about the troops without Lord Epitaph's constant watch. He claimed that these would be their first steps in their path to victory.

* * *

Cody had been cast into a metal shackle around one of his ankles and fastened to a ten-foot-tall metal stake firmly planted into the ground at the center of a deeply dug and extremely wide entrenchment. Cody looked around his position deep inside an entrenchment and found other Matrasus also chained to metal stakes all around him. Cody grasped his arms around the metal stake and tried to pull it from the ground but only pulled his own muscles in the attempt. He looked around again to all the other chained Matrasus, who seemed to have lost all hope as they either sat or laid in fetal positions around the stakes. The worse-off ones just walked out as far as their chains would allow then around the stake and back to it. They repeated the process almost as if they were mindlessly driven into mental despair.

Cody then looked up at the ledge of the entrenchment that stretched about twenty feet upward. Clawlow stood there with the support of a Matrasus at both his sides. Cody barked angrily up at him in the Canian language. He then followed his statement in common language and demanded to be freed at once. Clawlow yelled back in common response that he would deal with the beast when he returned. He was going to reclaim the Matrasus destiny and would be the new leader after he claimed his victory with his conquering of the great village his people referred to as Siber. Cody could hear several Matrasus chants of loyalty as Clawlow and his guards turned and walked away from the entrenchment edge.

* * *

Josh and Tana had gathered torches and, with the friction of what Tana called fire stones, had lit them as they walked through the passages of the underground caves with the accompaniment of awkward silence. Josh could feel Tana's stare burn into him. She was puzzled and angered at his rejection of her sexual advancements. Humans had never minded taking her in that way before. Josh was clearly a different human. Cody had mentioned to her before that Josh had a past and there was a definite darkness about him, but events had ripped him from that past into the man he was today. Josh tried to ignore Tana and put the incident out from his mind. It was not a difficult task as he was totally intrigued at the architecture in the cave. The walls were sculpted and engraved with very involved and elaborate designs. Each design was so distinct in its own but seemed to still perfectly flow into the next one. They were also deeply textured and resembled grand sceneries of water and trees and sunrises followed by highly detailed night skies. He was amazed that a culture so primitive could have done this much advanced works of art. Tana spoke up with a tone of pride as she claimed that her ancestors had carved out this entire cave.

Josh stopped and turned to face Tana. He apologized again for what had happened. It was unclear to even him of how his dream had been so intense that it controlled his bodily actions. Tana mentioned that she knew he liked her and would not stop. Josh replied that he had stopped.

Tana felt a burning feeling inside her. It was more than hate and rage. It was a desire for vengeance. She pressed on by saying, "You feel good to me. You not say you not want me. My skin, my fur not like Laylee, but you still fuck Tana. Dream not control you as you say. For moment, you want Tana."

Josh had enough and stormed closer to her. He said with all intent to hurt her, "It was Laylee that I thought of as you forced yourself onto me! Do not turn this around as my fault!" He did not know why he exploded this way onto Tana but stepped back when he realized that he had.

Tana only met the response with a scoff of Laylee's name.

Josh asked, "What is wrong with Laylee?"

Tana responded, "Laylee strange flesh, not even real human."

Josh pushed the question and response away. He turned to walk away himself. He added in a morally defeated tone, "It is of no matter anyway. I have only ever loved one woman and always will, my Emelia."

They had approached an inclined passage of the cave. Tana had motioned for Josh to take the lead. It was a sharp and narrow incline with little there than cave wall to grab onto for support. The ledge tapered off with a steep fall into what was total darkness.

Tana was native to the planet, and with better footing barefooted, she remained close behind him and helped to guide Josh along. As they traversed upward, Tana asked, "What fate became of this Emelia?"

Josh paused as if he had not wanted to discuss the matter, but Tana pushed on with the question. Josh slowly submitted with a deep sigh and stated that Emelia was once his wife. Josh turned to face Tana in the torch lit glow. He described her as beautiful but fragile. She was a Jaskan with long and wavy dark-blue hair. He had met her on a popular paradise planet called Tyzalon. He seemed lost in a brief state of happiness as he described his first sighting of her walking out of the ocean. She had lain down on her back on the sandy beach. He had brought over two drinks that the planet had dubbed Forever

Suns. He remembered that he had become frozen as he looked down onto her. Her long legs and firmly developed body with her long dark-blue hair falling over each shoulder and laid over each of her naked breasts. She had opened her green eyes and claimed that he was blocking her sun. Josh's smile seemed to grow with a small chuckle as he described his response. As he reached down to give her one of the drinks, he had told her that he brought a sun down to her beauty that had outshined it. He remembered that she had smiled in the moment. Josh claimed that was the very moment they had met and were instantly in love. They had quickly married.

His smile seemed to fade away. He mentioned that a great darkness had consumed him. He added that the darkness was the mental corruption from his former mentor, the Dark Lord Epitaph. Josh's eyes grew a cold stare, and his facial expression seemed to darken with sadness. He had been persuaded to kill her. He started to cry as he could now envision the memory of her cold and limp body held in his arms after he had strangled the life from her. Tana was shocked by the knowledge that she had just learned. She took a few steps back and away from Josh in disbelief.

Josh continued with his tale that it was long unknown to him that it had been Epitaph's plan to resurrect Emelia from the dead and make her his soulless bride. Their ascent of the cave continued in silence. They had approached the upper level of the cave and a dim light shined into it. They had exited the cave to see the sun just setting. Through the heavy vine and branch cover of the jungle, Tana pointed and said that her village was a half rotation away from here.

* * *

The four Honsho ships commanded by Sorlin Garrison had exited hyperspace. Sorlin was informed that one energy signature trail was present but was fading. It had an estimated course to a jungle planet. Sorlin asked the Honsho at the console if he was certain of his findings. Sorlin had not wanted to waste time or fuel on guesses. The Honsho brought up his readings on the monitor. He was positive that a ship the size of what they were looking for had been here within the last rotation or two, and a matching energy trail had left residue on a course straight to the jungle planet. He provided a 90 percent match that the energy trail was the remnants of a Janan crystal power source. Sorlin replied that the Black Guard ships also used Janan crystals as a power source. The Honsho claimed that this residue trail that he had discovered was only enough for a small freighter. He admitted that it could be a small troop transport or the freighter they were looking for. Sorlin considered his options and gave the orders to plot a pursuit course.

* * *

Lord Epitaph had disembarked from his personal shuttle onto his warship, the *Darkfall*. He was greeted by the ship's admiral and Fright Agent Maddo. Lord Epitaph ordered the admiral to have the ship ready to depart upon his command. He then looked to Fright Agent Maddo, who immediately began a detailed and extensive report on the interrogation of the Prophetess. He admitted that she had been extremely uncooperative. He also added that it would be much easier if they could directly torture her with physical means rather than the sonic bombardment. Epitaph had replied that he would be able to get close enough to provide the physical torture that was required. He added that it was a miracle that the Prophetess was captured at all. The ability to produce such a defensive field that created great and powerful illness upon approach had intrigued Fright Agent Maddo. Not much was physically known of the Shrow except that they were dwarf-like and all seemed to be prophets, which made them rare and difficult to locate. They were rumored to have magical abilities beyond their visions of the future, but the prisoner in question had not revealed any as of yet. As they entered the detention block and approached the cell, Epitaph had ordered Fright Agent Maddo and the cell guards to wait outside and have all the monitoring systems in the room powered down.

Epitaph walked into the cell as the metal door slid shut behind him. He slowly approached the dwarf-like woman with long gray hair. With her back against the metal cell wall, she seemed stricken with fear at the sight of him. She admitted that she had seen the day the dark lord would approach her with his immunity to her abilities and her magic. The Prophetess only knew of one other race that was immune to the aura of the prophets. It was knowledge that even Epitaph had not known or she surely would have been tortured long ago by his Luth Bik fright agent. She stated to Epitaph that she was prepared to die.

Epitaph's mouth grew wide with a sinister and reptilian smile. His forked tongue flicked in and out wildly from it. He reached out and stroked the face of the Prophetess. To see a prophet was a rare feat, but to actually stand before one and touch it without being debilitated was even more so. Epitaph claimed that he needed something from her before he could allow her to die.

The Prophetess defiantly, through her fear of him, stated that he would not get what he sought from her. Epitaph's sinister smile grew even wider as he replied that she knew that not to be true. He then stepped toward her with his open palms and a medium-sized crystal in each that he had pulled from concealment under his cape. The Prophetess was puzzled as to how Epitaph had obtained the transfer crystals, as she had not seen it in her vision. Epitaph dismissed his smile into an emotion of anger and disgust. He stated that he would be writing the visions from now on.

The Prophetess started a death chant on herself. She would perish before the dark lord would take her power. Epitaph displayed a sudden sprint of speed, and he was standing before her with the transfer crystals raised above him and put to touch each other. A spiral form of energy darted downward and consumed both Epitaph and the Prophetess. Her death chant had ceased as she dropped to her knees. The magical energy inside her was being transferred to Epitaph as she grew weaker. She finally collapsed as the spiral form of energy dispersed. Epitaph felt empowered; he could feel the magical power run through his very body. The Prophetess slowly stirred as she laid face first on the metal cell floor. Epitaph looked down on her with even greater disgust now as he placed his foot onto the back of her neck. The magic of light that ran through him was being converted now to a darker form. It was a power that he believed he should have had long ago. It was wasted on the likes of the Shrow. He pressed his foot harder against the back of her neck. He then raised it away and stomped it back down with all the hatred he could muster into the action. He reached down and pulled her head back as his foot continued to press against the back of her neck. Her limbs twitched until her neck snapped, and she was left motionless. Through the magic now coursing through his body, he could sense her death. He knew that all the other prophets, wherever they were hidden, could feel it as well.

* * *

Cody remained a captive with the other subdued Matrasus that had given up hope. Cody had not given up on his hope as he continued an attempt to break his chain from the tall metal rod. He was using all his strength to smash a jagged rock against the chain. Two Matrasus guards that Clawlow had left behind had approached toward him. One kicked him in the back as the other forcibly removed the rock from Cody's clawed hand. Cody lunged forward and grappled the legs out from under the second Matrasus. He had pulled the Matrasus guard to the ground. He kicked one leg back and, with strong impact, had kicked the other to the ground. Cody then, with no wasted motion, had jumped onto the Matrasus guard he had taken down first and clawed twice across his chest, before lowering his open jaws down and biting at the jugular of the Matrasus. With great ferocity, he continued to maul at his now defenseless victim. The other Matrasus guard had recovered from the kick and grabbed Cody from behind, as he tried to pull him off the fallen guard. The claws of the Matrasus were deep into the sides of Cody. Cody then reached back over his shoulder and clutched the Matrasus' neck.

Cody pulled the Matrasus guard over his head. The Matrasus guard's grip on Cody had been broken as the Matrasus hit the ground in front of him. The Matrasus guard quickly scrambled to his feet and took a physically defensive stance. He was face to face with Cody, who met him with a vicious snarl. The blood from the fallen guard still dripped from Cody's mouth and sharp teeth. The Matrasus answered Cody's snarl with an angered hiss.

The two charged at each other from only a few feet apart. They both landed claws and bites. They had both taken each other to the ground and continued their growls throughout the physical struggle. Cody had managed to get onto the back of the Matrasus guard and was able to utilize the long chain fastened to his ankle as an additional weapon. He had gotten the chain around the Matrasus guard's neck and had pulled back on it.

The Matrasus captives all around had started to unleash angered growls. Even though they were also prisoners, Cody was unsure if they were growling in support of his attempt to break free or if they were growling in defiance of him killing their own kind. Cody was not deterred as he pulled back on the chain he had wrapped around the Matrasus guard's neck. The Matrasus guard twitched and finally fell motionless under Cody's own body draped across him and exhausted from the battle. Cody looked around and found a short spear that one of the Matrasus guards had dropped in the struggle. He broke the metal head from the wooden handgrip. He used it to pry at the manacle around his ankle and was able to force it open and release himself from the chain.

* * *

Back on Xotosia, news was spreading with whispers among the denizens of a coming revolt against the Black Guard. One small band of several mixed races had taken the rumors to heart and had organized an assault on a small outpost lower on the highest mountain. The outpost was in the early stages of assembly and easily overtaken. The few Black Guard soldiers assigned to its construction were forced to flee up the mountainside to the Black Guard confiscated palace that had once belonged to Silos Taqoon.

Aboard the *Darkfall*, the admiral had reported the incident to Fright Agent Maddo and the Dark Lord Epitaph. Fright Agent Maddo had contacted his warship, the *Ripper* and ordered another full complement of troops and assault vehicles sent to the outpost location. Epitaph had ordered the admiral to have the rest of the fleet organize a blockade around the planet. He declared that the *Darkfall* would be leaving orbit on a special mission and rendezvous with the Fury Fleet. Epitaph added that he would be sending special enforcements to join the blockade of Xotosia. They would be special enforcements that were more suited to deal with insurrections.

Epitaph was sensing something. He believed that with his newly acquired powers, he was being guided or perhaps urged on his path to assure that his own destiny would not turn out to be as predicted by prophecy. He provided the coordinates for a hyperspace jump to be initiated once the *Darkfall* had cleared the far orbit.

* * *

Night had arrived, and darkness was becoming more prominent. Josh and Tana had pushed on instead of setting up a camp. As they walked over a hill and looked down below toward Tana's village, they were witness to the beginning of a siege on the village by a rogue force of Matrasus. Tana had recognized the flags of the aggressors and claimed that the invaders were under the command of her father's enemy called Clawlow.

* * *

In the village, the Matrasus warriors were running to action with spears, shields, and bows. Flaming arrows were being fired into and all about the village. Then the unthinkable—heavy explosions from mortar shots began to pulverize strategic points of village defense. The walls, the armory, and the infirmary huts were all heavily hit.

Bangalark was joined by Laylee wishing to help as he assembled his troops that were not fleeing. Garton had approached as translator. Bangalark was going to lead a commando squad out of the village toward the attackers. Garton had claimed that Bangalark wanted Laylee to help organize defense of the inner village circle. Garton seemed hesitant but returned Laylee's earlier confiscated blaster and stun pistols to her. Laylee agreed to help as Bangalark and his team moved toward the village entrance.

* * *

Tana and Josh had picked up a running pace as they were ensnared by a net that had fallen from the trees above them. Tana clawed and bit her way out of the net as she tore it apart with great savagery. Josh cut through the tangled remnants of the net with the use of his short sword. As they freed themselves, they looked around to find that they had been surrounded by several Matrasus. Their only clothing was the leather armbands with the logo of Clawlow that matched the logo of his flags at his camp and the ones carried by his flag bearers. Tana remained defiant and was fully determined to fight herself free. Josh tried to talk her down and calm her hostility. He had now noticed that many of the Matrasus had eye scope manacles and blaster technology rifles. Tana released a loud roar of anger and rage. Josh was forced to clutch both her arms tightly and turn her to face him.

Tana demanded with a snarling tone, "Let me go! I kill them all!"

Josh tried to convince her that surrender for the moment was their only move if they expected to survive. The savagery burned inside Tana like a river of high intensity flames. She insisted on killing them as she would not surrender. Josh repeated that they must surrender for now, but that did not mean that they could not fight their way out at a more opportune time. He begged Tana to trust him. Savagery in this case would be best fought with smartness.

Tana looked around slowly, but with a methodic stare. She seemed to be capturing the faces of all her enemies mentally in her mind as if she was formulating a personal kill list. Josh released her as she relaxed her stance. Josh slowly raised his arms into the air. Tana did the same as she released a long broken and stuttered growl, which in the language of the Matrasus meant "surrender."

They were escorted deeper into a jungle area with a crescent shaped terrain. The central part of the area was set lower from the rest of the terrain. The jungle terrain surrounded a large area that was layered with stones and bricks. In the middle, Clawlow was using loud roars to give orders to his loyal followers. He stood with a holstered blaster pistol and a sheathed longsword. He also had fastened to his lower left arm a highly technical-looking buckler. He noticed Tana immediately as she was brought forth before him. The two roared and growled back and forth at each other for a long moment.

Clawlow then turned his attention suddenly to Josh Broody. One quick and seeming out from nowhere swipe of Clawlow's over-furred claw cut across Josh's face. The action caused Josh to turn down and away as he held his face with the blood dripping through his fingers. Tana lunged forward at Clawlow but was grappled by three of his Matrasus soldiers and forced to the ground against her will. Clawlow looked back only briefly at her before he let out one loud roar. He then leapt forward with almost blinding speed and tackled Josh to the ground as well. The momentum of the pounce rolled them both over. Clawlow landed on top and proceeded to pummel away at Josh with tightly closed fists. He had also positioned his body and legs to pin Josh firmly on his back. He then opened his fists and started to slash Josh viciously with both of his claws. Tana let out roars of anger and almost concern as she begged Clawlow to stop.

* * *

As the attack on the village continued, Laylee was helping many of the Matrasus citizens to improvised forms of cover. Girassar was attending to many of the wounded. Garton had entered the center and watched on through the combat. Laylee noticed that Bangalark and his commandos that had charged the village entrance point had been pushed back inside. The attacking forces of Matrasus were well trained and coordinated as they were keeping the village defenders herded together. Garton pulled a high-tech grenade from the leather bag he had flung over his shoulder. The activation sound of the grenade drew Laylee's attention. She was shocked that he had any technology at all much less a grenade. He hurled it with great accuracy and directly at Bangalark and his commandos. She yelled at him more with shock and surprise than anger. Garton rushed forward into the impact area of the grenade. He picked up a wooden spear from a fallen guard and readied it as Bangalark staggered out from the explosion. Bangalark was shaken and unaware of his surroundings as Garton leapt forward with extreme precision and drove the spear straight through Bangalark's chest. The spear went completely through the body and out the backside. Garton then tripped Bangalark to the ground and stood over him. Bangalark was pinned to the ground with the spear through his heart as Garton twisted and pushed the spear with even greater force. Bangalark reached up to grasp the spear but was too weak to prevent Garton from twisting it. Bangalark could see the hate and resentment in Garton's eyes and was completely surprised by it.

Bangalark then asked in the Matrasus language, "You are with Clawlow?" He followed with, "You were my loyal advisor and my friend. I pledged my daughter to you. Why?"

Garton sneered before he replied that he was loyal, but he was sickened as he watched Bangalark lead their people into despair. Bangalark had always resisted technology even as Garton had tried to urge him into using it as defense against the enslavers. Garton continued to state that the banishment of Clawlow was the beginning of his own downfall. Garton claimed that only Clawlow would have them fight the enslavers that would come and rip them from their world. Clawlow had rebelled at Bangalark's lack of strength and commitment to him. When the enslavers came, Bangalark's answer was always to hide and mourn the loss of those taken. They would rebuild only to have the enslavers return and take more of them. Garton stated with his own strong conviction that Clawlow would not allow this to happen. He was convinced that once Bangalark was slain, their people would follow Clawlow. One last twist and push of the spear claimed the last of Bangalark's life.

Laylee had fought through the chaos and the combatants of both sides to get closer. She watched as Garton twisted and drove the spear into Bangalark. She saw Bangalark's arms drop from the spear to his sides. Laylee was unsure of what had happened but raised her blaster pistol. Still confused by Garton's actions, she was frozen. Girassar had also pushed her way through the battle and arrived as Garton pulled the spear from Bangalark's dead body. Girassar asked what he had done. Garton asked her to join him and Clawlow. Girassar refused in full support of Bangalark. Garton raised his spear with all intent to throw it directly at the helpless old medicine woman. Laylee snapped from her frozen state of confusion and reacted with three rapid blaster shots to the chest and one to the head. Garton fell to the ground dead with the bloodied spear at his side.

* * *

As Tana struggled to pull herself free from the Matrasus that now held her at each arm, more Matrasus in broken chains charged into the camp and initiated an attack onto Clawlow's soldiers. Cody then struck from behind and tore the two Matrasus from their grips on Tana.

Clawlow's attention was diverted enough for Josh to land a solid impact punch under Clawlow's jaw. Another two rapid punches were delivered as follow ups and Clawlow had rolled off Josh. He was shaken by the punches that Josh had just delivered but still rose to his feet and charged back at Josh. Josh had rolled away to create distance and was able to pull himself up to his knees when he saw Clawlow charging at him in a state of full rage. Josh waited with his own battle focus until Clawlow halted over him. Clawlow attempted to pull Josh up by pulling on his long hair. Josh defended with rapid and forceful punches solidly placed into Clawlow's midsection of his torso. As Clawlow staggered backward, Josh was able to get back on his feet. He moved in quickly and threw four more punches in the same area and forced Clawlow into a hunched-over position. Josh then delivered a spinning leg kick that caught Clawlow square in the jaw and sent him spiraling to the ground. Clawlow, with a tumble roll, quickly returned to his feet and drew the blaster pistol from his side holster. Josh had followed up on his combat action quickly as well and was able to kick the blaster pistol from Clawlow's hand. The two of them locked their arms into a physical struggle for strength. Clawlow stepped in and raised a knee into Josh's abdomen. He was then able to gain the advantage and push Josh again to the ground. Clawlow went to stomp on his fallen prey. Josh was able to roll away from three of the stomp attempts and reach his own fallen short sword. He tumbled by Clawlow and swung at the back of his legs. Clawlow's close combat skills and agility were superior, and he leapt over the swing. Clawlow then drew his own longsword from his sheath and used it to block the next incoming and upward slash from Josh. The two of them clashed their blades against each other and met each slash and thrust equally. Clawlow felt himself becoming winded as Josh's fury with a sword was extremely proficient. Clawlow now backtracked his footing and had switched more to a defensive swordplay against Josh.

The sudden switch in strategy slightly lapsed Josh's focus. Clawlow triggered his highly technical-looking buckler, and it lit up with fully encompassing electricity. Suddenly, it had shot a high voltage stream directly at Josh. The high-voltage shock threw Josh backward. He had been tossed off his feet and fell to the ground as the static charge coursed through his entire body. As the charge dissipated, Josh fell unconscious.

Clawlow took the moment to survey the battlefield and was witness to his soldiers falling to Cody and the former Matrasus slaves. Tana had also broken free and was defeating his soldiers in unarmed combat as well. Clawlow seen little room for a victory and ran off into the jungle. Tana had slashed through yet another of the soldiers, and as he fell, Tana had seen Clawlow's retreat. Without a moment of hesitation, Tana had started to give chase after him.

Josh had recovered and made eye contact with Cody, who was in fierce melee combat but holding his own and used his receipt of the eye contact to formulate a quick glance in Tana's direction. Josh followed the motion to spot Tana running into the jungle in pursuit of Clawlow. Josh followed after them.

* * *

Girassar confirmed to Laylee that Garton was dead. Laylee took notice of the battle. She noticed that the mortar fire had ceased and that the invading forces of Clawlow were beginning to retreat. She looked around at the several fallen village defenders. The village was clearly defeated, yet the invaders had turned away. The answer was quickly revealed. Laylee looked upward and saw four Honsho freighters pierce the sky.

* * *

Sorlin Garrison stood in observance in the command deck as his fleet was initiating landing procedures onto the jungle world. Sorlin had spotted a thinning jungle area, not exactly a clearing but open enough for a landing point. He directed his ships to land there.

The ships' repulsor lifts fired to slow their descent. The four ships landed in perfectly choreographed unison. Clawlow had run directly and unwillingly into the landing site. He staggered to a stop. The boarding hatches opened, and ramps lowered from each Honsho freighter. Clawlow had found himself surrounded.

Tana had hit the scene from the direction behind him in a full run and sudden stop. Josh ran out from his own jungle path and halted at Tana's side.

The Honsho pirates had disembarked from the four freighters and secured the perimeter. Sorlin then strode down the ramp with a sense of purpose. He held his Honshon stick at the ready. Clawlow unleashed a growl of rage directly at him, but Sorlin's attention locked on Josh. The Honsho pirates had all shifted positions and forced their quarries into a tighter formation. Sorlin raised his Honshon stick, fully charged and struck Clawlow with it as his followers did the same to Tana and Josh. All three victims were struck with stunning energy and fell unconscious.

* * *

In the far orbit of the jungle planet, a small fleet of Black Guard warships led by the *Darkfall* had exited from hyperspace portals. Unbeknownst to those Black Guard ships, a smaller form of a Honsho freighter had tucked into hyperspace with them and magnetized to the hull of the *Darkfall*. Gold Gatling stood with great pride of his accomplishment in the circular cockpit and asked if they were still concealed. The pilot stated that the cloak was still holding. He then commended Gold on his idea to let the Black Guard bring them to the prize. Gold's smile of confidence in himself widened. He ordered all comms and sensors monitored to detect anything the Black Guard would find on the planet.

Chapter Seven

Black Quest

LORD EPITAPH WAS experiencing a vision. He had been locked in a trance on the command deck and seemed completely oblivious to the attempts of the officers that tried to snap him out of it. In actuality he was quite aware of his surroundings, but his will had demanded he not break his concentration. He wished not to abandon the vision he was seeing. In the vision, he was pursuing Josh Broody as doors slammed in between them. With the final door, Epitaph was in complete darkness, but even with his dark vision, he was unable to locate Josh. Everyone on the command deck could hear Epitaph speak out his vision. He said, "The former general will be hidden to the dark lord in darkness." Epitaph then screamed out for Josh as his vision ended, and he was snapped back to reality.

He remembered everything. He then ordered full deployment to the jungle planet. His officers addressed the landing and exploration protocols of unknown worlds. Epitaph became greatly enraged and yelled out with great anger and determination that he needed Josh now before he was able to be hidden from him.

* * *

On the jungle planet, the Honsho pirates were dragging their stunned prisoners onto Sorlin's freighter. Sorlin ordered them secured as he was being notified of the Black Guard ships being detected in orbit. The Honsho pirate at the sensor station reported that it would not be long before the technology of their ships would be detected on this primitive planet. Another Honsho spoke out in suggestion that they turn over Josh Broody now. The praise and bounty would still go to Sorlin. Gold Gatling would still be humiliated because Sorlin had acted separately from the Gatling Legion and the desired clout would certainly levitate Sorlin in fame as he had originally planned. As an added bonus, they could also sell the two Matrasus prisoners as slaves.

Sorlin considered the logic and admitted that it sounded promising. He held back though with reservation. He admitted that he would feel more comfortable if he could turn Josh over more on his terms and perhaps on a more civilized planet with witnesses than a back hidden planet in a barely explored region of space. His own ego also wished for Gold to be present at the revealing moment. He ordered all four ships to lift off and fly at the lowest level altitudes closest to the jungle cover in effort to move to the other side of the planet. They would need a darker and thicker region to remain hidden for now.

* * *

Cody led the former slaves of Clawlow into the Matrasus village of Siber. They had also brought many of Clawlow's Matrasus soldiers in as captives. The Matrasus village guards took the prisoners and bound them to trees. Girassar attended to the wounded as she set up a triage. Laylee was assisting the Matrasus reassemble their sundered village. She noticed Cody as he entered the village boundaries and went to him. She explained the best she could at what had happened. The betrayal of Garton had upset all the village natives. Cody had not met Garton but did have the displeasure of meeting Clawlow. He explained that Clawlow fled like a coward but that Tana and Josh had given chase. Laylee ushered Cody away cautiously and explained that Bangalark, the leader of the village, was the one that Garton had slain. She added the relations that they both had with Tana. Girassar had overheard Tana's name and interrupted. She asked if they knew where Tana was now. She insisted that Tana must be brought back before her father's funeral rites.

The moment of recovery and reflection was interrupted by loud, booming sounds. The Matrasus villagers were again sent into a state of panic as starfighters, shuttles, and troop transports descended from the clouds and skies in massive formations. Laylee looked to Cody with a troubled expression worn across her face. It still seemed odd to him coming from an android, but Laylee was proving herself to be much more than her programming. Cody also shared the look of concern. He had recognized the ships as Black Guard landing and invading forces. He stated to Laylee that this was not a good thing.

* * *

Gold Gatling's freighter remained magnetized and cloaked on the hull of the *Darkfall*. It was operating on bare minimum functions and lighting to further avoid detection. Gold sat quietly in the captain's chair on the circular command deck. His hands were clasped, and his legs were tightly against the chair as Gold himself sat in a hunched over position. He was so tense and quiet. He was nearly holding his breath. It seemed he was hiding his ship by sure will. His confidence that he had upon arrival had been consumed by nervousness. He continued to watch the Honsho at the sensor station. He wanted some bit of information. The Honsho looked to Gold and, as if knowing the unspoken question, shook his head in a negative motion. Gold's second in command stepped to his side and asked what they were doing. Gold sighed and finally leaned back in his chair. He said that Black Guard ships were in full planetary invasion and orbit combat readiness mode. He explained that orbit movement among the fleet was now even more closely monitored than before. If they attempted to break away now, even under cloak status, they could very well be detected. He sighed in his own disapproval of the situation. They had no choice now but to wait for information from the Black Guard comms and confirmation that Josh Broody had been detected. The Honsho asked him if he believed they had Josh on that planet. Gold had seen many Black Guard maneuvers before but none with this much focus and effort. He believed that Josh Broody was down there on the planet. He also believed by the sure mass movement of the Black Guard that Josh was not getting away. The trick now was to get Josh before the Black Guard did. They would use the Black Guard's own scanning operations against them. Gold called it a very strategic game. Gold knew one other thing that kept his confidence well-hidden. Gold Gatling was very good about playing strategic games. None of the Honshos doubted him either. They all knew that if Gold could get to the prize before the Black Guard did, they would most certainly get away. They knew Gold well, and he had his escape plan and twelve contingency escape plans already in play.

* * *

Sorlin's four Honsho freighters had landed in a heavy mountainous terrain away from the jungles. They had nestled deep in the valley base of three adjoining mountains laced with shieldstone, an element of rock that disrupted sensor scans into it, but they could freely scan out from it. Sorlin had already formulated his escape plan as any good Honsho pirate would. He had ordered the other three freighters stripped of all necessities. He then wanted two of those freighters fully crippled. They would use the third freighter to exit the planet with life signs of Honshos and one falsified human. Sorlin planned on using that ship as his decoy for the Black Guard to concentrate on while his freighter with Josh Broody would plot a course from the planet's southern hemisphere and make a hyperspace escape.

Another Honsho stated that the prisoners were beginning to awaken. Sorlin ordered the human brought to him. He quickly belayed that order and stated that he would come to the black-furred beast's containment cell. His advisor and second in command looked at him in a state of confusion. Sorlin replied to the look of question.

He felt that perhaps the black-furred Matrasus was an obvious out-cast and might yet be of some use to him.

* * *

Black Guard ships had touched down on the jungle floor. The Black Guard starfighters were triangular shaped with the front point as they pilot and the two rear points were extended out as curvature formations. They were commonly referred to as schisms and patrolled the skies. Each pair of two schisms escorted a bomber conducting bombing runs over the jungle cover in a method of clearing away obstructions. The bombers resembled the schisms in triangular form but seemed to be more like two stacked together. Troop transport landers were much bulkier and more squarely built then followed in behind the bombings and dispatched Black Guard soldiers. They were also more heavily armored as their function was to fly into direct combat and deliver the troops and heavy gunnery. Among the Black Guard soldiers were squads of twelve Laser Heads. They were fully armored bi-pedal robots that hosted glowing pink spheres of energy where a head would normally be.

* * *

The Matrasus were well-practiced in running into hiding from enslavers that routinely raided their planet. Black Guard soldiers, though, were much different than enslavers. They would slaughter first and enslave what was left. Cody and Laylee were assisting the Matrasus in their fleeing movements. Girassar approached and was concerned that Tana would be left behind. There was already a real possibility that Bangalark's body would be lost or destroyed in the raid. Laylee had learned much from the Matrasus. Their dead were considered sacred, and they believed that a last rites ceremony was extremely important to escort the spirits into the afterlife. She despite being an android could feel the concern. This though was not a time to worry about the dead. This was a time to save the living. The last of the Matrasus had fled and Cody followed behind them. Girassar would not go without Tana. Laylee promised her that her friend Josh would keep Tana safe.

* * *

Josh woke up inside a containment cell aboard the Honsho freighter. He pulled himself up against the wall and walked slowly to the energy barrier that blocked the doorway. He lightly touched it and felt a low surge of energy snap back through him. He was growing weary of energy and electricity shocking him. He yelled out for anyone that would hear him or even respond. He looked out the barrier of yellow energy and could see Tana waking up in her cell across from him. She was panicked and charged her own barrier, only to be shocked and thrown back against her cell wall from the impact into the yellow barrier. She was screaming that she was not a slave again. Tana broke from her panicked state as she saw Josh. She could hear him clearly. Josh was assuring her that he did not believe they were enslavers. Tana responded by slapping the energy barrier in front of her. The low shock zapped through her body and she experienced a jolting motion. She said, "Seems like cage." Josh asked her to trust him. He promised her that they would not be held for long.

Just then, three Honsho pirates entered the room and approached the third cell that rested to the side of the two facing cells. That cell's door was deactivated at a wall panel, and Clawlow lunged outward at them. The Honsho that stood at the point position stood firmly at his ground and met Clawlow's lunge with a fully charged Honshon stick. Clawlow fell unconscious again. The two other Honshos collectively dragged Clawlow's limp body away as they followed the first Honsho. Josh yelled out his demand that they release him and Tana at once. The Honshos completely ignored him as they departed the holding cell area.

* * *

The Black Guard troops had begun to scour the jungle planet by foot patrol and air combat vehicles. Cody used the jungle cover and his natural hunting abilities to shadow their movements and at the same time he kept just out of scanning range. He was helpless as he watched two straggling Matrasus get gunned down by heavy blaster fire. He wanted to help them but knew it would have done no good. He would just be lying dead next to them as well. Cody looked around and grew an almost sinister grin across his snout and jaws. He had just recalled his position. He was not far from Clawlow's camp and arsenal. The Black Guard had not yet discovered it, and Cody figured he could get there first.

* * *

Lord Epitaph paced the command deck of the *Darkfall*. The admiral of the Fury Fleet had reported that full landing parties had quickly taken nearly 50 percent of the planet. He estimated full control within another rotation and guaranteed that once full control had been achieved, they would easily locate Josh Broody for capture. Lord Epitaph twitched nervously, and his forked tongue flicked even more rapidly. He informed the admiral that this was not a capture mission. What was done with anyone else on the planet was of no concern to him. Epitaph slowed his words and slowly lisped out his orders, "Josssh Broody isss to be killed on sssite and hisss dead body brought to me persssonally."

Even as his new prophet vision powers grew, he was still puzzled to how the prophecy of his death by the two brothers could come true. Jase Broody, the oldest brother of Josh, had been slain by Cage. Yet the prophecy, as Epitaph could see it, was still claiming that the brothers would be his demise. Epitaph looked to Fright Agent Maddo as he approached. Epitaph stated that the fright agent's particular mission had just changed. Fright Agent Maddo inquired, "What is your wish, my lord?"

Epitaph answered, "You will go to the jungle planet, and you will persssonally ensssure that Josssh Broody iss found and killed."

* * *

Clawlow awoke on the floor of the Honsho ship. He was groggy and slow to process his surroundings. As he gathered his senses and looked around, he found himself circled by Honsho pirates all with their Honshon sticks drawn and aimed directly at him. He quickly and instinctively reached for the blaster pistol that he had holstered at his side, only to find it gone. He spanned his head around his surrounding captors and then released a loud and rage-filled roar.

Suddenly the blaster pistol slid along the floor from behind him and stopped at his feet. He quickly reached down and retrieved it. As he brought it upward to bare a shot, he was witness to all the Honshos consolidating their arms and tightening their grips on their Honshon sticks. Clawlow spun quickly around and brought his blaster pistol to aim on Sorlin, only to find Sorlin aiming a heavy blaster pistol on him. Sorlin's remark was, "Good, you do know how to use it."

Clawlow replied with a snarl and pulled the trigger to no effect. He looked puzzled at it, only to see Sorlin toss the power pack at his feet. Clawlow slowly steered his gaze from Sorlin and slightly turned his wrist that held the blaster pistol to confirm that the power pack had been removed. He returned his gaze to Sorlin and unleashed a low tone growl of disgust before he threw his blaster pistol to the metal floor.

Sorlin responded by calmly introducing himself. He waited for a response, only receiving a strong glare even from Clawlow's bad eye. Sorlin then, with his other and steady hand, offered Clawlow another blaster pistol. Clawlow stepped toward him, and the two stood only inches away from each other, locked in a face-to-face stare down. Clawlow shifted his stare to the weapon and back to Sorlin. He unleashed a full roar with a heavy stench blown into Sorlin's face. Sorlin fought hard against its effects but remained steady and unflinched at Clawlow's attempt. Sorlin waved his fellow Honshos back that had moved in closer to the threat. Sorlin remained focused and, as a show of strength, never broke his gaze with Clawlow. Sorlin then spoke with a tone of firmness but still calm, "To wield great power, you must possess conviction." He again presented the blaster for Clawlow to take it.

Clawlow looked around, fully aware that he was surrounded by the strange-appearing human race offshoot. In human common language he asked, "Humans?"

Sorlin replied, "Honshos actually." Sorlin remained unshaken as Clawlow used the human common language to introduce himself. Sorlin asked if it was power that he desired. Clawlow replied in the affirmative. Sorlin then promised him power, and all Clawlow would have to do was join him.

* * *

Girassar was guiding Laylee through the jungle. They had strayed into a heavier jungle cover to avoid Black Guard troops slashing their way through the trees and vines with utilization of their axes. Under Girassar's guidance and assistance, they had laid flat to the jungle ground and watched the Black Guards walk by them from under thick vine and leaf ground cover. Once they had figured the soldiers had securely passed their position, Girassar motioned for Laylee to rise and move forward. They pulled back the thick vines and continued to push their way through the thickest of trees. They had remained far off any jungle trail, and even Girassar was finding it difficult to figure their location. Laylee continued to pull back on the thick vines and leaves. They had entered a clearing, and Laylee was relieved to see the *Fallen Star*. Laylee entered the access code into a control panel, and the boarding ramp started to lower.

It was a trap. Suddenly, Black Guard soldiers fanned out from the surrounding jungle trees with full blaster fire engaged as they moved out. Girassar was standing behind Laylee and was heavily gunned down. Laylee was grazed as she quickly ran up the ramp. She stumbled into the ship and fell at the head of the ramp. She pulled the heavy blaster rifle from the gun rack next to the boarding hatch and readied it to fire on whoever dared attempt to board. The Black Guard soldiers had moved closer to the ship. They started to move up the boarding ramp in pairs of two. The first two were immediately gunned down as they stepped foot onto the ramp. The other soldiers, with their blaster rifles already drawn, had retaliated with blaster fire of their own as they rushed the boarding ramp. Laylee had some cover inside the ship, but despite, that she took a few more hits to her shoulders. Being an actual android helped her remain defiant. She fired off several heavier blasts in rapid succession, which dropped four more of the Black Guard soldiers.

The Black Guard soldiers still on the ramp retreated backward, and as they did, the ship's engines roared to life, and the repulsor lifts fired as the *Fallen Star* began to lift off the ground. Two of the Black Guard soldiers charged forward with great leaps and used their black axes to grapple onto the still lowered boarding ramp. They pulled themselves up as the boarding ramp closed. They were inside. They heard the combined blaster and artillery fire impact the bottom of the ship as it ascended into the sky.

Laylee backed up to a section further in the ship, and from around the corridor wall, she unloaded relentless blaster fire onto one of the Black Guard soldiers. The other soldier had noticed that she had exhausted the power pack in her blaster rifle. He raised his black axe and charged at her as she tried to quickly perform a reload of a new power pack. Laylee had lowered her heavy blaster rifle but maintained a firm grip. She was able to physically dodge two of the Black Guard soldier's axe swings. She noticed the ship's engines hum louder and recognized the pause in the lifting of the ship. She then dodged another swing and shifted her position. The Black Guard soldier shifted his position as well. Laylee smiled as her regenerative skin started again to heal its wounds and conceal the exposed metal beneath it. She then raised her heavy blaster rifle upward and caught the Black Guard just under his helmet with the butt of her rifle. Laylee dropped the rifle and delivered a hard-impact kick at the soldier's chest that sent him falling backward. She charged forward as the soldier staggered to his feet. As she charged, she hit a control panel button that opened the boarding hatch. She had forced him to switch his position earlier to be directly in line to her plan. Laylee leapt off the floor of the ship and dove directly at the soldier and rammed him with her shoulders. The maneuver sent the soldier to the open boarding hatch. Laylee grabbed onto a rail on the wall as the ship made a turning motion and fired thrusters. The motion was enough to jar the ship and toss the soldier out the boarding hatch. As he fell from the low airborne ship, he was gunned down by friendly fire of the Black Guard soldiers shooting at the ship from the ground. Laylee resealed the boarding hatch as the *Fallen Star* streaked across the sky at a hurried pace.

* * *

Cody had arrived at Clawlow's former base camp. Despite his best efforts, the Black Guard troops had located it and gotten there just before he did. He watched from tree cover outside the camp as the soldiers stockpiled all the weapons and devices of technology and discarded the rest. The few Matrasus that Clawlow had left at the camp as guards had fled. Cody's plan to take over Clawlow's acquired armory had been taken out of play. He now needed a new plan as he watched the soldiers not looting the weapons take an abrupt and hurried stance of assembly. Cody recognized a highly decorated Black Guard officer approach, but the uniform was all wrong. He then realized that it was not an officer, but it was Fright Agent Maddo. The lower-ranked officers had approached and delivered their reports to him directly. Cody then noticed that the assembly was the distraction he needed as one small corner of the base camp had been left defenseless and unguarded.

Cody slowly moved from the tree cover and kept low to the ground as he hurried to the unattended base camp corner. He dropped to his stomach and crawled into the campgrounds. He crawled quietly up to a weapons cache that the Black Guards had opened and not yet emptied. He pulled out a blaster pistol and two frag grenades. He also scavenged four power packs. He then returned to his feet and moved about the campsite utilizing the rocks, crates and huts as cover. He watched as Fright Agent Maddo had finished with his briefing and was walking to Clawlow's former command hut. Cody had holstered what he had stolen but was now preparing to throw one of the frag grenades. He was close enough to hit Fright Agent Maddo. The assassination of a fright agent would ripple chaos through the troops. He pulled back the switch to activate it but froze as Fright Agent Maddo was turned away and rushed toward the campsite's main entrance. Cody reset the frag grenade and looked at the commotion that had stirred and saw an elderly naked Matrasus dragged into the camp. She was badly wounded from several shots of blaster fire. Whatever the case, she was important enough to detour Fright Agent Maddo's attention. Cody overheard another captive Matrasus was brought in at the same time. One of the Black Guard officers was translating—or at least trying to. The Matrasus language was similar enough to the Canian language that he was able to translate a good chunk of it. The officer said that the prisoner claimed the old Matrasus woman as Girassar, the village medicine woman. She had knowledge of the android Laylee that had gotten away. Laylee was reported to have been stolen from Silos Taqoon. It was Josh Broody that they were after, but Fright Agent Maddo knew enough that any potential lead to him would be useful. He also knew that the Matrasus that they did round up might be a little more cooperative if their medicine woman was threatened. He ordered the old Matrasus secured inside the main hut. Once they had Josh Broody, she would be of no further need, and they would kill her then. As she was dragged to the hut, Fright Agent Maddo had commed his ship, the *Ripper* in orbit. He ordered scans intensified and enhanced around this region for any non-Black Guard ship movement close to the ground. An open and heavily armed hover vehicle approached. Fright Agent Maddo told the officer next to him to keep the campsite secured until he returned. He then climbed in and ordered the vehicle's driver to take him to the other Matrasus village.

As Fright Agent Maddo was escorted away and with all attention diverted to that, Cody had managed to sneak into the rear former command hut or the main hut as Fright Agent Maddo had called it by crawling underneath the primitive structure. The old Matrasus woman had been thrown to the dirt floor inside and abandoned as the two soldiers took guard posts outside the hut's entrance. Cody knelt down to her side and assessed her state of health. She was near death, and the blaster wounds were quite severe. Girassar struggled to speak, and Cody could only make out some of it. He had picked up the Matrasus language pretty well over time spent with Tana, but many of Girassar's words were slurred from the pain of the blast wounds. He was able to make out that the non-human woman Laylee had gotten away on a starship. She then spoke of Laylee's promise that her human friend would keep little Tana safe. She used the last of her strength to clutch tightly at Cody's shaggy brown fur. She pleaded with him to help save Tana. Girassar's eyes then fell to a blank stare and her body went limp. Cody gently placed her on the dirt floor.

Cody carefully looked out the entrance and found that only one Black Guard soldier stood there now. He then ruffled the large leaf lined wall and shook the wooden post. The action forced the Black Guard soldier to look inside the hut. As the soldier peaked inside, Cody grabbed his neck and helmet with both arms. The helmet was thrown off, and Cody reapplied his headlock to the soldier. He had both arms securely locked around the soldier's head, with one slipped down and around the soldier's neck. Cody squeezed harder, and the pressure applied had choked the soldier unconscious. He then made a quick exit and was almost to an exit point when he was spotted and fired upon by two Black Guard soldiers. Cody kept his head down and kept running. Blaster shots hit the ground just below his feet and splintered the trees at each side of him as Cody made his escape. He could hear the Black Guard soldiers give a short chase on him through the trees. Cody had become familiar with a good portion of this jungle terrain, and it was enough of a familiarity to give him the edge. The Black Guard soldiers were blasting wild shots into the trees. Cody continued to easily dodge any blaster shot that came close to him. Two of the Black Guard soldiers had visually spotted him and ran through the trees at him, firing their blasters off on the run. Cody bore down and kept running. His focus was now off the terrain and on his pursuers. As a result, he did not see the cliff as he ran off the ledge. The Black Guard soldiers that pursued him ceased fire and slowly walked to the cliff's ledge. They peered over the ledge and were startled and instantly thrown backward to the ground as they dodged away from the *Fallen Star*. The ship rose up from the cliff and buzzed just over the Black Guards that had fallen to the ground. It then turned at a sharp angle and flew upward above the trees.

Cody had run off the cliff's ledge expecting to fall to his death but had fallen on top of the *Fallen Star* instead. He had slid off the side of the ship but had managed a steady hand grip and footing. As the ship flew away, the side boarding hatch opened. Laylee reached out and helped pull Cody inside. The hatch door closed behind him.

* * *

Sorlin and Clawlow entered the secured cell area on Sorlin's freighter. Tana jumped up in a rage and slammed her fists at the energy barrier, which flickered and zapped her with electricity upon contact and sent her staggering backwards. Sorlin's and Clawlow's attention was directed immediately toward her. Sorlin asked Clawlow if it would offend him if she was sold to enslavers. As Sorlin looked her over, he said she was in fine shape for labor or sex and she could bring substantial profit. Clawlow said that he would like to try her out sexually first and break her will. He then told Sorlin that he could do with her as he pleased after that. Sorlin looked at her and provoked a long undertone growl. Sorlin looked to Clawlow for a translation. Clawlow offered nothing back and simply turned away to observe the human in the other cell. Sorlin took a moment to check Tana out once more. Her naked body was tight and firm. He wondered what it would be like to have sex with someone layered with short-haired fur. He then pondered his own thought further. He stated out loud that she would bring a fantastic price.

Sorlin turned to join Clawlow in the observation of Josh Broody. Josh sat quietly with his back to the wall and facing the energy barrier. His eyes were wide open, but he was showing no reaction to their presence or to that of Tana's rage in the other cell. His blind stare continued. Suddenly explosions were heard outside, and the Honsho freighter trembled. Multiple and heavy explosions were heard all around the freighter. After the sounds of explosions finished the light trembling of the freighter, the larger explosions began to hit and shake the ship more violently.

Sorlin ran to a panel in the cargo hold and turned on a video monitor. He saw the other three Honsho freighters with heavy damage, fire, and trails of black smoke. Two of the ships had taken further damage than the sabotage from the Honshos. Heavier blasts hit Sorlin's ship again. He pressed another button as a comm to the command deck. All he could hear was, "We're under attack! Under attack by a—" The comms had gone dead, following an even louder explosion and an impact that collapsed part of the cargo hold. The energy barriers on the cells flickered before they were deactivated with the power loss in the cargo hold. The hull above Sorlin and Clawlow was then blown open. In a panic, Sorlin had led Clawlow to the sealed cargo hold door. He frantically tried the door control panel, but the power loss had affected that as well. Clawlow pushed Sorlin aside, and he pried at the sealed door. His brute strength forced the door to slide open just far enough for Sorlin and himself to push through. In the collapsed corridor, Sorlin climbed up the fallen metal to the exposed portal that had been forced open from the heavy blaster attack.

Sorlin climbed out and along the outside of his damaged freighter. Clawlow had climbed out as well and looked up at Sorlin scaling the surface of what was left of the freighter's hull. Clawlow easily made one single twenty-foot jump to the ground. Sorlin was now atop his freighter and surveyed the scene of all four freighters that had been heavily hit and severely damaged. The Lone assaulting ship was hovering above the crippled freighters. It was the *Fallen Star*. It fired off two more blaster shots at each freighter just to make sure they were completely disabled. Sorlin also watched his fellow Honsho pirates fleeing from the ships and running further into the mountainous terrain for cover. The *Fallen Star* spun around again to face Sorlin's freighter. Sorlin then saw Tana crawling out from a hole in the cargo hold that had been blown open from the *Fallen Star's* assault. She jumped down to the ground and tumbled from a roll to her feet and started running. Josh jumped out right behind her and instructed Tana on the direction of her run. Josh followed behind her the best he could against her animalistic stride. The *Fallen Star* maneuvered its flight overhead of them and unleashed rapid-fire blasts again onto Sorlin's ship. Sorlin struggled to remain standing from the impact. He then noticed the *Fallen Star* hover directly over and train its blasters on him. Sorlin ran along the top of his ship's hull just barely ahead of each shot blasting the surface behind his path. He leapt down to the freighter's lower section and then again to the ground—again, just barely dodging each shot from the *Fallen Star's* strafing run. The *Fallen Star* made a wide turn and fired again as it simultaneously lowered its boarding ramp. Sorlin had dove from the blaster shots and was pulled under his freighter by Clawlow, who had taken cover there. Tana leapt up to the ramp and used the railings to pull herself up to where Cody was standing and assisted her inside. Josh followed Tana with more of a jump than a running leap. The boarding ramp started to close, and Josh was tossed into a roll and landed at Cody's feet. The *Fallen Star* fired off four missiles as parting shots into the flame and smoke-filled freighter landing area and then made an ascent upward into the sky.

* * *

In orbit, Gold Gatling's freighter was still stealthily attached to the hull of the *Darkfall*. A Honsho monitoring the Black Guard comms informed Gold that they had something. Gold bolted from his command chair to the comms station. There had been an explosion in the planet's mountainous region, and Black Guard chatter was beginning over the comms. It was confirmed as multiple explosions. He also picked up a ship matching dimensions and signatures of the *Fallen Star* as it was headed for orbit. The Black Guard schisms had also detected it and were pursuing for an intercept. The Honsho plotting the trajectory also reported that the Black Guard warships already in orbit would have to change their positioning and would likely just miss the *Fallen Star*. The smaller freighter just then broke into near orbit from the planet on the exact trajectory projected. The Honsho confirmed a match to the *Fallen Star*. Gold ordered a full power up. As they powered up, they had also been detected by the *Darkfall*. The Honsho reported that the schisms were gaining on the *Fallen Star*. He had also picked up a distress call on the planet's surface across the Honsho frequency. It was Sorlin Garrison's call sign.

Gold was taken by surprise. He asked, "What is he doing here?! Was he not confirmed in the Tordrey system?"

The Honsho monitoring the system had interrupted and claimed that the *Fallen Star* had just entered far orbit and was well ahead of the pursuing schisms. He also stated that several schisms were being dispatched from the *Darkfall* to their location. Gold ordered his freighter detached and a pursuit course of the *Fallen Star* plotted. The Honsho freighter detached and started to move along the side of the *Darkfall* and drew laser fire from the warship's side mounted guns as it did so. The freighter jolted harshly as heavy laser impact was made. The Honsho copilot stated that rear shields were holding. Gold ordered the pursuit of the *Fallen Star* continued. The Honsho at sensors then reported that the *Fallen Star* was plotting a hyperspace jump.

Gold calmly ordered, "Plot ours and stay with it."

The Honsho at sensors asked, "What about Sorlin's distress call?"

Gold replied, "Sorlin is obviously playing his own game. Leave him there for the natives and the Black Guard."

The Honsho looked strangely at Gold.

Gold then firmly repeated his order, "I said leave him there!" The hyperspace portal ahead of the *Fallen Star* opened and closed again behind it. Gold screamed out for status of their hyperspace jump. The Honsho copilot answered back as their hyperspace portal opened that their course should be 90 percent along the same course as the *Fallen Star*. He added that it was the best he could do. Gold returned to his command chair and answered with a nod. The Honsho at sensors added that he had jammed Black Guard sensors and they would not be able to detect or follow. Gold acknowledged with another nod. Gold's freighter moved into the hyperspace portal, and it closed behind them.

Chapter Eight

Seven Asteroid Run

FRIGHT AGENTS KYRAK and Maddo stood at each side of the Dark Lord Epitaph on the command deck of the *Darkfall*. They could only watch Josh's ship, the *Fallen Star*, jump away into hyperspace and followed closely behind by Gold Gatling's freighter. Epitaph was furious at the escape and, in his rage, began tearing apart the consoles on the command deck with his bare hands. He was finally calmed by the aid of both fright agents and their assurances that they would use all their resources to locate Josh Broody again. Epitaph reminded them that he wanted proof of Josh Broody's death. The rest of Josh's crew they could do with as they would see fit. He then added to his standing orders that he now wanted the Honsho, Gold Gatling as well and he wanted Gold brought before him alive so that he may deliver the punishment personally.

Epitaph ordered the Fury Fleet admiral to plot a hyperspace course to pursue. The admiral quite nervously with his delivery reported that they could not plot an exact course through hyperspace. At best, they could get an approximate exit point. Epitaph ordered him to get it done quickly and to evacuate the planet of all Black Guard forces. The admiral had agreed to the order and then inquired as to what Epitaph wished to be done about the explosion area on the planet, as well as the Honsho life signs and indigenous race that they now had as captives. Epitaph considered the inquiry and responded to burn the jungles. As for the Honshos on the planet, Epitaph ordered an incinerator field deployed around the entire planet. Anyone trying to land on or leave the planet would be disintegrated. He then instructed the admiral to make sure a Black Guard Death Post beacon was also deployed as a warning. The admiral turned to his council to assign the orders he was given. He was then approached and reminded by a general of the situation on Xotosia. The admiral again turned to Epitaph with a bit of nervousness. He feared that any more bad news delivered would result in his death, but not delivering it would result in the same. He reported that they have received reports that the rebellion on Xotosia was becoming more problematic then originally believed. The blockade fleet was requesting support forces. Epitaph looked to the Teon, Fright Agent Maddo with new orders to take a portion of the Fury Fleet back to Xotosia. Epitaph then ordered the Luth Bik, Fright Agent Kyrak to again find Josh's ship as he had done before. The fright agents were then dismissed.

* * *

Aboard the *Fallen Star* and amid a hyperspace run, the crew rested in the central recreation area. Laylee asked Josh where they were going. It was clear now that Epitaph himself was so obsessed with the prophecy of his demise and Josh's role in it that he would track them even in the wild regions of space. Josh was confused himself over that fact because with Jase dead, there would be no more brothers to slay Epitaph. Unless there was another part of the prophecy that Josh was unaware of and if so, finding any safe haven would be difficult. Cody suggested that there was always Derth space. They would be hunted by Derths, but it would be a lot easier than trying to elude the Black Guard. Josh reminded him that Epitaph had formed an allegiance or may still control a good portion of the Derths. A warning on the autopilot sensors then sounded. Cody checked it and reported that they had a new problem. A single ship was pursuing them through hyperspace and was employing a dangerous method of trying to mask its signature or presence by utilizing a very dangerous tactic of skimming along the barrier wall of hyperspace. One slightest slip of speed adjustment or shield harmonics would shred the ship into pieces, and the only race risky enough to try it was the Honshos.

* * *

On the Honsho freighter, Gold hovered closely over the pilot to make sure the pilot was doing everything correctly in skimming the hyperspace wall tactic. The pilot was doing the best he could against the difficult pull of hyperspace. The copilot recommended pulling out from hyperspace. Gold knew the idea that was being suggested was out of fear of their demise. What they were doing was extremely risky, but one could not be considered a true Honsho pirate without risk. Gold asked the pilot if they were close enough. The pilot looked worried as he replied in the affirmative. Gold said if we are leaving hyperspace then they are too. He ordered, "Increase all shields slowly against hyperspace propulsion and matching wave direction, extend buffer sensors and stabilizers, and engage tractor beam on my command." Every Honsho had been in this method before, but it was always dangerous. All of them performed their tasks with great attention. One slip would end them all. Finally, the pilot acknowledged that all was ready. Gold ordered the tractor beam engaged.

* * *

The *Fallen Star* jolted and then slowed in movement. Josh had taken off the autopilot and engaged his neural link. The *Fallen Star* attempted to increase its speed and fluctuate its molecular hull binding. The action turned the ship to its side and the crew stumbled with it.

Aboard the Honsho freighter, the piloting consoles exploded. Other consoles followed. The resistance of the *Fallen Star* had thrown their carefully plotted movement off. Damage reports were coming in. The port side was experiencing minor tears. If they did not adjust, they were doomed. Termination of the tractor beam would only send them spiraling into the hyperspace wall and increase the rate of damage. Gold checked the tractor beam readings; all unification waves were off. Harmonics and engine fluctuations that should be at a forced match from the tractor beam employment were not conforming. Struts and energy dampeners were unable to maintain locks. Gold checked the readings on the *Fallen Star* at the snare end of his tractor beam. Standard ship locks and controls were not wired to the main drive that the tractor beam was targeting.

Aboard the *Fallen Star*, the crew had assembled in the cockpit and engaged energy binding restraints. Tana was filled with panic. She asked what was happening. Cody told her that the Honsho ship chasing them had locked on a tractor beam. Laylee interjected that tractor beams do not perform with such unstable reactions even when resisted. Cody responded that the initiating ship is normally not skimming a hyperspace wall. The entire interior lighting and controls blacked out briefly and several fires were detected aboard. Cody engaged all fire repellant devices. A surge raced through the ship's systems that Josh was able to divert. Josh stated that the tractor beam was trying to affect the ship's drive systems through standard ship systems, but standard ship functions were unavailable through ship access when his neural link was applied. Suddenly everything not secured by energy bindings in the ship started to lift. A warning light displayed that the ship's artificial gravity controls were damaged. Laylee pleaded with Josh to disband the neural link or they would be killed. Josh replied that the neural link was the only thing keeping them alive at this point. If he terminated it now, they would be crushed.

Aboard the Honsho freighter, more hull tears were reported and two portions of the port side hull had ruptured. All containment measures had been initiated. The pilot console exploded, and the pilot was burned from the blast. Gold threw the copilot from his chair and took over the pilot controls that still functioned. He danced his fingers across the console and ignited thrusters as he steered the freighter upward and to the port side. The Honsho freighter slowly emerged from hyperspace, inching its way out like emerging from a cocoon. Severe explosions resonated throughout the ship as it emerged prematurely from hyperspace. The tractor beam fluctuated, and an energy feedback wave reversed through it just before it was terminated. The Honsho freighter experienced a ship-wide energy wave that shut down all systems.

The final release of the tractor beam had an echoing pull effect. As it terminated, the *Fallen Star* was thrown outward through the hyperspace wall. It was tossed into normal space like a baseball crashing through a glass window. Josh had been forced to release the neural link or suffer brain damage. He held his head firmly with both hands as he experienced the pain of unjacking from the system prematurely without normal log off protocols. Cody detected pressure increase as the ship started to crush inward. With Josh impaired, Cody quickly decreased all pressure and venting flaps and ports. He had stopped the ship from crushing in on itself. The *Fallen Star* came to a rolling stop in the drift of space. Both ships with severe damage now sat adrift and facing each other.

* * *

Back at the jungle planet, Sorlin had gathered up the Honsho pirates that had fled from the *Fallen Star's* assault that left their fleet in ruin. The Black Guard was in full departure mode of the planet. Their only hope of getting off this planet was to form an alliance with the Black Guard troops. Clawlow was hesitant about the plan, but to gain the power he wished to have, he would have to follow Sorlin off this world.

They approached a Black Guard encampment under a flag of truce. The Black Guard forces were in a hurried state to get off planet and were ordered to attack any Honshos and natives. The Black Guard patrols opened up heavy blaster fire upon Sorlin and his approaching party as other Black Guard ships left for orbit. Sorlin and his men were forced to retreat. The Black Guard patrol boarded the last ships and followed their comrades into orbit. As the last ships were departing, a planetary bombardment was unleashed. Heavy fire bombs hit the surface and ignited the jungle terrain. Flames began to join and sweep in unison across large regions of the planet. The surviving Matrasus and those released from the Black Guard were sent running for cover as well from a final rain of rockets. Clawlow had ushered Sorlin and the Honshos into a cave. Sorlin watched the widespread devastation from the cave entrance. He also witnessed the last of the Black Guard ships vanish further into the sky from his sight. Sorlin's plan of freedom from the Gatling Legion and goals of his own leadership in the Honsho Piracy had led him to being stranded here.

* * *

The Black Guard Fury Fleet in orbit of the jungle world of Matrel was ready to depart this distant region of space. Fright Agent Maddo acknowledged his orders to take his assigned portion of the fleet back to Xotosia. Epitaph granted him the permission. Fright Agent Maddo and his portion of the fleet entered into hyperspace portals; the rest of Fury Fleet took another hyperspace path on a course plotted by Fright Agent Kyrak. He assured Epitaph that it would not be long before they would have Josh Broody dead and Gold Gatling would be begging for mercy before Epitaph's feet. Epitaph responded that the begging would be futile because he had several torturous plans that would make Gold Gatling consider death a merciful fate.

* * *

The *Fallen Star* was the first ship to move from its adrift stare down with the Honsho freighter that had yanked them from hyperspace. Artificial gravity had been restored along with internal pressure. The Janan Crystals had fared well and suffered less energy drain than expected. Weapons and shields were still offline. The neural link to Josh's mind was still severed, but priority was propulsion. The engine drives had suffered the greatest stress, but Cody was able to reroute all the engine systems to one drive. They had base speed of four, five if they pushed it. Josh recommended that they be as cautious as they could. It was clear that the Honsho freighter was in worse shape, so time was on their side. Cody fired up the ship's engine drive, and it slowly crawled away from the standoff at half standard speed. The *Fallen Star* slowly gained its speed as it maneuvered away from the Honsho freighter. It reached standard speed one and sputtered its way to standard speed two. Cody was sure they could increase to standard speed three, but Josh at manual pilot controls insisted on a slow and safe advance to prevent further damage. They were flying a glass ship at this point, but they were at least flying.

* * *

Gold was furious at the fact that his freighter sat within grasp of the *Fallen Star* and could not do anything but watch it limp away. The freighter was in total disarray. Consoles everywhere throughout the ship were blown out. Some sections were sealed to contain hull breaches, and all engine drives were offline. The technical crew was fighting just to keep life support from total failure. Smoke had filled most of the passages, and others were collapsed with debris. Suddenly partial engine function had roared to life. Gold was informed that the best they could do was standard speed two. It would be enough to stay on the *Fallen Star's* trail but not enough to overtake it. Attention was called to the heading of the *Fallen Star*. It was on course to an asteroid field. Gold smiled. He said that they were headed to Seven Asteroid Run, which just so happened to be an old smuggling route for the Gatling Legion. Gold knew his way around the seven large asteroid hosted field blindfolded. He knew how to get around and make up distance. With restored confidence, he said, "We'll get them there!"

* * *

In hyperspace route aboard the *Darkfall*, Epitaph had received a transmission from his bride Emelia. She had been resurrected from the dead by Epitaph some time ago but did not appear as such at first glance. She was a Jaskan with long wavy dark-blue hair that ran past her shoulders to just over her breasts. It was combed over to cover her left eye. The exposed eye was green. Her facial features were thin and she had full luscious lips. Around her left eye and the left side of her neck that was concealed by her long hair was of rotted flesh. Her left eye itself was layered in black ooze. She wore a leather jacket with sleeves down to her elbows. The leather jacket itself was fastened just at her breasts. It spread open from there and exposed a smooth and firm midsection of her bare skin. Her waist was very thin. Her legs were covered in skin tight leather pants that fit her lower regions like a perfect mold of second skin. Her holster around her curvaceous figure held two blaster pistols with the handgrips facing forward. She also sported a long similar to katana style sword in the sheath worn across her back. Her right arm from the elbow down was bare skin but covered with tattoos of claws and talons that ran downward to her hand. Her left arm from the elbow down was also bare, but it was the arm of a rotting corpse. Behind her stood the thorn covered Prah, Fright Agent Nehih.

Emelia asked Epitaph if he had found Josh yet. He reported that the search continued. Emelia revealed her position and wished to reroute to join him, but Epitaph denied the request. He needed her to divert to Xotosia with her skills in persuasion to end the rebel uprising. She hesitantly agreed. She reminded Epitaph that the death of Josh Broody would be upon her to deal. Epitaph bowed his head at her and replied, "I will make sure of that, my bride." Emelia ordered Fright Agent Nehih to adjust their plotted course to Xotosia and she ended the transmission.

* * *

The *Fallen Star* was the first ship to reach the outer edge of the asteroid field. There were seven large asteroids that lined the field among hundreds of smaller asteroids. The *Fallen Star*, thanks to Cody's mechanical skills, had regained some of its speed and maneuverability. Josh had turned the piloting controls over to Laylee, while he repaired the severed neural link between himself and the *Fallen Star*. The smaller asteroids crashed up against the hull as they entered the outer edge of the asteroid field. Cody engaged molecular shielding to lessen the blows. Cody took control of navigation and plotted a course through the thinnest part of the asteroid field and accounted for trajectory and speed of the asteroids in the path. The shielding that he had restored would be able to handle that course. He also highlighted on the monitor screen the asteroids that they would be able to deploy landing claws onto if they were forced to land. Laylee insisted that she could handle the pilot controls. She then turned the ship slightly to match course of the oncoming asteroid. The *Fallen Star* rotated and flew parallel with the larger asteroid, matching each slowed twist in flight perfectly. Josh commended Laylee on her flying skills, but that was just the edge of the asteroid field. He instructed her to take the ship further inside. Laylee utilized a bit of her android hand-and-eye coordination to match the course plotted. There were a few smaller asteroids that had not been accounted for, but Laylee was able to perfectly adjust the flight and sharply dodge them just as they came up on her view.

* * *

Gold's Honsho freighter had come upon the Seven Asteroid Run at a course above the asteroid field. He then relieved his pilot and took the flight controls himself. Honsho ships were extremely long and narrow in design for greater speed but sacrificed maneuverability as a result. Gold, though, was an expert at doing things with ships that others claimed could never be accomplished. He had also been flying Honsho freighters before he had learned how to walk. He instructed his crew to hold on and fasten in. He turned the Honsho freighter in a spiral maneuver and flew into the asteroid field between two of the large asteroids. The Honsho freighter turned to spiral in the opposite direction and as a result cleared between the two asteroids just before they collided into each other. He looked to the Honsho copilot that seemed filled with admiration on the maneuver. Gold called those two asteroids the clappers and then announced that was the easiest part of this maze of twisting rock. Gold then pointed to the identification blip on the sensors. He said, "There is our prize."

* * *

Laylee was able to skim the *Fallen Star* close and tight around another of the big asteroids with only a slight scrape of the shields. Tana had noticed the blip on their monitors and called Josh's attention to it. He put down the device he was working on and assessed their location with comparison to the plotted course. He realized there was a wide-open region just before the edge of the asteroid field. It was a clearing in the field. He instructed Laylee to fly into the clearing just long enough to reveal position then come back in under the asteroid and scrape the surface of it again. Tana looked at him questioningly, and the look was matched by Laylee herself. Josh answered the doubtful looks with confidence. He assured them that it would be all right because he had a plan.

Cody replied, "Now I am worried."

Laylee flew the *Fallen Star* into the clearing and allowed the Honsho freighter's scanners to detect them. The sensors detected that the Honsho freighter had adjusted course and was moving across the asteroid field to the closest large asteroid. Laylee then initiated a spinning maneuver as she took the ship back out of sensor detection and tucked in under the large asteroid. She looked once more at Josh. Josh nodded his approval. Laylee then skimmed the underside of the ship along the underside surface of the asteroid. Just as the *Fallen Star* impacted the surface of the asteroid, Josh launched and detonated two rockets behind the ship and at the asteroid that caused an explosion which caught the *Fallen Star* and propelled it away from the asteroid. At that exact instant, Josh took control of the ship with the now repaired neural link. He jettisoned the cargo hold of spare parts and hull plating. Following the explosion and the ejected debris, Josh cut all the ship's power. The *Fallen Star* spun on a drift created from the explosion and was thrown to the outer edge of the asteroid field. Josh used the gravity of the smaller asteroids to keep the *Fallen Star* concealed and flowing alongside them with matched movement. To any sensors, it would look like rogue asteroids separating from the field. Once Josh was convinced that the explosion decoy had been received by the Honsho freighter's sensors, he restarted the ship and flew the *Fallen Star* far enough away to avoid sensor detection.

* * *

Gold watched the monitors display the explosion. He then detected the debris and scanned it. The debris matched the readings of the ship they had been chasing. He slammed the pilot console with his fists in a state of rage. The collision had robbed them of their prize.

Chapter Nine

Mortigan's Price

THE BLACK GUARD Fury Fleet exited hyperspace and initiated a full sensor sweep. No ship either Josh's or the Honsho freighter had been detected. Fright Agent Kyrak struggled to find reasoning as to why there was no detection of either ship. He used a holographic map to display his charting of possible paths the two ships could have taken. He accounted for speed, known phenomena, travel distance at varied speeds, and hyperspace travel. He then pinpointed two more possible locations to search while still stressing the difficulty in tracking through infinite variables. Epitaph looked carefully at the two best choices Fright Agent Kyrak had selected. He instructed Fright Agent Kyrak to pick one and then reminded him that there were to be no more excuses.

* * *

The *Fallen Star* had escaped through the asteroid field, but its problems were not gone. The adjustments to the ship controls that Josh had made in order to reconnect his neural link to the ship had been hastened and resulted in an overload with several fried points of termination. The *Fallen Star* now sat adrift again. Whatever Josh had done to force his neural link had also disabled manual controls as well. Cody was able to maintain life support, sensors, and several minor passive running systems, but everything else was dead. Josh had scanned the Janan crystals and verified that they were producing the full charge required. Cody had ripped apart the engine drives and core systems. He had reconnected the drives to all function once power was back, and they would have full engine power again. Tana was left to watch the monitors, scanners, and viewscreens for any ships or possible approaching dangers. Josh and Laylee had physically climbed into the computer systems core to check the connections.

It was a long and narrow shaft lined with wires, circuits, and relays. It was a tight fit for two people pressing tightly up against each other. Josh was finding it extremely difficult to concentrate on the task with Laylee shifting up and down the terminals and her fabulous body rubbing up against him. She was trying to find an access point to plug in her cranial jack behind her right ear. It would enable her to directly interface with all the ship systems. She turned to face a possible connection point and placed her firm ass against Josh's lower extremities. She slid her body down along his and aroused his sexual desires. Tight quarters or not, he was enjoying this because he had wanted for so long to be close to Laylee. She turned her body again with her breast region in Josh's face. Laylee stretched to plug into the terminal above them. She slipped and caught herself by grabbing onto Josh's chest with one hand and his groin with the other. They locked their gaze upon each other. They both had wanted this and it was as if they could read each other's thoughts.

Josh could not resist any longer and pulled her back up to him. They were face to face, and their lips were drawn together. They embraced tightly and, with a fevered passion, had locked their lips together. Their kissing increased, and their embrace tightened. Josh tore open his vest and shirt as Laylee unzipped her jumpsuit. They could not disrobe fast enough as Josh undid his pants and Laylee slipped completely out of her jumpsuit that fell to the floor. Laylee stretched up to grab a tool support rail that she used to pull herself up. Her soft and firm breasts were in Josh's face as he licked them slowly with his tongue. Her nipples grew firmer and felt like they would fall off as he cupped them into his mouth. It may not have been real skin, but it was her flesh, and it tasted good to him. Laylee placed herself onto Josh's hard love rod and began to move up and down on it at a slow pace. Her body tingled like never before. They both moaned with passion. She had given pleasure to many and felt it in return, but not like this. This was pure bliss. Her body continued to shift and increase in speed as he matched her movement with his own. He had clutched her firm ass tightly to add support as their bodies moved as one. Josh's thrusting motions into her went deeper and harder. Laylee had never felt lost in such fascination before. She wanted this to continue forever. She believed her lust for him had been a mask. She mentally asked herself if this was what true love felt like. The passion grew and their movement had become wilder and almost primal as they shifted their bodies together even more rapidly until they had both reached their climax. They remained joined and tightly embraced in each other's arms.

Cody had inadvertently interrupted as he hollered over the comms for a status report. They frantically collected their thoughts and had again become aware of their surroundings. They quickly dressed back into their clothing. Josh helped zip up Laylee's jumpsuit as she pulled a computer cable from the terminal and plugged it into the small port behind her ear. Laylee hollered up that she was jacking in now. They smiled at each other with a mischievous look. Their gaze into each other's eyes was only broken by the sound of Tana running to the shaft and loudly yelling. They looked upward just as Tana looked down. The urgency in Tana's voice halted. She had frozen and was struggling for words as she watched the two separate from their embrace. Josh climbed out of the shaft and realized that his belt was still unfastened. Tana shook her head to clear her thoughts and told Josh that he had to see something. She turned quickly away and rubbed the strange feeling of tears from her eyes as she headed back to the cockpit. Josh followed behind her down the corridor. Laylee continued her connection into the ship's computers.

As they entered the cockpit, Josh finally put his vest back on over the tight shirt defining his great physique. He took the pilot seat, and Tana matched him by taking a seat at the copilot station. Josh was captivated by what he saw. Tana tried looking at it but found herself not being able to pull her stare from Josh. She was filling inside with an overwhelming feeling of dread that she could not understand why it had hurt so much.

Josh continued to observe a strange loosely formed mist moving across space ahead of them by a hundred meters. It was moving in a looping pattern and forming what resembled a misty giant spider web formation. His attention remained locked on the phenomenon as he initiated sensor scans of the formation.

The engines suddenly built up in a low humming and for only a few seconds roared to life, before sputtering and shutting down again. The brief display of power had frozen the mist formation in its path of movement. It then changed its direction flow and moved toward the *Fallen Star*. It would creep along at a slow pace then freeze and then continue moving again. It was repeating this process as it advanced ever closer toward the *Fallen Star*. The ship's brief show of power had also forced Tana's attention to finally be drawn away from Josh and to this mist form again. She recognized this movement and informed Josh that her people practiced this same movement when they were hunting. Her growing concern was genuine in expression.

The engines started again to switch on and sputter off again. The mist form seemed to be swaying from left to right as if it was searching for the *Fallen Star* and attempting to obtain a lock. One final burst of engine power drew the mist form right in front of the ship where it again stopped in its path. Josh and Tana observed the mist form then shifting its movement again from side to side and, this time, expanding outward and around the ship. Josh then commed his crew that he was shutting down all power and systems. He paused only long enough for Laylee to return the comm that she had jacked out of the ship's computer. With a simple flick of only two switches on Josh's console, the *Fallen Star* went dark. No interior lighting and no outward running lights. No signals of any kind and no fluctuating power sources.

The silky mist form had then started to rapidly shift its movement in a wild and sporadic motion as it moved just over the ship. It now circled around the *Fallen Star* still at a wilder movement than its

previous carefully stalking pattern. Tana also recognized this movement as a hunter that had lost its prey. After a few moments, the
mist form had seemed to have abandoned them. Cody had returned
to the cockpit. Cody told Josh to try it now. Josh started the *Fallen
Star* back up to minimal power and lighting, but Josh's neural link to
the ship was unstable. Laylee then entered and stood at the cockpit
doorway and dangled an electronic device from its thick wires. She
calmly stated that they needed a new pulse coordinator. The device
was responsible for directing energy pulses from the Janan crystals
throughout power relays of the ship. The activation of that path also
ran through the main computer port that hosted Josh's neural link
connections. They all looked silently at each other.

The silence was broken by Cody with a question. Cody asked,
"Despite needing a very sophisticated piece of necessary ship technology equipment, does anyone have an idea where we are even at?"

* * *

Gold Gatling stood behind his helmsman as they swiftly turned
the freighter ship along the surface of the twisting motion of the
largest asteroid in the field. The freighter followed along the asteroid
surface, twisting and turning in unison with the asteroid itself. The
freighter then entered a large and wide canyon surface of the asteroid
rock and shot straight across to a cave in the canyon wall. The passage was a long dark tunnel illuminated only by the exterior running
and spotlights of the freighter as it descended deeper into the asteroid
cave. The freighter flew through the passage and into a larger cave
that was scattered with ship parts and various other containers. This
was one of Gold's abandoned smuggling run encampments.

Gold pointed ahead to a clearing in the mechanical-layered
maze and said, "Land there, and we will make repairs."

* * *

The Black Guard Fury Fleet assembled in fleet formation at the
exit point of hyperspace. Epitaph inquired of their current location.

The Fleet admiral responded that they were in the Teniu System. Epitaph considered the answer and asked if the planet Kalilla was not in this system. The fleet admiral responded in the affirmative and, with a nod to the helmsmen, he added that they had already plotted course.

Fright Agent Kyrak stepped to Epitaph's side and addressed him. He said, "My lord, we can't go to Kalilla." He added that Black Guard presence in this area of space was minimal and even less around this system.

Kalilla was deeper into the system, and Black Guard presence there would be nonexistent. Kalilla was a scum world. It was more of a criminal haven than Xotosia. Even the criminals of the universe had etiquette and rules. Kalilla was left alone from the rest of Black Guard-controlled space simply because of the fact that there was nothing of interest. It was a world run by forces lower than galactic scum; even respectable criminals avoided it. Epitaph responded with a silent stare. Once Fright Agent Kyrak stepped back, Epitaph stated that he would go where he pleased and that Kalilla today did have something of interest. Fright Agent Kyrak turned to the fleet admiral and ordered all shields at full and all weaponry charged and ready to target. Epitaph looked back at Fright Agent Kyrak. He stated that they were most definitely not respected criminals, and if the name of the Black Guard alone did not install fear to those denizens of Kalilla, then it soon would.

* * *

The blockade around Xotosia welcomed the approaching smaller portion of ships linked to the Fury Fleet as they exited hyperspace portals. Fright Agent Maddo moved his warship, the *Ripper*, unobstructed through the assembled fleet and into the center of the assembly and announced that he was assuming command of the blockade and all ground forces. The fleet admiral boarded and reported on the organized rebellion attacks. Another Black Guard warship called attention as it exited from hyperspace. Over the comms came a visual transmission. It was the warship, the *Impalement*, commanded by the

Prah, Fright Agent Nehih, and with him was Emelia. She ordered all rebellion information sent to the *Impalement*. She also ordered four schism starfighters and two full troop transports readied to follow her to the planet. The fleet admiral flustered out the orders for rapid deployment of the specified forces. He then nervously asked if there was anything else he could do for her.

Emelia responded, "It is what I can do for you, Admiral Feese. I am here to solve your rebellion problem." She then asked if the rebellion had formed under his watch. The fleet admiral swallowed deeply before bowing his head in shame. He admitted that it had but begged for forgiveness. Emelia smiled. She then ordered Fright Agent Maddo to execute the admiral. One quickly drawn blaster shot to his head without hesitation sent the lifeless body to the floor. Emelia then begged of Fright Agent Maddo to make sure the former admiral's family was sent her forgiveness of his failure.

* * *

Aboard the *Fallen Star*, they had pulled out the paper star charts to determine their location and destination. They were able to gather that they were at the edge of the Gabree System. There was nothing there, but they would be able to plot a course through the system and to a planet of Jaltroo just at its edge. It was a planet full of salvage yards, and Black Guard patrols were loosely routed there. If you were looking for junk in the universe, Jaltroo was a paradise. Jaltroo patrol assignments in the Black Guard were usually given to soldiers and officers as reprimands for bad behavior, so few even cared about duty. Cody figured he could get small boosts from the engines, but they would be inconsistent. They could get to Jaltroo if they limped all the way there. Josh asked Laylee if she could get a transmission to the Honsho freighter that had pursued them in the asteroid field. Everyone displayed a look of shock at Josh. Cody reminded him that they had just recently tricked that very same Honsho freighter into believing they had been destroyed. Josh assured everyone that he had a plan. Another of Josh's plans did not bring ease or calm to Cody. Josh pointed out that the engine manipulation would put extreme strain on the Janan crystals. He wanted to use the run to Jaltroo as a backup plan. The best plan would be to try and strike some kind of deal with the Honshos that had pursued them. Honshos worked for fortune, Josh figured he could find something of more value to the Honshos. Laylee asked him what that something of more value might be. Josh smiled and said he had not figured that part out yet.

* * *

In the asteroid encampment, a Honsho came running from the freighter to alert Gold of the received transmission. Gold activated his wrist comm. The transmission was of Laylee. She declared that the ship the Honshos had pursued was disabled. She added that they were in need of assistance and promised fortune. Gold quickly pulled out a bottle of Abolish wine from the stash he had been searching through. He raised it in a toast to all the Honshos around him. He declared that their fortune had not eluded them. He then requested a repair time of the freighter. The Honsho reported that it would be two more aras, which was a term for "hours." Gold corrected him and said that he had less than half that. Gold then ordered all maintenance efforts tripled.

* * *

The Black Guard Fury Fleet arrived in far orbit of Kalilla. The guard satellites that were posted there and referenced as killer eyes opened fire on the approaching fleet. Killer eyes were a defense of many small outpost and unaligned worlds. They were armed with heavy lasers and strong deflection forcefields. They were well-equipped to stop one or two ships from reaching a planet, but they were no match for a fully armed Black Guard fleet. The killer eyes were shot down instantly and did little damage before their demise. Epitaph and Fright Agent Kyrak boarded a shuttle and departed for the planet with ten schisms and two troop transports as escorts.

Once in the atmosphere, the schisms with heavy blaster fire quickly eliminated the four air combat vehicles sent in engagement and sent them crashing to the surface. Epitaph opened a hail to the planetary defense fortress. He offered to not destroy their planet and assured them that the Black Guard would depart their world once he had met with Mortigan. A brief delay of silence was broken with provided landing coordinates.

The Black Guard ships landed. Epitaph and Fright Agent Kyrak disembarked. The Black Guard pilots and soldiers assembled in formations. The wind on the planet was heavy and blew dirt and debris around on the ground. There were few buildings, and they were spread widely apart from one another. Each building was as tall as the others. They were two stories tall and looked like they were about to fall apart. The appearance was a decoy. Each building had walls around them, and each wall was heavily manned with gunners of various races and heavy repeating blaster rifles. Epitaph ordered Fright Agent Kyrak to hold back with the soldiers. Four Laser Heads with their heavily black armored bodies and heads of spherical pink energy had emerged and walked with Epitaph toward the nearest building. They were met by six human men dressed in ragged cloths and scarves around their faces to protect them from the blowing dirt and rock. Epitaph was given a scarf, which he accepted and wrapped around his face as well. Until then, he had been shielding the heavy winds with his arms. The six men escorted Epitaph and his Laser Head guards down the wide-open street to the building at its end. The building looked better than the rest and had armor-plated walls. The building also had holographic doors that dispersed as they walked in and reconstituted again after they had passed through.

The inside of the building resembled an old western saloon and gambling hall. There were many ongoing different gambling games from circle shaped cards to holographic spin wheels and even a fighting pen with two oddly developed and armored creatures fighting while the patrons bet gems and mixed currencies on the results. The two creatures were called tredragons. They resembled featherless chickens, but also had long necks, four legs, and lashing wings, which along with their beaks were used as weapons. The patrons of the establishment were of various races. One thorn-covered Prah stood quickly up as Epitaph walked by. One of the Laser Heads darkened its spherical head of light energy from pink to red and fired off two short laser blasts. One dropped the Prah dead to the floor, and the other shot off from the side of the sphere, hitting and killing a Jaskan male. The room grew suddenly silent as the other Laser Heads also darkened their spherical heads to red and prepared to fire in any direction, not needing to even turn to do so. Epitaph ordered the Laser Heads to disengage, and they returned their spherical heads to the passive pink balls of light. Epitaph never broke his stride for any of the action and continued to walk as he passed the escorts.

He was ushered to the front of a stage as the dead were pulled from the floor and the various races resumed their gambling and drinking as if nothing had occurred. Mortigan walked out to stand face to face with Epitaph and introduced himself. He also declared more than questioned that Epitaph was looking for him. Mortigan was a humanoid, but his skin was layered and stitched with the flesh of many different races. He was actually a Sparbosan, which was a race essentially human but covered with brown splotches on their skin. Mortigan had none of his original skin exposed. He was a well-famed bounty hunter and known for his personal ritual of sewing a piece of skin from each of his bounties onto his own. He then apologized for the patronage of non-humans, admitting that he knew of Epitaph's hatred of them except of course for the most feared fright agents. He then declared that was why he had sent the humans as escorts. Mortigan then purposely displayed more of his knowledge by asking of the health of his bride, Emelia. He added that he had heard that Emelia drew even more fear from people than the fright agents. Epitaph took charge of the conversation and declared that Mortigan seemed to know much about him. Epitaph added that he knew much about Mortigan as well. He referenced the fact that Mortigan was the best bounty hunter in the business. Epitaph then added that he was in need of Mortigan's services. Mortigan countered by calling for two glasses of Takadish liquor. He then claimed to Epitaph that he only brought bounties back dead. If the bounty needed to be alive, then Epitaph would have to look elsewhere. Epitaph's forked tongue flicked wildly and he unleashed a hissing laugh. Epitaph then claimed that his bounty would qualify. Epitaph opened his palm, revealing a palm held mini holoprojector that displayed an image and data of Josh Broody. He then removed the disc and tossed it to Mortigan, who caught it with super-fast reflexes. Epitaph at that moment experienced a quick flash of a vision that put him into a hesitated trance. In his vision, Mortigan was shaking his hand, and in Mortigan's other hand was the head of Josh Broody. Epitaph recovered from his trance and widened his reptilian grin. He stated that Mortigan would do fine. Epitaph started to walk away with his Laser Head guards.

Mortigan hollered out, "We didn't discuss price!"

Epitaph turned only his head all the way back, displaying his amazing flexibility in body motion. He then declared 200,000 drekings. Mortigan claimed that Black Guard currency was not really valuable in his areas of dwelling. Epitaph countered the offer by offering to pay the value in gems. Mortigan accepted. Epitaph then turned his head back to the forward position and started walking away again. Mortigan hollered out once more. He admitted that he would like one of those Laser Heads. Epitaph kept walking, and without turning around, he hollered back that if Mortigan brought him the head of Josh Broody, then he could have two of them.

* * *

Gold's Honsho freighter had docked by boarding hatch with the *Fallen Star*. Gold approached in a wave of arrogance. Before he could gloat, Josh offered him twelve times what Epitaph had agreed to pay him for his capture. Gold was amazed at the offer and then clarified that the price would be 3,600,000 drekings. Josh promised to pay it only upon his ship being towed to the planet of Jaltroo and a procurement of a pulse coordinator. Gold agreed but wanted something else up front. He wanted Laylee and Tana. Everyone tensed up at the request. Josh declared that Laylee and Tana were both off the negotiation table. Gold walked around Laylee and Tana and expressed his disappointment of that statement while he visually admired both of them. He claimed that they both would fetch a high payment for bodies so fine. He then asked Josh what he would be using as payment. Josh claimed that he still had secret codes to Black Guard funds that even Epitaph did not even know about. He claimed he had been dipping into them when needed and promised to give the codes to Gold upon completion of the deal. Gold then stated that he would want to verify those codes were genuine during the installation of the device. Josh agreed. Gold then wanted one more thing before final agreement. Josh reminded him that Laylee and Tana were not for negotiation. Gold laughed and then admitted that he knew about Josh's neural link to the ship and he wanted that technology to forge his own. Josh did not seem surprised that Gold knew about the neural link but knew of Gold's resourcefulness reputation. He still hesitated and shared a look with Cody. It was a valuable tool, and in the hands of the Honsho Piracy, it would give them great power. Josh agreed to the codes and the schematics of the neural link, not an actual produced model. If Gold was going to have a neural link, he was going to have to build it on his own. Gold and Josh placed opposite hands on each other's shoulders as a sign of an agreement. Gold then commed his helmsman to prepare the *Fallen Star* for a tow.

* * *

Emelia's shuttle came under a missile attack as it prepared to land at the Black Guard confiscated mountain palace on Xotosia. The four schisms committed a strafing laser attack and blew up the missile launchers at two separate locations. The shuttle then landed with a troop transport on each side of it. The Black Guard soldiers disembarked at a hurried pace and secured the area. Emelia then disembarked from her shuttle with Fright Agent Nehih and two Laser Heads. Two ranks of soldiers filed on each side of Emelia and her entourage and marched them into the palace.

Chapter Ten

Sidetracked

EMELIA STRODE INTO the confiscated palace. As they entered the main living area, the Black Guard soldiers fanned out and took guarded stances along the walls. The two Laser Heads remained at Emelia's side while she instructed Fright Agent Nehih to the communications terminal to monitor planetary broadcasts. The commanding officer of the present force entered and protested this action. He then looked from Fright Agent Nehih to Emelia. Immediately upon sight of her, he quickly changed his attitude and position as he cowered to her side. Emelia encouraged him to state his opposition that he clearly had as he entered the room. He slowly regained his nerve to mention that he had everything under control and there was no need to replace his command, much less bring a fright agent. Emelia put her arm of rotting flesh around his shoulder and admitted that she understood his position. He grew more nervous and squeamish as she tightened her embrace. Emelia then asked if her arm bothered him. He was too scared to admit that it did and replied in the negative. Emelia maintained her half embrace and requested how the commander felt he had everything under his control. He was puzzled at the question but breathed a deep sigh of relief as Emelia broke her embrace and walked away from him. She kept her back to him as she calmly started to recite the most recent rebel attacks. She then turned quickly to face him and raised her voice in anger as she added the missile attack upon her shuttle as she arrived to the list. The commander groveled toward her and apologized for that attack. He quickly added that he was extremely grateful that no harm had come to her. He promised her that he could do better. Emelia replied that he was out of time. He begged her again and promised to do anything to receive her approval. Emelia considered the promise with a smile. She then pulled back the long blue hair that covered her left eye and revealed the rotting flesh and slimy ooze layered eye socket. Emelia then told the commander to kiss her. The commander looked around the room to all that had turned away from the conversation at this point. Emelia stepped closer and caressed the side of his face with her rotted hand. She asked him what was wrong as he appeared to be unnerved. He shook his head in a negative motion. She brought her lips closer to his and asked him why he now trembled. She asked if her disfigurement displeased him. The commander shook nervously and stuttered as he again replied in the negative. Emelia increased the caressing of the side of his face and told him again to kiss her. He stepped back from her, which drew a look of anger from her immediately. He mentioned that he should not kiss her because it would be a betrayal to his dark lord. Emelia again changed her expression from anger back to a seductive plea. She said that if he did not kiss her, he would offend her. He tried to step back another step, but she grabbed onto his arm with a tight grip of her good hand and pulled him toward her. She then screamed at him with insistence, "You will kiss me now!" With her rotted flesh hand, she pushed on the back of his head and forced his lips to hers. She maneuvered her luscious and full lips onto his with great passion. The passion of the kiss relaxed the commander as he surrendered to it and returned the emotion to her. Emelia tightened her grip on the back of his head, pushing his lips tighter to her own. She then increased the act of passion by slipping her tongue into his mouth. The kiss grew with more intensity. Suddenly something felt wrong. The commander opened his eyes and tried to pull away, but Emelia had him now tightly clutched with both her hands. He tried to move his head away from the kiss. Her once normal tongue inserted into his mouth was now a rotted tongue as she pulled it out and licked his lips before she kissed him again and forced the rotted tongue deeper into his mouth. His flesh started to rot at a rapid rate. He struggled with the last of his life, but her grip was too strong. She drained his life force from him as she forced the continuation of the kiss. As his life force was drained, his skin rotted. The kiss continued until he was motionless. Emelia broke the kiss and her grip on him and the commander's lifeless corpse fell to the floor. Fright Agent Nehih stepped quickly to her side and asked if she was all right. She smiled and replied that she felt renewed. She then ordered a soldier to remove the former commander's corpse.

* * *

Gold entered the cargo area of his freighter that Josh had claimed as his temporary quarters. Gold then, with no delay in words, inquired about Laylee's sexual performance. Gold followed with the admittance that Silos had informed him that Laylee was the best of his androids. Josh calculated his reply with caution. He told Gold that it was not of his concern and reminded Gold that Laylee preferred the term Simulent. Gold let out a half-hearted chuckle and a sneer took refuge on his face. Gold then changed the topic of conversation. He then asked if they could discuss the Honsho that held him captive. He added that the Matrasus seemed quite displeased when she spoke of her experience with those Honshos. Josh remained silent as Gold continued. Gold had mentioned that they had detected the explosions and had imagined that Josh's ship must have left the Honsho freighters pretty crippled if they had not pursued him. Gold's questioning then took a brunt tone as he asked if there were any survivors. Josh hesitated to answer as he was trying to read Gold's expression. Gold seemed to give nothing away as he remained calm and expressionless across his face. Josh finally replied that they should gamble someday. Josh had the feeling that Gold would be an interesting challenge. Gold quickly replied that he was an interesting challenge in everything he did. Gold then responded to his own previous and unanswered question. He said that it was of little concern anyway. He believed that if the Black Guard did not kill them, then they would just be stranded there. Josh sensed coldness in the remark and asked if those Honshos were not from his legion. Gold smiled. Josh then stepped forward to directly face Gold and asked if he discarded other people as easily as he did his own. Gold admitted, "Sorlin was my rival trying to underhandedly raise his status above mine and throw me under him as he made his climb. So you only did me a favor by removing him and my hands remain clean."

Gold started to walk out of the cargo hold and stopped at the doorway. He made a very clear and precise statement: "I only discard all those that have outlived their usefulness to me. You and your crew are still useful." Gold then departed. Cody, Laylee, and Tana entered as he was leaving. Gold unleashed his charm by complimenting the ladies on their beauty. Laylee turned away from him with no reaction. Tana followed with a growl. Cody looked at Gold and replied that it must have been something he said. Gold took his leave.

Cody asked Josh if they could trust Gold. Josh replied that they could trust him as long as he believed he would be getting paid. Cody countered by asking if Gold would be getting paid. Josh ignored the question with a glance by diverting to Laylee and asking what she was able to ascertain about the crew. Laylee started to talk when Tana interrupted by excusing herself with an annoyance tone in her voice. She went to keep an eye on the crew.

Laylee continued by stating the Honshos despite her rejection of their advances were still open to providing information as long as she moved her body just right and exposed just enough skin. She then added that even the female Honshos on other freighters and viewing over ship monitors seemed to like what they saw. She had gathered that most of the crew would turn on Gold to get ahead, but they also feared his retaliation if they failed. She also got the impression that Gold had measures in place in the case of just such circumstances.

Josh then looked to Cody, who had been given a tour of the freighter. Cody stated that the freighter was solid but had definitely seen better days. Suddenly, the entire ship, as if in response to Cody's remarks, had experienced a short jumping motion. Everyone on the ship was then slammed against the walls and floor as the freighter came to an abrupt and sudden stop.

* * *

Mortigan was boarding his ship, the *Dark Wish*. It was a sleek built ship with several forward slanted angles to its design. It was just a bit longer than the average freighter model but only had one level to it. It was black and had a stealth armor plating. The computer turned on upon his entry as well as all interior lighting. The computer voice was female in tone and welcomed him by name. There was a slight exotic accent to the voice that Mortigan found pleasing. As Mortigan made his way to the cockpit, the computer voice asked how he was feeling and if they were on mission or recreation. Mortigan referred to the voice as Binia and replied that he was feeling fine and that they were on mission. Binia offered a report that several Black Guard ships were leaving orbit. Mortigan thanked her politely as if the voice to him was a real person. Binia reported that she had fired up the rest of her systems and was preparing engines. Mortigan requested Binia to search her databanks for everything on Josh Broody. She replied that there were several files to browse and it would take some time to formulate a full and thorough report. Mortigan acknowledged her reply.

* * *

On Xotosia, Black Guard forces were in a gunfire pursuit of rebel soldiers. Black Guard combat vehicles, resembling tanks except with three treads and two turrets, each with two-gun barrels, had cordoned off the street corners and forced the rebels into separate buildings of the town called Mullich Valley. The Black Guard soldiers were using concussion grenades to clear buildings as the rebel fighters retaliated from those same buildings with heavy blaster fire.

Clad Byar and the other rebel leaders were huddled in an underground bunker and watching the incident on the allowed Black

Guard-controlled communication signals. The transmission seemed to be slanted in Black Guard favor as it appeared the rebel fighters were shooting without discrimination of soldiers or civilians. One of the taller buildings were hit with a strafing attack of laser fire from the schisms diving into the battle and swooping back up to the sky. One schism appeared to have been hit and crashed at the edge of the town, but transmissions terminated before confirmation.

The rebel leaders looked around the table as the Shapay male known as Ardicane Blivord attempted to confirm what they had just witnessed was through his private comm system. The transmission was reacquired in time to witness the execution of ten captured rebel fighters with their heads removed by the wielding of Black Guard axes. Another building exploded in the background as a result of a Black Guard bombing run perpetrated by the bomber ships called shutters. Ardicane had confirmed that the bombed building was one of his properties. He threw accusations at the green-haired male Jaskan, Arnvare Nixicine. Ardicane was asking if those slaughtered rebel fighters were not supposed to be Arnvare's personally chosen and elite mercenaries. Two of the other leaders chimed in with the human female Madaray Vilici siding with Arnvare Nixicine. Toxicus Forn took the side of Ardicane Blivord. The two sides argued back and forth as they accused each other harshly for the obvious loss of Mullich Valley. Silos Taqoon's efforts to play peacekeeper had failed despite his attempts to interject his laughter and humor and he abandoned the attempt when both sides forced him to choose. Silos remained neutral as the accusations and bickering grew louder. It was finally silenced by Clad Byar as he fired off his blaster to the floor. Clad told them that the infighting among themselves was not helping the rebellion. Silos counterpointed that nothing was working as fighting the Black Guard was proving insurmountable. The news that reinforcements had come with Epitaph's bride, Emelia to specifically deal with the insurgency was also not a good sign. The few victories that the rebels had achieved and any disorder that was created from them would be erased by Emelia's command.

Everyone was finally able to agree that once Emelia's fully inserted command cracked down, the rebellion would be on minimal life support. A look back at what had just occurred at Mullich Valley was just a sample of Emelia's command that had just begun. More defeats like that were soon to follow. What they needed was experience with someone that has actually fought against the Black Guard. Clad Byar agreed and stated that he was going to attempt to contact the Luth Bik Resistance forces. The mention of the Luth Bik name calmed the table. The Luth Biks have fought the Black Guard to more success than any other race. Clad Byar admitted that he had already reached out through his shadow contacts for Luth Bik communication and was awaiting a reply.

* * *

In the confiscated palace, updates and reports were piling into Emelia and Fright Agent Nehih. Emelia's redirection of Black Guard forces had already turned several battles around. Once Emelia was informed of the victory over Mullich Valley, she displayed the holographic map and marked another sector with a Black Guard flag. She then refocused to another area on the map and instructed the gathered Black Guard generals to move their forces along the highlighted line. She expected another sector by nightfall.

* * *

Gold crawled from the engine room of his Honsho freighter as the engines again roared to life. Josh and his crew had arrived through the ship's corridor, and Josh asked for a status report. Gold admitted that he had rushed the repairs in order to quickly get to Josh's ship, and as a result, the fuel regulator was down and they had lost fuel. He was going to have to cut the *Fallen Star* loose to maximize what he had left without straining the supply. Josh and Cody protested immediately that the *Fallen Star* was too important to be left behind. Gold reminded them that he also had interest in the neural link system. He assured them that they would install a stabilize field around it to prevent it from drifting away and he would deploy killer eye satellites around it to persuade away any potential salvagers, scavengers, and pirates.

Josh was still concerned but recognized it as the best option. He then asked Gold what his next plan of action would be. Gold activated a star chart on a monitor. He stated that Honsho freighters ran on a standard regenerative fuel for public knowledge. He then paused before admitting that they actually consumed Livafein, a term for liquid crystals. The process for refining it for fuel function was simple. The problem was that only a certain crystal could be crushed and liquefied. The Liva crystal itself was much more difficult to locate.

Gold pointed again to the star chart on the monitor. He proposed an alteration of course that would cost them only one rotation. They would then be able to reach a planet that was uncharted by public knowledge and authorities, but the Honsho Piracy had retrieved Liva crystals in the past from underground caves on this planet. It all sounded easy enough, and then Gold mentioned the problem. Josh responded, "That was not the problem?!" Gold mentioned that the dominant species that ruled the planet was not reasonable and would have to be avoided. He started to recite the danger element when Josh interrupted. Josh said he had enough of the buildup and asked what the threat was. Gold replied, "Giants."

* * *

Again, at the confiscated palace, a video transmission was received from Epitaph. Emelia greeted him with terms of affection and how she missed him. Epitaph responded in kind and then asked of the progress she had made. Emelia reported that Black Guard control would soon be back in hand. Epitaph inquired of the trouble that he had interpreted from her tone. Emelia apologized and admitted that she just wanted the mission over so that she could join the hunt for Josh Broody. She admitted further to having a great desire to slowly slaughter Josh. Epitaph stressed patience that all would come in time. Emelia reminded Epitaph that Josh's torture and execution would be at her hand. Epitaph assured her that he had not forgotten that promise.

* * *

The video transmission ended on Epitaph's ship as he stepped out from the triangular pads of the communications platform. Fright Agent Kyrak stepped to Epitaph's side and inquired as to what Epitaph would do if Mortigan got to Josh Broody first and reminded him that Mortigan was not known for bringing bounties back alive. Epitaph claimed that Emelia did not need to know about Mortigan. He also added that he had his spies in place to make sure he was notified when Mortigan got too close. Mortigan was merely a tool to flush Josh out. Fright Agent Kyrak then asked about the vision Epitaph had of Josh's head in Mortigan's hand. Epitaph explained that he had not yet written that prophecy and with careful manipulation he could still change it as he would with the prophecy of his demise. Although he admitted that he was still puzzled as to how the prophecy was still holding true that the two brothers would destroy him when there was only one brother left. Fright Agent Kyrak suggested resurrection. Epitaph countered that Josh did not have the means to such powers, and that was why it was important that they found him before he stumbled across such means.

* * *

Josh had returned to his cargo bay quarters on the Honsho freighter where he found Laylee waiting for him already naked and in the bed. Their eyes locked deeply. Josh had quickly undressed and lay atop her. They kissed wildly. Just to touch each other again had felt as if it had been forever. The caressing of each other's skin had led them to even a stronger desire of wanting more. He licked across her firm breasts before inserting himself into her. Their hands joined, and the clutch tightened with each thrusting motion that they made. They were joined and moving as one. Josh hammered his rock-hard cock deeper into her pussy as Laylee in a scream, begged for him to fuck her even harder. Josh did as she demanded and then finally rested his thrusts into her but never pulled out. They rolled over so that Laylee could take her turn atop of him and continued. Their shifting pace did not slow. They both gasped as their motion only intensified. Laylee screamed out one last time before they finally slowed to a stop, and while she still rested atop him, they kissed with tongues deep inside each other's mouths before closing to a long lip-locked kiss. Josh said to her that she was fantastic. Laylee replied to Josh that he was nothing less than incredible.

* * *

Cody and Tana had kept watch over their area of the ship as neither of them trusted the Honshos. Tana slowly worked the conversation to ask of Josh and Laylee's relationship. Cody was a little puzzled as to why Tana would ask. He admitted that Josh was attracted to Laylee from the first time he saw her on Xotosia. He also believed that it must run in the family to avoid real women. Cody told Tana of how Josh's recently slain brother Jase had also fallen in love with an android called Adrienne. Adrienne was not to the level of awareness that Laylee was programmed for. Adrienne knew she was an android programmed for pleasure and that was her path. Cody did admire that Laylee, despite knowing she was an android, still felt as though she was alive with a soul. Tana asked if he approved of the relationship. Cody stated that it was not is place to either approve or disapprove. If they were happy together and not hurting each other, then it did not matter to him. Cody did spin the topic around on Tana and asked why she was so concerned. Tana admitted that when captured as a slave she was used for tracking, fighting, and sexual needs of others. She admitted that she had always been made to feel that sex was random with no other purpose than to release tensions. She had always been forced and dominated by her captors and had grown used to it, although she had not liked being treated that way.

She then asked Cody to keep a promise and he agreed. Tana revealed that she and Josh had sex on her homeworld. The problem was that Josh had believed he was having sex with Laylee and grew upset when he realized what had happened. Josh had pushed her away and admitted that he had not yet been with Laylee but wanted to be. Ever since that moment though, Tana admitted that she had feelings that she had never experienced before in her life. Sex in that moment was not a task that she was required to do. She had a desire to be with Josh ever since and experienced pain inside her when she had realized Josh and Laylee had finally been together on the *Fallen Star*. That was another incident that Cody was also unaware had occurred. Cody wrestled with his response to Tana and finally admitted that he did not know what to tell her except to let Josh know of her feelings.

Tana then asked if Cody had ever experienced feelings like that. Cody paused in thought and then explained how he and his lover were separated by an attack from the Black Guard. He had gotten back to her only to watch her be killed. They were going to kill him next, but Josh saved him by declaring him to be his slave. Tana was shocked that Cody was once Josh's slave. Cody explained that it was a long time ago when Josh was with the Black Guard and his mind had been corrupted by Epitaph.

Chapter Eleven

Footsteps of Giants

IN THE REBEL headquarters, Clad Byar was brought an audio transmission that the Luth Bik Resistance had denied his request to aid Xotosia. His reputation as a druglord was a factor that the Luth Biks cited as preferring not to engage in an affiliation. Clad unplugged the device from its port and threw it across the room. He was out of options. Emelia's command was crushing the rebel forces and the blockade around the planet was starving off incoming resources. The rebellion on Xotosia would not be able to sustain its efforts much longer. Clad stood against a wall with his head and hands up against it. After a moment of contemplation, he moved to his messenger at the door and directed him to bring Silos Taqoon.

* * *

On Epitaph's ship, the *Darkfall*, in the Fury Fleet, schisms and shuttles were coming and going. Fright Agent Kyrak was monitoring the departures and arrivals as well as the patrol reports. Epitaph entered and approached him. Fright Agent Kyrak had reported no information had yet been gathered on Josh's whereabouts but added that he had doubled all efforts and patrols remained in a continuous state. Epitaph clarified his belief that Josh would be found. In the meantime, though it had come to his attention that some other planets and operations have grown too freehanded. He had also experienced some visions of planets breaking free from his rule. He announced to continue the search for Josh Broody while they enforced order at these other locations. Fright Agent Kyrak was given the order to oversee the Josh Broody search during the Black Guard operations. That search would also continue espionage operations left behind to monitor Mortigan. The Black Guard would let the bounty hunter do all the hard search work and then swoop in and snare their prey. Fright Agent Kyrak had inquired how they would deal with the systems breaking away. Epitaph had declared that he had already prepared the Fury Fleet to set course to the Irata sector where they would meet Fright Agent Paj on the *Grimm One*, where he was completing work on the Black Guard weapon known as the Breathtaker.

* * *

The female computer voice of Binia had awoken Mortigan from his slumber by announcing that they had arrived at Odebron. Mortigan activated his monitor and a map of the planet. He ordered Binia to plot a landing near the Pyramid of Gryy. Binia asked if he was certain that this was the course of action that he wished to take. She reminded him of the last time that he met with the Prophet Buis. Mortigan quickly and sharply replied that a history lesson was not needed. He then followed the statement by mentioning that Dark Lord Epitaph was not the only one with knowledge of the Books of Prophecy. Binia questioned again, "But a prophet himself?" Mortigan simply ignored the question and sternly ordered the landing course plotted.

* * *

Gold's Honsho freighter had entered the atmosphere of the uncharted and off-the-map planet. Gold reminded his Honsho helmsmen to get to and maintain a very low flight pattern. He also ordered a silent running and with the activation of a panel on the flight console, the outer engines of the freighter switched from a loud rumble to a low whisper. The freighter flew low and just above the ground and streaked across the terrain of the most gigantic mountains ever seen and tall grass blades that were taller than the starship itself. The backdrop of the sky was a jade green in color. The Honsho freighter flew over one last mountain and into a rocky canyon terrain. It flew along the side of the canyon wall and kept close enough to remain in the shadows of that wall. It finally slowed its speed on the course, and the repulsor lifts fired as it slowly descended to a landing.

The boarding hatch opened, and the ramp drew out to touch the rocky ground. Gold walked down the ramp first with two other Honshos behind him. Josh, before walking down the ramp, asked Cody and Laylee to stay with the ship. He still did not fully trust Gold and did not want to take a chance that Gold would double back to the ship, abandon them, and report their position to Epitaph. Tana was much more comfortable on land than on ships and was very anxious to explore. Josh followed Tana down the ramp. She surveyed the land by sight and scent. Josh noticed Gold and his Honshos checking Tana's body over and moved to stand and block their view. He asked Gold if they could concentrate on the task at hand. Gold stated that he would try but admitted that Tana was a fine distraction. Josh ushered Gold and his fellow Honshos ahead, and they took point in the march as Josh and Tana followed. Josh tried talking to Tana, but she sent the impression of a cold chill as she ignored him. He asked what was wrong. Tana claimed that she was trying to get a scent of any threats, and she stepped away from him.

Gold hollered back for them to make sure that they stayed in the shadow. Josh asked why. Gold mentioned that giants can see really well in daylight and complete darkness, but in a contrast of the two such as low light and shadows, they were as blind as a ruvivios file fly. Josh scoffed at the remark, still believing that Gold was making the whole giant story up.

* * *

Silos Taqoon was ushered into Clad Byar's quarters. The escort remained at the door as Silos approached. Clad informed Silos that the Luth Bik Resistance had turned down his request for assistance because of his reputation. Clad followed the statement by admitting that he had a new plan. He wanted to smuggle Silos off planet to go and personally, meet with the Luth Bik Resistance and plead their case in person. Silos had asked why he was chosen as his reputation was just as unsavory as Clad's. Silos further suggested sending Ardicane Blivord, the legitimate businessman of the rebellion founders. Clad responded by stating Blivord Industries may be a legitimate business corporation, but some of its practices throughout the known universe were in question of morality. Silos then suggested Madaray Vilici, but Clad pointed out her gambling collection methods were not always pleasant. Before Silos could continue suggesting names, Clad said that Toxicus Forn's smuggling and fencing operations had stretched into affiliations and races that have persecuted the Luth Bik race. He also mentioned that Arnvare Nixicine had sent mercenaries and assassins against the Luth Biks in the past. Clad admitted that Silos' name may not be clean, but the prostitution ring may be the least damaging of professions that the Luth Biks may be able to overlook. He added that Silos had the most welcoming and outgoing personality out of all them. Silos smiled and let out one very loud laugh.

Clad said, "You see, that is what I am talking about."

Silos had to master friendship in his line of work and could afford to be more accepting. His edge was not as harsh because he did not need to draw people into his trade. Clad admitted that everyone liked sex. He then handed Silos a computer chip and cited that it contained location details to his contacts. Clad would not even send his trusted messenger, because he felt it would be better with the least connection to his name.

Clad planned on creating a distraction that would hopefully draw even the blockade's attention and allow Silos to sneak off Xotosia unnoticed. Clad again stressed the importance and very survival of the Xotosia Rebellion to expel the Black Guard and added that the Luth Biks had proven to be the only force in the universe to have the greatest success. He advised Silos to play his plea on the Luth Biks anger of the Black Guard.

* * *

The *Dark Wish* had landed, and Mortigan walked down the ramp. The villagers and pyramid workers were of a race called Bakfurs. They looked human except that they were covered in short-haired gray fur, and each body hosted two necks and heads. They also had four arms with one pair off the shoulders and the other pair off the waist. They had rushed to Mortigan upon sight, and each shoved another away as they all pleaded to allow them to assist him in whatever he needed. They treated him like a celebrity. They all tried to just stroke his many different fleshes as if touching him was a deep privilege. They even offered him small gifts as he pushed his way through the crowd. The gifts were merely items they could pick up quickly, such as stones, tools, torn fabric from their own cloths, and even some flowers and grass. Mortigan politely refused each gift as he continued to push his way through the crowd and toward the Pyramid of Gryy. The pyramid guards assisted him away from the adoring crowd and allowed him access into the pyramid.

* * *

As they traversed along the shadow of the canyon wall, Tana had caught a strange scent. She ran to Josh and pulled on his vest to halt his stride. Josh yelled up ahead, and Gold also halted his two fellow Honshos. They stood perfectly still. Suddenly, the ground started to tremble. A giant human bare foot instantly stepped down just ahead of the canyon wall. Then another foot landed. They all looked up as the two giant feet stepped further away from them and the canyon wall. With each step taken, the ground trembled beneath them. He looked human except for his size. He stood near twenty feet tall.

The giant then stopped abruptly in the middle of the canyon where the daylight shined. He quickly turned to face the direction that he had just come from and took two thunderous steps before stopping again. To the giant, the canyon they were in was more of a small rocky outcropping to an even more awesome rock formation. They all remained still as the giant looked down and around his position as if searching for something. He then dropped very quickly to his hands and knees. The ground shook even more with the sudden thud, and all five members of the landing party were knocked off their feet and to the ground. The giant seemed like a young child. Despite being a giant, he had bare feet and long-legged pants but no shirt. He had short black hair and bright blue eyes. He crawled closer and peered intently into the shadow. He then let out a loud sneeze that shook everything around him. The tremble threw Tana out from the canyon shadow and next to the giant's hand, but she still remained in that shadow that the giant himself casted. Another sneeze followed and shook the ground. The giant raised his hand that Tana had just staggered by and rubbed his nose with it. As he did, a wave of slimy green ooze fell all around the area. Tana had rolled away from it but remained in the giant's shadow. The ground was covered with the slimy green ooze. They looked up as the giant wiped more of it from his nose and flung it to the canyon wall. The slime had covered Josh, Gold, and the two Honshos. The giant's hand then came crashing back down, covered in the green slime and landed just beside Tana. His gaze intensified, and he moved his hand again from Tana and placed it into the shadow. The giant fingers were outstretched and feeling around in the dirt and green slime. Josh and Gold were just between the outstretched fingers and moved as the fingers did to avoid being touched or crushed. Josh and Gold both rolled away from the giant fingers and pinned themselves up against the canyon wall. Tana remained calm and used the moment to run back into the shadow of the canyon wall. The giant hand then started to withdraw, raking the slime and rocky dirt in its dragging motion. The rocks that the landing party stood by were pebbles compared to the giant's hands. The giant raised both his arms from the ground and rested on his knees. He then moved one hand again back toward the canyon shadow and also toward Tana.

Suddenly a loud sound split the air and almost crushed the eardrums of the landing party. They placed their hands tightly to their ears to lessen the pain, but it did little good. The sound wave itself even slightly rolled the rocks and staggered their stance. The giant swiftly looked up in response, and the action was like a wind blowing against them. They were all off their feet and clutching tightly into the dirt. The sound from what they could make out was like a voice calling, "Dorogrove!"

The giant in front of them stood up quickly to his feet, still shaking the ground beneath them. The giant then shouted back, and the sound was just as shattering as the first. The giant shouted, "Coming, Mommy!" The giant's feet then lifted and they watched as the first foot hit just above the canyon ledge and knocked down around them more dirt and boulders. The second foot missed the canyon ledge and came down with the dirt and rock. The foot crashed down onto the other two Honsho pirates and crushed them instantly. The giant foot then rose up again and stepped over the canyon ledge. The ground trembled and shook the members of the landing party around as the giant boy ran away from them, and with each step, taken the tremble lessoned.

Even back at the Honsho freighter the impact was felt. Dirt and rock fell onto the ship and it forced the landing gear to give way. The ship fell to the ground as its landing gear collapsed. Josh's voice came over the comms and asked if everyone was okay. Cody looked around at Laylee and the other four Honshos. He replied in the affirmative. One of the Honshos claimed the repulsors had taken damage from the impact into the ground. They had the equipment and supplies to fix it, but they would have to dig under the ship for access. Cody offered his knowledge and assistance. Gold's voice cut into the comms. He told them to proceed but to stay with the ship. Cody mentioned back that the ship was partially buried by dirt, but he figured once the repulsors were fixed, the power would be enough to force the ship free. Gold then closed off his wrist comm and told Josh and Tana that it would take all three of them to retrieve the Liva crystals.

* * *

Mortigan was ushered through the pyramid corridors and down a walk ramp to a room where a male human dwarf-like form sat at a table. There were several open books gathered around him as the dwarf known as a Shrow or the Prophet hurried his writing with a long-feathered pen and vial of ink into another book. The male Shrow continued to write almost impulsively and verbally acknowledged Mortigan's presence by name and never looked up from his books. He instructed Mortigan to come forward. Mortigan slowly walked toward him. Mortigan addressed the Prophet by his name, Buis. Mortigan seemed to stagger and have trouble speaking as if he were trying to hold back vomit and was struck with dizziness. Buis asked what he could do to help Mortigan this time. He then stopped writing and looked up as Mortigan cautiously approached the table. Buis told Mortigan not to enrage him by vomiting on his books while he wrote again. Buis went back to writing as Mortigan turned away and vomited all over his boots and the ground around him. He collapsed to his hands and knees as his head throbbed even more now that he was closer.

Buis spoke as he wrote and mentioned that it was a shame that his friend got so ill in his very presence. Mortigan regained his stance and walked backward and further into the darkened halls of bookshelves. He felt a little better at this distance. The prophets had this effect on other races. Only the Dark Lord Epitaph and the Luth Bik race seemed to be immune to the illness forced in the very presence of prophets. Mortigan then mentioned that he was looking for a human called Josh Broody. Buis ignored the words and continued writing. Mortigan then added that he was looking for Josh Broody as a bounty for the Dark lord Epitaph.

Buis ceased his writing instantly and looked up at Mortigan. Buis made a motion with his hands and whispered a few words. The light in the room brightened in result and now illuminated the distant bookshelves in the area where Mortigan stood. Buis hesitated before mentioning that it could be one of the brothers. Mortigan had heard the basis of the prophecy of the two brothers that would kill the dark lord and in result end his reign. He wished to know more. Buis reminded Mortigan that it was against the rules for him to reveal the information on his visions. Mortigan stated that rules had not stopped Buis in the past. He relied on their friendship and asked Buis to just tell him the prophecy. Buis again hesitated before speaking. He mentioned that the prophecy has had varied wording as detouring events had occurred. As it was with all the Books of Prophecy, the words in the books magically changed as events happened. Buis mentioned that all prophecies were in flow. The prophecies all came true, but they were often detoured by mortals trying to prevent them. No prophecy was ever written with a time of conclusion as to allow for such flows. The prophecies' ends were inevitable despite mortal attempts. Buis then continued by speaking that the two brothers would bring about the death of the dark lord and his throne would be ended along with his reign of terror. The dark lord had recruited the made-up man who had killed the first brother. Mortigan then asked if the brother was to return somehow to ensure the prophecy. Buis stated that the prophecy holds true that the two brothers would be the destruction to the dark lord. He added that this could not be stopped. The dark lord would try to prevent this end, but the two brothers would still join to destroy him with one shielding the other. The knowledge of the resurrection of the first brother had not been seen. All that was certain was that the two brothers will be together.

Mortigan asked where he could find Josh Broody. Buis grew a look of annoyance directed at Mortigan. Buis declared that it would not be reading the prophecy and he had been warned by the other prophets. Mortigan then asked Buis to read it as prophecy to him because that would not be breaking the rules. Buis pulled a book from the floor beside him. He bowed his head and the book opened with a glow. He said that he had the vision of Mortigan coming to him. The book opened itself to a page, and Buis read aloud, "The last people that were lost for time will have the surviving brother's ship. The dark lord will learn this and will take the life from all the people's worlds. The dark lord will then have the surviving brother's ship and the weapon that takes away air of all that breathe. The surviving brother will survive the giant's feet and will learn of what the dark lord has done. The surviving brother will find tracking to his ship."

Mortigan thought about the words intently. He was lost at the words of the giant's feet but figured that taking life from a people's world was reference to a Black Guard super weapon. He would need to find where the weapon was at. The other wording of a people lost for time was yet a puzzle to him. Mortigan thanked him and tossed a bag of gems onto the table. Buis declared that all he did was read prophecy. Mortigan said, "I will see you again, old friend."

After his departure, Buis put down his feathered pen and looked up from the table and said aloud to himself, "No, old friend. This will have been the last time." He then continued writing.

* * *

Clad Byar had a missile fired from planet into near orbit and targeted the blockade. Another missile fired shortly behind it. Fright Agent Maddo was informed that both missiles hit a blockade warship in the near orbit flank, but the hits were insignificant because of the shield strength. Fright Agent Maddo contacted Fright Agent Nehih in the confiscated palace, and together they utilized their methods in the identification of the origin of the missiles' origin.

Emelia approached Fright Agent Nehih. She noticed something strange as he pinpointed the planetary location. He ordered a squadron of shutters to bombard the area. Emelia had examined the scans more closely and then belayed the bombardment order. She then pointed out that the missile attack had forced the blockade ships in both near and far orbits to adjust their formation. She then initiated a planetary scan of neutron and energy particles. The scan proved her suspicion to be correct. In addition to enhanced radar images, it was confirmed that a cloaked ship had left the planet through the blockade opening as formation was adjusted. She ordered the commencement of the planetary bombardment to the coordinates of the cloaked ship's launch location. She also ordered her shuttle readied before the neutron path detection had dispersed. She followed the order by instructing Fright Agent Maddo to come to the planet and assume command of the palace, as Fright Agent Nehih was coming with her to pursue the elusive ship.

* * *

They traversed along the side of the canyon wall and remained in the shadow. Gold was able to detect the cave with his handheld scanner. They entered with caution. The extremely tall cave divided into two tunnels. Gold had already activated a light sphere that was strapped to his wrist and traversed down one. Josh did not want to leave Gold alone and instructed Tana to take the opposite tunnel while he followed Gold. Tana's cold response of silence again triggered Josh into asking if everything was all right. Tana delivered an odd stare back at him. She shook her head as if from thought and replied that she was still shaken from the experience with the giant. Josh offered her his light sphere, but she reminded him of her dark vision. Josh hurried after Gold, and Tana sniffed ahead to detect any dangerous scent before traversing down the other tunnel.

* * *

Cody and two of the Honsho pirates had exited the top hatch of the Honsho freighter. They started to climb down the dirt and rock that had partially covered the ship. The ground began to tremble again, more rapidly and harder than before. The trembling had caused all three of them to lose their grip and slide down the slope.

Inside the freighter, Laylee and the other two Honshos were tossed around. The violent shaking motion increased as whatever it was drew closer. Suddenly outside the freighter, the shadow area grew larger. Cody looked up and saw two giants running. One had lost his footing and was now falling down upon them and the ship.

Cody issued warning and leapt away from the dirt slope. The giant fell, and his huge knee had struck the Honsho freighter and crushed the two Honshos that were outside of it with Cody. Another giant's shadow hovered as the second giant helped the fallen one back to his feet. The sound wave pierced Cody's ears as the first giant said that he had hit something with his knee. Being that the ship was still in the shadow of the giants, it could not be seen. The first giant reached down to the ground. His eyes strained to see in his own shadow as he used his hands to feel around him.

Inside the freighter, Laylee and the two Honshos had just regained their footing only to lose it again as the freighter began to be lifted up from the ground. They were tossed around again as the giant shook the dirt away that once partially covered the freighter.

Cody rushed to the canyon wall again has he dodged the falling dirt and rock that the giant had shaken from the shuttle. He remained silently in the shadow of the canyon wall and the two giants. The two giants were twenty-feet-tall boys. They started to talk excitedly over what they had found, and the sounds of their voices nearly crushed Cody's eardrums. He clutched his hands tightly over his ears to muffle the sound, but it was so intense that he dropped to his knees from the pain it caused.

The two giants began to shove each other as they fought over the freighter they had just found and believed it to be a toy. Laylee and the two Honshos inside with her were tossed around more intently now. They grabbed onto interior ship mounted structures to avoid falling as the ship shook and even turned upside down. The struggle stopped as the two boy giants ceased their fighting over their newfound toy. The giant that had won the struggle clenched the ship tightly as the interior slightly crushed. He then told the other giant that they should take it and show Dorogrove. The sound of the discussion continued to deafen Cody. The ground again trembled beneath him as the two giants ran away with the Honsho freighter.

Chapter Twelve

Living in a Larger World

FRIGHT AGENT NEHIH piloted Emelia's shuttle off Xotosia. Emelia was utilizing the ship sensors to continue her tracking of the cloaked ship's trail. Fright Agent Nehih suggested that the ship they were tracking could have made a hyperspace jump. Emelia was not so certain of that fact. A hyperspace portal this close to Xotosia would have been detected by the blockade ships just before it opened. Emelia figured that whoever was trying to sneak away was smart enough to get out of sensor range before attempting such an action. Moments later from her comment, the sensors that Emelia monitored had detected a hyperspace portal that had been just out of the previous sensor range of any Black Guard ships that were in orbit of Xotosia. Fright Agent Nehih started to prepare an intercept course, but Emelia steadied his thorn covered hand. The portal was being held open too long. Emelia thought that the cloaked ship may have picked them up on its sensors. She figured that the cloaked ship was close by and utilizing the hyperspace portal as a decoy. She instructed Flight Agent Nehih to mask their ship's signature.

Emelia intensified the scanning of the area. The original hyperspace portal had finally closed. Emelia than opened a hyperspace portal behind them. Once it was open, she adjusted sensors to scan around the portal and detected a slight flutter and a neutron trail shifting course away from the portal. Emelia locked the coordinates and instructed Fright Agent Nehih to fire there on target.

Emelia's shuttle shot off multiple energy blasts. With the impact of each hit, the cloaked ship was revealed. Emelia showed no weakness and ordered continuous fire. The effect repeated as the cloaked and badly outgunned ship started to flee. Emelia remained relentless and ordered a pursuit course with the continuous fire at maximum strength. The heavy laser blasts had weakened the shuttle's shields very quickly. The ship broke off its cloak and made a sharp vector turn to come around. An unexpected maneuver combined with a full-frontal laser assault only bounced off the shields of Emelia's shuttle. The larger ship then increased for ramming speed.

Emelia's shuttle took evasive action on her order and swooped just below the oncoming larger ship. Emelia raised her anger and determination as she ordered Fright Agent Nehih to bring them about as well. Emelia had the edge as her smaller-in-size shuttle was able to maneuver better and again approach under the larger ship. Fright Agent Nehih called the attention of another hyperspace portal opening. Emelia ordered him to follow the ship into it. The shuttle maneuvered extremely close and was caught in the drift and pull of the larger ship as both starships entered into hyperspace.

* * *

Mortigan had again boarded the *Dark Wish*, and after closing the ramp, he began startup procedures. The lovely accented and calming computer voice of Binia had welcomed him back and asked if they had a destination. Mortigan stated that they needed to locate Black Guard secret weapon construction zones. Even with her computer intelligence, Binia had asked how they were going to accomplish such a task. She pointed out that areas of secret weapon construction were not heavily advertised and there were too many rumors to evaluate which could be true. Mortigan firmly requested for a course to be plotted to Hortis Six. Binia responded with a tone of shock that would even make her sound more like a living being as she replied, "Not Gullivar!"

Mortigan repeated his request, "Binia, Hortis Six please?" Mortigan manually flew the *Dark Wish* into an atmospheric climb as Binia started to plot the course.

* * *

Cody had been trying to follow the two giant boys, but their size and stride of running was proving too great. He tried but could not open comms to Josh. Suddenly, he heard a loud screech just as deafening as the giants' voices but sharper and shriller. He looked up to the sky and saw a strange winged creature. It was very large and diving toward him with outstretched talons. The creature's massive wingspan had cast a shadow. Its giant three-pronged talons were like long daggers. Its silver feather covered body appeared jagged and sharp-edged, almost like a shiny metal. The beak was long and pointed. With the beak wide open, it appeared as two swords falling from the sky. Its massive sized head was rugged and stone-like with three eye stalks protruding upward from it. One eye stalk protruded at each side of the head and another from the top ridged brow. Each hosted a black eye that appeared to have a crimson pupil.

Cody started to run and dove to him what appeared to be a tall tree. The swooping giant avian creature just missed him with its sharp talons as it flew by the same tree, only to it, the tree was more like a small bush. It swooped back up into the sky and circled the area as it searched for its elusive prey. Cody remained tightly pinned up against the tree as he watched the giant avian creature circle a few more times and then leave.

* * *

In the caves, Gold and Josh had found the Liva crystals. It was a small amount, but Gold's scanner was detecting more down two more splitting corridors. They, against Josh's better judgment had to split up again. Tana was not answering on the comm he had given her. Gold stated that comms did not work in these caves because of the rock element.

Still with a large lack of trust, Josh reluctantly walked down his passage after Gold started down the opposite one. A few moments in and Josh had arrived at a dead end. As he turned around, he heard the unmistakable and yet echoing sounds of blaster fire. He started to backtrack his path. Gold had also double-backed on his corridor, and with a small blaster, he had collapsed the entrance point to Josh's corridor and sealed him inside. Gold returned the small blaster pistol to a concealed zipper compartment in his boot.

Tana was utilizing her dark vision to traverse another passage in the cave when she nearly walked off a ledge. She fell forward, but her clawed hands caught the ledge. Tana pulled herself up and took a deep, relaxing breath. She then heard something below, as she dropped so that her stomach was tight to the ground. She crawled forward and peered over the ledge only to witness that lower part of the cave light up with two torches carried by Gold Gatling himself. He carried the two bright fire burning torches toward a partially concealed Honsho freighter. After pulling back a cover of woven together branches from a boarding hatch, Gold opened it and stepped inside. It was shortly after the boarding hatch had been closed that the Honsho freighter's running lights lit up and its engines roared to life. Tana then back tracked her way down the passage in a hurried state to find Josh.

* * *

The two giant boys had run to a large house where they were greeted by their friend Dorogrove. They showed him the strange toy that they had found, but none of them could figure what it was. As the giant boys switched it between their massive hand grips and jostled the freighter around, Laylee and the two Honshos inside hung tightly to the mounted interior ship fixtures. Suddenly, a large giant finger had pried open the boarding hatch door. A giant eyeball then peered through the opening. The ship then got turned upside down and started to shake violently. The forceful shaking motion had caused the two Honshos to fall out the open boarding hatch. Their fall was extreme, and they were injured with broken bones from an over twenty-foot drop. The three giant boys saw them and threw the freighter to the ground on top of the fallen Honshos. The impact from the drop of the freighter also broke off several interior and exterior pieces of the vessel. The three giant boys had kicked the freighter over to its side and revealed the two injured and struggling Honshos underneath it. One giant boy picked up one of the Honshos and crushed him in his fist. The other injured Honsho was handled with more caution from Dorogrove. The three boys began to argue over what they had found as the injured Honsho wreathed from internal and external battered injuries while in Dorogrove's open hand. A physical struggle developed between the three giant boys as each wanted to hold the strange small man they had found. Dorogrove broke free from the struggle and ran off with the Honsho firmly gripped in his hand, as the other two giant boys ran in pursuit.

Laylee crawled through the collapsed corridors of the ship to the boarding hatch. The ship had taken much damage on both the interior and the exterior. She staggered in her attempt as the ground shook again in reaction to the giant boys running back. Laylee had crawled out from the boarding hatch and dropped to the ground. She quickly rose to her feet and ran to a large mound. To the giant boys, it was merely a clump of dirt. The ground continued to shake as Laylee scaled up the large mound. The quaking of the surface hampered her attempt and had knocked her into a large river, which compared to the giants was only a small and very narrow stream. The force of the rushing water carried Laylee away as she struggled against it.

* * *

Inside the cave, the Honsho freighter was fired up and lifted off the ground as it flew down a long narrow trench and out another cave entrance. Gold was on the comms in an attempt to reach his fellow pirates but received no reply. He piloted close to the surface and adjusted the course back to the original landing site.

* * *

Tana had found a torch and traversed back down her original passage and down the one that Josh and Gold had previously taken. She saw the fork and checked down the first corridor where she encountered the collapsed tunnel. Through the aid of her animalistic hearing, she had made out a faint sound of Josh calling for help. Tana wasted no time in pulling the large rocks and boulders away. She increased her speed in clearing the fallen passage as her desperation to get to Josh increased. As she pulled the large chunks of rock clear, she had come across a large black boulder. It was like a giant black gem that shined at the little light provided from the torch she had set to the side as she dug. It was almost hypnotizing until she remembered Josh. She called out for him on the other side of the collapsed tunnel. She then paused and listened. She could no longer hear him.

* * *

Gold had landed the Honsho freighter at the original landing site. He disembarked and saw the large dirt slide and, at the bottom, the two dead Honsho bodies over half buried and crushed by the dirt and rock slide. Gold looked around and wondered if the ship was buried as well and perhaps with the others. He turned to head back to the landed Honsho freighter and was met by a brown furry fist across his face. Gold dropped to the ground in an unconscious state. Cody stood over him.

* * *

Laylee had managed to swim to the side of the large river and pulled herself up a rocky embankment. She looked back and saw a giant crab-like creature. It had four pincers against the ground as walking support. Its two forward pincers were extended outward and clamping from open to close at a rapid rate. Its dark black spherical eyes were at the end of two extended eyestalks, and its jaw was open displaying muscle tissue that was rough texture in design. The mouth itself could stretch wider. The whole design was much like a snake on Earth to pull a whole body of prey in and slowly digest it.

Laylee climbed up the large rockslide and kicked rubble down as it hampered the creatures speed but did not halt its movement. As Laylee reached the top, she started to kick at the larger rocks. The large rocks were freed and rolled down the slope, engulfing the large crab creature in a downward rush. The crab creature was turned on its back side in the sliding motion down the slope and struggled to turn itself back upright. Laylee looked down at the creature. Once it had gotten upright and stabilized itself, it scurried away. She then looked around the large open and empty area as she wondered what her next move would be.

Her comm suddenly squawked, and she heard Cody's rough and growling voice break through the static. He told Laylee to hold position where she was at. He was using the ship's sensors to lock onto her coordinates. She asked as to what ship sensors in a fully puzzled tone. She then added, "What ship?"

Cody looked back and down at an unconscious Gold Gatling on the floor of the circular cockpit. He answered that apparently Gold had another Honsho freighter secretly stashed on the planet. Laylee, with undisguised concern in her voice, asked about Tana, and even more stress followed as she inquired of Josh's whereabouts. Cody replied that he was still unsure.

* * *

In the cave, Tana had broken through the stone and dirt rubble to find Josh lying in a motionless state. She knelt down and thoroughly checked the pulse in his wrist, chest, and mouth to find that he was not breathing. The air back in this caved in section was still much thinner even with the opening that Tana had made. She figured that Josh had suffocated as a result. Tana felt her furry face moisten, and tears flowed down from her eyes. She pulled Josh's face close into her breasts and held him tightly against herself.

After several moments of sadness at her loss, Tana had decided to not leave Josh behind. She was still puzzled at the heartbreak she felt. She knew that she had strong feelings for him, and she knew how other races expressed love. She realized now that her feelings for him were more than a lust for sex. She had to face the fact that she loved him now that he was gone. Tana pulled her emotions together and lifted Josh over her shoulders. She stepped through the opening in the cave passage that she had cleared and trudged forward. She rested at the large black boulder. As she placed Josh's body against it, the boulder seemed to pulsate in different shades of black. It was almost like it was fading into a dull black. Tana raised a torch to it and noticed that it had lost some of its earlier shine to the light against it. She put her hand to it and felt it literally pulsating as its shiny blackness continued to grow to a dull shade. It stopped suddenly and felt again as a solid stone. Suddenly Josh kicked to life and took a long deep breath. Tana jumped back in shock as Josh slowly rose to a seated position.

Josh asked where he was at and what had happened. He was totally disorientated to the moment where he had first entered the cave. It was as though the part of his life that led up to his death was erased from his memory. Tana explained what had happened from Gold's betrayal to her finding his dead body. They had collectively come to the conclusion that the large black boulder possessed resurrection properties. It was too large to take with them, but the incredible find could not be wasted. Josh pulled a hilt-like device from the side of his boot. When he turned the outer hilt covering one clockwise turn, a spiral mist form activated. He turned the outer hilt covering clockwise a bit more, and a pulsating sound vibrated the mist form. He called the device a sounbla, and when placed carefully against the boulder, it began to use its sonic energy to slice into the stone. Josh was able to cut off a sizable portion of the regenerative stone. The piece cut from deeper in the stone was again shiny compared to the now dull outer shell. It was a large chunk but small enough to place in a pouch pulled from the inner layer of his belt.

Tana had helped Josh walk from the cave. It was apparent that coming back from the dead left a person significantly drained of energy. They traversed down the tunnel to the fork in the cave when suddenly the dirt and rock began to fall from above them. Squeezing from the mouth and main entrance to the cave ahead of them was a giant burrowing rat-like creature. It looked much like a rat on Earth with pointed ears and dark coal black eyes. Its snout was much longer, with long and jagged teeth hanging like daggers out from the edges of the mouth. Its four claws were as sharp as metal blades and it had two long hairless tails. Its body was large and plump in size, but still like most rodents anywhere in the universe, it was able to squeeze its larger body through a smaller portal. The nose twitched at their direction and a loud, but still a low tone growl was heard coming from the creature. Like everything else on this planet, it would likely be a common size sewer rat, but everything here was larger, and to Josh and Tana it appeared like a giant ravenous beast. Tana continued to help Josh in his weakened state as they went down the other tunnel. The giant rodent creature had caught their scent and pursued them. Its large body and burrowing motion caused even more of the cave dirt and rock to fall as it continued after its newfound scavenged prey.

* * *

The Honsho freighter repulsor lifts fired and its landing gear lowered as it set down along the river bank. The ramp lowered, and Laylee ran aboard as it again lifted to a closed position behind her. Cody had greeted her at the entry, and beside him was Gold Gatling, secured with energy bindings to a chair. Gold was slowly regaining consciousness. Cody aided in the waking process with a heavy slap across Gold's face. Cody's sharp claws left bloodied scars. He followed the action by asking in a violent growling tone of common of what Gold had done with Josh and Tana. Laylee gripped Gold's throat tightly with one hand. Her android grip tightened when Gold refused to answer. The choking action restricted his air intake, and Gold finally broke, admitting through desperate gasps that he would talk. Laylee released her grip, and Gold took an even larger gasp for air to breathe. He looked up at both of them and smiled. Cody again raised his clawed hand.

Gold admitted to causing a cave-in to trap Josh. He admitted that Tana had already separated from them further into the cave. He had planned to abandon them and give the planet location to the Black Guard, which would be better equipped to deal with force against the giants of this world. The Black Guard would likely find Josh as dead by that time, and he would still get paid without all the hassle of conflict and physically having to bring the body to Epitaph.

Cody asked Gold to show them to the cave. The ship started to tremble. The ground was again shaking. Laylee said with a great haste in her tone, "We have to leave now!" Gold demanded to be unbound. Cody and Laylee, without a reply, left him bound as they ran off for the cockpit.

As they entered the circular cockpit, they saw an even larger giant than before. It appeared as an adult male giant almost forty feet in height. He possessed a large walking stick as tall as himself and was walking down the now apparent dirt path toward the river's edge. Cody wasted no time in firing up the engines and repulsor lifts. The giant man stopped in his tracks and watched the strange small craft lift and turn away from him. He swatted out at the Honsho freighter like it was a small insect or creature that had crossed his path. The Honsho freighter again turned and jetted away and over the river.

* * *

Tana had led Josh down the cave tunnel to where the hidden Honsho freighter once rested. The giant rodent creature was still burrowing its way at a rapid pace toward them. Josh pushed Tana away and fell to the ground. He told her to climb down and hide or get away, but no matter what, she had to save herself. Tana refused to go and pulled Josh again to his feet despite his resistance. They argued back and forth until Tana unleased a loud roar upon him and insisted that she was not leaving him because she loved him.

The giant rodent had entered the passage and strode onto the ledge. Tana pushed Josh over the ledge and down a slope in the cave. She quickly followed after him. The giant rodent sniffed and then scurried down the slope again in pursuit of his next meal. At the bottom was a long and deep trench to them but not to the giant rodent. The slide down the slope had done some injury to Josh's leg, and he was having great difficulty in standing. Tana took a strong fighting defensive position between Josh and the giant rodent. She stood ready to fight despite the size. Her claws were out, and she unleashed a roar of fury and rage.

The humming engine sound of a ship was heard, and the spotlights of the Honsho freighter lit up the area as it flew in. The giant rodent lunged at Tana but was thrown off its attack by the front laser cannons of the Honsho freighter fired at full intensity. The force of the lasers did not stop the creature because of its difference in size. Tana had ended up pinned under the weight of the front left claw. The giant rodent turned its jaws away from her to snap at the Honsho freighter that hovered in front of it. The continuous laser fire into the giant rodent's face only angered it, but its attention was drawn away from its former prey. Josh then fired off his blaster pistol at upward shots toward the creature's chest. The blasts did little more than increase the annoyance in the creature. It released Tana and turned back up the slope and scurried away as it found the effort was too much for a tiny meal. Tana struggled to her feet and moved to support Josh, who was now leaning against a cave wall. The Honsho freighter landed behind them, and Laylee rushed down the boarding ramp. She ran frantically into Josh's arms and tightly embraced him as Tana backed away. Josh returned the embrace but looked over Laylee's shoulders to Tana. Their gazes locked onto each other with unspoken question of what to do with the knowledge they now had over Tana's confession.

As they boarded the Honsho freighter, Gold had been unbound but was held at gunpoint by Cody. Cody explained the situation and suggested leaving Gold here on the planet. Gold seemed as if he was genuinely shocked at the comment. He then replaced the look of shock with a begging for them not to leave him. Silence from the others followed. Gold raised his voice and changed it from begging to anger and declared that they could not just coldly leave him here. He then smirked and followed with the comment that it would be wrong. Josh fought back his agreement that leaving Gold to fend for himself would be a proper response to his betrayal. Josh then declared that they could not do it. Gold's smirk turned to a full smile as Cody pushed him back into the ship at gunpoint.

The Honsho freighter quickly lifted off and flew out of the cave. Cody had secured Gold with Laylee to watch him. Cody took over the controls. Josh leaned back in the pilot chair in silence. He pulled the shiny black rock out from the pouch that now hung from his belt. He gently examined it as he remained silent in his reflection.

* * *

A hyperspace portal opened. The ship that had escaped Xotosia exited with Emelia's smaller shuttle tucked right underneath it. The bottom bay doors opened, and a tractor beam pulled the shuttle inside. Fright Agent Nehih and Emelia were fully armed and ready to put up a fight. The shuttle was rested as the bay doors closed beneath it. The shuttle door opened with Fright Agent Nehih and Emelia charging out with full blaster fire against an assembled rebel force of nearly twenty fully armored troopers.

Chapter Thirteen

The Pleas of the Kemyyon

FRIGHT AGENT NEHIH and Emelia, in a furious rage, had engaged their combined blaster fire attack against the twenty fully armored rebel troopers of various races that surrounded them in the hangar bay. Emelia had a tight grip on the blaster pistols that she held in both hands. Emelia's movements seemed superhuman as she jumped, twisted, and turned through the air with rapid blaster fire from both pistols against the heavy blaster fire that was being unleashed from the armored rebel troopers. She dodged every blaster shot against her as she started to leap from point to point, landing between her assaulters and blasting them. Her fast and furious assault had quickly exhausted the power cells on her blaster pistols. She holstered them and began to punch and kick her way through the remaining troopers. She then drew her long katana-type sword. The blade with a shiny silver coating gleamed against the light. She quickly engaged the troopers that were recovering from her melee attack. Her battlefield calculation and the weariness on her enemies allowed her to slice at the exposed joints between the armor. She sliced off arms and legs and even a few heads.

Fright Agent Nehih had taken cover under the captured Black Guard shuttle and engaged his blaster fire against the troopers after

Emelia had hit them and downed the ones that had not fallen to her attack. Once all the rebel troopers had fallen, he ran to Emelia's side. Another door opened, and ten more troopers in lesser armor rushed the room with heavy blaster fire. Emelia again engaged her reflexive attack and, even more quickly than before, had sliced through the new wave of assaulters. Fright Agent Nehih had accessed a console and found the route to the ship's command deck. Once he confirmed that he had it, Emelia stated that they must secure the ship.

* * *

The Honsho freighter had left the enormously large planet and had rerouted back to where they had left the *Fallen Star*. They had found the killer eye guard satellites had been destroyed with only floating debris remaining and Josh's ship was gone. Cody pointed out that Gold had assured them that the Honsho stabilize field and the killer eye satellites would be enough to keep the *Fallen Star* safe. Josh replied that it was only one more thing that Gold had lied about. He brought the Honsho freighter to a dead stop and stood from the pilot chair. He informed Cody that it was time to have another talk with their captive pirate friend.

Josh walked through the corridor and back to a small community area where Laylee still held Gold at gunpoint. Josh moved right past her with a direct charge to Gold and knocked him to the floor with one solid punch. Gold fell to the floor and rubbed his jaw. Josh screamed at him, "Where is my ship?!" Gold had believed it was right where they had secured it. Josh laughed at Gold's understanding of security as he explained that the killer eye satellites had been destroyed and the ship was gone. He further added his belief that Gold had staged the whole thing and that another Honsho freighter of the Gatling Legion had taken the ship after they had headed for the planet of giants.

Gold had made his way back to his feet and denied the accusation. He admitted that he was a scoundrel, a pirate, a liar, and a thief to some sense of the words, but he insisted that his word carried honor and integrity. Both Josh and Laylee laughed at the remark.

Gold claimed he would prove it by helping them track the ship down. Josh told Laylee to escort the honorable pirate to the cockpit where he could help Cody. He started to leave the room and paused at the archway. He told Laylee to keep Gold at gunpoint and, if he showed the slightest hint of betraying them again, to gun him down on the spot.

* * *

The *Dark Wish* landed on Hortis Six at a planet docking bay. Mortigan ordered Binia to secure the ship as he walked down the boarding ramp. The docking bay population was filled with a variety of different races, but the majority was human. As Mortigan traversed through the facility, he noticed several Black Guard security posts and tried his best to pass them at the farthest distance. He used the crowds in the area as his cover. He was quite adept at that skill.

Mortigan entered a tavern, which was filled with all humans. A sign at the entry written in many different languages read "Humans Only." Mortigan with his patchwork skin drew the immediate attention of the patrons. He firmed his stance and strode to the bar unaffected by the hostile stares of hate that he drew. He asked the human female bartender for a man called Gullivar. Two large human males approached and positioned themselves at each side of Mortigan. He was asked in strong and deep voices from both men to leave. Everyone's attention was now drawn to the bar even from the outer rooms. The loud chatter and music had stopped. Mortigan looked at the large humans at each of his sides and took a deep breath. He warned them that if they did not back away, he would find a spot on him to stitch their skin. The two large men stiffened their stance as the crowd widened to provide more room for the fight that was about to break out. Suddenly a loud voice yelled out from the back to ease the tension. The voice claimed, "It's all right. He is human. He is just confused if he wants to be." The man knew Mortigan was a Sparbosan but claiming that he was human was clearly the less hostile option.

The music and chatter resumed as the male human approached and waved off the two large men from Mortigan's sides. The man was human and dressed in colorful arrays of clothing. He was scrawny in build and with long brown hair and a scruffy attempt to grow facial hair. The only difference was the metal spikes he had grafted to the outsides of his hands and around his neck. Mortigan greeted him as Gullivar.

Gullivar ushered Mortigan back to a more private section of the tavern. He remarked, "It seems as though you have added some more skin patches since we last encountered each other."

Mortigan answered that he had added a few. He pointed to a particular stitched orange-scaled patch and added that he had finally gotten a Derth and it was most fun. They seated themselves at a small table. Gullivar instructed a scantily clad woman to bring them two glasses of a drink called Toxic Scum. He then asked Mortigan whom he was after now. Mortigan, with a strong tone of confidence, in his voice threw out the name Josh Broody. Gullivar seemed impressed and said, "The former general? That's some big shoes there!"

Mortigan quickly took control of the conversation back to his advantage and asked Gullivar if he was still retired. Gullivar replied that it was much safer that way. He added that being Mortigan's main rival in the bounty hunter trade was much too dangerous. Mortigan admitted that old times were fun, but they were no longer rivals for the same bounties. He had heard a rumor or two that Gullivar was more into the brokerage of information these days. He then asked straight out if Gullivar knew where the Black Guard would be developing any super weapons.

The waitress had just brought the drinks and served them from a tray she held at her hip. They were tall skinny glasses with a dark-green liquid and seemed to have a black foam that spilled over the top of the glasses. They each paused in the conversation and took the time to take strong and equal swigs of the Toxic Scum. It was a strong burning drink. The drink itself had been used often for a lubricant replacement in machinery. Each man drank without twitching and not wanting to show weakness to the other. Gullivar was the first to return to the conversation and asked what Mortigan was offering for payment. Mortigan tossed eight square tiles onto the table.

Gullivar examined them carefully. He bit on one and held it up to the dim lighting above them. He gathered them up and asked with suspicion, "Calavan tiles? Where did you pick up these rare things?"

Mortigan assured him that they were not cursed and gave his word on the statement. Gullivar looked intently at Mortigan, trying to detect a bluff. Once he was sure Mortigan could be trusted, he pocketed the currency. He then told Mortigan that he was looking for the Irata sector.

* * *

Emelia and Fright Agent Nehih fought their way into the command deck with Emelia slicing and Fright Agent Nehih shooting everyone there. Any rebels with melee attacks on Fright Agent Nehih were ripped deeply by his thorn covered body where they had no armor. Emelia sheathed her sword and replaced the power cells in her two blasters. Fright Agent Nehih had checked the computer records and informed Emelia that an escape shuttle was recently launched. She asked if he could track it. He replied that he could track it to a mass area in this region of space but could not narrow the location because of sensor disruption from a nearby nebula. Emelia looked coldly around the room at the few survivors. She declared them all prisoners of the Black Guard. She then instructed Fright Agent Nehih to secure the engine rooms and any crew found there. She continued, "We're taking her back to Xotosia. We will question the remaining crew on the way."

* * *

Fright Agent Kyrak entered the quarters of the Dark Lord Epitaph aboard the *Darkfall*. Epitaph immediately inquired of the intel on Mortigan. Fright Agent Kyrak had reported that his spies had confirmed sightings of Mortigan being on Hortis Six. He then added that he had something even better for offering. Epitaph stood and stared at him. Fright Agent Kyrak claimed that he had found Josh's ship. The wide reptilian grin grew even wider across Epitaph's face. Fright Agent Kyrak brought up a space sector on the computer. He reported that he had strong and reliable information that the *Fallen Star* was on the planet Kemyyo. He then displayed a visual of the ship landed on the planet's surface. Epitaph ordered course adjustments immediately. Fright Agent Kyrak declared that it would delay their arrival at the Irata sector by no more than three rotations. Epitaph acknowledged the delay and still ordered the course plotted.

* * *

On the Honsho freighter, Josh entered the quarters that had been assigned to Tana. She was sitting naked on the center of the floor in a state of meditation. Josh asked if he could speak to her about what she had said in the cave. Tana tried to dismiss it, but Josh pressed on the topic. Tana claimed that it was a confusion of feelings that she had never experienced before. Josh, to some extent, had felt drawn to Tana. He reached out and caressed the side of her face. He then displayed some form of regret and returned the hand to his side and said that he was with Laylee.

Tana stood from her seated position on the floor. She was still shorter than Josh but looked up at him and directly into his eyes. She then asked if he was with Laylee, then why was he meant to be with her? She claimed that through her meditation, she could feel her own incompleteness and that he was revealed to be a match for her soul. Her vision clearly showed that his path ran alongside her own.

The conversation was interrupted by Cody's gruff voice over the comms. They had been searching the sector for the *Fallen Star* but had found a large and long vessel that had also detected and hailed them. Josh stated that he would be right there and excused himself from Tana's quarters.

* * *

Silos Taqoon was piloting an escape pod. He had just entered the atmosphere of a planet and steadied the craft. Two Luth Bik diamond-shaped starfighters called shards had taken position with one at each side of his shuttle. The comms light flashed as he was being hailed. He acknowledged the hail that was in the Luth Bik tongue. Silos turned on the translator. The hail was calling for Silos' pod to present designation and mission. Silos sent a translated message back, claiming that he was Silos Taqoon from the planet Xotosia and was wishing to discuss with their leaders the salvation of Xotosia by requesting their assistance in driving the Black Guard from their occupation of his planet.

After a few moments, he was hailed to follow along a designated flight path, which was also transmitted over his screen. The Luth Bik ordered the shard starfighters to remain as escorts. He then added that they would shoot Silos' pod down at the slightest deviation from the provided flight path.

* * *

Josh entered the Honsho freighter's circular cockpit and asked where Gold was at. Cody replied that Gold had tried to wrestle the blaster pistol away from Laylee. He was now secured in a holding cell, and Laylee was standing guard. Cody flipped a comms switch as Josh seated himself into the pilot chair. The hail registered as translated and said, "Unidentified Honsho vessel, this is the Kemyyon vessel *Gy Naffa Fy*. Can we provide assistance?"

Josh mentioned that he had heard of that ship. Cody replied that to all historic accounts it was lost ten cycles ago. Josh replied to the hail that they were a Honsho ship unassigned to any specific legion. He then requested confirmation of their ship's designation. The reply again stated the ship as Kemyyon vessel *Gy Naffa Fy*. Josh and Cody looked at each other silently. Josh then replied that they were not Honshos and were merely searching for their ship the *Fallen Star*. He added that it was a Jaskan-built intercosmos-class freighter. The Kemyyon hail then asked if they would like to dock and come aboard to discuss terms of Kemyyon assistance in the locating of their lost ship. Josh abruptly silenced the comms. Cody was opposed to getting involved with a mysterious ship that had been missing for ten cycles. Josh reopened the comms and respectfully declined the kind offer of assistance. The Kemyyon hail replied that if Josh did change his mind, they would be in the area.

As the hail closed, Cody asked if Josh had been able to attempt a neural link. Josh made a strong attempt, but the *Fallen Star* was obviously still out of range or the neural link had been severed completely. Josh then pointed to the computer mapping system and plotted another course. He agreed with Cody that it would be best to stay away from the *Gy Naffa Fy*.

* * *

Epitaph walked onto the *Darkfall's* command deck, where Fright Agent Kyrak reported that they had arrived at Kemyyo. Epitaph had opened comms to the governments of Kemyyo. He stated that he was sending Black Guard troops and starfighters down to retrieve Black Guard property and warned that no resistance would be tolerated. He added that they would not be stopping at the docking ring that surrounded the planet's orbit. The response was clear that stopping at the docking ring was required procedure before any planetary entry. Epitaph countered with the fact the Black Guard was on a priority one mission and was not obligated to their rules. He then terminated the transmission and ordered Fright Agent Kyrak to maintain command of Fury Fleet while he himself went down to the planet. Fright Agent Kyrak immediately argued the safety of that decision. Epitaph proclaimed he would be well-protected by his landing forces. He added that he needed to see this ship. He needed to be in physical contact to try to obtain a vision. Fright Agent Kyrak requested that Epitaph wait until the ship could be brought aboard where it would be much safer. Epitaph could not risk further contamination of the ship by the Kemyyon people. He was also well aware that with the *Fallen Star* on the planet, the odds were very good that Josh Broody could be on the planet also and possibly hidden by the Kemyyon. Epitaph summoned four Laser Head soldiers as his personal guards.

Fright Agent Kyrak also admitted that he would have a life monitor lock on Epitaph as well for any sign of threat.

* * *

Silos Taqoon had landed his shuttle, and as he disembarked, he found himself surrounded by Luth Bik soldiers. Just like all Luth Biks, they had hard shell-like gray skin, solid black eyes, widened nostrils, and straggly long black or brown hair that protruded from the sides of the head. The shell-like forehead ran up to a point that rested flat on the top of the head. They escorted him to an approaching Luth Bik donned in long and regal robes. He introduced himself in the Luth Bik tongue. The translator that Silos wore on his belt had received the announcement as Kyg and his Captain-at-Arms Karys. The translator also allowed Silos to introduce himself and his explanation as to why he had sought them out. Silos did so in his most gleeful and welcoming voice. Silos was interrupted as Kyg claimed that they had already stated their refusal to the cause because of Clad Byar and cited the obvious criminal history that they did not wish their resistance movement to have as an affiliation. Silos spoke up and admitted that his affiliations and those of his fellow rebellion founders were colored in the criminal element, but he was here not for them but for the people that suffered under the Black Guard tyranny. Captain-at-Arms Karys then asked if he denied being sent here directly by Clad Byar. Silos turned up his charm and did not deny it but also stated that his provided opportunity to restate their case was not just for their interests.

He pointed out that whether they liked it or not, Xotosia and its enterprises represented a key world. Black Guard operations based on Xotosia were far reaching and the location alone was a strategic one. Xotosia had all the resources to sustain base-operated campaigns and with its clout and operations it could draw from other worlds and provide support financially to worlds that would benefit greatly. In that case, sympathy for the situation could set in and spread outward, which could convert many worlds to Black Guard support.

Kyg mentioned that even if they would agree to lend aid of the Luth Bik Resistance that their resistance had taken its own tolls. Their forces were stretched, and their finances were constantly drained in the struggle. Silos claimed that nonetheless, the Luth Biks were carrying on despite the setbacks and doing what others could not. The Luth Bik Resistance may be limited, but the Luth Biks were resisting. It was also because of their nonexistent binds to other races and lack of obstruction by politics that made them effective. Kyg interjected that it was that nonbinding and lack of obstruction by planetary politics that would also be at risk if they supported Xotosia. He added that it was not to mention the image of whom and what they supported would blemish their honorable and justifying reputation.

Silos could see that Kyg wanted to help and was teetering on the edge of what morals they would have to sacrifice. Silos opened up with joyful laughter as he added that they may not want to show affiliation with criminal forces, but those same criminal forces could provide the intelligence and the support that could also aid the needs of the Luth Bik Resistance. He pointed out that they would have access to greater smuggling routes through the more heavily Black Guard-controlled territories as well as better real time information on Black Guard movements and operations. There was also no denying that the criminal element could also seep into the Black Guard in many methods and be used against it without the Black Guard even realizing it. Silos sweetened his plea with a promise that the criminal enterprises on Xotosia would grant the Luth Biks free reign and assistance without enforcing any special interests in return once the planet was freed.

Kyg and Captain-at-Arms Karys looked at each other. Kyg then announced to Silos that they would meet with other Luth Bik Resistance leaders and re-evaluate the risks and reconsider the needs. Silos, in the meantime, would be encouraged to experience the hospitality that they could provide.

* * *

Epitaph had come to the surface of Kemyyo with heavy Black Guard troop numbers and a personal guard of four Laser Heads. He met personally with the planetary governor, who granted him full planetary courtesy more of fear than legitimate status. The Black Guard, for the most part, until now had ignored Kemyyo claims in this sector and had contained its operations to the very outskirts of Kemyyon space. This was because there was not much the Kemyyons could offer that the Black Guard did not already have in abundance. In this particular case, though, they did have what the Dark Lord Epitaph needed. Governor Samira, as all Kemyyons, was bald and humanoid in form with the exception of an orange skin color and small dark red bumps that covered his entire body. Because of the intense heat that the planet produced, the Kemyyons did not wear any clothing on planet. Governor Samira did, however, put on the scantily thin robes that his people did wear on the docking ring and offworld as a courtesy for meeting with others not from Kemyyo. He had nervously taken Epitaph to the ship they had found adrift in space. He also provided those special coordinates without waiting for a request or demand. They had found the ship abandoned and had recognized the value. It had been secured by various forms of Honsho technology, but they had gotten past it. The Kemyyon had also replaced the pulse coordinator that was needed, and the ship was operational again.

Epitaph did not believe the claims that the ship had been abandoned. The ship was too valuable to Josh Broody. Epitaph knew this because he had it modified to Josh's requests and specifications during Josh's service as his general. Added to that claim was the fact that the Kemyyon had gotten by Honsho technology that even seemed to outmatch the Black Guard's technology. Epitaph then quoted a Book of Prophecy passage to Governor Samira: "The isolated people would hide the brother from the dark lord until the two brothers could join for their destined task of ripping the dark lord from power." Governor Samira argued that he was telling the truth and would never cross him. He dropped to his knees and begged for Epitaph to believe him.

Epitaph held out an open hand with palm side up. Epitaph followed the action with a chanting of a strange incantation, "Ssaiyai lissith ffleess copssnaith!" Governor Samira, as a result, instantly clutched at his chest and collapsed to the heated rock Kemyyon surface, screaming in pain. Epitaph's head tossed back, and his mouth stretched open extremely wide. The thin cloth attire of the Kemyyon governor began to disintegrate away in burning flame. The flesh and muscle tissue then did the same as he twitched on the ground in agonizing pain. As Governor Samira suffered, his blood materialized and gushed from Epitaph's open palm to form a pool at his feet. Simultaneously, Governor Samira's bodily organs began to materialize one by one in the widened and opened mouth of Epitaph. Each organ then fell one after the other down inside Epitaph's bulging throat and disappeared into the digestive system. The brain was the last to go so that the victim would be aware that it was being devoured. Epitaph's head then flung forward, and his mouth returned to its normal state. The governor's confidants had watched the act in horror and shivered in their own fear as Epitaph strode past them. Epitaph commed Fright Agent Kyrak that he would be returning to the *Darkfall*. He followed his claim with an order of a significant force of troops and ships to remain behind for a thorough search of the planet.

* * *

Emelia and the thorn-covered body of the Prah, Fright Agent Nehih had returned from hyperspace to the near orbit of Xotosia. The humanoid skeletal Teon, Fright Agent Maddo was left in charge of the planetary blockade forces, while Emelia returned to the confiscated Black Guard palace headquarters on the planet.

Upon her arrival to the central command room, she was notified by a Black Guard captain that Dark Lord Epitaph had requested she make contact at once. She strode over to the viewscreen and the visual transmission was initiated. Epitaph in his reptilian lisp proclaimed his happiness at seeing her once again and his loneliness without her at his side. She claimed that she also longed to be with him. She then reported that she was unable to locate one small escape pod, but there were logs found on the ship she did capture of limited communication with the Luth Bik Resistance. Epitaph expressed confidence that she could handle the Luth Biks when they arrived. Emelia was puzzled as to how he was so certain that the Luth Biks would come to Xotosia.

Epitaph proclaimed that Prophecy had declared, "The bride of the Dark Lord would face down the gray skins at the planet of pleasure." He also added that he had seen her battle in a vision of his own.

Emelia had changed the topic and asked of the status on the search for Josh. Epitaph admitted that they were very close. Emelia wanted to be there. Epitaph admitted that he wanted her there, but he needed her on Xotosia to close her chapter in the prophecy that was written. He promised that Josh's death would still belong to her.

After his communication with Emelia, Epitaph faced several empty reports of Josh not being found on Kemyyo. He then ordered all Black Guard troops to use great brutality in annihilation of the surrounding villages and commence heavy bombardment on the capital city. He was convinced by prophecy that the Kemyyon were hiding Josh. He watched on the viewscreen as the Black Guard soldiers blasted and with their axes chopped the citizens as the villages burned. On another screen, he watched as the planetary bombardment struck the capital city and destroyed building after building.

* * *

The Honsho freighter was exploring another sector when the ship took sudden damage to its port side. Josh piloted the ship to its starboard side when its upper hull was blasted away. Cody confirmed that they had hit two Black Guard orbital or spatial mines. Laylee had announced over the comms that she had freed Gold and he was aiding her in pressurizing the damaged hulls. More ruptures throughout the ship were registering on the piloting console. Tana reported another hull breach at the rear, and she had sealed it with a forcefield barrier. Josh was losing control as the ship's hull continued to buckle and break apart. Cody initiated a distress call to the nearby Kemyyon ship.

Laylee and Gold were reporting damages and that they could not repair them fast enough. Tana's comm had gone silent. Josh gave the controls to Cody and bolted from the cockpit. He was detoured down the ship's corridors as hull breaches hit ahead of him. He was able to seal those sections as he ran. He entered the lower level, where a toxic vapor had spread from a ruptured ship coolant line. Tana was trapped on the other side and unconscious on the floor. Josh saw the hull behind her bending. If it blew open, she would be sucked into space. He grabbed a nearby emergency kit and pulled out a chemical retardant blanket and threw it over him as he jumped through the toxic vapor spraying into his path. He scooped up Tana's limp body into his arms and jumped back through the toxic vapor. He closed the inner hatch door just as the hull breach tore into the ship and started sucking everything that was in that section into space.

Laylee and Gold had thought they had sealed their section, but the weakened state of the ship and other hull breaches had blown through their pressurized lock. Laylee was caught in the drift and started to be pulled into space. Despite the fact she was an android and could survive in space, the pressure was still ripping away her regenerative skin. Gold had earlier donned his zero-gravity space gear and managed to grab onto her and pull her through a section of the ship that he sealed with a forcefield behind her, but Gold was pulled into space. The dark tone skin that had been torn from Laylee was now beginning its slow regeneration process.

Josh rushed through the ship corridors with an unconscious Tana in his arms as the ship's hulls ripped away behind him. Cody had ushered them into another corridor, but with no power, he could not seal the door. Josh had placed Tana on the floor and was trying to help Cody physically close the door as the breaching wave of the ship approached. Suddenly, Laylee, still with exposed metal under her regenerating skin, dropped from a vent shaft above and pushed them aside. She was able to close the door with her android strength just before the breaching hit. Tana was regaining consciousness. Laylee turned with her back pressed against the door she had just physically closed. She said Gold had sacrificed himself to save her. What was left of the ship shook violently. The engines had exploded, but the vacuum of space had consumed the flames. Josh said at this point, it didn't matter. There was little of the ship left and nowhere else to go. Tana was still groggy; she used Josh to pull herself up. She asked if they could use escape pods. Josh replied those sections were already gone.

The remains of the ship then jolted. It felt as if the ship was moving upward. The Kemyyon ship *Gy Naffa Fy* had moved into an overhead position. Its tractor beam pulled what was left of the Honsho freighter upward and into its ship's docking bay with a tractor beam.

What was left of the Honsho freighter was secured inside the larger ship. Laylee embraced Josh and kissed him heavily in relief that they had survived. If it would not have been for Gold, she would be floating as space debris. As they broke their embrace, Josh looked directly at Tana and could see the hurt in her eyes. Cody pressurized what was left before they opened the door to prepare for what awaited them.

Chapter Fourteen

Dark Plans

ANOTHER ASSEMBLY WAS occurring elsewhere in the universe. The Fury Fleet had arrived in the Irata Sector. The fleet formation was observed from a large space station. The fleet's ships had surrounded the base and through a view of large station viewing windows, the Black Guard soldiers stationed there were impressed by the size and ships that appeared to be right upon the station. The taller, dark black-skinned cyclops-like being, Fright Agent Paj called to the fleet with the aid of the station commander. They were instructed to prepare for Lord Epitaph's arrival. They watched as a small personal shuttle departed the *Darkfall* and headed for a docking port on the station.

* * *

Hidden in a nebula a ways beneath the Black Guard space station rested the small armed freighter, the *Dark Wish*. The female computer voice of Binia had mentioned that Mortigan's plan had been accurate with the Black Guard's feared Fury Fleet arriving here at this rendezvous point. Binia continued with praise of the Prophet Buis's vision. Mortigan leaned back in his chair at ease while reviewing holographic and flatscreen data of Josh Broody and Cody. Mortigan took a deliberated moment away from the images and informed Binia to keep open and active sensors. He wanted to be alerted as soon as anyone other than Black Guard affiliation entered the sector.

* * *

On Xotosia, Fright Agent Nehih had taken over the command station at the confiscated palace. He was in collaboration with Fright Agent Maddo over planetary bombardment targets from the Black Guard ships stationed in near orbit. After the heavy bombardment had been delivered, a variation of sky and ground combat vehicles had been deployed ahead of a wave of heavily armored and gunned Black Guard soldiers and Laser Heads. Emelia had taken the point of the ground assault. They moved in swiftly and with severe force. They blew up remaining structures and killed fleeing civilian survivors without mercy or regret. Emelia had set up a command post in the center of the fallen rebel stronghold fortress. Resistance leaders, Ardicane Blivord and Arnvare Nixicine were brought before Emelia. No introductions were needed as she named both prisoners and their assets. She drew her katana-style blade swiftly and removed the heads of the prisoners. With the Blivord Industries funding and Nixicine's assassin and mercenary contacts all severed, it would be a crippling blow to the rebellion.

* * *

The Luth Biks, Kyg and Karys, came out from their conference and approached Silos Taqoon and handed him an encased computer chip. They explained that it contained a list of their terms in exchange for the liberation of Xotosia. They asked that he take the demands back to his co-rebellion founders for review. Silos was also given a special comm code to contact them upon a decision of agreement or denial. Silos accepted the offer with a widened smile of relief and a joyous form of laughter. He enjoyed laughing and mentally recalled how he had not done much of it since this whole ordeal had consumed his life. The Luth Biks also provided him with a ship to return to Xotosia. Silos thanked them with enthusiasm in his voice and departed from them with a human hand-shaking tradition. His happiness was uncontained as he promised that he would personally make sure all their terms were accepted.

* * *

Lord Epitaph and the Luth Bik, Fright Agent Kyrak entered the weapon project station and walked by the Black Guard soldier formations that stood at attention with their approach. Lord Epitaph's long cape dragged on the floor behind him. Fright Agent Kyrak followed him with a Book of Prophecy clutched tightly in his arms. They approached Fright Agent Paj and the station commander. Fright Agent Paj reported with confidence that completion of the Breathtaker would be in less than ten rotations.

Epitaph responded that the projection of weapon completion was unacceptable. He added that he wanted it done in five rotations or less. The station commander slowly cowered forward and, with a great fear in his voice, pleaded that only five rotations was unreasonable. Epitaph rolled his reptilian eyes backward. He held out an open hand with palm side up. Epitaph followed the action with a chanting of a strange incantation, "Ssaiyai lissith ffleess copssnaith!" The station commander, as a result, instantly clutched at his chest and collapsed to the station floor screaming in pain. Epitaph's head tossed back, and his mouth stretched open extremely wide. The armor worn by the station commander began to disintegrate away in burning flame. Once the armor was gone, the flesh and muscle tissue of the commander did the same as he twitched on the floor in agony. The commander's blood materialized and gushed from Epitaph's open palm to form a pool at his feet. Simultaneously, the commander's bodily organs began to materialize one by one in the widened and opened mouth of Epitaph. Each organ then fell one after the other down inside Epitaph's bulging throat and disappeared into the digestive system. The brain was the last to go so that the victim would be aware that it was being devoured. Epitaph's head then flung forward, and his mouth returned to its normal state. With the usual lisp in his voice, he asked loudly for all witnesses to hear if there might be anyone else that felt he was being unreasonable. He made direct eye contact with Fright Agent Paj as he delivered the question.

Fright Agent Paj recovered from the sudden silence that had fallen over the room, filled with shock and fear at what had just occurred. Fright Agent Paj declared that five rotations would be most generous and guaranteed that it would be carried out to Lord Epitaph's pleasing. Epitaph's reptilian grin grew wider with his flicking forked tongue as he stated that he was certain of it. He then guaranteed his certainty by placing Fright Agent Paj in direct control of the project. He started to walk away and suddenly paused to remind Fright Agent Paj that any failure to complete the weapon in the allotted time would be directly on him and that Epitaph's feeding methods would be nothing to worry about compared to the punishment he would suffer. Fright Agent Paj gulped in his throat and assured Epitaph once again that all was under control.

Epitaph with his prominent lisping voice replied, "Sssee that it isss." Fright Agent Kyrak followed Epitaph out of the room as Fright Agent Paj ordered an escort for Lord Epitaph to his awaiting quarters.

* * *

In the nebula on the *Dark Wish*, Mortigan sat in his pilot chair as he observed the Fury Fleet and space station in silent contemplation. He broke his own silence as he spoke to Binia and claimed that whatever they were building must be near completion for Epitaph to visit the facility personally. Binia replied by announcing she had detected different energy signatures coming from the station. He instructed her to list them. As she defined each in its technical term and function, Mortigan turned to another console screen and again brought up an image of Josh Broody.

* * *

The cargo bay doors of the Honsho freighter slid open. Josh and party stepped out to a formation of soldiers. The soldiers were outfitted in dark-red battle armor, and the backdrop of the assembly room was filled with draping and oversized battle flags depicting a sword crossed by two clenched fists in decorated armored gauntlets. From behind the soldiers stepped a scantily dressed man and several mixed gender aides closely around him. They were also scantily dressed in scarves and thin cloth designs, but his seemed even more regal in color and design. They were human except for their thick orange skin covered with small but, dark red and pronounced bumps. Like all Kemyyons they were all bald as well. He declared them as representatives of the Kemyyon race. He introduced himself as Prince Steyvar and welcomed them aboard capital class ship, the *Gy Naffa Fy*.

Josh Broody introduced himself and his crew. Prince Steyvar turned the back of his hand to each one's cheek as a greeting gesture of the Kemyyon people. He seemed particularly enthralled by Laylee. Josh broke his frozen interest by explaining their ship's problems. Prince Steyvar offered to take them to his homeworld of Kemyyo, believing that his people may have a ship that can fit their needs. He added that they may even be able to assist in finding Josh's lost ship.

Cody stepped forward and directly asked where this ship had been for the last ten cycles when it had been considered to all records as lost. Prince Steyvar seemed surprised that they knew of his culture and its historic accounts. He quickly shook the surprise and offered to explain, but only over a grand meal as his honored guests. He offered his aides as escorts to their rooms while on board.

Tana's primitive senses seemed to display a nervous state. Prince Steyvar took notice of her and tried calming her with words of trust. Josh apologized for Tana's lack of clothing. Prince Steyvar declared that her naked body was not an issue. He added that the Kemyyon only wore minimal clothing offworld. At home, he explained that they too had no need to cover their bodies. He added that the Kemyyon did not cling to the customs of clothing like many other civilizations. As they were all escorted away, Prince Steyvar never broke his stare of Laylee or Tana.

Chapter Fifteen

The Sun Rises Twice on Albetha

Tana was pacing about in her provided quarters aboard the Kemyyon ship. The quarters were lined with soft fabrics of varied bright colors much like satin sheets that ran down each wall. The floor was covered in a soft and shaggy type material. The lighting was low, and a soothing musical sound was coming from speakers mounted in the corners. There was also a pleasant-smelling fragrance coming through the ventilation. It was clearly an environment the savage Tana had never experienced. Laylee was attempting to calm Tana's nervous pacing. Laylee had donned a soft thin fabric cloth that barely covered her curvaceous body features and was trying to persuade Tana to try the other that she had clutched in her hand. Tana took the cloth and tore it to shreds. Laylee again tried to calm her, only to be confronted with a serious and low-toned growl. Laylee took the growl as a warning and slowly backed away.

Tana lowered her aggression and claimed that she was feeling a bad sense coming from everyone on this ship and especially from Prince Steyvar. Laylee had responded that she had no such indication. Tana growled again, this time in a tone of disdain. She followed it with the reply that Laylee could not genuinely feel anything because she was an android.

Laylee hated the word and took a sharp offense toward it. She claimed that she may not have real flesh, but even she as a Simulent had learned to feel. The stress on the word of Simulent had indicated to Tana that she had offended Laylee. She smiled slightly with a feeling of satisfaction. She then shook the feeling off and refocused her attention to the matter at hand, which was not about her feelings for Josh. She then asked Laylee, "If there was nothing to hide, then why had they been caged?"

Laylee seemed to pause with a frustrated sigh. She answered that they were not caged. Tana stepped closer to Laylee and stood only inches away with a snarl of her lip. Laylee held her ground. Tana then slowly surveyed the room around them. She followed by stating just because something was pretty and softly decorated does not mean it is not a cage. Laylee seemed to consider the statement. Tana then followed by asking why they had been separated from the others.

Just at that moment, the door to the room slid open and a mechanical bipedal robot walked in, offering to escort them to the dining hall where they would meet with their friends. The robot, although fully mechanical, was built with the standard two arms and legs. Its build was a metal skeletal look including the metal face. It introduced itself as a ZX3 model. Laylee had seen them throughout the galaxy. They were nicknamed "Brainerd" because of the display of functioning metal gears in the clear dome shape at the top of their heads as they moved and talked. Its eyes glowed orange as its metallic voice again repeated that it was their escort to the dining hall.

Laylee stepped to Tana's side and said, "See, we will be rejoining the others. There is nothing to worry about."

Laylee walked to the entrance of the room and stood next to the robot. They both looked back at Tana, who defiantly refused to leave the room. Laylee asked, "If you believe it is a cage, why would you stay?"

Tana ignored the question. She walked to a corner of the room, and with her back to the wall, she slid herself down to the floor where she curled her body into a cowered position. Laylee said that she would bring back some food and proceeded to follow the robot out of the room with the door sliding closed behind them.

In the corridors, Laylee and her robot escort had met up with Josh and Cody. Both had acquired new clothing albeit scantily clad leather, but it covered more of their bodies than the material that Laylee had been given. They had a ZX3 model bipedal robot escort of their own. Laylee mentioned Tana's nervous state and how she felt distrust here. Cody countered that maybe one of them should stay with Tana. Josh replied in the negative. If Tana had felt a distrust, she could become easily enraged at any indication. He felt it was best for now to have her remain isolated to prevent any undesired altercations while they more closely assessed their newfound friends. Cody admitted that he too felt some distrust. Josh claimed his own gut feelings were questioning their situation but figured with their current status of having no ship and being severely outnumbered, their best course of action would be to play along. He then reminded them to not let their guard down and remain vigilant.

They were then brought toward two doors that opened inward upon their arrival. The dining room was extravagantly decorated with bright colored metallic statues and many different plants along each wall. The dining tables themselves were extremely long and seated ten Kemyyons in chairs at each side. Each table had white-and-silver-colored cloth covers that ran the length of the tables and draped over the edges to the floor. They were seated at the table where Prince Steyvar himself was already seated at the end. He did not hesitate as he inquired about the absence of the savage lady in their party. Laylee started to explain. Josh cut her off by claiming that Tana had felt ill.

Prince Steyvar was sorry to hear that and asked Laylee to please offer his well wishes to her. The doors to the dining hall then softly closed, and Prince Steyvar's guards and attendants took positions around the room. Prince Steyvar then accessed a control panel at the side of his chair that rang a soft-sounding chime. The bipedal robots at the sound of the chime had begun to serve the meal. The first course was a thick orange pudding that Josh moved around with a utensil much like a spoon, but with the spoon head on both ends. Prince Steyvar claimed it as a rare delicacy called applice. He then himself used a crooked knife to spread it onto a cracker-type food. The robot servants also poured a light purple liquid into tall and thin glasses. This drink was called foo. Prince Steyvar then claimed that the next course of food would be a fruit platter of habba berries and toli berries with shankas leaves. This would be followed by the main course of kartzi meat and, for dessert, a brittle, crispy stick-shaped food called rogs.

Cody interrupted Prince Steyvar's excitement over the banquet of food with the question again of where this ship had been for the last ten cycles while it was reported as a missing vessel. Prince Steyvar paused in his eating and scanned over all three of them with an intent stare and a look of caution. He then asked his guards, attendants, and robot servers to clear the room so he could talk privately with their new friends.

As the room emptied and the four of them were at last alone, Prince Steyvar asked if they had ever heard of a planet called Albetha. Josh and his team all seemed to be unaware. Prince Steyvar mentioned that a race called the Albejen were denizens of this Albetha. Cody had heard stories of beings called the Albejen, but looking to Josh, he claimed that they were just stories of cloaked figures in shadows that wielded weapons of fire. Prince Steyvar quickly grew agitated and slammed his fists onto the table. He then, with all the attention back on him, claimed that the Albejen and their homeworld of Albetha were very much real. Josh apologized for Cody's interruption in a successful attempt to calm their host. Josh then inquired as to what they had been doing on this Albetha and where it was located.

Prince Steyvar smiled as he responded that they had gotten there through a black hole and that they had also returned from the very same black hole. Josh, Cody, and even Laylee appeared to have grown looks of skepticism. Josh had as politely as he could do so pointed out that nothing can exist in or even escape the pull of a black hole. Prince Steyvar responded with a strong tone of conviction that there was a whole other universe beyond the black hole that was very much different from the one they exist in now. Josh expressed some curiosity as he inquired as to how they had escaped from the black hole. Prince Steyvar admitted that the Albejen possessed a greater technology than what any of them could imagine. Navigating in, through, and out of black holes was not even a scratch as to what the Albejen could accomplish. He then boasted that this ship, the *Gy Naffa Fy*, had been modified by some of the Albejen technology. It was enough to allow them passage through the black hole. Cody had heard enough and grew irritated. He claimed that from the stories he had heard that the Albejen did not share their technology. It was an important fact to be able to support the stories without any proof from those that had claimed to have seen the all-powerful Albejen. Josh waved Cody back with an outstretched hand and again apologized for his companion's interruption. Josh than pleaded with Prince Steyvar to continue his account of events. Prince Steyvar thanked Josh most graciously. He continued to declare that there was something else that lived on Albetha that even the all-powerful Albejen feared. He referred to it as a shiffo, a lady with great mystic power and practitioner of dark magic. He added that this shiffo had abducted half his crew by teleporting them from this ship to her fortress on Albetha.

An attendant of Prince Steyvar then burst into the room and declared that two of their own and the savage lady friend of their guests had been taken. He reported that they had vanished into thin air just has the previous abductions. Josh's team jumped to alert from their seated positions. Prince Steyvar had also stood and claimed that the shiffo could not have possibly been able to reach them here from beyond the black hole. He then turned directly to Josh and repeated the same, but in more of a question. Josh had sent Cody and Laylee to check Tana's quarters as he moved to stand at Prince Steyvar's side.

Cody and Laylee had later confirmed over comms that Tana was gone. Josh grabbed a hold of Prince Steyvar and pulled him close. He screamed his question as to what had happened to Tana. Prince Steyvar appeared to have been shocked and stricken with fear. He said in a shaken voice that she had taken them. Josh released Prince Steyvar from his grip and asked if the she that Prince Steyvar was talking about was this shiffo he had described. Prince Steyvar's mind seemed suddenly lost as he kept repeating that she could not reach them here.

The prince's guards had been summoned by the attendant and had entered the room as Josh stepped back and away from Prince Steyvar. The two guards checked on Prince Steyvar as he recovered and declared that he was fine. They started to move toward Josh, but Prince Steyvar waved them off.

Josh said that if Tana and more of Prince Steyvar's crew had been taken by this shiffo, then they needed to go back and get them and make sure she could not do it again. Prince Steyvar claimed that she was powerful, but he could never believe she was this powerful.

Josh responded, "Clearly she is this powerful, and we need to go there and stop her now."

Prince Steyvar was afraid and stated that they had no means to stop her or combat her power. He then received another report that four more of his crew had vanished. Josh again grabbed and shook Prince Steyvar, saying that they needed to try to stop her, because if she truly was this powerful, then they would not be safe from her no matter where they went. Prince Steyvar fought himself into a stature to agree.

* * *

On Mortigan's ship, the *Dark Wish*, the female computer voice of Binia alerted Mortigan to a Black Guard patrol nearby and scanning the nebula that they had taken refuge in. He asked if the patrol had detected them yet. Binia's reply was negative. Mortigan instructed her to remain at minimal operation power and maneuver them deeper into the nebula. The ship's dim interior lighting went completely dark with the exception of the consoles and few emergency lights. The *Dark Wish* retreated further into the nebula just as Mortigan had instructed. There was a long pause before Binia again reported that they had not been detected and the Black Guard ships had moved away.

Mortigan had grown tired of waiting. He commanded Binia to try to stealthily tap into Black Guard comms to monitor for any updates on Josh Broody. Binia, after some time, reported that she had something. She announced that orders had been received that a salvage crew had repaired Josh's ship, the *Fallen Star*, on Kemyyo and were ready to bring it to a Black Guard warship in near orbit there. Mortigan looked over the holographic star chart and ordered Binia to plot the fastest course to Kemyyo.

* * *

Aboard the *Gy Naffa Fy*, the crew under command of Prince Steyvar was weary on the return to the black hole and what awaited them beyond it. Cody was on the command deck, overseeing the ship's operations, and excused himself from Prince Steyvar's presence. He had just started to walk through the corridors when he realized that he was being slowly followed. He also became aware of two Kemyyon soldiers that approached ahead of him. Cody stopped and held his position as the four soldiers converged to a flanking position around him with their small blaster rifles drawn and tightly gripped in both hands. Cody had realized that he had still not received his blaster pistol back as he reached for it out of instinct. Cody then let out a low and steady growl. Blue energy in a spiral form shot out from a blaster rifle in front of him, and another hit him from the rear. A heavy double stun blast had dropped Cody to an unconscious state on the floor of the ship corridor.

Josh was pacing in his provided quarters. He could only wonder what had happened to Tana. Suddenly, he was distracted from his thought by the presence of Laylee. She admitted to having been looking for him. They discussed the mission to head into the black hole, and both expressed a hope that Tana was all right. Laylee noticed a body movement in Josh as the subject of Tana came up. She had been programmed as a seductress, and all her times of providing pleasure had trained her in the art of spotting hidden thoughts and feelings of others. Laylee may not have been a human, but her programming had evolved to make her think, feel, and believe like one. She could tell there was more to Josh's worry over Tana than just if she was all right. If Josh did have feelings for Tana beyond that of a fellow crew member, then this moment of Tana's absence could be a huge advantage into winning Josh's heart for herself and to evolve their relationship beyond just the state of sex. Tana was her crewmate as well and a friend, but Laylee wanted more of Josh. All of these feelings were wrong to have, and a typical android would not have any unprogrammed feelings or much less be in a state of conflict with her morals as Laylee was right at this moment.

Laylee walked in front of Josh and unzipped her one-piece slotted leather suit she now wore. She peeled the tight leather from her body to reveal her smooth and exotic-toned flesh. She moved closer to Josh and tightly pressed her now naked body against him. She blew seductively on his neck and ear before bringing her soft luscious lips to lightly touch Josh's own. She slowly removed the vest that Josh wore and the shirt under it so she could suck on his bare and shaven chest. Josh had given in and finished disrobing his own attire and picked Laylee up by clutching tightly at her firm and bare ass. She bent her legs around him as he took her to the bed and placed himself on top of her as they both kissed wildly and lost themselves in passion. Laylee moaned in pleasure as Josh continued to pump himself into her, and she matched each of his thrusts with her own vibrant body motion. Josh had become lost in the moment as he increased his thrusting motion into Laylee. She felt so good and so right as he began to hit his climax.

It was then that Josh's mind took over. He began to see Tana and think of her walking with him. He looked down at Laylee, who was pinned under him and enjoying this moment with a facial expression of true bliss and satisfaction. Josh shook the image of Tana from his mind, and as he hammered into Laylee, he started to kiss her harder and with more passion than he ever had before. He loved her and wanted her. Their eyes both opened and gazed deeply into each other as their shifting body motion moved faster and the passion grew heavier. They even called out each other's names as they began to climax together. Again, Tana's image entered the forward thoughts of Josh's mind, and now all he could see was Tana's face as they kissed. Josh reacted by suddenly pulling himself out from Laylee.

The sudden stop in the moment had caused Laylee to ask what was wrong. She raised herself to her knees at the edge of the bed and clutched at Josh's chest as he was quickly redressing. She told him they were perfect together. Josh broke away from her and applied his shirt. He grabbed his boots as he hurried to the door. Laylee asked Josh if she had done something wrong because she thought that he wanted to be with her and she admitted that she wanted him as well. Josh stepped back to the bed and delivered one last passionate kiss. She was what he wanted, but Tana's image continued to flash before his mind. He apologized to Laylee and promised they would be together again, but he had to check the status on the command deck. He promised her when they found Tana and knew she was safe, they could be together.

Josh took a deep breath of relief as the door closed behind him and he found himself in the corridor. He believed he had wanted Laylee but now realized he had deeper feelings for Tana than he had thought. It was not fair to either woman for him to be with them until he could clearly decide which one he wanted to devote his heart to. As Josh walked through the corridor on his way to command, he attempted to comm Cody and got no reply.

Prince Steyvar announced over ship comms that they had arrived at the coordinates for the black hole. The black hole was massive. It was one of the largest ever seen. The stars around its edges seemed to shimmer. The dark core of the black hole seemed ominous. The helmsman on the Kemyyon ship had reported that they were at the safest distance to avoid the gravity pull.

Josh entered the command deck just as Prince Steyvar announced again shipwide to prepare for black hole entry. He looked directly at Josh as if expecting a sense of awe at what they were about to achieve. He then quickly turned his attention to the lead helmsman and instructed him to initiate the Albejen stabilizers and proceed into the black hole.

The Kemyyon ship began to experience a deep tremor that lessened slightly as it moved closer into the black hole. The gravity pull of the black hole was pulling the vessel into its darkness, but the Albejen stabilizers were slowing and controlling the direction of its descent. The *Gy Naffa Fy* seemed to be on a slow sliding motion with minor trembles as it moved deeper through the enveloping darkness. The stars had vanished, and all that was seen was the darkness of a total black space. The slow, sliding motion repelled against the gravity pull for several long moks that seemed like eternity. A feeling of claustrophobia seemed to suppress the amazement. Suddenly, a small flicker of light seemed to snap around the ship as the *Gy Naffa Fy* pierced through it and initiated a severe electrical surge in the powered systems throughout the ship. The ship's lighting flickered out and snapped back on. Prince Steyvar looked to Josh and then followed Josh's gaze at the forward viewscreen to a single planet with two white suns providing a bright white light to the planet's furthest side and southern hemisphere.

Laylee had entered the command deck and walked directly to Josh. She wore her one-piece skintight, slotted black leather suit and knee-high heeled boots. She still caught the eyes of the males and even the females that had looked up from their assigned stations. She reported to Josh that she had been unable to locate Cody. Josh had no hesitation in the use of his comms and called to Cody again with no reply. A Kemyyon officer then reported loudly in a shouting voice that four more crew members had disappeared.

* * *

Elsewhere in a dark cave, a swirling dark reddish light appeared, and four Kemyyon soldiers walked through while dragging Cody's limp and unconscious body. They threw it down onto a rocky ground surface. Cody slowly awoke and used a jagged rock base to pull himself to his feet. After an initial grogginess, he looked around and saw Tana and Gold Gatling suspended in individual stasis fields. The last time that Gold Gatling had been seen was when he was tossed into space, saving Laylee. Cody staggered forward and approached Tana first when he was zapped by electrical energy from the stasis field. He then moved to Gold Gatling with the same effect. They both could see Cody through their eyes. They seemed to be fully aware of their surroundings but were frozen and unable to respond. Cody looked around the cave to see many more of various races also suspended in stasis fields just above the ground level. He then spotted the four Kemyyon soldiers that he had previously encountered on the ship, and he lunged at them, only to be caught in a stasis field himself and become frozen in his place.

The swirling dark reddish light pattern behind them had dissipated, and the four Kemyyon soldiers were caught by surprise. They were spread outward from each other as they all yelled out, "Salankra!" They were each slowly separated and trapped in individual stasis fields of their own.

* * *

The *Gy Naffa Fy* had maneuvered to the daylight side of the solo planet provided by the two white suns. The suns seemed to be in position of the planet, whereas for the planet, one sun set while the other rose. Prince Steyvar viewed the scenery from the command deck with Josh at his side. He called the planet Albetha where there were two days before each one night. Another Kemyyon on the command deck reported the detection of ships on approach from opposite side of the planet. Prince Steyvar ordered a shuttle prepared for them and upon departure to move the *Gy Naffa Fy* away from sensor range of the planet. Josh had asked if the ship could not cloak. Prince Steyvar claimed that the Albejen ships could detect cloak signatures.

Prince Steyvar with two Kemyyon soldiers hurried Josh and Laylee along to a turbolift. They exited into a docking bay and were ushered aboard a Kemyyon shuttle by its pilot. The shuttle quickly departed and headed toward the planet. The atmospheric entry was rough and shook the small shuttle. The flaps and stabilizers aided in easing the violent turbulence until the shuttle broke the atmosphere and pierced the sky and took a low pass of the tall brown grass terrain. A clearing was located and the shuttle landed gently. The first sun was currently beginning its sunset as over the horizon the second sun was just rising.

In the distance, a light fog mist dispersed to reveal a tall tower made of stone. Prince Steyvar claimed that it was the fortress of the shiffo called Salankra and it was also their destination. Josh asked why they could not have landed closer. Prince Steyvar claimed that Salankra had put up a magical forcefield to repel all technology and they were currently at the edge of it. The fact called all attention to be focused on Laylee. She may not have liked the term android, but she was definitely a piece of technology. Laylee walked to the boundary and stuck her arm through the magical barrier. She held it there for a mok and then stepped through the rest of the way. As all gazes remained focused on her, she theorized that her regenerative skin was a combination of biology and technology, maybe enough to confuse the spell. It was not a strong answer but the best they could come up with for now. The mission was to find their friends, not learn why Laylee could function normally in a technology-banned field. Prince Steyvar then seemed to smile as he crossed the boundary as well with two Kemyyon soldiers and one pilot. Laylee looked to Josh. Josh answered the silent question by stating that they had no choice but to follow.

From the shadows in the cave stepped a woman. She was dressed in rags and animal skins. She had a slender and very curvaceous but well-aged body. Her hands were exposed to reveal her wrinkled reddish-yellow skin. Her plunging *v*-line top exposed her wrinkled reddish-yellow skin as well. Her neck and face seemed even more old and wrinkled. Her long gray hair hung free. She cackled like a mythical witch of Earth story lore. She slowly surveyed her trophies held in the stasis fields, Cody, Tana, Gold Gatling, four Kemyyon soldiers, and various races. Her slow stride stopped suddenly as she sensed something. She spoke in a mixture of the common and kemy language and out loud with a harsh and grizzly-sounding voice. She sensed an approach on her fortress of four Kemyyons, a human, and something else not of life but yet living, more of a consciousness than a being of soul. She added, "Very interesting."

Prince Steyvar's party traversed with Prince Steyvar and his Kemyyons still in the lead. Trailing back just slightly, Laylee had halted for Josh to get footing next to her. She reached out and stopped his stride. She asked what she had done to force his silence and distance from her. Josh attempted to press on by stating that she had done nothing wrong. She now followed his stride more closely and asked straight out if he still wanted her. Josh pressed that this was not the time and motioned her ahead of him again.

Laylee was confused. She was an android whether she liked the term or not and had the consciousness of a live female human and a strong desire to be with Josh, not just sexually for relations, but she believed it to be love. Josh had seemed to share that desire before but now was keeping her at a distance. Perhaps she had misjudged him and he was just like all the other humans that wanted her just for sex. Laylee kept looking back at Josh. She again looked forward to match her march. She was quite sure that it was love that she felt for him.

Josh admired Laylee's body as she walked. She was so attractive with an exotic accent and skin and a tight, firm, sexy body with long black hair that passed her extremely tight ass. He wanted to take her right there and taste every inch of her body. He had begun to fantasize her on the ground as he licked with his tongue from her neck over her breasts and down below her waist. Suddenly, he realized that Laylee had changed to Tana in the midst of the sex. The thought was pleasing yet forced him to jump from his fantasizing mind and back to reality as he again was watching Laylee walk ahead of him. He wanted to be with Laylee, but even as he admired her from behind, he could not shake the thoughts and visions of Tana that continued to enter into his mind.

Prince Steyvar had halted his walk and allowed Laylee and Josh to catch up. Just over the next rise was the stone tower fortress of the shiffo, Salankra.

* * *

On the Black Guard station in the Irata sector, Fright Agent Paj had approached Fright Agent Kyrak and Lord Epitaph and reported the weapon was fully operational. Lord Epitaph ordered a demonstration of the weapon. The weapon ship would follow the fleet as they returned to Kemyyo. It was there that Epitaph wished to test the weapon on what was left of the Kemyyon people. Fright Agent Paj had interrupted the plan by reporting a distress call from the crew left behind to retrieve the *Fallen Star.* They were about to leave the planet to meet up with the fleet when they had been attacked. Epitaph claimed that they would solve two problems at once. He quoted a passage from one of the Books of Prophecy: "The dark lord would face two tests before the unveiling of his powerful achievement of terror that would steal the life of the universe before him."

* * *

Silos Taqoon had returned with a successful stealth approach to Xotosia and dodged all detection with the aid of Luth Bik technology and the provided ship. The ship flew low across the mountainous terrain and landed at a remote small town outside from Xotosia City and nestled into one of the larger mountains. Silos had disembarked from the Luth Bik ship and was met by the human male with the spider-like haircut and black mascara, Clad Byar, the human female, Madaray Vilici, and the Abolish with the crimson-red skin and a red mist around his body, Toxicus Forn. They were extremely nervous of being gathered in one place too long with the Black Guard push on their fragile rebellion.

They were ushered into a secured starship repair shelter. Silos wasted no time in throwing out the proposal of the Luth Bik assistance to their cause under the stipulation that once freed, all criminal enterprises on Xotosia would be disbanded and a new government would be elected under Luth Bik supervision. Silos ended his proposal with a slowly grown smile, but it was met with outrage from all three of the other rebellion founders. Clad spoke up, and his anger was directly aimed at Silos, who had now retired his smile. Clad screamed out by asking what good it would do them to fight for their planet haven if they would lose their interests anyway. His displeasure with Silos' negotiations was echoed by his statement that they were fighting to keep control, not to relinquish it. Silos tried to wrestle up his charm as he responded that the Luth Biks would allow them to leave Xotosia with their wealth and fortunes and, in addition, would not stop them from rebuilding their empires on separate worlds from each other. It was even more of a preposterous proposal to the other three than the original one. Silos' charm quickly faded. Madaray had countered with the point that their strongholds were united on Xotosia was the whole of their strength. She added that

the Luth Biks would no doubt expand their newly founded government with rules to outreached systems, and it would spread outward
and with regulations and laws that would eventually cripple their
operations wherever they set up. Toxicus proposed to increase the
smuggling of weapons and fighter ships from offworlds. He added
that they could also strip down the Luth Bik ship that Silos had
returned with and reengineer that technology onto their own arse-
nals. Clad seconded the proposal and claimed that they would then
continue their struggle with new technology and fight on their own
terms. Silos pointed out that there was not enough of the Luth Bik
technology to duplicate and not enough time for them to learn how
to adapt it. Clad disagreed loudly and claimed that they were capable
enough to do it. Silos used his negotiating skills to agree with Clad
that they could definitely adapt and duplicate the technology but not
under the pressure that the Black Guard was bringing down on them.
Silos added the urgency that their rebellion structure was crumbling
around them, and it would not last much longer under the intensity of the Black Guard assaults. He had looked around the table to
notice that his words had temporarily forced his three compatriots to
consider their situation logically. Silos used the reflection of thought
to add that they were as of now only fighting a small partial force
of the Black Guard. If the Black Guard would refocus more of its
forces and might, the rebellion would most certainly be over. He
added that they themselves would be imprisoned or executed. Silos
pressed the alternatives if they were defeated. He claimed that they
would fare much better under a Luth Bik-approved government than
they would under the reign of the Black Guard. The room paused in
silence. Silos allowed for the silence and the reality to set in before he
insisted that the Luth Bik deal was a good deal. Clad acknowledged
that Silos had valid points and added that they had already lost two
of their founders. Silos felt a confidence growing inside him.

Clad then called for a vote. The call for favor of the Luth Bik
offer was met with only Silos' hand raised. His confidence was false
and failed. With the offer rejected by a three to one vote, Toxicus was
ready to have the Luth Bik ship seized when from outside they heard
it explode. They all looked at Silos with accusations that he had the

meeting monitored by the Luth Biks. Silos swore his innocence of the charges. Clad then asked, how else than would the ship seem to self-destruct immediately on a denial of the Luth Biks' offer? He was searched by Madaray, who found a monitor detection in the Luth Bik provided comm. Silos insisted that he was unaware of the Luth Bik precautions. His claim was not believed, and Toxicus ordered him seized. The hired muscle for each of them had secured the much heavier Silos in a physical hold. Clad stated that he would be held and charged for treason. He looked toward Silos' own thugs as they all bowed their heads and refused to support their boss.

* * *

Elsewhere on Xotosia at the overtaken rebel fortress, the explosion had been detected by the blockade ships in near orbit of the planet and confirmed by the Black Guard forces on the ground. Fright Agent Maddo had communicated with Fright Agent Nehih at the confiscated palace who had informed Emelia. Emelia gave the order to send forces to the small village. Fright Agent Nehih then asked if he should lead the assault. Emelia ordered him to stay at his post and continue to oversee the daily operations. She stated that she would lead the assault personally. Fright Agent Nehih recited the Black Guard policy for her own safety that a Fright Agent was not to let a superior enter unsecured areas. Emelia didn't care. She reminded him that she wrote that very policy, and it was hers to break. She was growing weary and bored. This exercise would be just what she needed to respark her internal fire. She added an order for Fright Agent Nehih to continue attempts to contact Lord Epitaph. She felt that Epitaph was ignoring her and admitted that when she finished crushing the rebellion's heart, she was going to pursue her own hunt for Josh Broody.

* * *

On the planet of Albetha beyond the wormhole Prince Steyvar, two Kemyyon soldiers, one Kemyyon pilot, Laylee, and Josh Broody had approached and stood at the wide moat that surrounded Salankra's stone tower fortress. It was deep and filled with spitting acid. As they stood in contemplation of how to access it, the draw-bridge slowly lowered. At the now open entrance were two very large razorback-like dog creatures. They had thinning strands of fur and on all four legs managed to meet a five-foot-tall human face to face. They were growling with full ferocity, and the heroes stood defen-sively ready for a charge. The two large creatures suddenly retreated to the sides of the entry and lowered the tones of their growls. Everyone remained cautious to the sudden move. Josh took charge and the point position as he walked onto the drawbridge and into the entrance point. Laylee followed close behind him. Prince Steyvar and his Kemyyon party at his side protectively followed.

Inside the fortress, they looked around the torch-lit base and saw a door. Next to the door was a staircase that led up several flights to a narrow balcony or overhung banister. Standing there and looking down was the shiffo. She seemed to have a slender body build, but her hair was gray and her skin was stretched with age. She pleasantly greeted them to her "humble home," all the while making solid eye contact with Laylee. She introduced herself as Salankra. She asked what brave quest had brought them here. Josh stepped forward to talk, and from a chant in another language and of unknown words from Salankra, he tried to speak, but only silence would come out from his mouth. He tried to make sense of it and found Laylee in his face with an expression of worry.

Prince Steyvar took point and started to speak. Another chant from Salankra followed, and he was also silenced. His Kemyyon sol-diers tried to shoot up at Salankra, but with another chant, each energy blast dispersed just before reaching her as if she was sur-rounded by a forcefield. Laylee noticed that each chant was followed by an aura of dark red light. Salankra then spoke directly to Laylee with a look of fascination in her eyes. She said to Laylee that she would hear the story from her and her alone.

Laylee slowly pulled her attention away from Josh and stated that they were here for the return of their friends that she had taken. Another glow surrounded Salankra after yet another chant as she slowly strode down the stairs with a light gliding touch across the handrail. She walked to directly face Laylee and asked her name. Laylee introduced herself and the rest of her party. Salankra looked puzzled at Laylee and asked why she sensed a human consciousness and yet could not sense her as a human. Laylee paused before Salankra continued and asked, "You are an automated human, not real in body and soul, but yet you are in presence?"

Laylee mentioned that she was what many called an android, but she preferred the term of Simulent.

Salankra replied, "Yes, you are and a technological marvel at that. Yet your presence is strong enough to break an anti-technological field."

Laylee added that they had only briefly questioned her ability to function in the technology banned bubble or zone. Salankra chanted again, and this time, an aura of dark red light glowed around Salankra but transferred to and surrounded Laylee. Salankra claimed that she had previously placed a field around Laylee, and she had just now made that field visible. Salankra added that technology could exist in her zone if she allowed it to do so.

Salankra then motioned for everyone to go up the stairs. She claimed that dinner was waiting for them at the top of the tower, and all would be explained. Laylee looked at Josh and Prince Steyvar and brought her gaze back to Salankra. She asked if her friends could have their voices restored. Another chant and another glow around Salankra had returned the voices of Laylee's friends. Salankra again motioned them up the stairs and walked ahead of them. As they ascended, Josh whispered to Laylee to remain alert. He stated that this old woman seemed a little too much enthralled with her. Laylee whispered back to Josh that this shiffo was clearly all the power here and they had no choice but to play along with her until they could find the proverbial chink in her armor.

They climbed the stairs and, once they had reached the top of the tower, walked through a glowing portal of swirling red light. They entered from there into a long hall that seemed wider than the diameter of the tower. In the center of the hall was a long wooden table nearly twenty feet long. There were seven high-backed chairs.

Salankra motioned for all of them to be seated. Salankra sat at the head of the table and raised a glass of light green liquid. They all looked to Josh and followed his lead as he seated himself and matched Salankra's move. The table was filled with sliced meats and odd-looking salads as well as breads and creamy deserts.

As the banquet began, Josh asked about their friends, and Prince Steyvar added to the question by asking about his people. Salankra ignored both and spoke with her sole focus directly on Laylee. She asked if Laylee and her group would do her a favor, and in return, she would release their friends. Josh started to respond but was silenced by Laylee's hand motion to halt. Laylee addressed Salankra with all the expected etiquette and regard in addressing a highly royal being. With an admission of their weaknesses and a boasting of Salankra's obvious and superior powers, Laylee asked what it was that they could do for her.

Salankra went on to ask if they had heard of the Albejen. Laylee looked toward Josh, who nodded for her to continue the negotiation. Laylee claimed that what little they had heard of the Albejen was purely unsubstantiated tales and believed to be myth. Salankra admitted that most cultures that encounter the Albejen have the same claims. The reputation of their fire weapons, superior technological power, and impervious state to bodily harm lends to fantastic and unbelievable stories. Salankra continued by admittance that the stories and legends were true. She then added the one exception to the belief that the Albejen were invincible. It was a fact that nobody outside herself and the Albejen were privy to. Salankra paused before mentioning that it was true that an Albejen could be slain and would fall only to rise back into battle as if no damage had occurred at all. This was because no single Albejen could be killed. The race was unique as it was the only race to share one heart. The heart was one huge living organ, which was hidden and secured here on Albetha, the homeworld of the Albejen. Each individual Albejen was bonded to the one heart. The only way to kill an Albejen was to destroy the heart that gave life to all of them. Salankra admitted to being blocked to all access of the heart by ward stone bound to the single heart that repelled her magic. She then told Laylee that in return for her release of their friends, all she wanted was for Laylee and her team to destroy the heart of the Albejen and the Albejen themselves would fall instantly.

Laylee asked why Salankra wanted the Albejen destroyed. Salankra claimed that the birth of the Albejen drew off the life force of this planet that was her origin. Salankra claimed that she lived here first and that her unrivaled beauty was a gift from the once very beautiful world. She was to her knowledge alone but bound to the life essence of this planet. The Albejen were a creation of life born from darkness, and that siphoned off the planet's life essence and drained the planet and, as a result of her tie to it, of its beauty along with her own. It was all based on what others would call mysticism, but Salankra swore it to be true. Salankra claimed that the Albejen were evil. She admitted to a one time wish that the planet could be even more complete. The planet was then beautiful and peaceful and provided her with everything to live. Even through a state of pure serenity, she felt there was still something missing. The one thing that was missing was a balance of evil, and Salankra claimed to have unwittingly by her wish and a desire of the planet to provide for her allowed it to flourish.

Laylee again boasted of Salankra's importance, power, and regal status. She then followed by asking Salankra to consider their ineptness and lesser value and release their friends so that together they all might aid in this great and wonderful honor to help such a regal and valued lady such as Salankra regain what was taken. Salankra responded with laughter and by praising of Laylee's ability to con. Laylee insisted that she truly meant all the respect she had given. She also claimed that her Simulent programming did not allow her to lie. It was a good bluff except for the fact that Laylee had obviously over-rode or surpassed her programming. Salankra did seem to partially buy the bluff and laid out an agreement to release their friends only on the condition that Laylee would stay with her until the task was completed. Josh stood and started to defy the proposal but was again silenced by Laylee as she interrupted and agreed to Salankra's terms. Josh's face revealed his growing anger as Laylee requested Salankra's great wisdom and patience to allow her to speak privately with her friend Josh and ease his concerns. Salankra pleasantly agreed with Laylee's most gracious request. Salankra glowed as she spoke another chant and, with a wave of her arm, vanished.

Josh started to approach Laylee and was verbally in defiance of the pact that Laylee had just made with Salankra. Laylee rushed to meet him and called for an embrace as she clung to him and their arms tightened around each other. They kissed, and Laylee slowly adjusted her lips to the side of Josh's neck, where she whispered that she did not truly believe they were unmonitored and reminded Josh of Salankra's power. She could have turned invisible or been observing in another way. She added that she trusted him to find a way to save her. She had bought them all the time she could and broke from their embrace.

* * *

On Kemyyo, the *Fallen Star* was under attack. Mortigan was communicating with Binia as the *Dark Wish* made a strafing run over the *Fallen Star*. As the *Dark Wish* maneuvered, Mortigan ordered a wide spread of laser fire laid down and reminded Binia that they wanted the Black Guard soldiers away from the *Fallen Star* but did not want to damage their prize. The *Fallen Star* had started its engines and was beginning lift off procedures. Two of the Black Guard soldiers dropped from the *Dark Wish's* suddenly intensified blaster fire as the *Fallen Star* lifted from the ground and turned. It then positioned for an ascent and shot into the sky. Mortigan ordered Binia to match the ascent as the *Dark Wish* maneuvered around from its last approach. The *Fallen Star* wasted no time as it ascended into the higher atmosphere and adjusted for an orbital run of the planet. Black Guard groundfire had engaged the *Dark Wish*. Binia asked Mortigan if he wished retaliation. Mortigan angrily replied that he wanted a pursuit course plotted of the *Fallen Star*. The *Dark Wish* ascended and adjusted its flight path as it shot upward for its own orbit of the planet. Binia announced that the *Fallen Star* was in far planet orbit, but she had a lock on its position and pursuit course had been initiated.

* * *

Josh had been reunited with Cody and Tana, and despite the unpleasantries, Gold Gatling as well. Prince Steyvar and several of his reunited soldiers joined the assembly. After a brief explanation of their new mission, they were all teleported together out of the tower. At the drawbridge doorway, Salankra stood with Laylee. Salankra called out that they were to set course following her familiar to the Heart of the Albejen. The familiar was long like an alligator with its long body and heavy tail but its large head was more similar to a frog. It had a jagged fin crown across its neck and head. Its four legs were also long and springy like a frog as it leapt into the air. Long and thick leathery wings sprawled out from its back as it leapt upward. Once airborne, the familiar circled around the group before taking a slow flight ahead of them to give the direction for them to follow. As they began their journey, Laylee turned to face Salankra. Salankra attempted to ease any concerns by again promising to set Laylee free and then allowing them to leave her world once the Albejen were dead and she had her beauty and the beautiful paradise of her world restored.

Josh and Laylee had shared one last glance at each other. Prince Steyvar called for his party to follow the familiar. Josh followed with Cody and Tana at each of his sides. Cody pulled back on Josh's arm and stated that Prince Steyvar's men were the ones serving Salankra and that brought them here. Tana confirmed Cody's claim. Josh looked ahead at Prince Steyvar and his men on their march. He said to Cody that Prince Steyvar may be unaware of his soldiers' actions, or if he was aware, then they were clearly being played. Tana asked about Gold Gatling who was marching with Prince Steyvar's men but somewhat holding back. Josh sighed. He then responded that Gold Gatling was the wild card in all of this, and if they were watching Prince Steyvar's moves, they had also best be keeping a separate eye on Gold. The one fact was that they were not getting back to their region of space or even just off this planet without Prince Steyvar. Tana asked what they were going to do about Salankra. Cody followed up the question by asking if they were really going to commit genocide of an entire race if the story of the one heart was true just to save themselves. Tana added that even if they did follow through, it was no guarantee that Salankra would let them or Laylee go free. Josh admitted that he had the same feeling swimming around in his gut. He had noticed her fascination with Laylee and feared Salankra would not keep her word. He truly believed that the end result would be that Salankra would keep Laylee and kill them all.

Cody added, "Or worse, keep us as trophies and lifeforces to drain." He claimed that while in the stasis field, he felt something draining from him. Tana admitted the same feeling.

Josh admitted that their only play now was to go along with the plan. He did not trust or like it, but they had no choice. Josh told them to keep their eyes and ears open. Any chance they got to turn this thing around before committing genocide would need to be seized. Josh added, "We will play by Salankra's rules until we can change the game in our favor."

The journey had seemed to take a long time. They had seen the planets' two back-to-back sunrises and one short night. Gold Gatling had distanced himself more from Prince Steyvar's men and joined the conversation by pointing out something strange as the days and night passed, but he did not yet feel tired. Josh grasped it as well. Cody and Tana both said that it was like time worked differently here. Josh paused as he had a thought and then added that it could all be an illusion. Gold asked if it could be an illusion cast by Salankra. Josh looked to Cody and Tana, who in silent agreement believed Gold was still untrustworthy. Josh then responded to Gold that he was just thinking out loud. Gold smiled and delivered a light tap to Josh's chest followed by a comment to, "Keep it up."

The familiar had flown ahead and returned directly to Prince Steyvar. As they stared at each other from way back beyond all the Kemyyon soldiers, Josh watched curiously and stopped his pace. Gold had observed all this and walked closer to Josh and stood beside him. Cody and Tana stopped as well. Gold asked what was wrong.

They all looked toward Josh, who was continuing his observation of the familiar and Prince Steyvar from afar. They were still face to face.

Cody asked, "Is the prince talking to that thing?"

Gold now locked his gaze on them as well. Tana's animal-istic alertness kicked in and she listened more intently past all the Kemyyon soldiers. Tana answered the question by confirming that they were talking. All of them seemed amazed that she could hear even from that distance. Cody was considered to have extraordinary hearing, but even he was unable to hear them talking. Although Tana could hear them, she was unable to make out what was being said. The four of them gradually increased their walking speed to not call attention.

As they closed the gap between them and the Kemyyons, Cody noticed something else strange. It was something he had missed before. He could smell everyone's personal scents but was picking nothing up from the familiar. Gold had enough of the games and increased his pace forward and back into the Kemyyon formation. Josh tried to stop him but did not want to draw any further atten-tion. Cody and Tana each looked at Josh as he watched Gold further mingle through the Kemyyons. Josh said to let him go and maybe he would find something out. Tana asked if they could trust Gold. Cody was quick to reply in the negative but added that they had to for now. Josh added, "That, my friends, is the bad part of it all."

* * *

Laylee had been appearing to be enthralled and amazed by the presence of Salankra and continued to flatter her almost endlessly. Laylee used her deceit to lead into an inquiry of how she had become so powerful and how she had gotten her powers. She even further presumed that perhaps the planet had given the magical powers to her. Salankra kept smiling and basking in the flattery but revealed nothing to Laylee in the form of answers. Laylee was starting to become aware of something different with Salankra. It was different from before, but Laylee could not pinpoint it. She continued on with her flattery and threw in unanswered questions every so often. All the while, Laylee was trying to sense what had changed. Something was definitely different.

* * *

Emelia had brought her Black Guard forces; airships, combat vehicles, starfighters, and soldiers. The small town outside Xotosia City was now surrounded. Emelia coordinated the positioning of forces herself as a true strategist.

Clad Byar and Madaray Vilici were caught with the panicked civilians as they were leaving in a transport vehicle. Clad turned the vehicle around through the spreading panic as the Black Guard forces started to move into the town from all points around it. Clad raced the vehicle through the overrun streets back to a house lined with metal sheeting. He ran inside with Madaray, and they were met by Toxicus Forn. Clad claimed that the Black Guard was taking the town and they had no escape route. Toxicus ushered them through a secret wall passage and down a steep set of stairs that led to a dungeon style basement. Silos Taqoon was locked in a cell. Clad went to free him as Toxicus worked on clearing passage to a secret tunnel. Toxicus shouted back that Silos should be left to his fate for betrayal of their interests. It brought a strong argument between Toxicus and Clad over Silos' value until it was broken by a loud sound of troop invasion overhead. Madaray declared this was not the time for this argument and allowed Clad to free Silos while she assisted Toxicus.

* * *

The *Fallen Star* under Black Guard piloting had cleared far orbit of Kemyyo and had detected Mortigan's pursuit. Binia informed Mortigan that the *Fallen Star* was trying to contact Black Guard ships nearby. Binia then claimed that she was jamming all comms but could not guarantee for how long. Mortigan took manual control and piloted the *Dark Wish* to a frontal and underside position of the *Fallen Star*. He then fired a complement of concussion missiles designed to hit and intimidate but cause no damage. Binia reported a response hail from the *Fallen Star*. The Black Guard aboard warned of violation of law to fire upon a Black Guard vessel and added that this ship had been confiscated in the name of the Black Guard. Mortigan replied that the signature of the ship had not yet been changed over to one of the Black Guard. He added that therefore, under all legal laws and treaties, the ship was still open for dispute and still free to claim. The pilot responded in an angry tone that the orders came from the Dark Lord Epitaph himself. Binia silenced the open comm and reported that sensors detected two approaching Black Guard warships but still at a safe distance. She added that the *Fallen Star's* weapon systems were trying to be activated but were still on a locked-out access. Mortigan inquired as to how many Black Guards were on the ship, to which Binia replied that she had only detected two. Mortigan responded by firing one more complement of the concussion missiles followed by low intensity lasers. He then ordered Binia to open the hail to the ship.

Mortigan stated that he knew their weapon access was currently inaccessible and that Black Guard warships on approach were still too far away to assist. Silence was the only reply. Mortigan called for another hail and declared that he only wanted the ship, but he would not hesitate on its destruction if he could not have it. Silence was again the reply. Mortigan asked Binia if they were receiving the hails, and she replied in the affirmative. The ship was continuing to flee, and Binia asked for the next action. Mortigan increased speed and angled to pass the ship with a strafing attack of the medium cannons. The damage he caused was minimal but repairable. Mortigan again flew his ship into an intercept course. The *Fallen Star* came to a stop. Mortigan had another hail opened and instructed the pilots to return to the planet at his instructed coordinates or be destroyed. A long pause was held. It was unlike any veteran Black Guard action. This revealed to Mortigan that he had cornered rookies. The *Fallen Star* slowly adjusted its position as if to attempt a run, and Binia asked for instruction. Mortigan ordered Binia to hold. The *Fallen Star* made a course adjustment and slowly headed back to the planet, plotting for the instructed coordinates. Mortigan relaxed himself in the pilot chair as he turned over controls again to Binia. He instructed Binia to plot re-entry coordinates. Binia congratulated Mortigan on his success. He replied that they were not done yet.

* * *

Gold had maneuvered his way to the front of the Kemyyon assembly. Salankra's familiar had moved back and on a hopping run had flown ahead again as Gold approached Prince Steyvar. The soldiers moved to block Gold's path. Gold cordially requested an audience. Prince Steyvar then granted Gold access to walk with him.

Gold delivered a quick look backward to the rear of the formation. He then admitted that he had overheard rumblings from Josh and his people that when the time came to slay the heart of the Albejen, Josh's team may betray the mission. Prince Steyvar responded with a display of doubt and reminded Gold that Josh's friend was held by Salankra and would only be freed once the heart was destroyed. He also added that it was the only way for all of them to escape and be free forever from Salankra's grip. Gold admitted to that but still claimed to feel uneasy that Josh may try to pull a fast trick. He stated that he had been chasing after Josh for a bounty and that Josh had proven to be quite resourceful. Prince Steyvar was confident in their situation and could see no other way for Josh to achieve their common goal. Gold bowed to the prince and praised his wisdom but added that he just wanted to add the warning that he had told him. Prince Steyvar thanked Gold for his warning but felt very confident that all would play out exactly as planned. Gold took that claim as a lead in to inquire if Salankra could be trusted to hold up her end of the deal. Prince Steyvar had grown a bit irritated and stated that he had made sure of it. With that said, he then dismissed Gold to the back of the formation to watch Josh carefully for Gold's own sense of ease.

Their march had continued on a while longer before the second sunset and another night. Prince Steyvar had finally called for a halt and a camp to be set. He was sure they would be able to reach their target destination after a good solid night of rest. He assigned his Kemyyon soldiers to a rotating guard shift. Josh was still untrusting of the whole situation and requested that his team be added to the guard shifts. Prince Steyvar denied the request by declaring his people as totally competent and trustworthy. Josh argued, but Prince Steyvar held to his orders. Cody and Tana looked to Josh as he backed down and walked away. He then informed his team that each of them would take secret shifts while posing to sleep. Gold had approached and suggested the same distrust and plan for secret guard shifts. Josh then decided that two shifts would be fine. Tana jumped at the insistence that she be on the same watch with Josh. Cody had no objections as he did not trust Gold either. Cody declared that he and Gold could take first watch. Silently, he was thinking this would be the best way to watch the Kemyyons and keep a closer eye on Gold. Gold nodded, and Josh agreed.

Josh, Tana, Cody, and Gold had made their camp slightly away from the Kemyyons but within sight. The first watch had proven uneventful. Josh and Tana had just taken their second and secret watch. They appeared to be sleeping for the benefit of the Kemyyons on guard but remained awake and aware as Cody and Gold went to sleep.

Tana appeared to be watching the area but was actually watching more of Josh. She had these strong feelings for him that were more than the typical feelings of lust she would have for a male. She wanted to be with him, and she could tell that he had feelings of want for her as well but knew he had conflicting feelings to be with Laylee. Josh managed to catch Tana looking at him as he was sneaking his own looks at her. He decided with the others sleeping that this might have been the perfect time to talk things out with her.

Suddenly, though, a fluttering sound overhead drew their attention. They both looked up to spot a dark form fly over them and land at the other edge of the camp. They tried to remain as if they were sleeping yet turned to watch the guards awaken Prince Steyvar. Once he had been awoken, Prince Steyvar stood and approached the dark form just over the edge of Josh and Tana's sight. Josh, in a whisper, had asked Tana to be a lookout while he crept around the camp for a better view. Tana argued in a whisper tone that she was built for stealth, and her species and experience would stand a better chance at not being detected. Josh considered it and yielded to Tana. He told her to be careful. There was something more in his tone, as if his feelings toward her may be stronger than she had even thought. She stealthily crept away with increased inspirations of hope.

As the guards patrolled the camp, Josh had gathered together some rocks and covered them with his arm tightly over the cloth covering. He posed as if he was sleeping with Tana close against him. The guards assumed it was Tana under the cloth covering and moved on to check Cody and Gold, who were both still sleeping.

Tana had managed to stealthily maneuver to and around the outer edge of the camp. She used the darkness, brush, and rock croppings as concealment. Tana moved with extraordinary stealth, silence, and speed. She displayed all the grace and stalking of a predator species, which was obviously bred into her race.

As she got closer, she was able to make out that the dark figure was the shiffo's familiar with its large froglike legs hopping around Prince Steyvar with small creeping hops. It then surprised her as the familiar started to speak.

The familiar stated to Prince Steyvar that they were close. He retaliated by asking for guarantees that they would be freed and able to go beyond the planet forever. The familiar seemed to reach out and lightly stroke his open palm, as if a hand gesture of a pact between the two. The familiar then requested that once the heart was slain, Josh and his friends be killed. Tana jumped back a bit at the request. The familiar added that the Honsho was included. Prince Steyvar asked why. The familiar declared that the automated woman they call Laylee must remain with her. Prince Steyvar hesitated as he was trying to decipher the wording. He was suddenly grasped by a flash of knowledge or awareness to the words, "Remain with her." He asked the familiar if he was talking to Salankra through this creature. "Not exactly," was the hesitant reply, interrupted by its attention snapped to the large boulder behind it. With one long and sudden hop, the familiar had leapt onto the top of the large boulder. Tana had braced tightly against the back side of the boulder and slowed her breath as she looked up at the familiar perched atop the boulder but looking outward and not down at her.

Suddenly a streak of flame singed the boulder, with the familiar flying straight upward and just avoiding the flames. Flames appeared everywhere surrounding the camp. Tana had seen the humanoid forms draped in cloaks and hoods. Under the hoods, she could make out a pale white skin on the forward crescent moon shaped heads with its points at the sides. Along with the many figures were wielded fire swords and whips. Fireballs were also being hurled from them at the camp. From the many tall tales she had heard over her travels, she was able to believe that these were the mysterious Albejen.

The campsite members had all awoken to quick panic. Tana had looked back at the camp to spot that Josh, Cody, and Gold had now mixed with the Kemyyons in the alertness of the surprise attack. Tana had pressed back firmly against the boulder and readied her claws from her fingers as two Albejen moved at each side of her. She looked at both with a fling of her long brown hair as she swiftly turned to each of them. She growled, and her back hunched as if she was ready to leap into an attack. Suddenly, standing directly in front of her was another Albejen with his flaming sword raised above her. He swung down at her with moving flames trailing the blade of fire. She did not meet it with a scream but with revealed sharp teeth and a ferocious roar.

Chapter Sixteen

The Heart of the Albejen

CLAD BYAR AND his rebellion founders were running through the secret underground tunnels. The sounds of blaster fire and explosions trembled the tunnel ceiling above them. They continued to run toward an underground access point that seemed to distance the sounds of destruction above them. Clad ushered Toxicus into a small narrow passage. He then helped Madaray into it as well and followed her. Silos was the last to enter the narrow crawl space. They were tightly squeezed in the passage but managed to crawl through it at their best speeds and exited through a rock foundation rested at the side of a slow-moving stream. Due to his size, Silos struggled through the exit. In the background just over a rising were still the distant sounds of energy blasters and explosions continuing to level the small township. Clad led his fellow founders and companions to a narrower part of the stream, where they were able to easily cross to the other side and observe the rising smoke and flames coming from over the rise. They looked at each other and pondered on their next move. Silos drew all of their attention when he declared that he could get them all back to Xotosia City.

* * *

Emelia oversaw the destruction of the small town with a pleasant feeling of satisfaction in the destruction that she had unleashed. A Laser Head stood at each side of her as a Black Guard captain approached and reported that the township had been completely destroyed according to his assessment. He began to recite casualty counts when Emelia interrupted and inquired if any rebel leaders were found among the dead. The captain had responded that he had assumed all rebel sympathizers were slaughtered with the rest of the town's population. Emelia again interrupted him and stated that his answer was not the correct response to the question that she had asked. She slowly, with stress on each word, repeated her question. The captain paused questionably and admitted that he could not answer for sure without sending his troops into the damage for up close medical examinations of each kill. Emelia interrupted him yet again. She stated slowly and calmly with a gradual intensity grown as her soft words sharpened and turned into screams of rage. "Then I… suggest…that you SEND THEM IN, CAPTAIN!"

* * *

The *Fallen Star* had again landed not at the docking ring of the planet, but on the planet itself near a small clearing area atop a high mountain overlooking the rest of the terrain. Mortigan's ship, the *Dark Wish*, landed just away from it and the boarding hatch doors opened at the same time the *Fallen Star's* ramp descended. Mortigan walked down his own boarding ramp and hollered over to the inhabitants still on board the *Fallen Star*. The large blaster gun at the top of the *Dark Wish* rotated to target the *Fallen Star*. Mortigan declared that he had a death lock on the ship and ordered those aboard to disembark at once.

From the *Fallen Star*, two figures in the black and dark blue Black Guard armor and helmets slowly walked down the ramp with blasters drawn but pointed down. Mortigan bravely approached them as the large top mounted gun of his ship made a charging noise and cocked its position to a ready fire stage. Mortigan now stood before them with a grip on the hilt of his jagged blade short sword and his other hand tightly gripping his still-holstered blaster pistol but ready to draw. He ordered them to drop their blasters and slowly throw their sheathed axes and fastened whips to the ground. They, at first, seemed as if they would be defiant. Mortigan stated that Black Guard bravery was not what he was looking for, and he recommended that they disarm before he was forced to kill them. He calmly added that he wished not to kill today and respected their honor to duty but respected more their still yet undisplayed sound judgement. The troopers looked to each other and slowly complied with Mortigan's demands. He ordered their helmets off, and they complied as well. Before them stood a man with skin grafts from many different races, and the two different colored eyes of Mortigan sent trembles of fear through the rookie Black Guard soldiers. Mortigan spoke in a question: "Do I look like I fear you?" They hesitantly shook their heads in a negative motion. He tightened the grip on the hilt of his sword with one hand and poised as though he was about to draw and slash with a quick single motion as he released his other hand from the grip of his blaster pistol. Mortigan with that hand of a mixed grafting of fur and scales touched the cheek of his face. With a calm, intimidating tone, he said that he had already collected human. He reminded them that by their surrender, they would be marked under Black Guard law as deserters and wanted forever with Black Guard punishment awaiting them. He seemed to almost be hoping for them to take the bait and make a move. They both gulped and knew the words were true. They awaited a movement or something. Mortigan continued to silently stare at them for several moks, mentally torturing them as they awaited his attack. Mortigan then broke his silence and instructed them to flee. They seemed to be caught by surprise of the order and hesitated as if unsure what to do. Mortigan again grasped the hilt of his short sword and slowly unsheathed the jagged blade a quarter of the way before pausing. The Black Guard soldiers fled around Mortigan at opposite sides to meet again behind him and continue their run.

* * *

On the planet beyond the black hole, the first sun had set, and the second sun broke the horizon and began to rise. Charred and slain bodies of Kemyyons lay everywhere. Josh, Cody and, Gold slowly returned. They walked through the dead as Josh called out for Tana. Cody, through all the smoldering bodies and death, was unable to lock onto her scent. Gold had started to kick his way through the spread of dead bodies as he searched for something worth salvaging. Josh was growing more desperate over Tana's absence.

Above them approached a winged shadow, and in a downward dive flew the shiffo's familiar. It halted at a hover over the ground before them and stared at them with its large and round stalked eyes. Josh approached cautiously and slowly matched the stare. Cody and Gold stepped to Josh's sides as he asked in a demanding tone where Tana was at. The familiar looked all three of them over before it replied in the language known as common.

The familiar claimed that it had followed the Albejen and that the Albejen had taken Prince Steyvar and the savage one that they called Tana. "Josh asked, "Taken them where?"

The familiar answered back, "To the heart of the Albejen race." It added that in order to save Prince Steyvar and Tana, they would have to strike now. Gold spoke out loud in more of a questioning tone stating the convenience of the situation. Josh merely looked at Gold in a disapproving way yet seemed to agree with the statement made. Cody then asked what they would do. Josh moved his stare directly to the familiar and asked for it to guide them. The familiar turned and hopped twice before leaping into the air and taking flight. It circled around them overhead before suddenly flying off in the direction that they had been marching in the day before. Josh spoke to Cody while never breaking his watch on the familiar. He said they were going to rescue Tana by any means even if they had to kill the Albejen by slaying the heart.

* * *

At the top of the stone tower fortress, in another mystical room, Salankra watched from a large crystal ball, her familiar flying and leading Josh's party. The shiffo turned away from the viewing globe and, with the aid of a chant, started to walk and slowly dispersed apart like a vapor. She then coalesced from the vapor into a solid form in a room, which Laylee now entered. Laylee had mentioned that she had been looking for her. Salankra replied in a questioning tone, "Are you quite certain you were not looking for perhaps an escape?"

Laylee shuddered in shock at the very accusation and assured Salankra how she would not even think in that manner. All the while, Laylee was still trying to figure out what exactly seemed off with Salankra.

* * *

Aboard his Black Guard ship, the *Darkfall*, Epitaph was asleep and lay across a spiral upward coil bed lined with rough burrs. He was more in a trancelike state with his eyes open as opposed to sleeping. He was experiencing a vision. It was such an intense vision that he had become paralyzed during its occurrence. He was pulling back a curtain of space, and a glow of light was shining brighter as he tore back the starfield further until the bright light fully encompassed him and he was awoken abruptly. Epitaph stood up quickly and almost stiffly before he rushed to a Book of Prophecy and turned to a blank page. He started to write quickly and at a super speed. When he was finished, he calmly put the pen down. He read aloud what he had written as if he was aware of it for the first time. He had written a prophecy that declared of the Dark Lord would tear the fabric of space as he stole the breath from a world. Through this, he would become aware of the brothers reuniting. The Dark Lord will be out of time as once the shiffo cried out, the brothers would be together, marking the Dark Lord's end.

Epitaph put down the book, and Fright Agent Kyrak entered. He reported that they would be at Kemyyo within an ara of time. Epitaph, in response, commed Fright Agent Paj and ordered him to check over the weapon again and make certain it was ready to test on Kemyyo as soon as they arrived there. Epitaph then turned swiftly back to Fright Agent Kyrak and asked where Josh Broody was at. Fright Agent Kyrak responded that he had still not been found. Epitaph answered in an angered tone that somehow the prophecy was still intact. His vision was that somehow, the brothers would soon unite and destroy him. Fright Agent Kyrak stated that it was impossible because Jase Broody was confirmed dead. Epitaph reached out, clutching tightly at Fright Agent Kyrak's throat. He screamed in anger that the vision was his own. He released the grip from his fright agent and insisted in even more rage, "We need to find and kill Josh now!"

* * *

Josh, Gold, and Cody had reached a cliff that overlooked a large elephant type creature minus the tail and trunk. A hooded and cloaked figure was in a large saddle atop the creature. The familiar descended behind them as they observed the mounted patrol. Gold offered to sneak down the steep and rocky slope and gain further insight into the terrain below. The noble act suggested was met with total surprise mixed with slight skepticism by Josh and Cody. Despite the fact that he had helped them, he was still untrusted, and Cody insisted that he would be the one performing the scouting. Before either of them could solidly decide, Gold had begun his descent down the slope. Along the rocky surface were several patches of wild brown bushes that Gold was able to use as cover.

Josh turned to the familiar and asked for a distraction. The familiar displayed a wide grin before it hopped into the air and took flight over the canyon, drawing the attention of the mounted Albejen below. Gold continued down the side of the canyon wall. Josh motioned for Cody to follow him down another similar slope to gain a better vantage point.

Gold had steadied his traverse down the cliffside slope by using the spiratic, but thick bushes along his path to maintain his balance. He had reached a more level ground along the cliffside and took cover within a large tree growing out from the cliffside wall. He observed two other cloaked and hooded figures with their backs toward him.

They stood in a guarded stance. Gold took the time to listen to a slow moaning sound coming from beneath his perched location.

Josh and Cody had gained a better and more concealed location at a slightly higher elevation across from Gold's position. They could see that Gold had come to a rest at the highest peak above a cave entrance. From deeper inside that cave came the slow moaning sounds and also an eerie white glow. Josh and Cody also saw the two guards in black cloaks and hoods. It had become clear to Josh that the familiar had led them not to Tana and Prince Steyvar but to the original destination of the Albejen heart.

Gold moved slowly and cautiously down to and over the cave entrance. He had gained a dangling position just above the two Albejen guards still with their backs toward him and the cave entrance. Across from the cave, Josh and Cody took his cue and started kicking the rocks down their slope to cause a small avalanche. The attention of the two Albejen had been captivated as Josh and Cody each ran down separate sides with the cover of the avalanche. The two Albejen had spotted something and drew their whips in response. They snapped the whips to engage the flames and stepped slowly away from the cave entrance.

Gold continued to grip onto the stalactites of the inner cave as he scaled upside down across its ceiling. Once deeper inside the cave, he climbed down along the ribbed cave walls to once again a normal footing on the cave floor. Gold used the divided rock walls to maintain his concealment as the moaning sound grew louder with his advance. He had also stepped into the full eerie white glow that filled the entire inside of the lair.

Outside the mouth of the cave, Josh and Cody had used the element of surprise to attack the Albejen from behind. The two Albejen turned to face their attackers. It was now that Josh and Cody could both see the forward crescent moon-shaped heads and pale white skin of their faces from under the hoods of the guards. The two Albejen had struck at both Josh and Cody with their fire whips. Josh and Cody were each able to dodge the attacks and they ran into the cave with the Albejen in a close pursuit.

* * *

Mortigan was able to board the *Fallen Star*. He powered it up and inserted a device into the control system. The device was a computerized rod that contained Binia's remote access program. It commanded the ship to tap into Josh's neural link and trace itself to Josh's current location. It also overrode all locked out systems. Binia informed Mortigan over his ear comm that the ship was unable to detect Josh's current location, but she had it locked onto his last known point. The *Fallen Star* sealed its hatches and lifted off the ground engaging its repulsor lifts and flaps as it went upward through the planet's atmosphere and into orbit. The docking ring around the planet had attempted communication, but it was ignored as the *Fallen Star* continued away from Kemyyo.

Mortigan's ship, the *Dark Wish*, followed on autopilot. Binia informed Mortigan that several Black Guard ship signatures were exiting hyperspace portals and approaching Kemyyo's far orbit. Mortigan instructed Binia to adjust the flight paths of both the *Fallen Star* and the *Dark Wish* to evade both sensor and visual detection. Binia announced that she had done so and that the *Fallen Star* was still locked onto its destination. The two ships increased speed and fled Kemyyo at the opposite side of the planet as the Black Guard warships exited hyperspace portals and entered far orbit. Binia announced to Mortigan that neither the *Dark Wish* nor the *Fallen Star* was detected by the Black Guard.

* * *

At the village on Xotosia, the Black Guard captain reported to Emelia that no remains could be positively identified as rebel leaders because of severe burn damage. He proclaimed that he was quite certain that nobody could have escaped, and he was positive that everyone in the village was killed in the assault.

Emelia asked if he would stake his life on that claim. He hesitated at the question and replied back, "Ma'am?" With one swift action, Emelia's sword was drawn and sliced the captain's head from his body. His head rolled across the floor as his body dropped. Emelia then looked to the captains that were next in command. She stated that making such a claim would require confidence without any doubt. She addressed one of them as the new captain of command, and asked if he would stake his life on the claims of his predecessor. The new captain stiffened his stance and firmly declared negatively. He assured her that he would double confirmation and identification efforts.

Emelia was interrupted by a comm from Fright Agent Maddo on the lead blockade ship. He declared a stealth flight entry was detected nearby her position. He followed by sending the approximate coordinates. Emelia ordered her new command captain to assemble his most elite soldiers to those coordinates. She also added that she would lead them personally.

* * *

A Luth Bik-designed shuttle approached and landed outside a thick woodland area. Toxicus, Madaray and Clad Byar looked to Silos questioningly as they approached it. Silos admitted that he had detected the monitoring device planted on him by the Luth Bik Resistance and, through that device, had been in contact with them. He stated firmly that they had no choice but to accept the Luth Bik-provided offer, and he turned and continued walking toward the now opening boarding hatch of the shuttlecraft. The three crime bosses exchanged looks with one another and hesitantly followed Silos on board.

Once on board, they were greeted by Luth Bik soldiers and the Captain-at-Arms Karys, who pledged the aid of the Luth Bik Resistance if the offer was truly accepted. Silos stepped forward and accepted the offer himself on behalf of the Xotosia revolution founders. Karys followed by replaying the acceptance over a secure comm to the resistance leader, Kyg.

* * *

In the stone fortress tower, Laylee was searching for Salankra again. With the aid of her android vision, she had found a peculiar shaping or coloring in the wall. Through the method of touch and examination, she was able to access an entrance switch that slid the portion of the wall to the side. She was shocked to find Tana there, secured in an energy stasis field.

* * *

At the cave, the Albejen guards from outside the cave continued to pursue Josh and Cody deeper inside. Josh and Cody ran into a more secluded section of the cave. The Albejen entered and disengaged their fire whips. Josh and Cody remained hidden as they observed their pursuers. Cody in a whisper asked Josh why the Albejen had lowered their weapons. Stepping out from the shadows, Gold answered the question, stating that they could not risk the damage to their heart. He pointed ahead to a narrow passage and led them inside, where they were forced to walk the narrow path in a single-file formation. As they walked, the loud moaning noise they had been hearing only grew louder.

* * *

Back at the stone fortress Laylee was examining Tana in the stasis field and trying to find a way to deactivate it. Tana was aware and with eye contact drew Laylee's attention behind her. Laylee turned to find Prince Steyvar standing there with a longsword. She asked what was happening. Prince Steyvar claimed that his Salankra had teleported them back here. He added that very soon, his lovely Salankra would be free once the Albejen heart was slain. He commented on how he had fallen in love with Salankra when he had become trapped here. He was unable to bring her from beyond this black hole because the very existence of the Albejen was what bound her and her magic here on this world. He claimed that Salankra was a dark mythos goddess trapped on the planet to contain her dark magic by the creation of the Albejen by another god. Laylee deduced that although Salankra could not leave this planet by the binding to the Albejen, she was able to send Prince Steyvar out to find strangers and abduct them so the shiffo, Salankra could manipulate them into doing her bidding. Laylee asked the prince why he did not just slay the Albejen heart himself. He replied that he and Salankra were in love and that any strong tie to her that would affect the Albejen would cause her agonizing death. The slaying of the Albejen heart would wipe out all the Albejen and free Salankra from the binding spell, but it had to be done by someone with no strong emotional ties to Salankra herself. Laylee asked how many of his own Kemyyons had died this way. Prince Steyvar added that there was nothing he would not do for his true love even at the expense of his own people. Laylee angered him by accusations that Salankra had been manipulating and controlling him with a love that was not real. She had firsthand knowledge of this because of her history as a pleasure-serving Simulent. She had used this tactic on many men and women before in regard to her own needs and programming. In the angered response she had generated, Prince Steyvar swung at her with his longsword. Laylee's android reflexes allowed her to quickly and easily dodge the attack. The sword struck the stasis field instead and exploded in a strong blast of blinding light. The stasis field was disabled, and Tana fell to the floor. The blinding light distraction was ineffective on Laylee's android eyes, and she was able to take the advantage. She grabbed Prince Steyvar from behind and locked his arms in a brace with her own. By using the momentum and strength she possessed to swing him and, with a quick release, tossed him with hard impact against a stone wall.

* * *

Josh, Cody, and Gold had exited the narrow passage and walkway into a huge chamber with the loud moaning noise growing inside their heads. There was a circular ledge with other passages that accessed it at all points. Below them, embedded in a crater of stone, was a colossal throbbing gray matter. It was a giant heart that moaned versus pounded its beats. Gold noticed its size and tissue thickness and wondered how they could destroy it. The two Albejen guards had now exited the passage. Cody charged one of them, and Gold followed suit by charging the other. Josh seemed mesmerized by the heart. He was lost in deep concentration, while Cody and Gold fought side by side in hand-to-hand combat with the two Albejen guards. Cody was even surprised by himself as he quickly gained the upper hand and threw his Albejen opponent over the ledge. The Albejen guard was able to catch onto the ledge with both hands and dangled there as Cody moved to attack the other Albejen guard from behind. That Albejen guard had already forced Gold to his knees. At the last instant of Cody's charge, the Albejen guard was able to turn and clutch Cody at the throat. Cody snapped his snout jaw at the Albejen that held him up off his feet and at a safe distance away from even Cody's swinging claws. Gold took advantage of the opportunity provided and pulled on the legs of the Albejen guard. Cody fell to the ground after being released from the Albejen's grip. Gold and the Albejen guard rolled in a scuffle on the ground. Gold was able to grab a hilt from the Albejen's belt and activated the fiery blade of the fire sword. The Albejen slid away from him on the ground as Gold took a standing position over him and readied to swing the fire sword. Gold took one swift and powerful swing and, trailing flames in that motion, had struck his fallen and defenseless opponent. The Albejen guard screamed out a loud, echo-like, and agonizing cry as he was not only pierced by the blade, but its fiery component had set him quickly ablaze and the catching fire with such heat and intensity had reduced him to chalky white dust within a mok of time. Cody was shocked by the intensity of the fire weapon and the effects he had witnessed. With Cody's momentary distraction, Gold limped back up to the ledge overlooking the colossal heart with the fire sword readied to throw at it. Cody followed Gold's path back up to the ledge. He noticed the other Albejen had pulled himself back up and drawn a fire whip as he positioned himself to swing it toward Gold. Gold looked back at him and stated that he would throw the fire sword into the heart. The Albejen guard looked at Gold and then at Cody, who by only a facial twitch seemed to confirm Gold's threat. Cody saw past the pale white skin of the forward crescent moon-shaped face with the hood now thrown back. The very Albejen look that seemed to provide a natural intimidation to Cody now seemed cracked. Cody saw the fear in the Albejen guard's cold gray eyes. The Albejen disengaged his fire whip and placed it and the hilt of his deactivated fire sword before him as he offered his own surrender. The Albejen that had been disintegrated by the fire sword that Gold had wielded had now started to coalesce. The white dust started a slow regeneration of the Albejen's body.

Josh had now broken from his concentration and yelled at Gold to stop. Josh had a feeling that something was wrong here. Two more Albejen stepped out from other and separate passages and both had their fire whips drawn. Everyone froze as they all gazed around. Josh calmly and politely told Gold to deactivate the fire sword. Gold refused and again made a quick motion that he would be throwing it down at the heart. He still had the fiery blade in full flame and the sword ready to throw. Cody ran toward Gold to stop him, but he had released his grip and sent the fire sword hurling down toward the colossal heart. Josh had also made a run and diving tackle to Gold. As Josh took Gold to the ground, Cody simultaneously dove over them and over the ledge. He was able to catch the ledge with one hand and the hilt of the flaming fire sword in the other.

Gold wrestled himself free from Josh. Josh looked behind Gold to see Cody crawling back up from over the ledge and tossing the deactivated hilt on the ground in front of him, where a cloaked Albejen moved forward and stepped on the hilt. Josh, Cody, and Gold had all made it back to their feet and slowly stepped closer together. They looked around to find themselves surrounded now by several Albejen. One of the Albejen stepped forward and claimed that Salankra's agents had been halted. The voice was calm and in a heavy whisper. Josh was relieved they spoke common language.

The Albejen stated that they spoke many different languages. Josh used the open dialogue to claim that they were not Salankra's agents by choice. He claimed that all they wanted was the release of their friends and to leave this world and return to their part of the universe beyond the black hole. He introduced himself and his two companions. Josh waited for an Albejen name.

No reply came from any of the Albejen, but they all clearly looked to the speaking one. Gold asked Josh what he was doing. Josh ignored Gold without even a glance and looked directly toward the lead Albejen. Josh hollered out loud enough for all to hear, and it echoed throughout the cave. He said that something was not feeling right about all this. He followed his statement with a question. He asked why the shiffo known as Salankra could not come here herself even with all her great power. He noted that nothing magical seemed to be here to prevent it because of the fact that they had gotten so close to the Albejen heart. The lead Albejen stared long at Josh before answering again in a heavy whisper, that the heart that provided life to the Albejen was immune to her magic. He added that her magic would also be drained the closer she would get to the heart. Without the heart, all Albejen everywhere, even those beyond the black hole, would die instantly. He continued to claim that the heart was a gift from their god of creation, and in addition to providing their race life, it also bound Salankra, who was an enemy of their gods, from taking her dark magic off this world of Albetha, where she would be unchecked in power and fill the universe with darkness like no other that had ever been seen.

Josh was beginning to piece it all together. There had been no recent contact with the familiar that had led them here. He then asked where their friends were located. He described Tana and Prince Steyvar. Salankra's familiar had claimed that they had been taken here. The lead Albejen replied that the last they had seen of any of them was at the Edge.

Josh questioned, "The Edge?"

The lead Albejen described the Edge as the boundary to where Salankra's magic could reach without being drained by the heart. He then claimed that Salankra had most likely taken their friends to the Center.

Josh took a quick moment to think. He then asked, "The Center? You mean her tower?"

The lead Albejen explained that the Center was the base of her power. Her magic cast on other living beings other than Albejen who were immune was all that could pass the Edge and did not last long after the crossing. He sensed that Josh, Cody, and Gold were not under her spell. He added that the shiffo herself could not maintain her mirage outside the Center. Between the Center and the Edge, she was forced to revert back to her true form. Josh guessed that her true form was what they had called her familiar. The lead Albejen stated that her true form was magic-free but impervious to harm of any kind. It could also exist separately from her mirage form. He added that it was only in her shiffo or mirage form that Salankra could be killed, but the Albejen could not enter the Center, and even if they could, Salankra's magic in that form was extremely powerful. The Center was the only place in the universe that the Albejen were prevented to go because of a pact between the shiffo and their gods.

Josh just realized now the danger their friends were in. He asked if Salankra controlled Prince Steyvar and followed the question with a repeated description of the prince. The lead Albejen claimed that Salankra could link herself to one living being and only until that being died at which time she could link to another. He added that besides the Albejen heart binding her to Albetha, the only way she could leave would be by linking herself to a being without a soul, but every being, no matter if they were good or evil, had a soul. Josh's thoughts raced to Laylee. He asked how they could slay Salankra, understanding that it could only occur in her mirage form in the tower. The reply was only the fire of the Albejen bonded with a res- urrection stone. The Albejen had their fire, but the resurrection stone was inside the tower. It would normally bring the dead to life, but it would kill Salankra if it would be destroyed by fire. Josh pulled out from his belt pouch the black stone that he had retrieved from the planet of giants and said that he had his own. The Albejen recognized the stone, and all present seemed to back away from it in fear of its great power. The lead Albejen explained that the rejuvenation stone was even more powerful than a resurrection stone. If used with the correct ceremony, it could bring back any dead to full life, no matter how long they had been dead. It, however, was not meant to be used because its price was so catastrophic to all other life around it when it was used in this manner.

Cody interrupted and asked if it could bring back Josh's brother, Jase. The lead Albejen raised his heavy whisper in panic that it must not be used. The temptation to restore life was too great. The dead would live again but would constantly be draining all other life around it. The longer the person had been dead, the more powerful the draining of all other life around it would be. Josh's own death was in moks and would likely not cause a drain. Josh said that they could not use it to restore life but changed to more of a question as he inquired if they could use it to kill Salankra. The lead Albejen believed it would work. Josh followed by asking for a fire weapon. The Albejen were very powerful but still seemed to be leery. Josh said he could kill their shiffo if they gave him their fire to do it. Upon the death of the shiffo, the Albejen by their god were required to perform one favor to those that killed it. Josh did not even need to look to his comrades. He said they wanted to go home. The lead Albejen stepped forward and offered his hand with the palm facing toward Josh. Josh did the same with his and the two palms pressed together. The human felt the coldness of the Albejen flesh, and the Albejen felt the warmness of the human touch. The deal in this manner had been sealed, and the lead Albejen with his other hand gave Josh a disengaged fire whip.

* * *

In the tower as Laylee confronted Prince Steyvar after throwing him into a wall, between them, a portal of dark-red light swirled, and from it, a mist coalesced into the shiffo known as Salankra. She stood between Prince Steyvar and Laylee as Tana made her way to her feet behind Laylee. Salankra claimed that she had no spell and that her love for Prince Steyvar was real. Prince Steyvar stepped to her side and suddenly, after a chant from Salankra, began to convulse and choke. Laylee moved toward him, but Salankra shifted her own stance to remain between them. Prince Steyvar fell backward and died as Tana stepped to Laylee's side.

Laylee screamed out at Salankra, "You killed whom you claimed to love!"

Salankra responded pleasingly, "An artificial lifeform with emotion? How rare." She continued, "Your friends have failed. I can sense that, but it is of no more concern." Salankra stepped to the side and Laylee rushed to the fallen Prince Steyvar. She confirmed to Tana that he was dead. She then used her hand to motion for Tana to step away from Salankra. Again, Salankra seemed amazed. She asked, "Compassion too? I must simply get in there."

Laylee asked, "Get in where?" Salankra claimed that she had killed a true love. That was the price, and she was now ready for her reward. She chanted and again turned to mist and surrounded Laylee in a swirling motion. Suddenly Laylee closed her eyes and reopened them as she screamed and fell to her knees. She screamed out, asking what was happening. Tana knelt beside her and tried to help by holding her. She was pushed away by Laylee's great strength. Laylee continued to scream and appeared to be in great pain, but she could not feel pain. Salankra's magic was bonding with the machine, but the machine's emotion programming was fighting back against the bonding and trying to repel the magic.

* * *

Dark Lord Epitaph was in his chambers and had found a passage in one of the many Books of Prophecy he had acquired. He read that the brothers would become united and there was a mention of one brother that would use the rejuvenation stone. Epitaph was frantically searching through the other books for some more prophecies that could add to it and make sense. He only grew angrier when he could find nothing.

He was interrupted by a comm from Fright Agent Paj stating that they had arrived at Kemyyo and that the weapon was being prepped. Epitaph calmed his rage and responded that he wished to bear witness. After one more calming breath, he stated that he would be on the command deck shortly.

* * *

As Emelia was on approach to the coordinates with her Black Guard forces, they saw the shuttle lifting off. It was a Luth Bik-style shuttle with its designation unknown. There was also no planetary registration for any Luth Bik vessel in this area.

Fright Agent Maddo was monitoring the situation from orbit in the lead blockade ship and projected an approach vector plotted to enter toward the lower levels of Xotosia City. Emelia ordered a precise planetary bombardment around the shuttle. She reminded him that she was on the ground as well and that the bombardment needed to be very precise as to avoid her assembly of forces. Fright Agent Maddo assured her that she would be safe. Two laser Head soldiers had joined Emelia with one at each of her sides. There was heavy impact of the bombs dropping from orbit of the planet and screeched like angry ghosts through its sky. The bombs seemed to hit close to the Luth Bik shuttle, but the shuttle was practicing aggressive evasion tactics and dodging each bomb. Despite the effort, the shuttle still headed toward Xotosia City. Emelia ordered the bombardment ceased for starfighters to enter and take the shuttle. She ordered her captain of command to proceed with troops and vehicles to Xotosia City.

* * *

Josh, Cody, and Gold rode at a hurried pace on creatures provided by the Albejen. They were called mystees and resembled large wolves with sharp quilled fur all around the saddled area. Their tails were without the sharp fur but hosted a thick skin and three prong-like daggers rested at the end of the tail. They had easily traversed the hills, and the tower fortress came into view. Josh ordered the riding pace increased. They each crouched down tighter against their mounts and jostled the reigns to summon the increase in speed, and the mystees responded.

* * *

Laylee continued to scream out as Salankra's mist form had fully consumed her and intensified its bonding attempt. Laylee's programming was still fighting the bonding process of the magic but was beginning to fail. Tana had taken a club weapon, moved in and attacked Laylee with a vicious savage rage.

The mist form abandoned Laylee's android body as it collapsed, and Laylee's own programming was shutting it down as a final defensive action. The mist reconstituted to Salankra's female form. With both hands outstretched and a chant, a force of strong gusting wind hit Tana and tossed her firmly against the wall with enough impact to shatter the stone bricks.

Salankra slowly walked toward Tana, who was stunned by the impact and shook her head to regain her senses. Tana then fell into convulsions as Salankra chanted and mentally choked her. Salankra suddenly stopped and became alerted to something. She used another chant and opened a viewing portal in the air ahead of her. Through the viewing portal, she saw Josh, Cody, and Gold dismount from their mystees and approach the moat around her stone tower fortress.

They stood at the edge of the moat. The drawbridge was up, and it appeared that this time they were not going to be allowed in without force. Cody asked how they would get inside. Josh said the Albejen had secretly given him a few toys besides the fire whip. Josh pulled out a thick but flat device and pulled at each end of it. A shadow fell from it and crawled to the edge. It stretched over and above the moat and created a bridge made of solid shadow to connect to the drawbridge door. Josh then pulled out a small metal sphere. It was cold to the touch like the handle of the fire whip. He activated the sphere with the pressing of three buttons. He directly faced the door and threw the sphere upward. It exploded in midair into an intense fireball shot toward the drawbridge door and set it aflame. The fireball was so powerful that it burned through the door quickly and started to slowly dissipate after its target had been destroyed. Josh activated the fire whip. Cody and Gold readied their weapons as well and charged inside. The two razorback dog creatures came running directly at them in full rage and attack mode. One of them leapt at Gold with his fangs ready to bite but was stunned and temporarily paralyzed by Gold's raised honson stick. The other quickly pounced onto Cody. Cody had dropped his longsword in the attack but had fangs of his own to his defense. The two rolled across the floor, snapping and biting with their snouts of sharp teeth. Cody was able to get the lethal bite and was helped back to his feet by Josh's open hand.

Salankra arrived before them in her mist form and coalesced back to her aged woman appearance. She followed her magical appearance act immediately with a chant, and Gold was encased in a red glowing energy sphere that started to collapse around him. Cody quickly drew his blaster pistol, and Josh again engaged the fire whip. Salankra again shifted into her mist form with a slightly different chant. Josh stepped forward to the swirling mist and struck it with a lash from the fire whip having no apparent effect. Cody moved to examine the collapsing red sphere and devise an escape as it was beginning to crush Gold inside its shrinking form much like a singularity. Cody dropped his blaster pistol as he was snared by surprise by a long red serpent that had risen from the floor behind him and quickly entwined itself around him. The spiked head of the serpent poised for a strike then stabbed into his left eye. He screamed out in pain and fell to the ground as the red serpent released its grip and burrowed back into the cracks on the stone surface floor. Josh had disengaged the fire whip and rushed to Cody's side on the floor as blood poured from where his eye once rested. He placed the whip to the floor and looked back to Gold, screaming for help as the red singularity sphere continued to collapse in on itself. In one bright flash of crimson red light, the sphere was gone and so was Gold. As soon as the singularity sphere had vanished and taken Gold with it, Josh started choking and clutching at his throat as if he was being strangled by some unseen force. Salankra's swirling mist form had again transformed to her old woman form, and she stood there in full defiance to their attempted attack.

Josh looked up at Salankra as she stood over him and with another chant intensified her mental choke on him. He was starting to black out when he was suddenly released from the mental grip when Salankra presented a most agonizing scream. Tana had reached the tower's base level and stabbed into Salankra's back with her clawed hands. Salankra pulled free and turned to face Tana with a chant that produced an incredible stream of red acid that shot from her mouth and scorched Tana's body. Tana dropped with smoldering burns across her fur-covered body, and Salankra again turned to finish Josh off, but Josh was gone. She walked to where Gold had vanished and back to Cody, who was coiled up and still clutching at his gouged-out eye socket. She turned again and hollered out, "Where are you?"

She then felt his presence. Josh had moved to the staircase and was slowly trying to crawl up the stairs. Salankra performed another chant that collapsed the staircase. It fell to the floor with Josh under it. Salankra looked around again at all the fallen then slowly strode over to the staircase debris. She stood over the debris that pinned Josh. He struggled to pull out the rejuvenation stone. Salankra was surprised but still laughed and followed with a chant that caused the stone to levitate into her awaiting palm. She let out a cackle more than a laugh and asked, "Was regeneration in reverse seriously the Albejen plan?" She clutched the stone tightly, and with a chant, it crumbled in her hand and fell as black dust to her feet. Another chant flung the staircase rubble from Josh. A different chant now seemed to cause Josh even more pain as he felt himself being ripped apart from the inside.

Cody had recovered, although still bleeding from his left eye socket. He heard the screams from his friend Josh. Cody grabbed the whip that was at his side and crawled along the stone floor and moved closer toward Salankra. Her concentration was focused heavily on ripping Josh apart and she did not notice Cody activate the fire whip. He pulled himself up to his knees and readied the fire whip. With a single lash, he had struck the crumbled stone dust spread out around Salankra's feet. The stone dust ignited in flame instantly. The flames rose up all around her and turned black as they did. The black flames engulfed her and seemed to constrict like vines around her body. She was dragged to the ground, and as the stone dust burned away, all that was left was black and red ash where Salankra once stood.

Josh had fallen silent. Cody stood up and walked to Josh. He knelt beside an unconscious Josh and looked back at Tana. She had rolled around on the floor and neutralized the burning acid. Her naked body had only singed fur. Cody then looked back at where Gold had vanished. He was a bit shocked but relieved when Josh reached up and clutched at his arm. Tana also rushed and knelt to Josh's side. The ripping pain he had experienced had ceased with Salankra's death. Tana told them that Laylee was upstairs.

* * *

The weapon at Kemyyo was transferred from the *Grimm One* to Epitaph's ship, the *Darkfall*, and was fired onto the planet. Something else in the wave emitted from the weapon also occurred. The weapon started to suck the atmosphere from the planet. The docking ring built around the entire planet that was once an engineering marvel started to break apart and each piece burned up as it did. The planet itself started to slowly crumble away. Fright Agent Paj spoke to Epitaph over a crackling ship's comms system and stated that there were unusual readings. Epitaph ordered the process continued. As the crew on the ship watched the planet crumble away, they heard a loud female scream that sounded more like a cackle. The Black Guard fleet of ships started to tremble. The planet had crumbled completely away, and now a wide and long tear seemed to be ripping at the fabric of space. The force that was ripping apart the stars and space itself to a white glow was also starting to affect everything else. The ships in the fleet reported shield failure as they too started to be shredded. Epitaph ordered the helmsmen of all ships to pull away.

Chapter Seventeen

Raising a Rebellion

THE BATTLE FOR Xotosia City had begun as Emelia led a Black Guard foot soldier army. Black Guard schisms provided air support and attacked the Luth Bik Shuttle, while Emelia marched in with combat vehicles at each flank of her Black Guard soldiers and Laser Heads. A squadron of Black Guard schisms, intensified the attack on the Luth Bik shuttle. The Luth Bik shuttle revealed its pulsar cannon weaponry and flew off as two more undetected Luth Bik stealth shuttles flew in and engaged the Black Guard squadron with a surprise retaliation.

Luth Bik Captain-at-Arms Karys was on the first shuttle and directed the assault. Another surprise was on the ground. Silos Taqoon and the rebellion founders had rallied their ground troops and poured out from the buildings to clash against Emelia and her Black Guard troops under the ongoing air battle. Emelia ordered Fright Agent Maddo to unleash a planetary bombardment around the perimeter of the battle as a distraction for the rebel forces.

* * *

The echo of the dead shiffo's screaming cackle was heard again as coming out from her ashes began a white light tear expanding upward. With the staircase destroyed, Tana and Cody had jumped up to the next level. Josh stayed back and looked directly into the tear and saw a figure which briefly appeared to be that of Gold Gatling, but the image quickly blurred. Josh reached into the tear. The pain was intense and burnt with some kind of radiation. He saw a shadowed male form just as he was about to pull his arm out. Josh cried out for Gold to grab onto his hand.

* * *

Mortigan was on the *Fallen Star* and had arrived at a safe reach from the black hole. Binia as the autopilot had rested the *Dark Wish* alongside the *Fallen Star*. Mortigan and Binia got no readings from the Black Hole. The homing system between the neural link of Josh Broody and the *Fallen Star* was last detected here at this point. The question that Mortigan and Binia had discussed was if Josh had somehow entered the black hole by choice or not, and if so, what lay beyond it.

The conversation was aborted when two tears of white light in the fabric of space, one on each side of the black hole, started to open and started consumption of the area around them including the black hole. Space was ripping apart in front of them. Readings on the ship scanners were off the chart. Mortigan and Binia felt the pulls toward the tears and used all evasive maneuvers and power strains to retreat with their ships.

* * *

The Black Guard blockade in space around Xotosia was taken by surprise as from hyperspace portals, exited a fleet of mixed-race starships. They were led by Luth Bik battle cruisers and engaged the Black Guard blockade ships immediately upon entry. Fright Agent Maddo ordered all still-docked schisms to be launched and a full retaliation with all gun ports. The space battle became fierce fast as all warships and starfighters opened up with all the firepower and maneuvers within their arsenal and tactics. The Black Guard was taken by surprise initially and caught off guard, but they were far better armed and war ready to hold their own. Fright Agent Maddo ordered the planetary bombardment halted in order to focus on the attacking forces and strengthen the defense of the blockade ships.

* * *

Fright Agent Nehih in the confiscated palace was monitoring the ground battle when the planetary bombardment halted. He was then made aware of a communication loss with the orbiting blockade after the initiation of the space battle had been reported. Emelia was screaming over the operating comms for reinforcements from the palace and for the planetary bombardment to continue. Fright Agent Nehih continued to assess the ground and space battles on his scanners. The Black Guard forces on both fronts were holding strong for the moment but taking heavy damages. A Black Guard captain had reported readiness to take reinforcements to Emelia. Fright Agent Nehih held the order and instructed the captain to have his forces remain and strengthen the defense of the palace. He then commed for Emelia to fall back with her forces. Emelia refused to retreat and surrender the city. Her path back to the palace was through the rebels, so she could not retreat if she had wanted to do so. She ordered Fright Agent Nehih to have the palace forces attack the rear of the rebel formation. Her call for assistance from the blockade ships remained unanswered.

In the palace, the Black Guard captain declared to Fright Agent Nehih that it was a good and possible strategy to move on the rebellion's rear flank as Emelia had suggested. He added that his forces were ready to act. Just then, a report came in of a Black Guard warship that had been destroyed and was falling through the atmosphere. Emelia had seen it firsthand in the sky through the dueling Black Guard schisms and Luth Bik starfighters referred to as shards because of their diamond-shaped appearance. The Black Guard schisms departed the skirmish with the Luth Bik shards in pursuit.

The schisms flew upward through the falling debris to the recall orders from Fright Agent Maddo to defend the blockade.

Despite her screaming orders over the comms, Emelia could only watch her air support flee through the falling debris in the sky. All around her, the Black Guard forces were dropping. The Laser Heads had tightened formation around her as the combat vehicles and soldiers fell. Emelia's tone of anger was cracked and coming across the comms more now as a desperate plea for any support. Reports followed of another Black Guard warship losing orbiting control and doing all it could to pull away and not fall into the planet's atmosphere. The scanners and displays continued to show Black Guard starships and ground forces depleting from the screens. The Black Guard captain was still ready to take his ground forces to aid Emelia but was shocked by Fright Agent Nehih's orders to hold the palace until he was clear. He also ordered a security detail to assure his escape and a shuttle to be readied at once.

* * *

The Black Guard warships at the former position of the planet Kemyyo were reporting more tears created all around them and Black Guard warships being torn apart. Epitaph ordered a full retreat. He again heard the cackle and screams and recalled a prophecy he had read: "The cackling laughs from a fallen witch will be the sign of the ripping end." He was then frozen in a trance amid all the chaos across the command deck. He experienced another vision. This vision showed Josh Broody pulling someone from the other side of a spatial rift. He could not see whom Josh was pulling through, but the prophecy of uniting brothers seemed to be ringing clear in his thoughts.

* * *

Josh was screaming for Gold to grab his hand as the rift became increasingly more painful and his arm was burning. Cody and Tana were on the ledge on the level above him and pleaded for Josh to let him go and pull out. Suddenly, Josh saw the blurred form clearing as the shadowed form fell from a cliff. He could also hear other voices screaming for the loss of this person, but he was unable to make them all clear. The shadow human form was falling, but Josh was able to grasp it. He believed it was Gold and hollered out for Gold to stop struggling so he could pull him through. Cody and Tana had jumped back to the main floor, and both of them grabbed onto Josh and pulled him from the tearing rift. Josh had pulled someone else out with him, who was thrown free from Josh's grasp and landed face down away from them. Josh's left arm was scarred with radiation burns, and the fallen person he had pulled through seemed to be smoldering from the burns on his backside. Josh, Cody, and Tana huddled together as they watched the male humanoid form slowly stand up as if unaffected by the radiation burns. His back remained toward them, and the armor burned away from his right arm revealed a full metal arm. There was also a heavy technical-filled gauntlet fastened to his lower left arm. He had long black hair that ran to his shoulders, and his remaining but tattered armor was two shades of green. He turned and saw Josh, Cody, and Tana standing before him. His facial skin seemed to be healing before their very eyes. He was clean-shaven and very handsome. He asked what had happened and where he was at. Josh did not know what had happened but remembered a passage he had read in a Book of Prophecy of a tear through space where one would come.

The man seemed shocked and angered. He asked Josh, "How do you know of the Books of Prophecy? Are you working for the Dark Lord Epitaph?"

Josh claimed he once did but had seen his errors. He then asked the human male stranger, "How do you know of the dark lord? Who are you?"

The man answered, "I am the Minister of the Books of Prophecy. You can call me Slade."

Chapter Eighteen

Prophecies Come to Pass

THE TEAR OR rift in space from which Slade was pulled was beginning to expand. Slade looked back at it and simultaneously with Josh said, "We have to go!" They started to flee, but Josh remembered Laylee. Cody and Tana leapt back up to the next floor and told Josh and Slade to run. Cody and Tana found Laylee still powered down. The tower was beginning to collapse with the energy tear. As the tower crumbled down around them, Tana became lost in thought. If she would leave Laylee here, she could be with Josh. It was a split-second thought, but she knew it was wrong to think that way. She was snapped out of her thoughts by Cody pleading with her to help him. Tana threw one arm over her shoulder, and Cody did the same with the other as they dragged Laylee's feet across the ground. They had leapt downward to the main floor and rushed through the stone and wood debris falling down all around them.

Cody's excellent hearing could hear Gold's voice calling for someone to help him even through the entire tower collapsing. The rift was opening wider, and they were feeling the pull. There was nothing they could do for Gold. Cody and Tana pushed forward, still dragging Laylee. They ran across the solid shadow bridge as the rift swallowed the last of the crumbling tower behind them. Josh and

Slade ran toward them as the rift opened wider and seemed to pull on them. Josh pulled Cody free and took Laylee's arm. The rift was like a wave and rushed down on them. Slade and Cody jumped forward as the rift raced over them and seemed to consume Josh, Tana, and Laylee.

Suddenly, Josh and Tana found themselves displaced and were now running down a starship corridor. They each still had one of Laylee's arms draped around their necks as the corridor behind them was being consumed by the rift. There was no time to wonder how they had gotten here, and Josh told Tana to keep moving. They rounded the ship's corridor to find several Derths fleeing for escape pods and paying no mind to them. The Derths were more worried of saving themselves than their new food supply. The Derths were large lumbering humanoid forms, a carnivore race with a deep hunting culture. They were a bit taller than the average human. They were a reptilian type of species with dark-orange skin. They had two sharp claws on their two-pointed toes of their feet. They had two very muscular legs and a long, heavy-looking tail dragging behind each warrior. The tails hosted a large spear-like tip. Their roughly scaled skin grew smoother at the chest level, which seemed to be protected by a hard-smooth shell. Their two arms were very muscular as well, and at the end of each were hands with a thumb and four fingers. The claws at the tip of each one appeared to be razor sharp like those on the toes. Running from their shoulders up to each side of their head was a hard-red bone fin type appendage. Another one ran from the top of their head down along their back spine. Their eyes were narrowed with vertical pupils. Their ears and noses were without lobes. Their savagery was even more heightened by the saliva that dripped from their sharp razor formed teeth and matched as well with a viscous hiss and snarl.

Josh and Tana found an open lift tube shaft as the rift rounded the corner behind them. The rift had split and another rift was coming up the shaft as well, but there was another open door about two levels down and still above the rising rift. Tana took Laylee's arm from around Josh's shoulder and flung Laylee over both of her shoulders. Josh looked at her and Tana told him to climb down. Josh grabbed onto the service rungs at the inner walls of the shaft and climbed toward the open passage two levels down. Tana looked down at him and back at the approaching rift behind her and the rising rift below her. Tana yelled for Josh to hurry.

Josh lost his grip on one of the climbing rungs and started to fall. He reached out to another one. Despite the pull on his shoulders, he was able to reach it and pull himself up. The fall had actually gained him ground as he stabilized his balance and side stepped into the open doorway. He looked up two levels and across toward the opposite wall. Tana had already begun her leap with one rift descending behind her and the other upward. Josh grabbed onto a loose and power-free cable as a tether and wrapped it quickly around his foot before reaching outward to catch Tana from her downward plunge. Tana's leap was impressive. Josh had to be swift and reached out, gaining a hold of her waist and pulled her in from the shaft. She fell from his arms and rolled forward, releasing Laylee's unconscious body from her shoulders upon impact with the floor.

Josh's successful catch of Tana had pulled her inward but sent him off the ledge. He dangled just above the rising rift that ascended the lift tube shaft toward him with another in descent from above. The cable that had entwined around his foot had prevented him from falling into them. He reached back upward and grabbed onto the cable with his hands and loosened the hold on his foot. He then used all his upper body strength and, with one hand over the other, climbed up the cable and into the doorway where Tana stood and helped pull him through.

* * *

As the rift in space continued to expand, all ships in the area could only back away from the epicenter which was where the planet of Kemyyo used to be. Despite the chaos and retreating ships, the Black Guard scientists were still on task and taking readings on the event. Fright Agent Paj was overseeing the scientific part of the weapon results. Epitaph continued to watch the event, recalling the prophecy now of a tear in space that would unite the two brothers. He now realized that he may have unleashed his own undoing. He ordered the Prophetess that he had earlier killed to be brought to the command deck immediately. After her death, Epitaph had her body secured because Shrows were granted two lives, as long as their bodies remained intact. The regeneration process from the first to second life was lengthy, but he had been informed that she had regained consciousness and her broken neck had finally regenerated just a rotation ago. The Black Guard soldiers that stood at each of his sides moved off to fulfill his command. Epitaph then commed Fright Agent Kyrak and inquired on the search for Josh Broody.

Amid all the ongoing chaos, Fright Agent Kyrak aboard the *Bloodbath* was shocked that his dark lord commander was still concerned about Josh Broody. He replied back with a question of why the search for Josh Broody was a bigger concern than the disaster Epitaph himself had just created.

The reply was heard by Fright Agent Paj as well over Epitaph's comms. The response of questioning the dark lord was unheard of by a fright agent, but the addition of blame upon Epitaph was even more unthinkable.

Epitaph's response was one of irritation and anger. He responded, "The sssearch for Josssh Broody isss your only conccccern! I want the sssearch exxxpanded for any evidenccce of Jassse Broody'sss resssurrectttion from the dead asss well! If you can't perform thisss sssimple tasssk, I will find sssomeone who can!" The last sentence was the only warning Fright Agent Kyrak would get. Replacement of a fright agent only meant death by execution before a new one would be named. Fright Agent Kyrak groveled over the comms with an apology cited in a trembling voice.

Epitaph left the apology open and simply added, "Find the brothersss by the end of the rotatttion and I will disssregard your accusssatttion toward my fault in thisss crisssisss." The remark was taken more as a warning than a deadline. Everyone, especially fright agents knew that the accusation would not be forgotten. Fright Agent Kyrak's inspiration to find the brothers had grown, as he could only hope that finding them would alleviate the level of his punishment. Epitaph then hollered out to Fright Agent Paj without looking back at him and asked if he had found any way to stop this event. Fright Agent Paj replied in the negative. Epitaph then calmly strode down the ramp and back toward Fright Agent Paj, who was struck with a nervous state upon the approach. Once they were face to face, Epitaph screamed at him to do so. Fright Agent Paj bowed his head and cowered away from Epitaph. Once back at the science station, he regained his stature with the scientists and threatened to have one of them spaced out every half ara the crisis was not solved.

* * *

Mortigan sat on the *Fallen Star* at his position at the black-hole with space tearing around it. Binia was taking rapid readings of the event aboard the *Dark Wish*. Binia reported several distorted and overlapped transmissions. The tear was growing closer to the black hole, which may have been the cause of the disruptions. Mortigan asked Binia if she could clear the transmissions up. Binia reported back that she had already begun to separate the overlaps, but the rift was still distorting them. Mortigan ordered them sent and played on the *Fallen Star* so he could hear and evaluate them. As the garbled transmissions sounded, he was able to make out one word: "Gatling." He had Binia cross-reference the name as it sounded familiar. Upon the view screen, the image of the famed Honsho pirate called Gold Gatling was displayed along with his datafile.

Suddenly, the lights on the *Fallen Star's* consoles flashed in an alert. Mortigan's attention focused on them. He reported to Binia that Josh Broody was somewhere just over the Derth spatial border at sector 51-52-19-4B. He ordered her to take the *Dark Wish* there as the *Fallen Star* was already preparing to engage a plotted course. It changed on its backward moving flight path, sharply turned, and darted into a hyperspace portal. The *Dark Wish* piloted by Binia had started to plot the course and also jumped into hyperspace shortly afterward, leaving the tear to consume the black hole.

Literally the entire planet of Albetha was trembling and slowly falling into the rift. Cody and Slade had made their way over a rocky hill and managed to ride the panicked mystees just ahead of the ripping rift in their pursuit. They managed to gain control of the mounted creatures just as a large Albejen warship flew over them. It was long with a curled-down vulture-style beak at its front and lined with several forward pointed wing formations that could reverse to a backward point formation as needed to adjust for planetary atmosphere. It also seemed to have a circular armored shell-like formation for its topside. It turned at a high elevation in the sky and swooped back down toward them. It slowed its descent and leveled off to hover above the ground in front of them as it swirled around the dirt, loose rock and dry grass beneath it. A tunnel-shaped boarding ramp was lowered. Cody directed Slade as they rode up the ramp and entered the ship. The tunnel-shaped boarding ramp detracted, and the ship began a backward ascension as it rose away from the oncoming rift, eating the planet and space in its path.

* * *

Well removed from any of the space ripping events at least for the time being was the planet Xotosia. The Luth Bik-aided rebellion had broken through the planetary blockade as the Black Guard ships fell and retreated away. More forces were making their way to the planet's surface, where they joined Xotosia's citizens in resistance. Androids and living denizens of the planet were rising up against the Black Guard and being armed by the Luth Bik Resistance movement.

Emelia was not ready to surrender and fought more fiercely through the lines with the Laser Heads around her using their full red glowing spherical heads to fire in all needed directions. As robots, they were programmed to never retreat or surrender without high ranking orders. Some of the Black Guard soldiers and vehicles had fallen back, but a squad remained up front with Emelia.

A Black Guard combat hover tank moved forward with a thunderous and heavy blow to the Luth Bik ground forces. A Luth Bik commander was caught directly in the blast. The Laser Heads surrounded Emelia and barricaded her with their armored bodies and 360 degrees of angle for laser fire from their red energy spherical heads. Their robotic and armored bodies moved with her stride and acted as shields.

Emelia had holstered her blaster pistols, and with her anger as her strength and her blade as her weapon, she was cutting her way straight forward to the fallen command center. When needed, she drew on her hatred for Josh Broody to inspire or to carry on, but her motivation to not fail seemed strong enough for the moment.

Clad Byar and Toxicus Forn had been the first to escape the command center rubble and came out shooting with a full barrage of heavy blaster rifle fire. The Laser Heads around Emelia shifted position and zoned in as they intensified their own laser blasts and dropped Toxicus Forn with no mercy. Clad Byar was heavily wounded and knocked free from the blast effect and utilized the smoke and debris as cover to crawl around the back of all the rubble from which he had previously escaped.

Emelia pushed through and leapt forward over the dead body of Toxicus Forn and landed down and inside the narrow passage rubble made tunnel. She hollered up her orders for the Laser Heads to secure the perimeter. Four Black Guard soldiers jumped down to Emelia and followed her through the passage.

This passage was the only way out, and Emelia was slashing down the rebel fighters with her katana-like blade as they could only flee toward her. She made her way deeper inside, where there was a wider range of movement possibility. She easily slashed her way through two charging male model androids sent at her by Silos Taqoon, who himself cowered behind a sultry female model android. Emelia quickly drew her blaster pistol with her rotted hand and blasted away at the android's head several times until it staggered away. She then blasted at it again working her way down the construct's form until it collapsed and its internal blinking lights shut down. Emelia then ordered the Black Guard soldiers onto Silos as she claimed she did not slay cowards. The Black Guard soldiers did as ordered and blasted away with heavy firepower at Silos Taqoon.

Emelia had leapt up to an elevated walking ledge that appeared to be stable. She stood over the Luth Bik Captain-at-Arms Karys, who was pinned by debris. Emelia shot him a long stare before thanking him for returning her fury. As a reward, she promised him an honorable death as opposed to slowly dying in a pile of rubble. She then holstered her blaster pistol again and, with both her hands, tightly gripped around the hilt of her katana-like blade, and in one downward swing, she swiftly removed his head from his shoulders.

The four Black Guard soldiers had been identifying the other dead in the fallen bunker. They were able to identify the other resistance founder as the druglord, Clad Byar. The only founder that had managed an escape was the gambler crimelord, Madaray Vilici. Despite that, Emelia ordered the soldiers to get the news of all rebellion founders found dead into the communication network.

Emelia was then commed from Fright Agent Maddo, who declared that a strange rift had opened in a far orbit of the planet and had hit many of the Luth Bik Resistance ships. Although the tide of battle had turned against them, he noted that it could grow worse as the rift was widening and moving closer toward Xotosia. Emelia ordered him to withdraw and reassemble at the other side of the planet and at a safe distance. She also ordered the fleet to keep any resistance ships engaged as long as they could during the action of withdraw. She then ordered the Black Guard soldiers to follow her back out. Their next objective was to return to the confiscated palace. Emelia commed Fright Agent Nehih to no reply. She knew that she needed to get to the palace for secure communication with Epitaph, and she ordered the soldiers with her to pick up their pace.

* * *

Epitaph's presence on the command deck of the *Darkfall* had cast like a shadow of overlooking doom onto Fright Agent Paj and his scientists busily at work trying to reverse the effects of their super weapon. Epitaph looked past them and outward through the viewport as the Black Guard Fury Fleet retreated away from the growing tear in the fabric of space.

Epitaph's focus was broken as two Black Guard soldiers brought the female dwarf-like Shrow Prophetess to him at a distanced gunpoint as instructed. She looked outward as well at the impending doom to the universe. She remained with her stare on the events in space around them as she stated the blame for unleashing the universe's end rested solely on Epitaph. Epitaph slowly stepped toward her, towering above her and let out a stern and prolonged hiss before stating that this couldn't be the end. He followed the statement with his usual lisp in voice by asking her how to stop it. She replied in a confident tone that only the brothers would stop it, and once they had done so, his downfall would then be inevitable.

Epitaph replied, "So it is true? They are together?" After a pause in thought, he stated that together they will die this time. He believed that once he destroyed the brothers, the prophecy would be broken and all would be set back rightly. The Prophetess laughed. Epitaph hissed and flicked his forked tongue at her as he asked what she found so amusing. The Prophetess had her powers return with her second life and claimed she had a clouded and unclear vision that the brothers were alive, but they were not the brothers he thought them to be.

Epitaph grew enraged and hissed again. He stated, "Josssh and Jassse were mentttioned in the prophecccy!"

The Prophetess smiled. Although the vision she had was clouded, she admitted that Josh was a key, but his brother was another. Epitaph had grown tired of her riddle speak as he now experienced a blurred vision of his own in her presence. He could see Josh, but the other was a blur. He ordered the two Black Guard soldiers to remove her from him for now.

* * *

As the rift had nearly consumed the black hole, one large Albejen warship was taking heavy damage as it attempted its escape from the phenomenon. Albejen tech to escape the pull of a black hole was severely hampered by the growing rift. Cody and Slade could only stand on the command deck as the Albejen worked diligently to save their ship.

Cody told Slade that they would need to find Josh once they were free. Slade mentioned that Josh could not have survived. Cody had recalled a prophecy of the two brothers that would rise against the dark lord. Slade looked at Cody in a puzzled state. He asked Cody of how he knew of this specific prophecy. Cody dodged the question and replied not with an answer but a statement that Slade should know of it as well. Slade had not read of it in his Book of Prophecy but was somehow at that exact moment recalling a memory of it. It was a new memory, not one he had but almost newly implanted into his mind. He questioned back to Cody, "Josh is not my brother?"

Slade, with that remark out loud, had suddenly become aware. He was a brother. The prophecy that he had never read was now clear. The two brothers would destroy the dark lord. It never said that they were brothers to each other.

Chapter Nineteen

Mortigan's Fall

ON THE DERTH ship, Josh and Tana had escaped the lift tube shaft, but the rift was tearing rapidly through the Derth ship. It was strange to see the Derths ignoring their primal instincts of devouring the meat source and being in more of a panicked and fleeing mode. Josh and Tana had again scooped up Laylee's powered down body state and thrown one arm around each of their shoulders as they dragged her away. Laylee may have appeared to be skinny and sexy, but her Simulent body was a heavy load to carry.

All escape pods seemed to have been previously jettisoned, and the last shuttle in sight had just been boarded by Derths and about to lift off. A run to the shuttle as a food source running up to a shuttle full of carnivores did not seem like a great idea. Tana looked to Josh, who had still not reacted to her declaration of love for him. Even now in their moment of despair, Josh was attempting the best he could to avoid eye contact. Tana asked what they were going to do just as the rift tore further into and started to devour what was left of the Derth humpbacked shaped warship. Josh's attention remained focused on the Derth shuttle that had lifted off and was departing the launch bay that was also crumbling down all around it. Josh told Tana not to worry. He was not sure how it was operational, but he had a ride coming.

The *Fallen Star* had exited a hyperspace portal across the Derth border and was in sight of the crumbling humpbacked Derth warship. It seemed to pick up speed as it approached the distressed vessel. Mortigan had been letting the small freighter ship fly on autopilot with its destination controlled by Josh's neural link. As the *Fallen Star* approached the Derth humpbacked ship, it opened a full barrage of its laser fire on two Derth shuttle ships. It was enough to not make them retaliate with an attack but to force them to dodge from the *Fallen Star's* path. The small freighter ship then made a sharp turn vector and flew directly into what was left of the collapsing Derth ship's launch bay. Mortigan's excitement grew alongside that of his adrenaline rush from the *Fallen Star's* maneuvers as he knew the ship would be retrieving his elusive bounty prize. Mortigan decided to hide in the ship's engine area. The freighter entered a low hover over the floor of the Derth launch bay. The rampway was extended downward as Josh and Tana both leapt onto it still with Laylee's motionless body draped over their shoulders. The ramp retracted and the boarding hatch door closed. Tana took Laylee from Josh and laid her down across a long lounge seat in the ship's commune center. She then began to use the ship's med center to treat the acid burns over her body and singed fur. Josh ran to the cockpit and released the neural link and took direct control of the ship's flight controls.

The ship made a jagged flight path outward as the rift split, expanded, and consumed the last of the Derth ship behind it. The *Fallen Star* was now in a direct conflict with the pull of the rift. Josh had plotted a quick hyperspace course, but the ship was unable to pull free enough from the now multiple rifts in order to engage. Tana had entered the cockpit with minimal burnt fur and acid scarring on her naked body. Josh told her to strap herself in at the copilot chair. As she did so, Josh released an array of rockets from the rear of the freighter. Each rocket had a simultaneous self-detonation that caused a large enough explosion to push the *Fallen Star* free and directly into an open hyperspace portal. The hyperspace portal closed behind the ship, and the *Fallen Star* was safely away as the rifts consumed the previous position of the hyperspace portal. Mortigan's ship, the *Dark Wish*, had exited its hyperspace portal directly into the now crossing rifts in that area of space where the *Fallen Star* had just fled. The *Dark Wish* was crushed and pulled into the rifts. Binia's programming, as a result of the ship's impending destruction, was also shutting down.

* * *

Epitaph had approached Fright Agent Paj with the scientists and asked if they had found a solution yet. Fright Agent Paj respectfully admitted that they had not yet but needed more time. Epitaph started the reply with a chanting of a strange incantation, "Ssaiyai lissith ffleess copssnaith!" One of the scientists, as a result, instantly clutched at his chest and collapsed to the floor, screaming in pain. Epitaph's head tossed back, and his mouth stretched open extremely wide. The clothing of the scientist began to disintegrate away in burning flame. The flesh and muscle tissue of the scientist then did the same as he dropped and twitched on the floor. The scientist's blood materialized and gushed from Epitaph's open palm to form a pool at his feet. Simultaneously, the scientist's bodily organs began to materialize one by one in the widened and opened mouth of Epitaph. Each organ then fell one after the other down inside Epitaph's bulging throat and disappeared into the digestive system. The brain was the last to go in order for the scientist to be aware that he was being devoured. Epitaph's head then flung forward, and his mouth returned to its normal state. With the usual lisp in his voice, Epitaph declared to Fright Agent Paj that he had another half ara or he would be short yet one more scientist to continue the project.

The chief helmswoman at the pilot station reported the rift intensity was growing and the rift itself was again splitting. She suggested a hyperspace jump away. Epitaph stated that they needed to stay ahead of the now multiple rifts but could not leave the central epicenter until they could stop it. The chief helmswoman insisted. Epitaph ordered the senior command deck officer to terminate the cowardly pilot's life. After a heavy energy blast was heard over the comms, Epitaph declared that as long as the rifts were tearing through space, there was no place to go. You could not plot a successful hyperspace jump if your destination would be torn apart before you would get there. He looked back again at Fright Agent Paj and stated even more firmly that they needed that solution soon.

Fright Agent Kyrak commed in on Epitaph and stated that he had broken coordinates on a transmission involving the bounty hunter Mortigan that he was closing in on Josh Broody, but the rifts were causing distortion and hampering communication. Fright Agent Kyrak admitted that he felt they needed to leave this area. All eyes were on Epitaph. Epitaph surveyed his surroundings in the room. He looked back toward Fright Agent Paj and ordered him to continue to search for a closure of the rifts. Epitaph then through the comms instructed the command deck to plot a hyperspace course at least six sectors away and double check the stability of the path and exit. Despite the danger he had cited before, Epitaph knew he had to find Josh Broody.

* * *

The rifts continued to rip into the black hole, and the Albejen warship caught in the storm was breaking apart, nearly crumbling in on itself. Many of the Albejen crew were now dropping into piles of a chalky white dust. Cody was realizing that the single heart on their planet that they all drew life from must have been in the process of destruction by the rifts.

One thing that Slade knew about the Albejen warships was a secret that the Albejen thought only they knew. There was a battle in the orbit of Slade's planet that he stated was literally named "Home" after a long journey there from many other previous worlds taken by the Ubides and Derths. During that battle, there was an encounter with an Albejen warship. Slade had managed to board it and witnessed that the ship had a secondary feature beyond its incredibly powerful weaponry. It could actually separate into two different ships. Slade told Cody to follow him as they ran to a shaft, and they climbed up to the next level. The Albejen here were also rapidly dropping into the chalky white dust, but Slade and Cody made it into a room before the doors slid securely closed and locked. The lighting was flickering about the oval-shaped deck. Slade was able to navigate to the central control panel and, with his knowledge of the ship functions, was able to initiate the ship's separation process. Cody took position at the pilot console as the upper shell formation of the Albejen ship broke away and lifted upward. At that instant, the rifts had fully consumed the rest of the Albejen warship.

Cody was still somewhat unfamiliar with the Albejen tech, but with what he and Slade both knew, they were able to identify basic ship functions. Slade had taken position at the copilot console. The Albejen consoles had no chairs. Everything seemed to be manned from a standing position. Slade ignited the thrusters that shot with a sonic blast and propelled the movement of the upper Albejen shell ship. Slade then asked where they needed to go in order to find Josh. Cody said he was already on it. Each hyperspace course he plotted seemed to be unstable or the exit point was no longer in existence. He fumbled through many of them before finding a stable course, at least for that moment. As long as it did not break apart while they were in it, they should be fine. Every aspect of the hyperspace that was unstable was becoming so at an alarming rate. Slade agreed that they really had no choice. Cody selected the hyperspace course. A jump portal opened, and they flew into it as it closed behind them.

* * *

The sky over Xotosia cracked with dim light as the rifts were consuming the planet. The warships from both warring factions were falling to pieces in orbit, and the pieces that fell to the planet from near orbit were burning in its atmosphere. Despite the burning metal rain and cracking sky, Emelia had managed to fight her way into the Black Guard confiscated palace. She slashed and blasted her way inside, still thriving on her hatred of Josh Broody for motivation. She was followed by Black Guard soldiers and Laser Heads.

As she entered the palace, she found Fright Agent Nehih lying dead. His body of thorns was covered in a white pus like blood. A Black Guard captain approached and informed Emelia that Fright

Agent Nehih was arranging his own attempt to flee. The captain admitted having taken the action upon himself to execute the coward for his crime. Killing a fright agent was a serious offense, but the very duty of a fright agent was not to flee. They had taken solemn vows of loyalty to die if needed in order to hold ground.

Emelia gave the captain pardon as he directed her and her team to a shuttle. Before boarding the shuttle, Emelia tried to contact Epitaph with the enhanced comms of the palace, but the destruction of the planet was proving too much of a disruption. Emelia boarded the shuttle. It lifted off and through heavy static-filled comms and obstructed navigation, somehow was guided to the Black Guard warship, the *Ripper* at the far orbit and other side of Xotosia. Emelia was welcomed aboard by the much-relieved Fright Agent Maddo. Emelia was even unsure how they had made it as they watched Xotosia be torn apart by the rifts. Fright Agent Maddo claimed they had been brought in by tractor beam. He also admitted that he had a hyperspace course already plotted for them. Emelia nodded her approval. Fright Agent Maddo gave the order to proceed.

The hyperspace portal opened with a heavy detection of rift disruption deeper inside. They could not risk entry. Fright Agent Maddo ordered an escape course. The *Ripper* flew away, fighting a heavy pull from the rifts that destroyed Xotosia and the rifts now reaching out from the hyperspace portal that was unable to close. The rifts collided with each other and created an even greater force of consumption. The *Ripper* took heavy damage but had managed enough power and speed to escape the disastrous pulling force.

* * *

The hyperspace trip was rocky. The *Fallen Star* was having trouble holding a steady flight path through the hyperspace tunnel. Hyperspace itself even looked different as it appeared lined with small ripples and cuts. Josh kept a close monitor on the readings, which seemed to fade away and return. With the unsteadiness and uncertain future of the existing hyperspace journey, Josh did not dare to engage the autopilot, but he needed to attend to Laylee's powered down state. They needed her reactivated. He told Tana to hold position. She had a previous knowledge of space flight from her travels but admitted that she had never piloted before now. Josh fixed her hands on the flight controls and told her to use all her strength to hold the ship steady. The effects of the hyperspace crisis pulled the ship with great strength, but Tana was able to hold it steady. She asked why Josh could not just use his neural link. He said it was too dangerous. He claimed that the rift disruption would overpower the ship's drive. He entered an alternative hyperspace course into the computer. The ship adjusted, and Josh opened up an exit point.

The *Fallen Star* exited just a bit prematurely from hyperspace to a strong jerking stop. It was a shorter jump than originally plotted. Tana asked where they were at. Josh checked the scanners and figured they were in a very distant area of the sector. He identified it as the Sillulite System. It was a more desolate and wildly unexplored area of space. This area seemed calm, and no rifts seemed to be present. Space was cold, but it was reading at much colder temperatures than that of normal known space. The system had a bluish and white sun that gave off a frozen chill as opposed to heat. The closest planet to this sun was, in fact, an ice-covered world. Suddenly, the *Fallen Star's* engines sputtered. Josh took the controls and locked the ship into the far orbit of another planet further from the cold sun, but still covered with snow. He told Tana to stay in the cockpit as he rushed down the hall through the living area. He took a quick glance at Laylee's motionless body. He then took a slide downward supported by two pole supports and threw up a lever to open a side hatch. He then stepped inside to the engine chamber of the ship.

Josh attempted to turn on the lighting at a panel near the hatch door, but the room remained dark. He engaged the small lights on his shoulder strap and holster. He navigated through the dim-lighted path and the low humming sound of engines. Suddenly he had a feeling. Something felt wrong. He then saw a shadow movement coming from behind the light. He quickly looked back. From a rafter above the engine, Mortigan jumped down behind Josh and onto his back, taking Josh to the floor with a jagged dagger blade edge held to the side of Josh's neck. Mortigan used his knees to improve his leverage to the under arms of Josh and essentially pinned him to the floor.

Tana had come down, unhampered with her dark vision and jumped onto Mortigan's back. She used her claws to tear through the leather he wore and scratch deeply into Mortigan's multigrafted skin. The clawing was followed by her sharp teeth digging deep into his neck and forcing Mortigan to release his pin on Josh. Mortigan stood up with Tana on his back. Her claws were dug into his shoulders and torso while her teeth were tearing away at his neck. He ran backward and slammed her body between himself and a ship's wall. The impact was enough for her to release her clutches, and Mortigan broke free. Josh now stood to his feet and had initiated a running charge. Mortigan dropped a smoke grenade, and Josh charged into the visual obstruction, choking on the smoke and losing site of his target. The distraction gave Mortigan enough time to draw his longsword and stab into Tana, who had also tried to charge at him. Tana fell off the blade and to the floor as Mortigan pulled the blade from her. Josh was through the clearing smoke and locked sight with Mortigan. Josh went for his blaster pistol, but Mortigan released a snare line from one of his wrist gauntlets. He pulled at the snare line after it had entangled Josh, and the pull took Josh to the floor. With Josh secured, Mortigan grabbed a cable from the wall of the ship and tied Tana up as well. He put a sonic head band onto Josh's head. The sonic waves would prevent Josh from initiating his neural link to the ship. Mortigan then made his way to the cockpit and took control of the ship. As an added measure, he broke into the ship computer systems and, after a thorough search, was able to locate the neural link there as well and severed the connection by pulling out that cable. Mortigan then accessed the comms. With all the spatial disturbances, he enhanced them the best he could. The *Fallen Star's* computers were almost as good as those of the *Dark Wish*. Binia could have done better, but Mortigan no longer had that option. He initiated his hail on all Black Guard frequencies and prioritized the message specifically out to Fright Agent Kyrak. He claimed that he had Josh Broody as his prisoner and requested drop coordinates. He normally brought bounties in dead but this time he wanted to kill Josh in front of Epitaph.

* * *

Epitaph was in the holding cell talking with the Prophetess. She continued to mention another brother. He nodded at the Black Guard officer, who upon the gesture injected her again with several needles mounted on a remote device. They punctured into her brain and heart. The pain was excruciating. They also injected a burning chemical into her bloodstream. Epitaph asked for what he said would be the last time, "Jase is dead. What brother?" His tone was even more threatening than any before. She confirmed that Jase was dead, but there was a third brother that neither Jase nor Josh had knowledge of existence. The third brother statement was a bluff, but Epitaph seemed to have believed her—for now at least.

Fright Agent Kyrak interrupted the interrogation stating that Mortigan had made contact and that Josh Broody was in his custody. Epitaph smiled with his reptilian grin growing wider. He asked the Prophetess if Josh's death would sever the prophecy. He used prolonged hisses and lisps in the question. She bowed her head and hesitantly agreed with him that Josh's death would guarantee that the reign of Epitaph would last forever. She added that the third brother would become insignificant. Epitaph quickly turned back to Fright Agent Kyrak and instructed him to arrange a rendezvous on Mezagayzia. Fright Agent Kyrak said that he had suggested that, but Mortigan had refused and insisted on a more public and a less Black Guard-held planet. Fright Agent Kyrak suggested a meet at Mega City on Wrol. He reasoned that the city was a free city, but the Black Guard had a light presence there. He added that there were also many shadow operatives there as well as sympathizers to their cause. Epitaph's reptilian smile grew even wider. He ordered Fright Agent Kyrak to proceed.

* * *

Cody was monitoring all transmissions that he could through the spatial disturbances. He had the computer searching specifically for any mention of Josh Broody through Black Guard frequencies. He found something and reported it to Slade. Slade was working with his own communication project in an attempt to reach his bride and his sister through the rifts. Cody mentioned that it sounded as if the Black Guard was going to meet Mortigan at Mega City on Wrol. He added that Mortigan was a well-known bounty hunter and that there were many rumors of Mortigan searching for Josh. Cody also stated that he did not believe there would be a meeting if Mortigan did not have his bounty. Cody added that it was also troubling because Mortigan had a reputation for bringing his bounties in dead as opposed to alive. He stressed the importance to the prophecy that they needed to make sure if Josh was the bounty, even if he was alive, that he did not end up in Epitaph's grip. Slade agreed they needed to head to Wrol. He then asked Cody for all the information on Mega City.

* * *

Emelia was aboard the *Ripper* as it and a few other Black Guard warships made their way through space in an attempt to get far away from the rifts that had destroyed Xotosia. With the hyperspace access threatened by the rifts destroying the universe, regular space was the best they could do. All of the ships had suffered major damage either from the rifts; the space battle with the Luth Bik Resistance or both and the tech crews on all the ships were working diligently to get as much speed as possible.

Fright Agent Maddo brought reports to Emelia of the Luth Bik Resistance regrouping at the planet Grayden. He added that many planets in that system may be inclined to support them. The Black Guard had always had problems establishing clear dominance in that sector of space. He also reported that space seemed to be stable and unaffected by any rifts at this point in that region.

Emelia ordered all Black Guard ships between here and Grayden to assemble there. She included the ships that traveled with the *Ripper*. As she understood, the *Ripper's* repairs were the furthest along. Fright Agent Maddo confirmed that fact. She ordered repair efforts doubled around the clock as the *Ripper* would continue on its own path. Emelia answered Fright Agent Maddo's unasked question. She would find her former husband Josh Broody on her own while the Black Guard fleet that assembled at Grayden and under her orders would end the Luth Bik Resistance once and for all. She declared she would do what her husband, Epitaph, had been unable to do. She then declared full command of all Black Guard forces at this time. Emelia injected Fright Agent Maddo with an antidote to neutralize the fright agent chemical compound injected in them at time of service from turning volatile if a fright agent would turn against Epitaph. Emelia's antidote would also maintain the enhanced skills and traits provided from the original injection. Fright Agent Maddo was fearful of Epitaph's wrath but would side with her. He did point out, though, that no other fright agent would dare oppose Dark Lord Epitaph. She added that she would instate her own fright agents if the others did not follow her rule. She then added that she would start by making the human Black Guard captain that killed the cowardly Nehih her newest fright agent. She added into the ship's log that Captain Riscarro was immediately promoted to Fright Agent Riscarro. Fright Agent Maddo stated that no human has ever served above the rank of admiral or marshal. Emelia stared directly into Fright Agent Maddo's skull facial features and asked if he was already beginning to question her orders. Fright Agent Maddo stiffened his stance and replied that he would never question her and that his loyalty to her would be unmatched. She thanked him. Emelia then claimed that with her vengeance fulfilled and the Luth Bik Resistance gone, the Black Guard dominance would be able to deal with Derth territories more intensely and finally rule the universe.

* * *

The *Fallen Star* had begun to fly through a space lightning storm that surrounded the planet of Wrol. The freighter was struck several times as it passed through. The electrical charges were sent throughout the ship's interior and shorted out many systems. Mortigan's attention was on trying to reroute ship power to repair needed systems. He was unaware of the charge sent through the ship that struck and reawakened the android body of Laylee.

Laylee walked to the cockpit and spotted Mortigan frantically dealing with the power surges as the ship came into near orbit of the planet. Laylee quietly moved back unnoticed by Mortigan. She accessed a console in the rear of the living area and detected two other lifeforms in a locked cargo hold. One was human, and the other was Matrasus. Laylee disabled the inner ship's motion alarms and entered the cargo hold, where she unlocked the section that held Josh. She removed the sonic band from his head and untied him from the snare line that had entangled his entire body. They kissed briefly in relief of seeing each other at last until Josh pulled away and told her to unlock the other section that held Tana and tend to her wound. Laylee asked what he was going to do. He realized that the ship's computer end of his neural link had been severed, but he had a backdoor protocol that his neural link could access in just such an occasion. He told Laylee that he was going to get control of his ship back. Through his mind, he had activated the neural link's backdoor protocol. It would take only a few moks to come fully online. It was enough time for him to reach the cockpit before Mortigan would become aware.

In the cockpit, Mortigan had already stabilized the ship's functions and requested landing protocols on Wrol. He was using forged Black Guard credentials in an attempt to avoid docking at any of the sky stations as he flew the *Fallen Star* out of the atmosphere of the planet. He was granted approval to bypass the sky stations and land at platform 1951 in Mega City.

Laylee had used a med kit and her knowledge of first aid to close the wound to Tana's midsection and stop the bleeding. During the process, Tana had spoken of her love for Josh. As she became more alert, she realized what had happened and that Laylee, not Josh, was healing her. Despite Tana's declarations, Laylee was glad that Tana was going to live. She broke the awkward silence as she admitted that she too had feelings of love for Josh that overrode her own programming. Tana snarled but was struck by more pain from her just healed wound. Laylee told her to rest, and when she was well, they would have to talk.

As the *Fallen Star* prepared to dock on landing platform 1951 at Mega City, a cascade of phosphorus gas was released into the cockpit. Mortigan was surprised by the incident until the ship swooped upward from its descent to dock. He realized that he had lost control of the ship. Somehow, Josh had reactivated his neural link. Mortigan began choking on the phosphorus gas and his exposed various grafted skins started to blister as he drew his blaster pistol and fled the cockpit. Down the corridor from the cockpit, Mortigan entered the living commune area and saw that Laylee's body was gone. He was then shot at by Josh and forced into the dining chamber. Mortigan found cover and waited as Josh advanced. Mortigan took careful aim at Josh's head and fired. Just before he pulled the trigger, the ship had made another and sudden upward swoop that threw off Mortigan's balance and aim, causing him to miss his lined-up lethal shot.

The shot hit a regulator and pierced inside the unit. A thick black smoke spread out from the freighter as it ventilated itself during a streak over the region cloaked in its own dark black smoke outside Mega City known as the Deadly Mountains.

Inside the ship, Mortigan had dropped his blaster pistol and charged through Josh's layer of low intensity blaster fire. Mortigan dove forward and tackled Josh to the ground as Josh also lost the grip on his blaster pistol. The distraction caused the *Fallen Star* to slip into a short spinning motion that was quickly stabilized, but the brief wild spin did throw everyone around. Once positions were again gained, Josh pulled on a lever that opened a floor hatch beneath Mortigan's feet. Mortigan fell out of the freighter and dropped from the sky into the black smoke covered mountain region.

The *Fallen Star* was losing altitude. The coil to a power cell was hit by the blaster fire inside the ship. Josh used his neural link to again vent the smoke from inside the ship and stabilize its flight motion. He leveled the freighter off and flew away from the Deadly Mountains and toward Mega City.

Chapter Twenty

Swing of Momentum

THE *FALLEN STAR* had docked on landing platform 1951 at Mega City. Josh, Laylee, and Tana disembarked from the freighter and were arrested by the security forces for suspected terrorism because of the ship's sudden and erratic flight path. There was also evidence that the Black Guard credentials utilized to gain passage and bypass the sky stations were forged. Josh tried to explain what had happened with Mortigan, but the panic that had struck the city had nobody listening, at least until a level of calmness could be restored.

* * *

There was still some distance from Wrol in a distorted but stable hyperspace route. Two Black Guard soldiers held the Shrow Prophetess at a distant gunpoint, while Epitaph meditated with her to gain a future vision to clarify if by killing Josh, the prophecy would truly fail to come to pass. He could feel her trying to deceive him, but he was finally able to see the faces of Josh and Slade. He recognized Slade from a previous prophecy that mentioned a human that was not human of a conquered world. The vision faded out as Epitaph realized the two men were standing over him before he saw only blackness. The Prophetess said to Epitaph that it was his own death that he saw and that the prophecy would come to pass.

Epitaph became deeply enraged and attacked the Prophetess. Her prophet defense ability still clearly did not work on him as he physically choked her with both his hands around her throat. Fright Agent Kyrak interrupted over the comms as Epitaph released the Prophetess and she fell to the floor gasping for air. He reported that they had been forced to exit hyperspace because of rift intrusion into the hyperspace stream. He added that there was detection of a small rift opening ahead of them.

* * *

Slade and Cody were aboard the Albejen shell ship and traveling in regular space to Wrol. They found their path through the stars by several shard-shaped starfighters. Both Slade and Cody recognized them as Luth Bik starfighters. The lead starfighter hailed them and identified herself as a member of the Luth Bik Resistance. They were unaware of the origin of the ship that Slade and Cody traveled in and demanded a response. Slade introduced himself and Cody. He explained what had happened and stated that they were no threat. The lead pilot claimed that the Albejen were just a myth. Silence filled the comms. Slade broke the silence by stating that he had previous relations with the Luth Biks. It was with his best friend long separated from the Luth Biks but named Rayk. After another brief silence the lead Luth Bik starfighter pilot asked if Rayk was the son of Lekar. Slade responded with an affirmative and added that Lekar was the son of Jak and he was the son Krok. Another silence fell until the Luth Bik starfighter pilot admitted that she was impressed with Slade's knowledge of a Luth Bik family. She then instructed Slade to adjust course and move into the fleet assembly of a variety of different Luth Bik starships. Slade mentioned the urgency that they got to Wrol. The lead Luth Bik starfighter pilot now identified herself as Laka and promised that they would be allowed to continue as quickly as possible, but her Luth Bik Resistance leader wanted to speak with them. Cody detected that the shards had charged all their weapons. Slade looked at Cody as he acknowledged over the comms that they would be honored to be escorted.

* * *

On the planet Wrol and in the Precinct of Mega City Authority, the security forces had identified Josh Broody as a former general to Epitaph and the Black Guard. Josh insisted that it was a long time ago and that he was not with the Black Guard any longer. The security officers seemed in dispute over their choices. The Black Guard had a small presence on Wrol and those that supported the Black Guard were in favor of turning Josh over to them. Josh appealed to those not in the favor of that choice. The problem escalated when they received a list of crimes Josh had committed where he was with the Black Guard and another list of crimes he was wanted for in opposition to the Black Guard. The warrant for his arrest offered by the Black Guard, along with a 200,000 dreking bounty, had only sealed his fate. Josh was put into a holding cell while they awaited contact with the Black Guard.

Josh was thrown into a confinement cell with Laylee. She stated that she was unaware of where they had taken Tana. Josh pounded on the sealed door with one closed viewing hatch. Laylee had tried to pull on the door, but even her android strength had no effect on Kimen steel. They sat together in a close huddle. Their embrace comforted one another. They admitted their love for each other. Laylee claimed that Tana had also loved him and that she could detect that he had feelings for Tana as well. Josh took Laylee and pressed his lips to her own. He told her that he wanted to be with her more than any other. Their kiss grew stronger and with more passion until they ripped off their clothing. Josh ran his tongue around her breasts, and Laylee felt the passion as he went further down and licked out her already-wet pussy. He then positioned his rock-hard cock deep inside her passage. He hammered into her with increasingly powerful thrusts. Her body shifted in motion with each thrust as she begged for more. Their screams and their moans became louder as they both climaxed together. They simultaneously produced deep sighs of relief at their fully-achieved encounter with pleasure.

* * *

Fright Agent Maddo again, came to Emelia in private with his concerns of her appointment of a human to the title of fright agent. Emelia stated that all the Black Guard soldiers and officers except for fright agents were humans. Fright Agent Maddo admitted that fact, but he felt humans should not be given any higher power as the race already considered themselves superior to all others including his race of Teon and her race of Jaskan. Emelia stated quite firmly and with great authority that as long as she was running the Black Guard, loyalty such as that displayed by Riscarro dispatching the coward of former Fright Agent Nehih would be rewarded. She added that Riscarro had acted more like a fright agent than Nehih when the situation arose. The conversation was over at that point as far as Emelia was concerned. Fright Agent Maddo was then notified over comms of a message from Dark Lord Epitaph.

Fright Agent Maddo had the message played at Emelia's comms station. It was very garbled, but Emelia could make out that Epitaph was announcing to all his subjects a warning of death as punishment for any further betrayals to the Black Guard rule. He claimed to be headed to Wrol to make an example of the trader Josh Broody and to insert his authority by breaking the rumored prophecy of his demise.

The very thought of gaining revenge on her former husband was her primary drive, and she was furious that Epitaph might kill Josh before she could have the chance. She ordered their course adjusted to rejoin the fleet and the assembly at Grayden. Despite her desire to kill Josh, she knew now that her rule of the Black Guard would be sealed with the defeat of the Luth Bik Resistance. She decided to let Epitaph play his games while she took control of the Black Guard from him. Once others would hear of her victory, there would be nobody that would dare deny her rule. Epitaph would likely kill Josh anyway before they could get to Wrol. While he stole her vengeance, she would steal his army.

* * *

Elsewhere in the universe, a very beautiful and well curved human woman with long black hair running all the way down to her ass and garbed in skintight armor with two shades of green had led a rescue mission into the mountain hole. She and three others, two human males and a Helven female, had descended on cables into the hole. Helvens were of humanoid form but with an extremely skinny build. They had long pointed ears that protruded just above their head. They resembled elves from Earth fantasy lore except for their cat-like formed nose. The male Helvens had white hair and pale white skin, while the females had black hair and dark brown skin. The rescuers had detected a life sign and grabbed onto the hand of a humanoid form.

At the top and outside the hole, an encampment of various races awaited. They were led by a beautiful blond human that they addressed as Eva. She was a sexy built woman as well but was currently displaying a pregnant form. Over the comms in her ear, she heard the woman in green armor claim that they had someone. She called the woman Erikai and asked what she meant by someone. Eva was notified that they were climbing back up. She rushed to the opening of the hole where the others were helped out. Erikai came up last, but ahead of her was the person they had found. Everyone was confused and disappointed that instead of the male they expected to find, they pulled out an unconscious Honsho. Erikai seemed even more disappointed almost disgusted that she had not just saved a Honsho but one that she knew. As he was sprawled face down across the ground, Erikai kicked his body over to his backside. She introduced everyone to Gold Gatling, the most despicable Honsho anyone would ever meet. Eva asked what happened to Slade. It was Slade that had fallen down the hole. Gold Gatling should not even be here. He was left at the other end of the universe when they had sealed the wormhole that led to their planet, Home.

Chapter Twenty-One

Mortigan's Return

GOLD GATLING HAD awoken and was surprised to see Erikai again, calling her Princess Erikai. It was a title she declared that she had forsaken. He then inquired of his old friend Rayk as he slowly stood to his feet. The name still brought unrest to Erikai. She loved him and Rayk being of the Luth Bik race, his kind had never experienced love but he had loved her deeply. Erikai informed Gold of Rayk's noble sacrifice to save her and all the people here on the new world they had found and named Home. Rayk, along with the Hispanic human Enrico Dalchez and the Teon General Kullen Tok, had destroyed the Black Guard warship known as the *Claw* and created a radiation blast that sealed the wormhole and cut this area of space off from the Derths, Ubides and Black Guard. Erikai then stepped within inches of Gold's face and followed her statement with the question of how it was possible that he had gotten here. Eva claimed that they would have detected if the wormhole had reopened. She asked if another one had breached their seclusion.

Gold rose to his feet and tried to backstep away from Erikai, but she matched his pace and stayed inches from him with her hand tightly gripping the handle of Gold's Honshon stick that she now had holstered at her hip, along with his jumpband. Gold declared that it was not a wormhole. He explained what had happened and hypothesized that when he fell through the portal, Slade must have fell back through Gold's own origin point. Eva asked if she was correct in understanding that her husband and Erikai's brother was at the other end of the universe. He acknowledged in the affirmative. Eva asked how they could get Slade back and Gold seemed to be clueless on the solution. Erikai had backed away while Eva spoke but was again directly in Gold's face. She asked, "So we are stuck with you in place of my brother?!"

Gold admitted that he had interests he wanted to get back to as well. The Gatling Legion was fragile at this point and he needed to be there to hold it together. He then sighed and thought about the fact that if he was stranded here, he could start all over and figured he could fill the void left by Slade. He admitted that once they got to know him, they would love him. One solid and hard-fisted punch from Erikai knocked Gold back to the ground and unconscious again.

* * *

Lord Epitaph's remnants of his Black Guard fleet of ships were on an approach to a small but rapidly expanding rift. The fleet of ships had halted and began to reverse away from it. Epitaph ordered a course plotted around the rift. Another rift started to open nearby, and special readings of yet another rift formation was detected behind the fleet. The fear of uncertainty had surfaced. Fright Agent Kyrak broke and through all ship comms had again, accused this all of being Epitaph's fault. Epitaph stood to counter him on the command deck. He ordered Fright Agent Kyrak to get off his ship and return to the *Bloodbath* and await punishment for disobedience and insubordination. Fright Agent Kyrak claimed that thanks to Epitaph he no longer had a ship. As Black Guard officers and soldiers started to stand behind him, others stood behind Epitaph for support.

* * *

Josh and Laylee had just finished their moment of passion and were hurried in their redressing efforts as Mega City security officers were pulling them from their cell. Josh asked where they were being taken and for the whereabouts of their Matrasus companion, Tana. After what they had just done and how Josh claimed he wanted to be with her, Laylee seemed somewhat threatened by the tone of his concern for Tana, but their current situation was the immediate threat. The guards ignored Josh as they restrained him and Laylee at the wrists and ankles. They were then thrown into a prison transport hovercraft vehicle.

* * *

In a world of darkness consumed by a thick black smoke, something had stirred as Mortigan was awoken and realized that he had been snared by a dead and rotting tree. In addition to the several pieces of grafted skin of other aliens over his body, he had also had his eyes replaced and his left eye was that of a Kro, a species resembling that of fantasy orcs. Through this eye, Mortigan used dark vision to climb down from the tree to the marsh layered ground around it. He had seen mountains towering above the field of dead trees all around him. There was something else as well. Nearly twenty feet away and knee high in size spider-like creatures had come from the dead trees and slowly surrounded him. Once he was completely surrounded by the creatures, they started to close ranks and move inward toward him.

* * *

Epitaph had ordered Fright Agent Kyrak and the officers and soldiers that supported him to all stand down. Fright Agent Kyrak could feel the chemicals that the Black Guard had injected into him and provided his enhanced abilities. He could feel them start to burn at his betrayal of Epitaph, but suddenly, the sensation ceased. He could still feel his enhancements, but the Luth Bik body had found its own way to neutralize the chemical from becoming volatile. He remained defiant and refused the order. Epitaph threw out terms of "Shell Face" and "Rock Head," which were racial insults used to describe the Luth Bik race. Epitaph used the terms in his excuses as to why he should have never trusted a Luth Bik, much less one that he called a trader to his own race. The ship shook as the rift grew and took another ship from the fleet. Epitaph took advantage of the distraction and moved in on Fright Agent Kyrak. He was not going to use his incantation powers. He was going to dispatch with this trader in a more physical display. He had lunged forward and wrapped his arms tightly around Fright Agent Kyrak's waist. The squeeze was powerful, and Fright Agent Kyrak was gasping for air as he threw rapid punches onto Epitaph's back. The action also caused combat throughout the supporters of both sides. So far, the combat was only aboard the *Darkfall*. Black Guard soldiers shot blasters at one another, while those in melee combat used their axes.

* * *

Gold Gatling had been carried back to a treetop fortress. It was an entire society that thrived around the trees below and within the treetops. Gold had awoken in one of the larger treetop huts. He was taken with a guard on each arm across the connecting rope and wood bridges that linked the trees. He looked down at the commerce activity on the ground. He asked where he was being taken just as Erikai approached. She relieved the guards that escorted him and guided him into a larger wooded constructed hall that stretched around three large trees that ran through it. Reluctantly, Erikai introduced Gold to President Eva and the governing council of the League of Unified Worlds. Her words doubted his trust. Gold claimed that he had changed. He added that his old life was behind him anyway as long as he was marooned here. Erikai and a pregnant Eva were not ready to abandon hope of getting Slade back, and both agreed that if they had to swap Gold for Slade, they would not hesitate in that choice. The Helven scientists declared that they would begin working on the retrieval efforts of Minister Slade immediately. President Eva asked Gold if he would be willing to provide his knowledge and experience as assistance. He promised that he would do whatever he could to help. Despite his bolstering of staying here, he did have his own investments at his end of the universe. He then saw a small boy enter, about four cycles in age, and approach Erikai. He had a hard shell-like skin. He appeared to be a mixed breed of human and Luth Bik. His hardened-skinned forehead ran to a point and flattened at the top of his head, just like all other Luth Biks, but the color was not gray. It was a human Caucasian color. The boy hugged Erikai as she picked him up and noticed Gold was staring at them. She answered his inquiry before he could ask by stating the boy was the son of her and Rayk. Obviously, due to the boy's age and the last time that Gold had encountered Rayk and Erikai with no child, some time had passed within the portal transfer. Gold displayed a saddened look across his face. It was a look of sorrow that the boy was being raised without his father. It was a look that Erikai could read but seemed shocked that Gold could express it.

* * *

Mortigan was rescued by a thin humanoid-shaped shadow creature that scared off the large spider-like creatures. Mortigan sensed something he had not sensed for a long time. It was a feeling of pure and cold fear. The creature had created a mental and telepathic link with Mortigan. It explained that its purpose for creation was to install fear and corrupt others, but it was bound here in the darkness region of the Deadly Mountains by a Saca woman. Sacas were humanoids that wore armored suits that bound their bodies of sentient sand. The creature called itself an Incurro. It claimed it was one of many, but its species had no individual name like Mortigan. It claimed that it must escape from here and spread its fear and corruption. Mortigan tried to mentally combat this creature's influence from his mind, but the creature was not ready to be rejected so easily. Mortigan felt a bombardment of his long-buried internal fears and painful memories that he had cast away long ago.

* * *

Epitaph continued to increase the squeeze on Fright Agent Kyrak, whose punches to break free had lost much of their strength and intensity as he was finding it even more difficult to breathe with each passing sec. The Black Guard followers of both men were still engaged in furious blaster fire and brutal melee combat, but Fright Agent Kyrak's supporting officers and soldiers had gained an upper edge and had control of the *Darkfall's* weapon systems. The officers were calling for the other Black Guard warships to denounce Epitaph and join Fright Agent Kyrak or be fired upon. The commanders of the other warships seemed to be more preoccupied with the destructive rifts tearing through the fleet of ships. The officers on the *Darkfall* ordered all weapons ready to fire on any Black Guard ships that did not pledge allegiance to Fright Agent Kyrak in the next thirty secs. Epitaph had caused Fright Agent Kyrak's body to fall limp within his squeeze as he sensed the mutiny growing. He released his grip, and Fright Agent Kyrak's unconscious body fell to the floor. Epitaph then rolled his eyes back to reveal a ghostly white glare, and his head flung backward as well. His forked tongue flicked as he had initiated his dark powers. Epitaph held out an open hand with palm side up. Epitaph chanted the incantation, "Ssaiyai lissith ffleess copssnaith!"

The armor worn by Fright Agent Kyrak began to disintegrate away in burning flame. Once the armor was gone, the shell hard flesh did the same. His blood materialized and gushed from Epitaph's open palm to form a pool around his unconscious body. Simultaneously, his bodily organs began to materialize one by one in the widened and opened mouth of Epitaph. Each organ including the Luth Bik's two hearts then fell one after the other, with the brain being last down inside Epitaph's bulging throat and disappeared into the digestive system. After the gruesome act was completed, Epitaph's head flung forward, and his mouth returned to its normal state.

* * *

Josh and Laylee were taken from the transport vehicle and about to be handed off to the Black Guard base in Mega City. Suddenly, they were all under heavy assault of rocket fire. The explosions all around them had thrown a blanket of chaos upon the situation. The rocket fire was brief but effective. The rocket fire had halted, but before the Black Guard soldiers or the Mega City security forces could regain composure they were charged upon by members of many different races. As the melee combat began, Josh and Laylee were able to free themselves from their energy binds thanks to an unconscious security trooper's controller device. They started to run from the battle, but something else was overlooking and following them. Their path was cut off by a few different alien races. Josh moved Laylee to a position behind him as an elder and naked female Matrasus jumped down in front of them from a ledge. She seemed to be one of the leaders of the assault.

Josh asked, "Who are you?"

A voice from behind them claimed it as her mother. They turned toward the voice and saw Tana standing there naked as usual except for her fur.

* * *

Mortigan's mental battle with the shadow creature continued. He was trying to fight the fear and stop the mental link. In the process, Mortigan discovered a power from more than his patchworked skin, mental shielding. He was able to repel the darkness and fear from his mind. His eyes grew black. He had enough of his own darkness and a remnant of what was just inside him. The Deadly Mountains began to moan loudly all around him. This time, though, the darkness that had been previously tempting him was pulled inside of him by Mortigan himself. He smiled with a frightful grin as he was now controlling the darkness from the Deadly Mountains. So, he thought.

* * *

Epitaph had used his dark powers to dispatch of Fright Agent Kyrak. He then received a vision of Mortigan's growing darkness and a worded prophecy that stated when the dark lord would kill one of his trusted own, a new darkness would become aware and once united these two dark forces would be the last chance for the dark lord to defeat the two brothers before they could destroy him.

Epitaph took over the ship wide comms between the fleet and declared Fright Agent Kyrak dead. He ordered all of Kyrak's supporters to cease their assaults and they would receive his graceful forgiveness. All combat slowly halted as there was no directed defiance toward Epitaph as all that had sided with Kyrak knew it was over and chose to heed the call of Epitaph or lose their lives. Epitaph then ordered the fleet of ships to plot courses to Wrol. Because of the growing speed of the fracturing rifts, the ships would obviously be setting upon different courses. Fright Agent Paj had entered the *Darkfall's* command deck and stated that he believed his team had found a solution to the rifts. Epitaph looked to him without words spoken. Fright Agent Paj moved to the science center and over comms requested the process control sent to the command deck. He then started to explain the science of it but was quickly pressed by Epitaph to move on. Fright Agent Paj accessed the computer and aligned the satellites of the ship to exact coordination. The *Darkfall's* satellites then emitted a fluctuating tachyon energy beam into a rift that started to create a slow-growing seal as it literally started sewing the fabric of space back together.

* * *

Inhabitants of Mega City were captivated by the loud moaning sounds that came from the Deadly Mountains and that of the black smoke seemingly creeping from the mountains and toward the city. The event caused the multi race attackers and the security forces to hustle to the nearest found shelters. Josh and Laylee were engulfed in the panicked crowd and separated from each other. Once shoved into a street tent shelter, Josh found himself grabbed by Tana's clawed grip.

* * *

Gold was helping in the day-to-day activities of the community and seemed welcomed by the people. Erikai and President Eva kept a close watch on him from the treetops. Despite his claims of changing, Erikai still distrusted him. President Eva was willing to give him a chance and benefit of doubt. Erikai suddenly broke from Eva's side and dropped down to the ground on a strong vine. She moved with purpose toward Gold and pulled him aggressively from his walking approach to her son. She warned him that Rico was off limits to him. She then took her son by the hand and rushed him away.

Eva, in the meantime, had made her way to the ground from a pulley and vine system elevator. She approached Gold and wanted him to discuss further with her of his so-called changed self.

* * *

Tana with Josh, had fled from the small shelter to the awning covered side of a much larger building. She explained that her mother had been taken from Matrel long ago. She added that her mother, Shalree, had escaped her enslavers here just outside Mega City. She had been unaware for several cycles of her mother's whereabouts until now when she was rescued by her mother.

Laylee and the other alien races had found them. Tana seemed to barely acknowledge Laylee's presence with only a quick yet dismissive glance. Laylee had sensed the desire for Josh in Tana's voice and the lack of eye contact that Tana was willing to make with her. As a result, Laylee slid under Josh's arm and clutched tightly with both of her arms around his waist. Tana seemed to sneer briefly before her mother urged her that they had to move. Tana told them to wait here. There were other random races that would keep them safe. Tana then stalked off with her mother around the corner of the building.

* * *

The emitting beam from the *Darkfall* was healing the rifts, but they were still being detected as unstable. Fright Agent Paj stated that the process would take more time to completely heal the rifts.

Epitaph was already impatient to join with this newly discovered darkness and to destroy the two brothers. Communications and hyperspace paths as well as scanner detections were all clearing up. Epitaph had decided that the solution was good for now and wanted to depart. He ordered the entire fleet to follow the *Darkfall* to Wrol. Fright Agent Paj urged the importance of taking more time to fully heal the rifts and make certain all the damage that they had done was repaired. Epitaph refused and called for his orders to be followed. Fright Agent Paj stood directly in front of Epitaph's path and insisted that Epitaph take the responsibility for the destruction caused by the weapon he had instructed to be made.

Fright Agent Paj's argument against Epitaph halted suddenly. Fright Agent Paj seemed mesmerized into a trance-like state. Epitaph's head flung backward, and his eyes rolled back to reveal a ghostly white glare. His forked tongue flicked as he had intitiated his dark powers. Epitaph held out an open hand with his palm side up. Epitaph chanted the incantation, "Ssaiyai lissith ffleess copssnaith!" The armor worn by Fright Agent Paj began to disintegrate away in burning flame. His already boiling blood materialized and gushed from Epitaph's open palm to form a pool around Fright Agent Paj's slowly collapsing body. Simultaneously, his bodily organs began to materialize one by one in the widened and opened mouth of Epitaph. Each organ then fell one after the other, with the brain being last down inside Epitaph's bulging throat and disappeared into the digestive system. The crew watched helplessly as the process played out. When it was concluded, Epitaph's head flung forward, and his mouth again returned to its normal state.

Epitaph then called for an open comms announcement to all Black Guard forces. Epitaph declared that he had effective immediately disbanded all ranks of fright agents. He mentioned the betrayal and his forced killings for that betrayal of Fright Agent Kyrak and Fright Agent Paj. He ordered the remaining two fright agents taken into custody immediately, and if they refused, hostile action would be granted. Epitaph named Fright Agent Maddo and Fright Agent Nehih as enemies of the Black Guard. Epitaph, of course, was still unaware that Fright Agent Nehih had already been terminated and that Emelia had taken over the fright agents as her own, as well as declaring Nehih's replacement by the human named Riscarro. Epitaph then set his ship and the rest of his fleet back on course to Wrol.

* * *

President Eva Cusping of the League of Unified Worlds had called for a meeting in her governing chambers. It was another wood-constructed hut built high in the treetops. Her intent was to patch differences between Erikai and Gold Gatling. He seemed more preoccupied with the fact that a Luth Bik and a human could reproduce and was much more amazed that Erikai would have survived as even normal pregnancies among Luth Bik women were considered extreme in effort. Erikai had stood from the table in anger but was pleaded with by Eva to be reseated. Erikai stated that she would consider working with Gold only for the purpose of getting her brother Minister Slade back. She demanded though that her child and any relation of herself and Rayk be left out from the communication efforts. Gold offered his apology and did his best to put it out as genuine, but Erikai could not help her doubts. She had known Gold Gatling, and sincerity was not one of his traits. Eva again pleaded with Erikai and added that she wanted Slade back as well. He may have been Erikai's brother, but he was also her husband. Erikai was reseated, but her stare on Gold remained cold. The meeting was then again interrupted by a Helven scientist with news that the portal where they had lost Minister Slade and pulled out Gold Gatling now seemed to be hardening.

* * *

Mortigan and that darkness he controlled inside of him had directed the dark black smoke that had now encompassed and consumed most of Mega City. The city's security forces and the Black Guard soldiers surrendered to Mortigan as he strode in from the thick black smoke. He corrupted their minds with his aura of darkness and claimed them all as soldiers in his army. He vowed to do the same to all of Mega City's inhabitants.

Chapter Twenty-Two

Disassembly

SLADE AND CODY had joined the Luth Bik Resistance and had been given ranks of lieutenants. Slade had talked with Kyg the resistance leader at great depths. Kyg had been much impressed with the tales of Slade's friendship with the lost son of the Luth Biks, Rayk. It was sorrowing to hear of his death but pleasing to know that Rayk died with honor by giving his life to keep others safe.

Slade had also given Kyg a tour of the Albejen shell ship and shared what he knew about the race that the rest of the universe regarded as myth. Kyg was fascinated with the mass of knowledge he had obtained over the rotations of visiting with Slade and Cody. Slade though had his own agenda and again brought up the possibility of Cody and himself taking their leave and continuing on their mission to Wrol to join with their companions, Josh Broody, Laylee, and Tana. Kyg admitted that he was well aware of their wish to rejoin their companions but stated that he wished for them to stay only a little while longer. He admitted that they had reports of Black Guard ships headed here toward their assembly around Grayden. Kyg admitted that Slade's experience would be a great asset to their stand here. Slade and Cody exchanged a glance and decided that they would stay and aid the Luth Bik Resistance. They had walked through the Albejen shell ship and reached a boarding hatch. Slade offered to escort Kyg back to his Luth Bik command ship, but Kyg did not want to burden them any longer. He entered the boarding hatch and declared that once their ships separated, Slade and Cody would be provided coordinates for their ship to take in the fleet. Slade again bid Kyg farewell and closed the boarding hatch.

* * *

Emelia was notified by Fright Agent Maddo and her newly appointed Fright Agent Riscarro of the order given from Lord Epitaph to disband the fright agents and take those remaining into custody. They also notified her of Lord Epitaph's claims to the killings of Fright Agents Kyrak and Paj. Fright Agent Maddo had verified the authenticity of the comms and order. Fright Agent Riscarro added that the Black Guard officers and soldiers aboard the ships in her fleet have been rumored to be organizing against them.

Emelia recognized the importance of this new situation. She could not allow this to happen during her takeover of the Black Guard. She issued an address to all the Black Guard troops on the ships in her fleet. She dispelled the disbandment order and any further orders given by Epitaph. She stated that her fright agents would continue to serve her Black Guard. She claimed that Epitaph was still unaware of her move to take leadership of the Black Guard. She claimed that Epitaph had forgotten them and ignored advancements of the Black Guard for far too long. She firmly stated with great conviction in her voice that she would not forget them and that she would lead them further than Epitaph could ever take them. She promised them complete control of the universe once she was in full command. She reminded them of the recent defeats they had suffered since Epitaph's questionable alliances with the Ubide clone Cage and the brief alliance with the Derths. Emelia added that the failed blockade at Xotosia was all the fault of Epitaph. She had been sent to take the reins of his already too far failed plans. She continued and blamed the failure of Epitaph's weapon design for the chaos that had torn space apart. She again stressed her words and promised to lead the Black Guard to the prosperity its servers and followers rightfully deserved. It was reported that her message was received with cheers on all ships. Emelia ordered the course maintained to Grayden where the Black Guard would finally crush the Luth Bik Resistance.

* * *

Mortigan had taken a throne position at the Mega City Central Security Station. The former city security and Black Guard forces had been filled with corruption and fear and bent to serve Mortigan. He referred to them, the men and the women as the Darkest. Mortigan had given orders to have all the inhabitants of Mega City brought to him. As they were brought to him and thrown at his feet, he unleashed a shadow from himself into each of them. One by one, men and women, he filled them with fear, which corrupted their souls and bent their wills to serve him.

* * *

In the tunnels underneath, Mega City, the various races of beings had taken refuge. Josh and Laylee made their way through the overcrowding passages. Josh led Laylee into a secluded area. They embraced quickly. They kissed wildly as they began to disrobe each other. Josh lifted Laylee upon a stone formation and pressed over her. He kissed her neck from behind. His hands guided her waist as she clutched the sides of the smooth stone formation. She moaned with pleasure as he inserted his thick cock into her from the rear position. Josh then thrusted his cock into her throbbing pussy and pushed harder with each thrust. Laylee was overtaken with a feeling of deep pleasure and satisfaction as Josh fucked her harder and faster until she released her synthetic internal fluids. She was programmed to release like any other female and to make others feel pleasure, but when she evolved past her own programming, she was allowed to feel the pleasure herself and it pleased her much.

When Josh had finished, he crawled onto the flat stone formation and lay beside her on his back. Laylee then placed herself on top of him. She took his still sperm-oozing cock back into her dripping wet pussy and sat up on it. She rode it hard with a rapid up and down motion. Josh had thought that he was spent but realized he had more to give her. They clutched each other's hands tightly as they shifted their bodies and released into each other. Unknown to both of them as they were lost in their sexual bliss were the crying eyes of Tana as she watched them from a thin gap in the stone wall.

* * *

Aboard the *Darkfall*, Black Guard scientists had come forward pleading urgently to speak to Lord Epitaph. He granted them an audience, and they nervously showed multiple readings of how the patch to the spatial rifts was weakening after a certain amount of time. They believed they could strengthen it and make the seals more permanent, but they needed to remain stationary at a site of repair. Epitaph responded with the fact that he could not stop the fleet. The mission on Wrol was more important. He promised that once they reached Wrol, the science ships would be allowed to work on a sealed rift and complete the process. Neither of the scientists believed they had that much time. The earliest seals were already growing thin and about to bust open. They also warned that when a sealed rift busted back open, the original rift would expand further and faster. Epitaph strongly advised them to stop wasting his time and find a way to strengthen the seals as they were made. He was still allowing them to seal encountered rifts along their journey, but they were not stopping. The scientists could interpret his irritation with their pleas. In order to spare their own lives, they agreed to return to their work. One scientist did speak out and declared that they would stand a better chance at success if they still had Fright Agent Paj working with them. The pause put a sense of coldness in the air. Epitaph though broke it quickly by declaring that they would have to make do. A gasp of relief was displayed that Epitaph had not taken another life.

Epitaph walked to the holding cell in the detention block and entered. He did not have to speak. The Prophetess warned him that the scientists were right and that the spatial rifts would return even more aggressive and widespread than before. She claimed that he would have nothing left to rule. Epitaph asked if the brothers' killing of him would stop it. She paused until he demanded she answered him. She hesitantly admitted that his movement to unite with a new dark power was pushing the brothers and their destiny away. Epitaph's wide reptilian smile grew. His forked tongue flicked wildly as he turned toward her with his hissing voice and claimed victory over the prophecy.

She cautioned his excitement by stating that the prophecy of his demise could still occur. He had only possibly evaded it. With so much happening, even her vision of now several separate futures was unclear as to which one was true. A comm interrupted them by declaring that the fleet was on final approach to Wrol. She then asked if Epitaph would kill her now. He left her cell without a response. She smiled as if she had experienced a new vision. She said out loud to herself, "The brothers were still separated, but events were moving them together. The brothers' destiny was in flux, but it may still play out after all."

* * *

Epitaph commed his Black Guard in Mega City on Wrol. He viewed on screen the black smoke that now covered the Deadly Mountains and the entire Mega City. Mortigan answered by visual hail and claimed that Epitaph's Black Guard were his Darkest now. Epitaph requested a meeting and Mortigan refused. Epitaph revealed a Book of Prophecy. It glowed as he opened it and read aloud a prophecy. "The two evils that embraced their darkness would clash. Refusal of a truce would bring about a splinter of light." Epitaph closed the book and stated that a meeting would be in their shared best interest.

Mortigan agreed to the meeting, but Epitaph would have to come to him and come alone. The hail was terminated. Mortigan sat on his throne and listened to the darkness tell him that Epitaph was coming to take his power. Mortigan first responded with a dark laugh. He then stated that he would not let that happen. The darkness warned Mortigan of Epitaph's power. Mortigan asked if theirs was not stronger. The darkness replied with a tone as if it was offended by the question. It stated that they were strong, but Epitaph was from an evil source and the epitome of darkness itself. Epitaph also had powers from a prophet that may cause alarm.

* * *

Tana went to her mother, Shalree. The mother asked what troubled her daughter. Tana told of her feelings for Josh but that Josh and Laylee were together. Shalree told Tana that they were not feelings, but desires and as discipline should not be acted upon. Shalree held Tana's face between both her hands and declared that her daughter was meant for more than to be with a human.

A young green-haired Jaskan boy ran in and claimed that the soldiers had found an entrance and come with the darkness. Shalree and Tana helped the young boy spread the alarm. Mortigan's Darkest began a storming through the tunnels with dark smoke following in their trails. They were armed with black solid shadow staffs and with their strikes ensnared and stunned the rebels to be taken to Mortigan. The screams and warnings forced Josh and Laylee from their passion. They quickly dressed and ran into the tunnels, shooting at the invading Darkest.

* * *

The darkness informed Mortigan of the tunnel discovery and invasion beneath them as the thick black smoke cleared a path for Epitaph's landing shuttle. The darkness stated that it would stand with Mortigan and they would overpower the Dark Lord Epitaph. The thick black smoke closed behind the shuttle's flight path and surrounded its landing spot.

Once landed and before he disembarked, Epitaph heard something. It was not words of prophecy. It was the darkness that welcomed him and declared it was pleased he had come home. The darkness promised to help him overpower Mortigan. Epitaph asked the darkness if it was not with Mortigan. The darkness replied that

Mortigan wanted to keep it here, but it must spread throughout the stars and only Epitaph could truly harness it.

* * *

In the underground tunnels, Josh and Laylee were shooting their blasters at the Darkest, but the darkness power was bringing more backup and pushing them forward. The black smoke was choking all that were not corrupted by it. Tana and Shalree were clawing and biting at the Darkest, but they were rising too fast for the Matrasus mother-and-daughter team to keep up. Shalree called for everyone to retreat. As the various races not choked out by the smoke itself or stunned by the Darkest retreated, they crowded through the passages, causing Josh and Laylee to again become separated and forced down different corridors.

* * *

The Prophetess sat in a trance in her cell aboard the *Darkfall*. She had a vision of darkness and an evil using Epitaph and Mortigan, promising power to both, but when the victory would come, the darkness could only choose one. She deepened her trance but could not see which one the darkness would choose. Many variables were now in play. It clouded much of Mortigan's path as he seemed to run with smoke wrapping around him. Epitaph still had a confrontation with the two brothers while the fabric of space tore behind them. She also had seen a woman that had departed from Epitaph but had also been taken from one of the brothers and would be the one that would unknowingly bring the brothers together when space cracked open again.

* * *

Emelia's Black Guard fleet arrived at the far orbit of the planet Grayden. The various styles of Luth Bik ships fired blasters, lasers, and missiles as the Black Guard warships approached. The Black Guard warships returned fire in equal measure on Emelia's command. Kyg on the Luth Bik command ship called for the shards to be deployed. The diamond-shaped Luth Bik starfighters deployed fast and hard as they moved in and attacked launch areas from Black Guard warships. Fright Agent Riscarro declared the Black Guard schisms to be launched, but Emelia held that order. Fright Agent Maddo stepped to Emelia's side and declared that the longer they waited to deploy schisms, the more damage to the launch bays would prevent the ability to launch at all. Emelia sharpened a glare at him and ordered to intensify all guns on the warships. She added, "Make it look like we are trying to launch schisms to keep the shards busy. The longer they attack launch ports, the less damage they will do to vital areas."

Fright Agent Riscarro physically pulled Emelia away from the command table display and screamed at her that it was a mistake to not launch schisms. Emelia swiftly drew her katana-like sword without warning and, with one swift stroke, removed Riscarro's head from his body. She looked toward Fright Agent Maddo and declared him as the only fright agent she would need. He then reinforced her orders.

* * *

On the other side, Kyg was observing the battle on his own overhead display. He ordered all warships to shift to Altta One positions. All Shards were to continue to hit launch ports. Damage reports were stating massive and rapid damage, but most shielding was holding. Another Luth Bik brought to Kyg's attention that the Black Guard warships were holding a tight formation. Kyg ordered the attack pattern changed to Deeda Six. The Luth Bik warships started to spread out and surround the Black Guard ship formation.

* * *

Once the Luth Bik ships spread out to surround the Black Guard fleet formation, Emelia smiled at her table display. She ordered fuel tankers five and six blown and the warship *Warshow* sent toward the three command ships. The fuel ships at the sides of the battle started to explode from the inside. The distraction caught the Luth Bik ships off guard, and their attention was diverted away from the schisms launched from two warships behind the fuel ships that were masked to scanners as ground troop deploy ships. The schisms shot through the explosions and caused increased shockwaves on the closest Luth Bik ships. The schisms were then able to flank around to the rear of the Luth Bik warship formation. The Luth Bik warships were, in effect, blocking off their own shards now caught in the middle of the space battle. Once it was realized what had happened, Emelia called for all other schisms that could launch to be launched.

In the meantime, the Black Guard warship, the *Warshow*, moved on the three command ships. Two of the Luth Bik command ships adjusted to engage the *Warshow's* approach. Emelia watched closely, and as the two made adjustments, she ordered missile fire on the third command ship, as she declared Kyg on that one. Fright Agent Maddo looked to her and acknowledged, "Well played."

* * *

Epitaph was greeted by Mortigan after his departure from the shuttle. They were both compelled by darkness filling their eyes to bond arms and hands. When they did, a darkness bound them together as one, and the thick black smoke started spreading further outward and began to cover the entire planet. Epitaph and Mortigan both felt a tremor in their bodies as they joined. A spiral shadow formation came from both of their bodies and swirled about them increasing speed as it did so. Epitaph and Mortigan had become completely engulfed in the spiral shadow and their bodies merged together as one. With the evil and darkness entities joined, Epitaph's physical presence was allowed to take the lead and Mortigan was pushed to a background voice.

* * *

The battle in the underground tunnel had suddenly grown more intense and the feelings of fear increased. Josh called out for Laylee amongst the sounds of screaming and rebel gunfire and those choking on the thick black smoke. Suddenly, the passage he was forced into collapsed down all around him. Josh was able to push some rubble from him, but the passage was blocked and there was no movement from the others in the passage with him.

Laylee was hit by the solid shadow staffs of two Darkest with only damage but no stun effect from either. Not even the smoke was a factor. She shot her blaster at the two Darkest. They went down, but two others advanced on her. The Darkest could breathe in the smoke without condition as well. Their staff weapons again only did damage and could not stun. They realized as they pierced her synthetically exotic-toned skin that they were dealing with an android. They grabbed a hold of each of her arms as others came forward to grab her legs. She was strong enough to pull free twice, but the advancing numbers game had eventually subdued her. They began to hit her continuously, causing bludgeoning damage. Tana had come around at a higher-level position still choking on the smoke. She was remaining conscious but frozen by contemplation. She could have leapt down to help Laylee or let them bludgeon her to fatal system damage. The smoke was doing something else to her as her eyes filled with darkness.

* * *

The power of the joining of Epitaph's evil and Mortigan's darkness was being felt everywhere. Emelia's Black Guard ships were joined by newly arrived Black Guard ships. Their commanders were still unaware of Emelia's Black Guard takeover and saw her yet as an ally to Epitaph. The overwhelming ship numbers and firepower began to take its toll. The Luth Bik Resistance had not fully assembled and many of their ships on route were still too far away. Some of the Luth Bik allied ships were beginning to crumble under massive damage. Shielding was no longer holding on any of them. Some of the ships were fleeing from the battle but still taking heavy damage as they did.

Kyg commed Slade on the Albejen shell ship and started talking about honor. Reminding Slade of Rayk's sacrifice and what he must have felt. Kyg was proud to be an honorable man and willing to die for that honor. His ship was reaching critical failure, and he was not even considering abandoning it. He asked Slade to not let his honor be for nothing. He asked Slade and Cody to use their Albejen shell ship and take command of those ships that could still fight. He pleaded for them not to let those ships lose hope. Slade accepted the order and replied that he would personally see that Kyg's honor lived on through a victory. Cody began to move the ship into position as Slade made contact with the Luth Bik allied ships still able to fight. They all maneuvered in a pattern through the ships falling in combat and retrieved what escape pods they could. Several shards were also still able to combine firepower on the bigger Black Guard warships despite the newly launching schisms. Slade ordered the shards to cut a path for all operational ships. Kyg's command ship finally fell into another, and both ships began to simultaneously explode.

Chapter Twenty-Three

Allegiance of Evil and Darkness

As THE SPACE battle continued, Slade wrestled with his promise to Kyg. That Kyg's honor would be upheld with a victory. They were doing damage as the Albejen shell ship led the other ships through the space battlefield, but they were taking more than they dealt. The only option was to retreat in order to be able to fight again. There were still other ships aligned with the Luth Bik Resistance on their way, but if they got here, they would fall almost instantly as Black Guard ship numbers were still increasing. Slade called for comms to all Luth Bik aligned ships in battle and those headed to the battle. He needed a new area to regroup. Cody recommended a shooting retreat. The best they could do now was during the retreat hope that only a few ships would pursue. They would stand a better chance against thinning numbers. Slade ordered parting shots delivered and all shards in attack mode until further away from battle to be recalled.

Emelia had observed the battle from her monitor display and ordered Fright Agent Maddo to pursue the strange, unknown shell-shaped vessel. Fright Agent Maddo dispatched orders to the ships remaining in the fleet to hold position here. He then ordered the helmsman to pursue and plot intercept courses on the unknown vessel. He added, "That ship is the priority ship."

* * *

Tana observed the Darkest continue to bludgeon Laylee. She was still pinned as they continued to beat on her with the solid shadow staffs, but her fight of resistance to break free had diminished. Tana was able to fight the darkness that tugged at her and her eyes cleared. Tana jumped down from her overseeing ledge and clawed and bit in a full animalistic rage at the Darkest. Tana took a defensive stance position over Laylee's motionless body. Her quick reflexes aided her to dodge the swings of the staffs that would definitely stun her. Her roars grew more in ferocity as she grew angrier; she swiped her claws and snapped her teeth at any that got too close. She was able to take down her targets and pulled Laylee's body from the ground. She dragged Laylee away before more reinforcements arrived.

* * *

Josh had dug through the rubble with his bare hands searching for anyone still alive. He managed to uncover Shalree and noticed despite several wounds that she was still barely breathing. He noticed another opening under Shalree's body and dug at it to further clear an escape. He initially thought that he was digging deeper down, but the collapse had disoriented him, and he realized that he was actually going upward as he removed the last pieces of debris. He pushed Shalree through first and followed after her.

Once free of the underground tunnel, Josh activated his neural link to the *Fallen Star*. His ship activated and lifted off under gunfire, quickly diminished by its own retaliation. It headed for his coordinates at the edge of Mega City.

* * *

Elsewhere at the other end of the universe, Gold Gatling was walking along a dirt path with tall grass at each side of it. He halted his stride suddenly as he noticed Erikai up ahead seemingly paused in a moment of reflection. He hesitated in his approach, but Erikai had sensed his presence somehow and called him forward. He stepped to her side, and they both observed a grassy plain at a slightly lower level from their point of view. Erikai said that she was on that battlefield when she last saw Rayk's ship ascend back into the sky. She admitted that she watched the ship fly upward and never took her eyes off it until she had lost sight of it because of altitude.

Gold was not good at comfort talk. He knew how to inspire his fellow pirates, but consolation was not in his skill set. He tried anyway by bringing up his memories of Rayk, mostly of Rayk attacking him, but admitted he deserved it. She remained looking away and accused him in a calm manner of never liking Rayk. Gold admitted that he never did. Erikai turned to face him, surprised by his honesty. Gold said that just because he didn't like Rayk, it did not prevent him from admitting that Rayk was a good man and a worthy adversary.

Erikai remained silent but smiled slightly at the comment. Gold explained that he was chasing a bounty and during their pursuits and struggles, he was forced to aid this bounty, and he admitted with a smile that the bounty found him untrustworthy. He continued though when the moment came that he was falling through the singularity and was caught in the rift, even despite all the pain, pursuit, betrayals and filled with distrust, this bounty could have let him go but instead tried to save him. Gold claimed to have been in a state of limbo between his falling through the rift and when they pulled him out from it. In that state of limbo, Gold admitted to remembering Josh's act to save him and reflect on his own life and choices. He had tricked and betrayed many without a second thought but there, stuck in a moment that seemed like eternity, he had a self-realization that he did not like whom he had become. Gold then added that she could believe he has changed or not, but he had just told her the truth. To Gold the truth had been a concept he had put away a long time ago.

Erikai took her own moment to look deeper into Gold's eyes. She admitted that she could see he wanted to change, but she still saw the Gold she knew. Gold then surprised her again. He asked her to give him the chance to show her the Gold she did not know. He was not asking for forgiveness, because he knew he would not get nor deserve that. All he wanted was a chance to show that he had learned from his past. She paused still with doubt, but he could also see that Erikai wanted to believe him. Gold pressed on and claimed that if he could switch back locations with her brother Slade he would gladly do so, but he would still wish to bring Rayk back for her as well. She was not one to break, but she shed a small tear. Erikai replied that she saw that was true and thanked him for it. Erikai returned Gold's Honshon stick and jumpband to him.

* * *

The darkness grew as the union between Epitaph and Mortigan—controlled by the darkness-planned departure from the planet of Wrol. The darkness in full control was using them as its puppets to consume more of space with its fear and replace good with overwhelming and unbridled evil. They were still both conscious of events around them, but something else was in control. Mortigan screamed to be released from the back of Epitaph's mind as the darkness moved Epitaph's body.

Reports came over the comms of an unsecured ship's flight path through the smoke engulfed city. Mortigan recognized it as Josh's ship. The darkness sensed it through Mortigan's memory as a threat and used Epitaph's body to secure a schism. The schism sensors locked onto the freighter's flight path and predicted a destination.

The *Fallen Star* had landed at the edge of Mega City, but despite that, the entire planet was engulfed in the thick black smoke. Josh managed to guide the ship to him through the neural link. He carried Shalree aboard as they choked on the black smoke. Once on board, he grabbed a respirator mask for each of them. The *Fallen Star* lifted back up from the ground and had initiated a scan for Laylee and Tana.

* * *

Cody was in communication with a Luth Bik captain and given the coordinates for a rendezvous of forces. The Albejen shell ship was then fired upon by two decloaked Black Guard warships. Cody instructed the Luth Bik warship to head to the rendezvous. As it moved away, Slade piloted the Albejen shell ship to a strafe attack directly between the two Black Guard warships, hitting both with the rapid-fire shots. The warship guns retaliated, but the Albejen shell ship was already past them and adjusting for an escape path opposite the direction taken by the Luth Bik warship. Slade's desired result was achieved as the two Black Guard warships took pursuit after Slade and Cody.

The rear guns were hit by the pursuing and attacking Black Guard warships. Slade had taught Cody everything he knew about the Albejen tech and turned the pilot controls over to him, while Slade moved to the computer in an attempt to bring rear guns back online. The Albejen shielding was fluctuating on and off, allowing several hard-hitting shots to cause more damage. Slade had given up on rear gun firing repair and tried to divert more of that power to shields. The two Black Guard warships had overtaken the Albejen shell ship and assumed flanking positions. Emelia's video hail from aboard the *Ripper* had called for surrender and boarding. Cody hesitated before returning a video hail of his own and declined Emelia's request. The very sight of Cody fueled Emelia's thirst for vengeance and demanded the immediate surrender of Cody and Josh Broody. Cody replied that Josh was not here right now before terminating the communication.

Slade was still attempting to restore shielding by pulling what power he could from other systems. He said in a surprised tone, "Oh that's how that works!" He made a few more quick adjustments. Cody asked if he had restored shields, and Slade replied that he got them something better. Cody looked at him as Slade accessed gunnery control and declared he figured out the activating sequence for the Albejen main gun. Cody thought that was inaccessible, and Slade replied that it was just before he hit the controls. The main Albejen weapon from the entire ship had another gun on the shell ship. It was only good for one shot—not multiple like they would have had with the full ship, but one shot from this gun was all they needed. The Albejen main gun fired onto the Black Guard warship opposite the *Ripper*. The blast hit and with a shimmering blaze across the whole ship, in an instant, the warship was reduced to ash and started to spread apart in space. Emelia ordered Fright Agent Maddo to back them away. The *Ripper* launched schisms as it pulled away from the Albejen shell ship. Emelia had correctly determined that a powerful weapon like that would not be as impactful against several fast and more evasive starfighters.

The Albejen shell ship turned and Slade fired main cannons at the approaching schisms, taking a few out before Cody was able to fly the ship away. The remaining schisms took pursuit. Emelia ordered the *Ripper* to rejoin the pursuit. Several at the helm were afraid of the strange ship's powerful weapon it had just deployed. Fright Agent Maddo ordered the helm techs to follow Emelia's order but stay behind the schisms. The schisms could engage and the *Ripper* would provide fire from the rear. The helm techs were still frightened. Emelia swung her katana-like sword at one and removed his head as she shot the other one point blank in the chest. The Albejen shell ship opened a hyperspace portal and escaped through it. Emelia ordered it tracked and pursued once all schisms were recalled. Once the last schism was retrieved, the *Ripper* opened a hyperspace portal and jumped through. Emelia's message had installed more fear into the remaining helm techs than the strange ship's powerful weapon could do.

* * *

Tana had dragged Laylee's body into a secluded tunnel chamber and dropped her to the ground. Tana pushed her back against a stone wall and slid her body down along it to a seated position. After several moments, Laylee's systems came back online, and she was able to perform small movements which increased slowly. Her regenerative skin was already repairing itself. She crawled to the wall opposite Tana and sat against it. They sat face to face. Laylee announced that she had begun an internal diagnostic that should not take long, and once finished, if no severe damage was recorded, they could continue.

Tana was still fighting against her own dark feelings. She snarled and growled at Laylee. Laylee knew what it was about and asked Tana why she did not just let her die, and then Josh would have been left to her. Tana gave a feline hiss at Laylee, revealing all her sharp teeth in her open jaw. Tana then followed with the admission that she wanted to do just that. Silence fell over both of them for the next few moments.

Laylee was the first to stand, and Tana followed her out of the chamber. They walked through the tunnel passage and up a flight of stairs. Both remained silent toward the other. They exited from the stairs to the outside, Tana still coughed from the smoke all around them. The thick black smoke ahead of them was pierced by the lights of the *Fallen Star*, which hovered before them. The freighter turned to expose the open boarding hatch and extended ramp. Josh greeted both of them as they entered. He gave Tana a respirator mask, which she just swatted away.

Five schisms approached with firing lasers. The darkness controlling Epitaph's body and Mortigan's mind was in the lead ship. The *Fallen Star* turned to return parting fire before initiating evasive maneuvers. Josh rushed to the cockpit to shift ship controls to manual. Epitaph's lead schism's lasers tore a hole in the side cargo wall. Shalree was caught in the exposed section and pulled outward by the sudden air drift. Tana had leapt forward to grab onto her mother and was able to pull her back inside, but Tana fell out as the freighter turned away from another glancing hit. Tana fell backward out of the exposed section and was grabbed literally from midair by Laylee's right arm. Laylee had a hold of the ship with her left arm and used her android strength to pull Tana and herself back inside. Shalree grabbed and cradled her daughter in her arms as Laylee welded the damaged section. The freighter shifted position several more times, but Laylee's android perception and agility helped her stay stabilized long enough to finish the welding repair. Laylee looked at Tana as Shalree tightly held her. Before Laylee exited the room, Tana looked up at her and asked why she did not let her die and have Josh all to herself. Laylee, with no facial expression, simply stated that she wanted to do so. She then exited through the door.

The *Fallen Star* moved in an upward swing into near planetary orbit, and the five schisms followed, firing lasers all the way. The *Fallen Star* with five attacking schisms right behind it had flown into far orbit and directly into a Black Guard fleet formation. Josh asked out loud to himself, "You are kidding me, right?"

Chapter Twenty-Four

United Brothers

As THE *FALLEN Star* flew into the fleet of Black Guard warships with the five schisms in attacking pursuit, more schisms were launched. Josh had flown his freighter right directly into a swarm of starfighters. Josh maintained manual flight control but through his neural link initiated a hailfire of forward energy weapons, which caused the schisms ahead of the *Fallen Star* to disperse to the sides.

The laser fire from the squadron behind the *Fallen Star*, however, had hit vital functions. Rear shields were down, and remaining shielding was at 50 percent. All port side maneuverability was lost and they would not be jumping into hyperspace anytime soon.

The Black Guard warships continued to intensify fire on the weakening shielding. Josh had no choice. He had to fly in closer and tight along the side of one of the warships. The move was stupid or daring depending on the outcome. It did have the effect of halting schism laser fire as well as causing the warships big guns to lose targeting on the *Fallen Star*. The squadron of five schisms led by the darkness-possessed Epitaph and Mortigan did not care about damage to the warship and engaged with full laser fire hitting the warship and the *Fallen Star*. Shielding was now down to 35 percent. Inner lighting and targeting systems were lost, and internal computer panels began to explode and catch fire throughout the freighter. Tana kept her mother close, while Laylee took position at the rear guns. Lasers, pulsar cannons, and the neutronic phaser were out, but she was able to access control to the rocket and concussion missiles. Once access was granted, she fired randomly and without hesitation.

The darkness-led squadron was joined with the other schisms as they followed the *Fallen Star* off the side of the Black Guard warship. The darkness-controlled Epitaph and Mortigan broke off and entered the launching area on the *Darkfall*. Epitaph's body stumbled out and fell from the schism. Black Guard officers and soldiers rushed to help him up from the floor. His long black cape was swung back, and he ordered them all away from him. A spiral shadow formation exited from him and swirled about him increasing speed as it did so. Epitaph's voice screamed out, "Two are better to serve." From within the swirling shadow around him, another shadow in humanoid form stepped from Epitaph's body. The two shadow forms merged again, then dispersed, leaving Mortigan on his knees and side by side with Epitaph. Once again, Epitaph and Mortigan were separated. They looked at each other, and both of them still had their eye sockets filled with shadow form that was pouring out and dissipating around the outer eyes. It was an action that continued to repeat. The darkness began to speak internally to both of them simultaneously. It claimed that it was still in control, but it required their individual talents. Both Epitaph and Mortigan seemed compelled to obey. The darkness spoke through both of them now. Epitaph instructed Mortigan to take command of all the schisms. Mortigan instructed Epitaph to take the command deck.

Epitaph had walked onto the command deck. His crew had already feared him, but now with shadow pouring from his eyes, he had become even more sinister to them. The science station reported that a sealed rift here was weakening. Epitaph asked for the coordinates and had the *Darkfall* turned to face that direction.

The *Fallen Star*, still without any of its own port-side maneuverability, had rolled and made another pass along the *Darkfall's* starboard side. Mortigan had again taken the schism squadron to full attack in the pursuit. They once again hit both the *Fallen Star* and the *Darkfall*. Epitaph ordered Mortigan to veer his squadron off.

Epitaph ordered the science station to repair the rift again once it broke open. The scientist at the station screamed in a panicked state that they would not be able to seal it again. Epitaph ignored the comment and focused on the battle around the ship. Once the *Fallen Star* was again away from the *Darkfall*, Epitaph again ordered Mortigan to take his squadron off the attack. There was no response, and Mortigan continued to direct the assault on the *Fallen Star*. Epitaph ordered the *Fallen Star* targeted with all guns as it flew onto the *Darkfall's* starboard side. The scientist warned that it might hit the weakened seal. Epitaph took control of the weapons station himself and fired everything in that direction. The barrage tore through the *Fallen Star's* fifteen percent shielding and hit the schisms pursuing it as well.

The multiple explosions tore open the weakened seal, and the rift ripped open quickly and wider than it had been before. All ships in the vicinity felt the pull of the rift, but the *Fallen Star* was the first affected as the force ruptured hull plating on the port side of the ship, and a small section blew open and pulled Tana's mother from her arms and into space. Tana screamed out but was able to grab onto a ship fixture and prevent herself from being pulled out. Equipment and air were sucked outward from all around her. Tana was drastically trying to maintain her grip but was losing the struggle.

With no port-side maneuverability, the *Fallen Star* went into a spinning motion as it was sucked toward the rift. Many of the schisms passed by the *Fallen Star* with no resistance power and were pulled into the still-widening rift. The Black Guard warships were also being drained of all power as they resisted the pull of the rift. Josh was doing all he could at the cockpit. The neural link was offline, and he commed Laylee to get to the stabilizer and increase all repulsor engines.

* * *

The hyperspace path of the Albejen shell ship was random and rushed. Slade was monitoring the rift's opening again in hyperspace as the Albejen shell ship became stressed and systems began to fail. Stress points in the hull intensified. Navigation was impossible as each attempt at location became distorted. The hyperspace passage was collapsing as well. They would have to exit prematurely into a rift or be crushed. Cody put everything he could into a speed increase and shields after gathering distance to a safe exit portal.

The *Ripper* was following the course and detected the disaster as well. The clear option was to cease pursuit and drop out before they reached the critical point. Emelia's hatred for Josh Broody and chance for vengeance was commanding her over reason. Josh may not have been on that ship, but she knew Cody was, and she was confident that Cody would lead her to Josh. She ordered that they stay in pursuit.

* * *

Hyperspace ruptures had ripped and tore at one of the Black Guard warships in the far orbit of Wrol. Another warship's hull was buckling under the stress and being evacuated. The *Darkfall* was also feeling the effects as it strained from being pulled into a still widening rift. Epitaph ordered Mortigan to take his squadron of schisms to one of the unaffected warships that were positioned further away.

The Prophetess had come to the command deck in a state of chaos. Epitaph looked around her in question. She stated that the detention block had been damaged and lost all power to cell containment. She admitted that she could have sought out an escape pod, but she felt she had to be here. She observed the chaos through the massive viewscreen and said that it was happening. The time was at hand. Epitaph laughed that the prophecy was not coming true. He pointed to the *Fallen Star* and watched as the rift started to tear it apart.

A scientist interrupted by stating that he might be able to close the rift and seal it again with a nearby opening hyperspace portal. He started explaining the radiation and gasses from the rifts and the hyperspace elements that cause the opening and closing of those portals. He went into further explanation of the scientific reactions and calculations that seemed similar. Epitaph stopped him and told him to begin on his command. Epitaph turned to the Prophetess, shocking her with the shadow still pouring from his eyes. Epitaph stated that his victory over the prophecy of his demise was in full occurrence at that very moment. Once the *Fallen Star* was destroyed, Josh would have no chance to find Slade but would only join his brother Jase in death.

* * *

The *Ripper* was beginning to crush inward upon itself from the collapsing hyperspace passage. Emelia was notified by the sensor officer that the strange ship they had been pursuing had exited hyperspace and added that they would not make it to that point. He urged that they exit now.

Emelia screamed angrily in response, "No! I will have my revenge on Josh!"

The alarm of escape pods and ship evacuation sounded. Emelia watched as her crew fled. She looked back to find Fright Agent Maddo, but he was not at his station. The command deck started to collapse at both turbolift exit points, and Emelia was forced to flee through an escape hatch in the floor.

* * *

A hyperspace portal opened a short distance below the tearing rift. The Albejen shell ship exited, and Cody immediately recognized the *Fallen Star* breaking apart. He scrambled to detect life readings, but the rift was distorting all scanners. Cody flew closer as Slade activated a tractor beam to snare the pieces of the *Fallen Star* as it fell apart. Internal sensors of the Albejen shell ship were more stable, though there were no life signs yet to what they had so far retrieved.

Laylee had lost all stabilization and the repulsor engines had been torn away. Josh was running back toward Laylee's area of the ship when he felt a tractor beam lock on to and pull at what was left of the *Fallen Star*. Ahead of Josh, he saw the hull in Laylee's area of the ship break open, and she was screaming as she tried to grab onto something while her area was being sucked into space from all around her.

Josh screamed out to her. He then saw Tana in another area of the ship, still struggling against her own vacuum pull of space. He could reach and save Tana, but Laylee was slipping away; he could not save her. Laylee's scream fell silent as the vacuum of space won and pulled her from the ship and toward the rift. Josh knew that she could survive in space but not long enough for him to find her and was in a state of terror over losing her. He heard Tana's screams that broke his trance of terror that had frozen him. Josh dove over the railing and grabbed onto Tana's hand just as she had lost her grip. She grasped onto Josh's hand with both of her own. Tana's claws dug into him deep enough to draw blood. The ship around her started to collapse, and as it did, the pieces were sucked into space. Josh pulled her in just as his portion of the ship was snared by the tractor beam and pulled into the Albejen shell ship.

* * *

Epitaph's fleet of warships was crashing into each other as they were pulled into the rift. He watched the strange vessel pull the wreckage of the *Fallen Star* and slip free from the pull of the rift. The Prophetess stood next to him and laughed. Epitaph asked what was happening. She ceased her laughing and claimed that the prophecy was back on track. "A woman that was lost from Epitaph but also taken from one of the brothers will be the one that unknowingly brings the brothers together when space cracks open again by chasing one brother into another. The brothers would be united."

Chapter Twenty-Five

Eye of the Storm

ERIKAI AND EVA were on a stroll through a forest path, discussing Gold Gatling's claims of change. Erikai knew Gold much better than Eva did. She admitted that people could change, but Gold Gatling was—well, for lack of a better word—complex. Suddenly three wolf-like creatures were in the path ahead of them. It was rare for the olfs to be out in daylight. They were night hunters. They were a bit taller than wolves. They had longer snouts filled with more teeth than that of a wolf. Their snouts were almost as long as half their legs. They were feeding on a creature that they had drug into this area. The three olfs had ceased their ripping of the animal carcass and snarled their teeth at the young ladies in the path. They hunched up their backs as Eva and Erikai slowly backed away. Erikai cautiously readied the heavily technical gauntlet called a war arm on her lower left arm.

One olf lunged suddenly at Erikai. She raised her war arm and shot it with a heavy blast of pulsating energy just as it landed on her and took her to the ground. Erikai quickly threw the dead olf off from her and rose quickly to her feet. The other two had already run forward on Eva. One had its teeth around her right leg, and the other had just obtained a solid bite on her upper left arm. They were trying to drag her to the ground, but somehow, Eva was still standing. She was pregnant and knew that if they took her to the ground, there was a greater chance to harm her and her unborn child. Erikai readied her war arm to shoot the one on Eva's leg and then noticed Gold Gatling running toward them. He hollered out to distract the olfs. They released Eva and charged at him. Eva collapsed into Erikai's arms. Erikai guided her gently to the ground and pulled a tube container of healing ointment from her war arm to apply to Eva's wounds.

Erikai looked up to see Gold use his Honshon stick on the first olf. He struck the olf hard with the Honshon stick that delivered a full stunning voltage, and the olf fell limp to the ground. The other olf jumped him from behind. They fell to the ground together. Gold rolled over and tossed the olf away from him. The olf instantly jumped to its feet. Gold was on his knees as the olf snarled and then charged at him. As the olf charged forward, Gold used his jumpband worn on his upper arm and teleported by rolling into a yellow and white light ahead of the olf. He then leapt out of another light portal behind the charging olf and again used all his strength to strike the olf and delivered another full stunning voltage blow from his Honshon stick.

Erikai and Eva thanked him as he walked toward them to check on their condition. He helped Erikai lift Eva up to her feet, and they each took one of her shoulders as they helped her walk. As they walked, Gold noticed Erikai shooting him a strange and puzzled look. He asked her what was wrong. She smiled and said that the Gold she knew would have robbed them and left them. He replied to her that he was just working on that chance of redemption. Eva then asked what he was doing running out to them in the first place. Gold claimed that one of the Helven scientists had discovered that the portal he came through was opening again. Eva and Erikai looked hopefully at one another.

* * *

Space tore again in multiple rifts all around Epitaph's Black Guard fleet. A hull breach occurred over his head, and he braced against the command console as the pull of space tried to drag him away. The darkness that possessed him and bled shadow from his eyes was pulled from him and dispersed into space. The Prophetess had tried to hold on as well but voluntarily released her grip and accepted that this time she would truly die and do so with the prophecy back on track. Two Black Guard soldiers in full zero-gravity gear had grabbed a hold of Epitaph and pulled him from the command deck. They closed the sliding door and informed Epitaph as he gasped for air that his shuttle was ready. They guided him to a docking bay.

Once launched in his shuttle and moving away from the rifts, he looked back at his decimated fleet. He commed for Mortigan to move in with the warships from the further and safer distance and assist with rescue and recovery missions. Mortigan replied that he had assumed the command of his own Black Guard fleet. He added now that the darkness was solely with him, that there was no more use for Epitaph.

Mortigan showed his crew the site of the Black Guard ships being destroyed and asked if anyone wanted to die today. The crew was silent as Mortigan called for the warships now under his command to retreat. The officers and soldiers of the Black Guard did not hesitate to follow Mortigan's orders and the remaining undamaged Black Guard ships left the crumbling fleet behind.

Epitaph was enraged at Mortigan's betrayal and could only watch as the *Darkfall* blew up and the pieces of it that survived were pulled into the rift. A retreating Black Guard warship had approached and opened its docking bay. Epitaph piloted and landed inside. As Epitaph disembarked his shuttle, he was greeted by a human female Black Guard captain. She identified herself as Captain Krissondra Gwen, commanding officer of the warship *Mayhemic*, and requested further orders. Epitaph asked for a damage report on the ship. She handed him an updated comm pad that listed all current damage and repairs that were underway. Epitaph commended her on her efficiency. She was a young, beautiful white blond female of average build. She wore her long blond hair behind her head in a tightly held bun style. She followed up with another comm pad reporting all surviving ships that refused to follow Mortigan. Epitaph again commended her on her loyalty. She then was unsure if he wanted it, but she had a scan on the strange ship that came through the hyperspace portal. She presented him another comm pad and apologized that they were unable to learn much about it, but she had scanned that the ship made several attempts to access hyperspace but was unable to lock onto any stable portal. Epitaph's reptilian smile grew and his forked tongue flicked as even his posture stiffened. He commended her on her resourcefulness. She stood at attention, awaiting further orders. Epitaph noticed on the last comm pad that there were three estimated courses that the strange ship could have taken. She acknowledged in the affirmative and pointed to the one that she had thought most likely because of ship damage scanned, territorial safety from spreading rifts, and an assumption of the most advanced and full fuel system. She admitted that she applied that considering that they knew nothing of the ship's origin, so she just accessed information on best and longest lasting known fuels. Epitaph ordered her to plot the course she chose for pursuit. His forked tongue flicked more rapidly. Her attractiveness and her efficiency and loyalty had aroused him sexually. He hissed softly at her and asked, "Do you have plansss for promotttion?"

She smiled at him seductively. She then offered to meet him in the quarters she had provided for him to discuss it. Epitaph smiled, and his body twitched like a rattle snake, but he was all about business first. He told her, "Catchch me that ssship firssst."

She smiled and swore that she would. She then directed an officer to escort Epitaph to his quarters.

* * *

With space tearing all around them, Slade was maneuvering with information provided to him over comms from a Luth Bik Resistance warship. He told Cody to go back and see if his friends had survived. The Luth Bik officer claimed that they had intercepted some communication through Black Guard channels. He claimed that various reports seem to indicate a power struggle for command of the Black Guard. With that being the case, the Luth Bik officer hypothesized that the Black Guard would be splintered and less effective until one true leader could take full command. Slade acknowledged that as good news, but he had still scanned lightly damaged Black Guard ships in this area, and splintered or not, until he could link up with Luth Bik support ships, his fate and that of his crew looked grim. Slade stated if they did not make a hyperspace jump, the Black Guard ships in the area would definitely over take them. He was still unable to access a stable portal. The Luth Bik officer claimed they still had stability and offered to come and retrieve them. Slade was against that plan. He could not risk the Luth Bik Resistance as it was struggling to reassemble. Slade claimed he had no choice but to enter a random fluctuating portal and hope for the best, but he had to believe that those odds were better than staying here and awaiting capture. Slade picked up a probe alert that registered as Black Guard and was forced to sever communication to avoid detection.

* * *

Epitaph had taken temporary command of the *Mayhemic* and monitored a hyperspace jump detected at coordinates near the projected course of the strange unknown vessel. He ordered a pursuit course set. Multiple officers warned Epitaph that the portal was random and fluctuating, following through was too dangerous, and there was no way to determine an exit point. Captain Gwen stepped forward and reprimanded the officers for arguing with the dark lord's decision. She offered to engage the course personally and begged for him to spare her officers, swearing on her loyalty that it will not occur again. Epitaph rescinded his own order and reminded her that she couldn't make such a promise as most under her were not as gifted.

An entry alert sounded, and an officer detected a Black Guard signature entering back by the rifts from a hyperspace portal that just closed behind it. Epitaph recognized the signature as a special prototype shuttle that could utilize hyperspace unlike standard shuttles that could not. Captain Gwen expanded the scan and detected an android signature nearby the shuttle. Epitaph wondered if it was the android reported to have been traveling with Josh and perhaps not retrieved. He ordered the *Mayhemic* to continue on course. He instructed Captain Gwen to send one of the other warships for the shuttle and android and have them brought to him here aboard the *Mayhemic*.

* * *

Aboard the Albejen shell ship, Cody had brought Josh and Tana to the medical bay and was providing aid to their wounds. Doing the best, he could with what he knew of the Albejen provided med lab. Josh was able to say that he could not save Laylee before he passed out. Tana was already unconscious.

The ship jerked as Slade entered the med bay. Cody asked what had happened. Slade reported it as a hyperspace portal situation. He added that they had just exited. He then corrected his statement to claim that they were more like thrown out. Slade went to a console and checked the autopilot coordinates. He could not believe it. He told Cody to meet him at the command deck when he was through with his friends. Slade rushed back to the pilot station and scanned for a rocky or desert type planet in the region. There was such a planet, but sensors were distorted from scanning the surface. Cody had made his way up there and observed the scan. Cody said that the distortion must be from the spatial rifts. Slade said it was not from the rifts. He brought the planet up on the viewscreen. He was in a state of disbelief. Cody asked again, "If it was not the spatial rifts distorting the scan, then what could it be?"

Slade shook himself out from his disbelief and called it shield-stone. He claimed it was a natural element that blocked or hampered scanning of the planet. Cody had never heard of it before and Slade responded that he only knew of it on one planet. Cody asked where they were at. Slade replied, "I believe we are on approach to my homeworld."

Cody asked, "The planet you settled on and named Home?"

Slade was still shocked. He replied, "No, the one before that, the one I was born on."

Chapter Twenty-Six

Homecoming

SLADE STOOD AT the command deck on the Albejen shell ship with a long and silent look at the dusty and rock covered planet that he once called his homeworld. Slade listed off coordinates to a canyon. Cody was unable to detect any formations. Slade said it was there and there was a palace carved into the canyon walls. Cody responded, "A palace? Like for a king?" Slade said that his mother had taken it from the king. Cody tilted his head in confusion. Slade apologized for not mentioning he was once a prince. Cody was without words for a reply.

* * *

Captain Gwen approached Epitaph and reported that the android and Emelia were secured in the sickbay. Epitaph asked about tracking a Black Guard code on the ship that Mortigan had taken. Captain Gwen declared that they had sent out probes and tapped into communications. She added that she was personally calculating the data retrieved. She was confident that she had pieced together enough information to plot a course, but the destination was at least four rotations away at the best speed the *Mayhemic* could achieve at the time. She noted that it would take the other ships slightly longer. Epitaph ordered that course plotted by her personally. He reminded her that there was neither room for time or errors. She acknowledged the order with a salute. Epitaph said he would be in sickbay.

* * *

Reports of a spatial rift in orbit were brought to President Eva Cusping at the newly reactivated portal site. The Helven scientists at the site reported that there was only a 10 percent chance to retrieve Minister Slade form the portal. Erikai was willing to take the chance. So was Eva, who argued over who should try. Many of the people of various races working at the site had volunteered. Gold Gatling stepped up and said it had to be him. Erikai explained that with only a 10 percent chance, they could not guarantee Gold would be put back where he was taken from. He claimed he would have to go much further than that anyway. He admitted he was lost before the portal incident.

* * *

Cody was helping Josh out from the Albejen med bed when Tana awoke. She looked around as they stood over her and asked where they were at. Cody explained everything to her and Josh. Tana then looked around again and asked about Laylee. Josh claimed he could not save her even if he had tried. He told her that he had to choose between them and that she was the best chance for him to succeed.

Slade entered and Josh looked to Cody. Cody had made updated introductions but then added that it got complicated from this point. Josh asked what he meant by complicated. Slade jumped in with the declaration that he and Josh were the brothers of destiny. He then asked if Josh was well enough to join him. Josh from the past had heard many prophecy tales and was no stranger to those that threatened his former master, Epitaph. He had always assumed the brothers of prophecy were his brother Jase and himself. Josh never considered the possibility that it would be two different brothers to someone else. He stood to walk with Slade. Slade asked Cody to stay with the ship now that he was familiar with it. Tana asked Josh if she could come with him. Josh held out his hand for her to take, and she did.

* * *

Epitaph's walk to sickbay was a long and dreaded one. The wrath of his bride, Emelia, met him at his entry. She expressed her anger and feelings of betrayal for leaving her out of the hunt for Josh Broody. Epitaph redirected the accusations by questioning her attempt at taking the Black Guard from him. She seemed surprised that he knew but displayed no remorse. Epitaph asked her which she wanted more, either the control of the Black Guard or her vengeance on Josh Broody. She paused before admitting her vengeance was strong, and she had been so close before, but never quite satisfied. He then directed her to the disabled female android. He stated that her name was Laylee and she had been rumored to be traveling with Josh Broody's crew. He then stated that through Laylee, they may yet still kill Josh.

* * *

Mortigan was notified through comms that Epitaph was alive and had a small Black Guard warship fleet still loyal to him. The officer on the comms added that Epitaph was aboard the warship, *Mayhemic* and that ship was on a tracking course toward their current location. The darkness controlling Mortigan commanded him to wait for Epitaph because there was something here he may wish to see. Mortigan gave the order to hold his fleet here and monitor Epitaph's ships as they approached. Mortigan then looked out the viewing window at a planet.

* * *

A single Luth Bik Resistance ship had arrived at the far orbit of the planet that Slade was calling Aklowda. Slade had pleaded with the resistance to reassemble their fleet and not waste resources for him. Despite the pleas, the Luth Bik code of honor would not leave a warrior in need. It had been done, and Slade knew from experience that Luth Biks had a hard time refusing to help friends and allies.

Slade, Josh, Tana, and two Luth Bik soldiers landed in a Luth Bik shuttle in the center of the canyon and approached the palace carved into the canyon wall. Their approach was attacked by soldiers in green and yellow armor and helmets that resembled that of a ram on Earth. The soldiers soared in from the sky and landed in a blocking formation. Their metal wings retracted back into the packs on their backs. There were six of them, and they had drawn longswords that spread apart to form parallel blades. The weapons were charged with a humming sound, and two soldiers had fired off electrical streams from them into the air as warning shots. Josh was impressed with swords that doubled as ranged weapons. Slade explained that the soldiers were called Gomen Satys, humans in a living armor, which was an additional weapon itself that had many abilities. He called the swords stingrippers. He then said that the Gomen Satys were the least of their worries. Josh, Tana, and the two Luth Biks looked to him in question. Slade nodded his head forward. They followed the nod and looked behind the line of Gomen Satys soldiers for the answer. A giant robot with smooth armor plating had emerged from the palace. It was wide with massive arms and legs and a hulking stance. The giant robot straightened its stance and stood fourteen feet tall. Josh, Tana, and the two Luth Biks looked back to Slade again. Slade called the robot a brute. Slade told them that this would be easy, because that brute was one of the smaller models.

* * *

Epitaph entered the cybernetic and robotic lab aboard the *Mayhemic* with Emelia at his side. They stood in an overhead observation unit as they watched Laylee be disassembled. Epitaph spoke over a comm unit to those scientists taking her apart. He told them to make sure that the memory banks were thoroughly probed. Emelia was anxious to see how this would help them find Josh. Epitaph explained that everything the android knew about Josh would be in its memory if it was not damaged during the exposure to space. Epitaph claimed that they could possibly learn more about Josh then Josh knew about himself.

* * *

Mortigan was observing the fluctuation readings near the temple on the planet with the shadow still pouring from his eyes. Epitaph was still just under an estimated four rotation arrival at maximum standard speed. Mortigan wanted a shuttle and schism escorts to land at the temple on the planet. He called it the God Planet and the key to his further ascension of power.

* * *

Slade waved his companions back behind him as he stepped forward. He revealed the highly technical gauntlet called a war arm that he wore on his lower left arm as he focused his attention to the Gomen Satys general identified by a red sash. The general called for surrender. Slade slowly and cautiously removed his war arm and gently placed it on the rocky ground. Josh and the Luth Biks behind him followed his move and did the same with their blaster pistols and rifles. Slade then introduced himself as Prince Slade of the Kylde Kingdom. Luth Biks and humans in the same two shaded green armor that Slade wore had then poured out from hidden positions as well as common citizens. All seemed to be spreading joy among each other. The Gomen Satys general yelled out in a great tone of happiness and declared it as the return of Prince Slade. Slade's companions rallied behind him.

Josh smiled and asked, "Prince?"

Slade replied in the affirmative.

Josh said with an even wider smile, "Destiny's brother!"

* * *

Epitaph received a report delivered personally from Captain Gwen that no information on Josh's current whereabouts could be retrieved from the android's memory. All past activity pulled from the memory had been placed on a comm pad, and anything pertaining to Josh Broody had been prioritized. He ordered the android destroyed, but Emelia countermanded the order as she looked over the data and discovered that the android was having a sexual relationship with Josh. Emelia claimed that Laylee may still be useful. Epitaph asked Emelia if she could reprogram the android. Emelia nodded and matched it with a sinister smile. Epitaph ordered Captain Gwen to have the android rebuilt. Captain Gwen smiled back at Epitaph with a little flirt in her grin and walk as she left the room. Emelia noticed and asked Epitaph if he was taking another bride. Epitaph grinned at her with his own reptilian smile. He said, "Nobody could replaccce you, my love."

Emelia stepped closer to him and reached up to caress his scaly reptilian face. Epitaph bent down as Emelia stretched upward, and they open-mouth kissed each other heavily with intertwining tongues and tight groping of each other's asses.

* * *

Slade, Josh, Tana, and the two Luth Biks were escorted to and greeted by the Council of High Citizens that Slade had put in place to run the planet when he left to help a planet called Earth from a Ubide invasion. The council provided Slade's companions free run of the palace. The Council of High Citizens was exactly what Slade had envisioned. It was made up of three chosen individuals and two elected individuals. All were from both sides of the war and consisted of one human female, two human males, one Luth Bik female, and one Luth Bik male.

As the others departed and the crowd dispersed, Slade held back at the council's request for a private meeting. They first asked about his sister, Princess Erikai, and Slade informed them that she was doing well and was even a mother now with the son of Rayk. He then dispensed the bad news that Rayk had given his life to save many others. All the council members seemed pleased and wished for their condolences to be given to Princess Erikai. Slade promised to do that. They cautiously approached the reason for his return and asked if he had desired to resume his rightful place as ruler.

Slade assured them that he had no desire to seek a throne. He admitted that he was pleased with the success the council had achieved at governing his former kingdom and the progress of unification between his people and that of Queen Arrara's people and the peace they have obtained. He announced that he had become separated from his new home, wife, and child yet to be born. His only intention was to find his way back to them. The citizens on the council knew that some would be angry that he was leaving again. Slade expressed his confidence that the council could calm them and maintain peace and order.

The two Luth Biks had assembled with the Luth Biks in the society while Josh walked off alone through the palace halls. Tana followed and wished to apologize for Josh's loss of Laylee. Tana admitted that she felt bad for two reasons. She was genuine in her sadness for his loss. She also admitted to feeling wrong that she was, in a way, glad that Laylee was gone. Josh looked at her strangely as he stepped backward a bit at the comment. Tana admitted that she still wanted to be with him but not in this way. Josh also expressed sadness for the loss of Tana's mother, whom she had just been rejoined with, and he was sorry he had not expressed that to her before now. The two embraced as friends but got lost as they gazed into each other's eyes. They began to kiss, and the kiss grew with passion as neither wished to break away.

* * *

Emelia had completed her reprogramming of Laylee's directives. All her previous directives of pleasure and self-survival had been erased. Laylee had now only one purpose, and that was to kill Josh Broody. Emelia accessed the computer and began a probable search for Josh with her newest ally.

* * *

Slade was walking through the palace when he was stopped by two council members, one female human named Kileen and a human male named Delonian. Kileen was a tall human woman at six feet in height. She had long dark brown hair and a very curvaceous and firm body. Delonian stood only at five feet eight and was slightly heftier than an average weight for that size. He had wildly grown and ungroomed gray hair. They had four soldiers with them. Kileen expressed their concern that they still believed Slade was here to take back his throne and did not believe the story he told the council. Delonian asked if he remembered the man named Nacaab. Slade recalled the name of the man who tried to assassinate him in Queen Ararra's name. They admitted to being instrumental in Nacaab's capture and trial and used that fame to gain their seats on the council. They admitted that they were defaming the reputation of the other council members and about to take over the council to rule as the new king and queen. Delonian stepped closer and yelled that Slade's return has put their plan in jeopardy.

Kileen stepped behind Delonian. She reached around and slit his throat with a dagger. Delonian fell dead at her feet. Kileen then claimed, "I guess only a queen will rule." Slade raised his war arm to shoot a pulsating blast, but nothing happened. He tried to engage the dagger and the comm, but nothing worked. He checked the charge quickly, and it seemed in order. Kileen laughed. She admitted to sabotaging it while it was removed when he first took it off and before it was returned to him. A quick magnetizing was all it took. The four soldiers with her then opened fire on him with their war arms. Slade dodged the pulsating energy blasts and barreled past them, only to find this section of the palace was locked down and the alarms deactivated. Kileen was proud of her preparation. Slade ran down another hall as the four soldiers pursued on her order.

* * *

Mortigan had brought two Laser Heads with him as they broke into the temple. As the door was forced opened, a large axe swung down and impaled one Laser Head. Electricity shot out from its circuits as the oversized axe kept swinging with the Laser Head still attached. Mortigan pressed on and threw the other Laser Head in front of him to take the flames that shot out from a forward wall. The fire burned briefly on the Laser Head only singeing the metal armor. Mortigan sent the Laser Head into the next chamber first. The walls sprung with spikes and closed in on it. Once pressed together, the walls again retracted. The Laser Head was damaged and sparking from its joints but was able to continue down the hall still ahead of Mortigan, where poison sprayed out at it, and as a robot, the Laser Head was still unaffected. Mortigan again made the Laser Head enter the next chamber. The floor gave way, and the Laser Head began to wildly shoot laser fire from its spherical head in all directions as it fell into an acid pit and began to disintegrate. The acid had eaten through the armor and circuitry, and the Laser Head stopped its laser fire as it was further disintegrated by the acid.

The chamber led nowhere, and Mortigan tried the next chamber. Mortigan cautiously and slowly walked across the cobblestone floor. He made it all the way across. He stepped on the last stone before the door and felt it sink. From the left side of the door, a long and sharp blade swung downward. The darkness inside him told Mortigan to jump, and he did. Mortigan had excellent reflexes and jumped over it. He also had great hearing, and after the first blade missed him and stopped its swing, he heard a small click followed by another blade that swung upward from the right side of the door in an attempt to take his head off, but Mortigan had again heard the darkness tell him to drop. He dropped to the floor and evaded that as well. The door ahead of him opened after the blade traps had sprung. He believed he had found the God Chamber, but as he lit the torch at the door, he found it to be a library. At first, he was disappointed until he realized it was not a regular library. He had found a Library of the Books of Prophecy. This knowledge of events to come was the ultimate power that Epitaph had been in pursuit of for so long.

A portal abruptly started to rip open. It did so just as the Black Guard had warned Mortigan over the comms that a rift was opening in space above the planet. The portal opening in the library seemed to be in sync with the opening of the rift. Mortigan stood ready with the shadow pouring from his eyes, and now black rings of smoke encircled his wrists. He further embraced the darkness in order to use it to fight the gods that he believed would exit the portal. It was no god that crawled from the portal, it was Gold Gatling.

Chapter Twenty-Seven

Mortigan's Rise

As GOLD GATLING crawled out from the portal, Mortigan realized that the darkness had made him a god. The incubation process was complete, and he was now fully aware. He knew of Gold Gatling and demanded Gold to serve him. The thick black smoke reached out from Mortigan and began to go inside Gold. He choked on the smoke at first before realizing that it was trying to control his mind. Gold fought it as much as he could, but he collapsed as it overwhelmed him. The smoke darkened Gold's eyes and then retreated back into Mortigan, who again demanded Gold to serve him. Gold staggered to his feet and shook the disorientation from his head. He looked at Mortigan's shadow pouring eyes and called him Master.

* * *

The disappearance of a council member and the absence of Prince Slade had caused some concern from the Council of High Citizens. Kileen claimed that she had the sealed-off section of the palace searched. She was asked by the Luth Bik female High Citizen Ashik and the Luth Bik male High Citizen Docar how the repairs in that section were progressing. Kileen admitted that she had not yet had the chance to fully assemble a construction team. Kileen redirected the conversation back to Prince Slade's and Delonian's disappearance by stating she had just learned through a comm that Prince Slade had returned to visit what was left of the underground caves, being he had spent most of his life there. She added that Delonian had offered guidance. The explanation did make sense. Delonian had been reconstructing small portions of the underground caves. Kileen smiled and sighed in relief that she had most likely solved another crisis. She moved for the emergency meeting to be adjourned, and her motion was granted.

Slade was on the run and trapped in the section of the palace that Kileen had sealed off. He was trying to remain hidden as the four soldiers loyal to Kileen methodically searched for him. He had learned of many hidden areas in the palace that had not been revealed to everyone and had accessed one of those passages through a false wall panel. He figured he could traverse the narrow passage to another point beyond the sealed section. He walked along, trying to remain quiet as he crept through the inside of the walls.

He heard a rustle and a moan up ahead in the curvature of his path. He carefully and quietly approached an air vent only to find Josh pounding himself into Tana. Josh was braced against the wall with Tana grappled in his arms and her legs tightly around his waist as he pounded his cock hard inside her, as she moved in an up-and-down motion. Both were moaning in deep states of pleasure as they finally climaxed. Slade pushed open the air vent and jumped down from his position on the opposite wall. Josh and Tana were equally surprised. Tana released her legs from Josh's waist and stood on the ground between Slade and Josh as Josh quickly redressed himself. Slade apologized and used his hand to shield his eyes. Tana would never understand the obsession other races had with covering their bodies with materials so that others would not be offended or judge. The Matrasus believed the naked body made them free, not to mention provided them with greater prowess and agility.

Once Josh had been situated, Slade explained what had happened. Josh asked if he had any supporters that he was sure he could trust. Slade was unsure. He admitted that he had been gone for a long time. Josh showed him where they had sneaked into and could lead Slade from there back out from the sealed-off palace section. Slade did not think he could make any accusations against Kileen until he was sure he could trust other council members or even some guards. Even if he did accuse Kileen, he was sure that Delonian's body had been removed.

* * *

Emelia had entered Epitaph's quarters aboard the *Mayhemic* with a new plan to find Josh and forever stop the prophecy. She also unveiled the new and improved Laylee. Epitaph was in awe and inquired as to the difficulty to reprogram these units. Emelia laughed with conceit of the confidence of her own skills and desire to kill Josh Broody. Epitaph seemed frozen in puzzlement of Laylee. Emelia asked if there was something wrong. Epitaph shook his attention free and said that there was nothing wrong; he was just wondering if it was that easy to catch a Broody. Epitaph recalled Josh's brother Jase was attached to another android by the name of Adrienne. He asked what Emelia thought that the Broody brothers found so attractive about them. He admitted that they were top of the line and the most advanced models. Emelia thought it was much simpler than that. Epitaph looked at her, and Emelia claimed that the Broody brothers just did not like to play with real girl parts. Emelia removed her garments and offered her body to Epitaph. She then placed herself across his bed. Epitaph positioned himself atop her and began to flick his forked tongue across her firm breasts. Laylee remained silent in observation.

* * *

Mortigan was reading through the Books of Prophecy that he had found. Despite being a library, it still seemed that many books were missing. It did not matter anyway because Mortigan was having trouble deciphering their meanings. He assumed that would come natural to him now that he was a god and the gods had made the prophets. Mortigan though grew more frustrated by the moment as he tried to interpret them. He needed an edge against Epitaph. All he knew for sure was that Epitaph feared a prophecy of uniting brothers. What Mortigan was able to decipher was that the brothers were the key. Mortigan pondered hard on the question of Josh and who, because his brother Jase was already dead so the prophecy should have already been stopped.

Gold admitted that he too was unable to ever understand the writings, but they did make great profits when he sold them, and Epitaph was always top bidder. Gold did admit to hearing something once about how prophecies could never be truly stopped, just delayed and forced to change, but still with the same end result. That could not be true, though, because otherwise, why would people try? Gold continued to ramble on as Mortigan searched through several books.

Gold suddenly became quiet as Mortigan read aloud something that described the hidden world that Gold had come from in perfect detail. There were also many prophecies about a made-up man, and a lot of them crossed with the hidden world and conquered worlds. He found many references to a dark brother that lined up with Josh Broody and a human that was not human that lined up to what he learned from Gold's knowledge.

Mortigan also made the connections with what he knew about Josh. Josh and Slade were prominently important in more than a few prophecies. They were also brothers, just not to each other. Mortigan realized they really had to find Josh more than ever before.

* * *

Epitaph was again on the command deck as the *Mayhemic* and a small warship fleet navigated through disrupted space. Captain Gwen brought to his attention of a crippled Honsho freighter that had been detected by long-range sensors about an ara and a half ahead in their path. He ordered it ignored. Captain Gwen admitted that they had just learned its registration to the Gatling Legion. Epitaph recalled his dealings with Gold Gatling, known throughout the galaxies as the most resourceful pirate. Epitaph considered his desired payback for Gold's play at the planet, Matrel. He was remembering a prophecy: "A passenger would be found amongst what was once a pirate stronghold. This passenger's role to play will be significant." There was nothing else that Epitaph could recall. It was not even specific to which prophecy this passenger would affect. He reversed his order and instructed Captain Gwen to put a tractor beam on it once they reached its location.

* * *

Once back on his Black Guard warship, which he had renamed *Dark Wish 2*, Mortigan was updated by his Darkest on Epitaph's approach, which was now three aras away. Gold stood with his master and detected a Gatling Legion Honsho freighter in the path. Mortigan claimed to care for the interests of his newest slave and decided that they should meet Epitaph halfway and do so by rescuing the Honsho freighter.

* * *

Cody had been waiting on the Albejen ship for some sort of transmission or report on the status of his companions. The shield-stone seemed to hamper communications much like it did the scanners. He was working on the sensors and trying to adjust them to detect through it. A hail from the Luth Bik warship called for his attention. They informed him of a bright spherical light on an approach near Aklowda. He put it on his screen as well. There were detections of energy around it and something familiar to a lifeform inside. The readings were inconclusive as to what lifeform, but it was a 98 percent match that it could be a sentient lifeform. The light was on an approach vector not headed directly toward Aklowda but seemed to be veering toward a specific rift away from Aklowda's far orbit. Cody moved the Albejen shell ship to Aklowda's far orbit and enhanced scans on the light and its path. As the light moved closer to the rift on screen, it seemed unaffected by its pull.

Slade, Josh, and Tana had exited the sealed-off section of the palace. They were attempting to stay hidden but were fired upon with pulsating energy blasts by two soldiers in dual shaded green armor and brandishing war arms. Slade led his friends to another secret passage. They dodged around the corner, and the two soldiers pursued. They hid behind some crates as the soldiers passed by them.

Slade then led Josh and Tana in the opposite direction. Slade reached a doorway and reached up above it to trip a section in the ceiling. A rope ladder dropped as the section opened. Slade climbed up first, followed by Tana and then Josh. Slade claimed that this passage was deeper in the palace but could be traversed to the council chambers.

The pulsating energy blasts had been heard by citizens, and the news grew rapidly to the attention of the Council of High Citizens. Kileen warned that the shots heard could have been anything from a training soldier or a misfired weapon by even a civilian. She urged the other council members not to escalate the situation out of control. They needed to learn the facts first. She assured them that she would check with security forces and review the area of report. She reminded them that with Delonian's absence, security did fall under her responsibilities.

One of the security soldiers entered and delivered a scout report directly to Kileen. It was purely fabricated by Kileen herself and delivered as she expected. She read the report, and with credit to her acting skills, she seemed very shocked. She read that Delonian's body had been found dead. His throat had been cut by the blade from a war arm. The council members were filled with horror as a response. Kileen then showed them a map and plan to kill the Council of High Citizens and take control. The map and plan were on a videocom chip found under Delonian's dead body and displayed for the whole council to witness. As the council examined the video displayed map, Kileen identified the author code on the chip. It was an older code registered to Prince Slade. The plans were dated just before he had left Aklowda. Kileen claimed it an obvious long-term plan to execute on return from his long absence.

The council members found this all hard to believe, but Kileen verified the authenticity. She mentioned that Princess Erikai was listed as a key involvement in the plans. Kileen further drew her conclusions that by Princess Erikai not returning with Prince Slade, might indicate why he had not moved on them yet. She added clearly in an attempt to further spread fear that perhaps Princess Erikai had returned and had already infiltrated the palace.

The council of High Citizens delivered a panicked vote to send forces to search for and apprehend Prince Slade and his companions, including Princess Erikai. Kileen did state that she had already called for a brute robot to be stationed at the doors to the council chambers in the interest of their security. The human male High Citizen, Brosin, added that the palace should be on a full lockdown as well.

* * *

Mortigan and Gold learned that Epitaph was poised to reach the crippled Honsho freighter before them. Gold recalled a female Honsho as he started to peer through the darkness. This lady was on the freighter. He could not place her name or gain a clear look at her appearance but he had the feeling that she was very important to him somehow. He informed Mortigan of what the darkness had allowed him to see. Mortigan felt the darkness inside him confirm that they needed this female Honsho. Mortigan ordered their fleet speed increased.

* * *

Cody had been reviewing an energy signature trail that the spherical light had been leaving behind its path. He matched the last three detected areas of space where the spherical light had been with the same three areas that reported the rifts had now closed. Cody also noticed the energy trail was weakening. A dissipation in the trail from over the period traveled was expected, but this seemed more like a faster draining of energy than dissipation. He observed the light still unaffected by the pull of the rift but entering into the rift under its own power. As it passed through, the rift slowly closed. The light reappeared after the rift closed, and the energy level had indeed dropped from the previous recording before entry.

Cody hailed the Luth Bik warship and gave it coordinates and a course. He was going to follow this thing and see where it went. The Luth Bik commander asked about Slade on the planet. Cody said they would return for Slade. The Luth Bik warship followed the Albejen shell ship's course.

* * *

The passageway that Slade, Tana, and Josh were crawling through was attacked and blasted open. All three of them fell to the floor under heavy pulsating energy blasts. Josh was severely hit. Slade held his hands up while Tana threw herself over Josh's body to further protect him. The soldiers were then shocked to unconscious states by streams of electricity fired from two Gomen Satys soldiers armed with stingrippers behind them.

The soldiers asked if their majesty was okay. Slade reported the situation to them and implicated High Citizen Kileen as the head conspirator. Two other Gomen Satys soldiers had run into the area. Slade asked them to take Josh and Tana to the medical facility. Slade then asked the first two that had saved them to follow along with him again.

Slade realized that anyone in the conspiracy could not have been in the Gomen Satys. They wore living armor that bonded with the soldier inside like a symbiote relationship. The armor was also linked like a sect or hive mind. The person wearing the armor could only hide the knowledge briefly before being discovered by the others. Slade's newfound knowledge brought him a smile. He had an ally now, and better than that, his ally was an army.

* * *

In the council chamber, news was brought by a security officer that Slade and two others had been stopped from an advance through a secret passage that appeared to be leading to this council chamber. The Luth Biks that had come with Slade had already been arrested. Josh and Tana were taken to the medical facility, but retrieval would be a problem as they had Gomen Satys guards with them. It had also been reported that the Gomen Satys were the ones that rescued Slade and his companions. Kileen asked for Slade's current status. The officer reported that Slade was still at large and with Gomen Satys soldiers.

He asked Kileen if she wished the medical facility taken. Kileen said no. She was not ready to engage the Gomen Satys and start an internal war inside the palace. She ordered that Slade be stopped first and any Gomen Satys with him. Until that goal was achieved, Kileen recommended that the Gomen Satys believe the medical facility was in their control. Kileen called the brute into the chamber. This brute was the larger twenty-eight feet tall model. She suggested that the other council members go out and calm the people. She would stay in the council chamber and use it as her command center.

As the council members flooded out from the chamber, the female Luth Bik High Citizen Ashik stayed behind. She suggested that she wanted to keep this conversation private until they were certain that she was correct. Kileen asked Ashik, "Correct about what?" Ashik claimed that she had suspicions that the previously found evidence had been falsified. Kileen hid her reaction well and urged Ashik to give her explanations. Ashik claimed that the plans could not have been made just before Slade had left Aklowda. She pointed out that the videocom chip itself to her inspection was only a cycle old. Kileen had placed herself behind Ashik as the videocom chip was displayed for further inspection. Kileen stabbed Ashik with a blade from the rear straight through her chest, piercing one of the Luth Bik hearts. She pulled out the blade as Ashik fell to the floor. Kileen then plunged the blade through Ashik's lower left midsection, piercing the second Luth Bik heart. Kileen summoned a bipedal light metal servant robot frail in build from the side wall to clean the blood up. She instructed the brute robot to remove the body and, when the servant droid had cleaned up all the blood, to crush it and remove it as well. The servant robot started by wiping the blood from Kileen's hands. When they were clean, Kileen motioned for it to get the blood on the floor.

Chapter Twenty-Eight

Prizes

EPITAPH WAS INFORMED by Captain Gwen of the tractor beam engagement on the Honsho freighter. She added that the Black Guard ships that Mortigan had stolen were headed toward their position and slowing speed from a previously hastened approach. This knowledge was well received. It was clear that Mortigan had an interest in the Honsho freighter as well and was trying to retrieve it before they did.

Epitaph ordered the tractor beam halted and shields up. Captain Gwen asked about the freighter reminding Epitaph that if Mortigan wanted it, they could not let him have it. The ships under Mortigan's control had arrived and were already firing upon them. Epitaph ordered Captain Gwen to adjust position ahead of the freighter. He then asked for arrival time of the slower ships in her fleet. She admitted that they were on their own; the others were still an ara away. Epitaph then ordered all schisms launched and to send Emelia to the Honsho freighter.

Five Black Guard warships to one were good odds as Mortigan observed the battle and liked his chances. It was announced that the *Mayhemic* had begun launching of schisms. Mortigan replied with the order to launch their own. He was informed by one of the Darkest that the *Mayhemic* was primarily a schism carrier warship and did possess a much larger complement of schisms than what all five of their ships had combined. Mortigan repeated the order to launch their own.

Gold was monitoring the freighter and announced that Epitaph had sent a boarding party to it. Mortigan ordered Gold to stay focused at gun controls. Gold was beginning to mentally fight against the darkness that had taken control of his mind. Gold was actually reverting to his older thinking of where he could get to with his jumpband. He had no good options. The darkness in Mortigan warned him of Gold's mental conflict. Mortigan ordered Gold to remove his jumpband. Gold struggled with the command but did as he was told. He placed the jumpband at the gunnery station within his reach. He then replied, "Yes, Master."

* * *

Emelia had instructed Laylee to come with her on the shuttle. Laylee was feeling something like an internal conflict. She had an urge to contact Josh, but her programming was telling her to kill him.

As Emelia docked the shuttle to the boarding hatch of the crippled Honsho freighter, she noticed Laylee frozen in her reactions. She yelled at Laylee to unlock the hatch. Laylee did and started to stand. Emelia stood at the boarding hatch with her katana-like sword already gripped tightly in both hands. She ordered Laylee to stay on the shuttle and perform another self-diagnostic on her programming. Emelia then stepped onto the Honsho freighter.

* * *

A battle of purple flames and streams of electricity shot from stingrippers and pulsating energy blasts shot from guns and war arms had erupted. Slade had been given a stingripper but wished his war arm was operational. The battle spilled over and into a community gathering area in the palace. Several of the citizens trapped there from the total palace lockdown were taking cover.

Slade kept his head low and moved out under cover fire to help direct the citizens back behind the battle lines before returning to his firing position. The palace lockdown alarms started to sound causing a widespread panic. The male Luth Bik High Citizen Docar pushed his way into the Gomen Satys formation and next to Slade. Slade continued to shoot the stingripper, but his purple flames were depleted and he had switched to electricity streams. High Citizen Docar stated that he saw Slade save people stranded here. He admitted that he doubted the evidence that Slade was going to kill all the council members and assume power. Slade shot one more stream of electricity from his cover position. He then turned to Docar and said, "I was, huh? Doesn't seem like a good idea, though." He then asked Docar if he could get as many people possible away from the council chambers for safety. He replied that Kileen had locked herself and a brute inside to make her stand. Docar asked if Slade thought Kileen was behind it.

Slade replied with laughter he could no longer contain, "You might be on to something there. Maybe she wanted to be the next bitch queen since my mother's demise apparently left the position open." He then shot off another electricity stream and hit the last of the soldiers. The battle was over. The human male High Citizen Brosin, who had been among the people that Slade had just saved, came running to express his loyalty to Slade and apologize for believing the charges against him.

* * *

Emelia was forcing the Honsho and Wobmat refugees, most of which were children off the Honsho freighter and onto the Black Guard shuttle. Wobmats appeared human except for their yellow eyes. Emelia was unsure which one Epitaph found important to prophecy. It had to be a Honsho because Wobmats were mostly ignored and considered insignificant of attention with nothing of value except to the Honshos. She was also looking for anything of value. She stuck a pile of gems into the inner pocket of her jacket. As she moved away, she tripped something. She recognized a trap instantly. She began to push the refugees harder and commed Laylee. Laylee stated that there was a bomb just detected. Emelia acknowledged the detection and told Laylee to pull the refugees aboard. She then instructed Laylee to detach once she was on board. Emelia was the last through and closed the boarding hatch. She hollered out for Laylee to detach now. Emelia rushed to the pilot controls as the shuttle was floating away from the Honsho freighter. She engaged the engines and flew a curving motion away from the Honsho freighter just before it exploded in two large blasts.

* * *

Gold had reported damages in the engine room. He claimed he could help. The Black Guard warship just took a heavy barrage of laser fire from a full squadron of schisms loyal to Epitaph. Mortigan dismissed Gold to the engine room. He did not notice that Gold had reequipped his jumpband.

Gold took the turbolift down to the engine room. He continued to think evil thoughts along the way to keep the darkness inside of him from realizing that he was slowly regaining control of his own mind. An explosion occurred in the engine room as Gold was walking toward it. The fire, smoke, and debris were shot down the corridor. Gold had seen it coming toward him and activated his jumpband just as it poured over where he was at. Gold entered a teleportation portal with a mixture of yellow and white light. The portal closed behind him. He then walked out from another portal that opened in the shuttle bay. Between the explosion and the jump, Gold had felt the darkness that had corrupted him disappear. He ran for the Black Guard shuttle and lifted off. He made a turn, and the shuttle flew from the docking bay.

* * *

Despite the advantage of schism starfighters, the *Mayhemic* was outgunned by the force of five other fully operational Black Guard warships commanded by Mortigan. The *Mayhemic's* damage was reaching critical. Emelia was headed back to it in the Black Guard shuttle as the escape pods launched. She was forced to adjust her flight pattern and try to flee the battle zone. Two schisms loyal to Mortigan had targeted her shuttle. Just before they could fire, a squadron of nine schisms from the *Mayhemic* and loyal to Epitaph flew over her shuttle and combined laser fire on the hostile schisms, blowing them apart. The lead schism pilot assembled the squadron around Emelia's shuttle and offered safe escort from the battle zone. She accepted and flew her shuttle in the middle of and protected by the schism squadron.

The *Mayhemic* was left behind by the shuttles, escape pods, and schisms as it was beginning to fall apart. Epitaph had climbed up a ladder as an explosion threw debris all around him. He maneuvered upward through the falling debris and entered into a compartment that housed a one-seated ship shaped much like a missile and it sealed as he entered. The missile ship launched upward and away from the final explosions that claimed the last of the *Mayhemic*.

Mortigan watched the *Mayhemic's* destruction and gave orders for his schisms and shuttles to corral all the escape pods and shuttles. He was then notified that additional crews had been assigned to engine repair. Mortigan looked back at the gunnery station and realized that he had not heard from Gold. The darkness inside him could not link onto Gold either. Mortigan asked the sensor officer to locate Gold Gatling. After a few moments, it was reported that Gold Gatling was no longer on ship. Security cameras had been run through, and they had found Gold departed with shuttle identification number 67976 from docking bay ten. Mortigan ordered the shuttle beacon activated. It revealed his coordinates. There were two small squadrons of schisms in that sector. Mortigan ordered them to destroy that shuttle.

* * *

The Albejen shell ship had lost track of the mysterious spherical light that it had been following. Suddenly, an attack came from above the ship. It was pounded with multiple and rapid hits of solid light energy. The recently repaired shields were holding. Cody sent a distress signal. The Luth Bik warship that had been following the spherical light with Cody had just caught up and entered the sector.

Cody called for retaliation. The shields were holding on the Albejen shell ship, but the rapid fire and relentless pounding of solid light energy had prevented the ship from any offensive moves. The Luth Bik warship opened up all its forward guns.

On board the Albejen shell ship, Cody noticed his body shimmer and start to vanish. The spherical light ceased its attack and seemed to have taken no damage from the Luth Bik warship's most powerful guns. It streaked away in the blink of an eye. The Luth Bik commander hailed Cody to no response. They detected no life signs. The Luth Bik warship docked with the Albejen shell ship and a boarding party was detached and searched the ship. They reported back to the Luth Bik commander that Cody was not on the ship.

* * *

The announcement was sent throughout the palace for everyone to surrender to the guards stationed at either the palace gate or the council chamber door. The palace would remain on lockdown until all citizens had been processed. The Council of High Citizens effective immediately had been disbanded. Those former high citizens still alive would be charged with treason if they did not surrender at once. The same went for Prince Slade and his companions. The Gomen Satys was also ordered to stand down or vow their service to the new ruler of Aklowda, Queen Kileen.

The Gomen Satys general informed Slade and the council members that the Gomen Satys would not stand down. Slade told him to have the Gomen Satys stand down but remain ready to move on the soldiers that had sworn loyalty to Kileen. Slade figured once Kileen had been taken down, the soldiers that supported her would most likely surrender. High Citizen Docar estimated that the actual number of soldiers that had taken action with Kileen was quite small. Those that did not have either lain down arms or went into hiding to plan a rebellion. Slade said it would be over once he killed Kileen.

Capture was not going to work; she had proven to be too dangerous. High Citizen Brosin asked how he would enter the council chambers. Slade admitted that knowledge of secret entrances was his secondary specialty. He then asked Slade what the first specialty was, and he responded that it was taking down ruling bitch queens.

* * *

Gold's shuttle was fired upon by twelve schisms. He attempted evasive maneuvers, but the shuttle was bulky and slow. He fired its low-level lasers, but he was already outgunned and outmaneuvered. The shuttle was hit multiple times, and what was left of it would burn up in the atmosphere of the planet it was falling into.

The schisms reassembled into squadron formations and headed back to Mortigan's controlled Black Guard ships. Critical damage alarms were sounded as the body of the shuttle continued to heat up as it plummeted through the planet's atmosphere. Gold was calculating distance as he prepared to do what Gold Gatling did best. The distance had to be exact for the teleport jump to work. He activated his jumpband and jumped into a portal of yellow light just before the shuttle remains burned away. Gold dropped from an opened teleport portal just above a swamp and fell into it in his solid form. Gold yelled out loudly, "A messy landing, but another amazing escape!"

* * *

Slade had slid away a wall panel that was once behind where the old queen's throne once rested. He crept along the wall keeping his body tightly against it. He took cover behind a tall curtain that hung from the high ceiling and observed self-declared Queen Kileen redesigning the layout of the room. A highly decorated chair was the best she could do with for now. She wondered out loud though what had ever happened to Queen Ararra's throne. Slade stepped out from his hiding spot and declared that he had ordered that throne burned.

Kileen slowly walked to the side of the giant brute that jumped to an alerted stance to Slade's arrival. Kileen admitted to hearing that

Slade had taken down a brute before. Slade admitted that it was actually his Luth Bik friend Rayk and his sister Erikai that had done most of the work on two of them. He had just cleaned up what was left.

Kileen then said, "Let us see how you can do on your own against one then." She ordered the brute to crush Slade. The brute readied its charge forward. Slade raised his war arm and activated a beam from it that shot out at the brute and encompassed it in a circle of energy. The brute slumped forward just a bit and powered down.

Kileen was shocked. Slade apologized, but he had gotten a new war arm before he had snuck in the room. He added that these new gadgets developed here were top-notch. He liked the robotic suspension field. It would only keep a full robot neutralized for ten moks before the field would shut down, but by that time, she would be defeated and the brute could be given new commands. He claimed that he was going to keep this war arm. Kileen raised a blaster pistol from a table she stood by. Slade was disappointed. He had thought she was more of a blade person and had been looking forward to a blade battle. Kileen said that she was sorry to disappoint him. She followed with four quick blasts.

Slade still had his war arm up and deflected all four blasts with an energy shield that covered his entire body and was projected from the war arm. Slade said, "Yes I do love these new features."

Kileen threw her pistol away and grabbed a longsword from the wall. Slade smiled and activated the dagger from his war arm. They charged each other with their blades out. Kileen had the advantage with the longer blade, but Slade was a more proven melee combatant and able to dodge her swings and drop and tumble past her before she could readjust. They thrusted and slashed at each other for a few moks. Kileen mentioned that his time was about up. The brute would soon be back in the battle, and she would keep on him with her sword skills to prevent him from pulling that trick again. Slade jumped back from the combat and launched two smoke pellets from his war arm at Kileen's feet. He rolled back in and under the rising smoke around her that was now obstructing her sight. Slade was able to cut her twice before rolling back out again. Kileen stepped out from the already thinning smoke with her midsection sliced open.

She dropped the longsword and fell to her knees with blood gushing out from her midsection as she clutched tightly at it.

She mustered all the breath that she could to laugh and claim that if she survived, she would find a way to escape and others would still follow their queen. Slade reached down and removed the metal control box from her belt. The brute had reactivated and stood to its full twenty-eight feet height. Slade started to walk away from Kileen as she gasped out her declaration that he could not stay and guard her, and he could not let her die. Slade walked to the wall and stood to face Kileen as she laid there bleeding out. He admitted that she was correct—that he could not stay here and guard her from escaping. He then activated the brute control box he had taken from her belt.

Slade said, "Please step on that bitch in front of you." The brute raised its giant foot and stomped once. The foot was nearly seven feet round on size all around her. Kileen was crushed to death in one stomp. Slade then commanded the brute to power down and it did. Slade then looked upward and thanked whatever god was presiding over his actions for forgiveness. He then opened the chamber doors and walked out. He said he would be in the medical facility with his friends.

* * *

Prisoners were covered in hoods and chained together as they were ushered for display before Mortigan at an assembly stage aboard his warship. He ordered the hoods removed. He added that the gags over their mouths were a nice touch. He walked down the line of the ten prisoners and examined each of them closely. They were lined up in order of Honsho, Wobmat, Honsho, and Wobmat until the last two. Most of the Honshos and all the Wobmats were children. In fact, only two adult female and one adult male Honshos were present. Mortigan's shadow still poured from his eyes, but he smiled at the last two prizes as he called them. He pulled the blue hair back from the rotted flesh around the Jaskan's left eye and side of neck. "I have the bride of Epitaph, the infamous Emelia." He was very satisfied with this prize. He admitted that his mind was filling fast with too many thoughts over what he could do with her. He then looked at the android called Laylee. He recognized her from the holograms he had seen as he had pursued Josh across the starfield. He commented that the dampening bolt strapped to her neck to subdue her strength was a clever thought. The one male Darkest that escorted them in added that it would self-destruct if anyone tried to remove it by entering the wrong release code.

Mortigan cupped his hands together and said, "Boom—no more android." He pulled his hands away in an exploding motion as he said it.

Mortigan cupped the chin of the scared and crying little Honsho girl lined up next to Emelia. He pulled her long blond hair back from covering her eyes. He spoke again with a smile, but the pouring shadow from his eyes and his patchwork makeup of multiple and different skins frightened the little girl even more. He said that he needed this one secured in his quarters. He then ordered Emelia and Laylee locked up in separate cells far away from each other. The one male Darkest asked what to do with the others. Mortigan said, "Space them" and walked out of the room.

* * *

Cody had awoken inside the spherical light. He was surrounded by light all around him that was blinding but slowly dimmed. In the center and ahead of him was a translucent humanoid form. Its voice was reverberating and undistinguishable by gender tone as it spoke. It claimed that it had been waiting for him for a very long time. The spherical light continued on its flight.

* * *

Gold Gatling was pulled from the swamp by several Honshos and Wobmats that had crash-landed there. Their Honsho freighter was traveling with another one, but its fate was unknown to them. Gold informed them that the other freighter was crippled and the

Black Guard had rescued the others from that freighter. Gold thanked them again for pulling him from the swamp and wanted to check on their crashed freighter. He suddenly recognized a female Honsho. She looked like any other Honsho, but not many females wore their hair tied back as she did. Gold was shocked to see her. It had been nearly ten cycles. She was once the love of his life, but as the Gatling Legion had grown larger, they had grown apart. He spoke her name as if it was fragile and would break once spoken—"Vally."

The Black Guard comm device Gold still wore sounded an alarm. He activated the visual hail. Mortigan was stroking the long blond hair of a little Honsho girl. He called her a great prize and stated that maybe she could help him in ways that Gold could not. The transmission was terminated at Mortigan's end.

Gold was confused and even more so when the other Honshos tried to calm Vally as she had started crying and shaking. Gold asked if Vally knew the little girl. She replied with a trembling voice that the girl was their ten-cycle-old daughter, Dyam. Gold was filled with shock, an emotion he had not experienced for a long time. He had never known that he had a daughter.

Chapter Twenty-Nine

The Serpent Slithers Still

THE SPHERICAL LIGHT was traveling through space at its own provided light speed. The translucent humanoid form was the pilot. The
reverberating tone it spoke in seemed more stressed as the sphere
moved but clearer when it would be still. It took breaks of movement
with short periods of stillness, but it seemed the movement motion
lasted longer. The pilot explained to Cody that it had been imprisoned in a dark holding zone created by the Dark Lord Epitaph. It
had been told by prophecy. It added on its mission to heal what was
torn. What Epitaph had done to imprison it, would be undone by
the very action Epitaph had taken, leading to the brothers uniting
that would free it. It had again been told by prophecy. The brothers
had united, and now it was traveling through space again and seal-
ing critical rifts. It was literally pulling the fabric of space back into
cohesion. It also spoke of the healing of the universe, which drained
its own life, and to heal everything, it would have to die. It had been
told by prophecy.

Cody was unsure how he had been chosen. Deciphering prophecies had always made his head hurt. It sounded as if the light had
healed space before in the past. The actions that captured it led to the
actions that would cause the actions that would free it. Once freed,

it would do its healing again. Cody clutched at his head. The pilot claimed that Cody had understood. Cody thought that was good and then asked the light to explain it to him what he understood because he was still confused.

* * *

Gold Gatling had helped the stranded Honshos salvage compatible parts from a long-crashed and older-style Black Guard shuttle. It would not be a permanent fix, but it would be enough to get off the planet. He left the Honshos to make their repairs but urged them to rush so they might be able to save the others. They were unsure how they would get the others away from the Black Guard. Gold reminded them that all Honshos were pirates and that pirates always found ways to win. He added another bright spot stating that they were not any ordinary pirates; they were of the Gatling Legion. It was clearly his best skill to rally his followers even when he knew the situation was bleak at best.

Gold had taken Vally off to the side of the swamp and asked her about his daughter. She was still beautiful to him and still his only distraction. Vally explained that she was going to let him know, but Gold was strengthening his legion and building his fame, favor, and reputation to ascend the Gatling Legion to the top of the Honsho Piracy. Gold claimed he would have made time. Vally lightly caressed the side of his face and laughed. She asked him if he believed that. She stated the facts that all Honshos were pirates and belonged to the Honsho Piracy, which was the governing body of their way of life. The stronger the legion, the more sway it held in the piracy. She also reminded him what Honshos had been taught from birth was that it was the responsibility of every Honsho to make the piracy strong. The Honsho Piracy came first, the legion second, the individual third, and the family last. It was the principles of the entire Honsho race. They were the same principles she had been teaching Dyam.

Vally explained that she knew they had grown apart, but she had also seen how Gold had emerged and forged his own legion. She reminded him that the Gatling Legion was the highest-ranking legion in the Honsho Piracy because of his leadership. Vally knew the best thing to do was let Gold go. She stayed within the Gatling Legion for the benefits of strength. She just decided to let her role drift to the lower ranks within it. This allowed Gold to not have to worry about them and kept anyone that wanted to move up in the legion from using them against him. The Honsho Piracy code, after all, was "Always watch those below you." While moving up in any legion was what was expected, she decided to slide down. The further down in the legion she was, it meant less notice.

Gold asked if Dyam knew he was her father. Vally replied that she would not keep that from Dyam. She had explained the dangers of that knowledge to Dyam. She had also given Dyam the same last name she had taken, which was Wait. It was a forged name, but she had taught Dyam the meaning of it. It literally meant "wait." Vally was giving Dyam the chance to grow, and once Dyam became an adult, it would have been up to her alone of how high she wanted to climb in the legion. If Dyam had chosen to rise through the ranks, she could also do it by her own name.

Vally blamed herself for allowing Dyam to go on the freighter with her friends. She either should have kept Dyam with her or gone on that ship as well. Gold thought back to when he was ten cycles of age and remembered that as the age of independence and the initial stage of adulthood for Honshos. The age of ten was when a Honsho was expected to break away from the parents and lay out the ground-work for their own path.

Vally asked how they would get Dyam back and if Mortigan would truly hurt her. Gold leaned back against a tree and sighed. He was truthful that they had to get her back because Mortigan was truly a dark and evil man even before a dark power possessed him. At least Epitaph had a guiding code. It may have been wrong, but it was something that Mortigan did not have. As for how they would get her back, Gold was calculating a plan. Vally asked how far along that plan was at. Gold smiled and said he had just found the word calculating, but he was confident it would go well from there. They laughed and cried together as they embraced each other.

* * *

Emelia had managed to pry open a panel on the inside wall of her cell. She was able to reach through that access point with her left rotted hand and manipulate the outer locking control from the wires in the wall. Emelia laughed as she started to feel for wires and circuits. She asked herself how big of a fool Mortigan could possibly be. She knew all the Black Guard schematics inside and out. She did not even need to see what she was working on. She could do most by touch. It did not matter whether it was a flight control, food cooker, or security lock. She kept looking out and shaking her head at the fact there was not even a guard posted. She felt around the back of the press pad code lock. She did not need a code when she was already into the circuitry. Emelia reached down lower and smiled. She had found the conduit she had desired. She moved her hand along the conduit and felt for the control box. It was an electrical overload switch inside that she was after. She then pried it open and tore out the switch. A strong electrical shock fired through to her hand. The rotted flesh did not feel the shock and also blocked the shock from traveling any further back toward her.

She removed her hand from the wall and tried the door. It had worked and overloaded the computer lock. Emelia simply walked out of her cell. She looked around, and still no guard seemed to be present. She moved silently to the guard control panel and switched off the alarm light that indicated a power failure to her cell lock.

Emelia then identified the cell that Laylee was in. Emelia used her master code to open Laylee's cell, again stunned by Mortigan's stupidity to not even erase previous codes. The next bit, though, would be her challenge. Emelia examined the dampening bolt strapped around Laylee's neck very carefully. It did have a trip for any tampering attempts. She needed the correct code to unlock the strap. According to Mortigan, even an entry of the wrong code would set off the explosive. She told Laylee to follow her. They would have to go get someone with the code.

* * *

The missile escape ship had crash landed on a desolate world. Many odd-looking creatures had surrounded it. They scurried away as the door slid open and Epitaph stepped out. There was little water around. The water that was around was gathered in only small puddles. A dull, gray soil covered most of the surface. Epitaph started to walk across the terrain. This was also a dark world. Epitaph did have dark vision, which helped as the only light seemed to come from the two close orbit moons.

* * *

Cody asked the pilot why he had been waiting for him. The pilot stated that it had been declared in a prophecy. Cody sulked to himself. More prophecy was not what Cody had wanted to hear. The pilot stated that there was prophecy that spoke of a Canian that could take the charge of the light, once the light dimmed out. Cody suggested that perhaps it had the wrong Canian.

The pilot claimed it had the right Canian. It quoted another prophecy, and Cody wished he could gnaw his own ears off to not hear any more. The other prophecy stated that the light would be found by a one-eyed Canian separated from his friends. Cody admitted that it sounded like him.

Cody continued to try to grasp his importance to the scheme of prophecy and destiny. The pilot explained that prophecies had discussed Cody's past with Josh, Josh's betrayal of him, and their reunion. Cody asked the pilot if it was a prophet. It laughed and stated that only Shrow could be prophets. It claimed that it was one of the gods from God Planet.

* * *

The Council of High Citizens was down to two and had decided to call for elections of the three open vacancies. This would make all five of them elected positions. The two current high citizens had again wished for Prince Slade to stay as did the people. Slade declared that he still had faith in the council. Slade's destiny rested elsewhere. The council could accept that but requested Slade and his companions stayed for a festival in their honor. Slade agreed. Josh and Tana had decided that they would return to the Albejen shell ship and brief Cody. They would return with the shuttle in the morning. The two Luth Biks said they would stay with Slade for the night as well. Josh and Tana walked toward the Luth Bik shuttle.

* * *

Emelia and Laylee had moved silently from the detention block and crept around the outer corridors. They came across an officer walking down the corridor with his eyes scanning a datapad. As he rounded the corner, Emelia leg-swept him, and he fell face first to the floor. She jumped down and turned him on his back. She sat on his chest to hold him down and jammed her right forearm hard against his throat. Laylee stood over him as well with her foot pressed against his groin.

The officer looked relieved more than panicked. Emelia noticed that his eyes were normal. She asked if he was not infected by whatever source Mortigan used to control the others. He claimed he was not and had been hiding for rotations. She asked how he had managed that task. He admitted to working night shifts and lesser populated areas of the ships. He added that keeping his head down and moving around without calling attention had helped a great deal. She slowly released her pressure and stood to her feet. Laylee also backed off as Emelia helped him to his feet.

He introduced himself as Lieutenant Mont. He was of average build and ordinary in appearance with short-cut brown hair. He asked if they could get him off the ship. As far as he could tell, he was the only one not yet infected at least until he had run into them. Emelia asked if he had the code to the dampening bolt strapped to

Laylee's neck. He utilized a scanner from his belt. It provided him the code. Emelia watched as he entered it but had the last two numbers inverted. She stopped him, and he said it was okay as he deactivated the dampening bolt and removed it. He explained to Emelia that the scanner could read the code, but the last two numbers were always inverted from his scanner read. It was a security precaution in case the wrong person got a hold of his scanner.

Emelia was impressed. Lieutenant Mont claimed that security precautionary measures and deterrents were his primary duty. Emelia had admitted to never have heard that title. He admitted that it was pretty low-level stuff, but thankfully, his low-level credentials actually helped him stay hidden. Emelia then figured he was unable to get them a shuttle. He corrected her in that error. He was also a computer tech and pretty good at it as he sung his own praise. He even stated that he could gain retrieval of their weapons. He would need protection to the shuttle bay and asked if either of them could pilot because that was not within his skill set.

They had used the cargo turbo lifts to get to a smaller docking bay currently undergoing routine maintenance. Lieutenant Mont accessed a computer and cleared shuttle 6161 for scouting missions. They only needed to get past the two Black Guard armored Darkest that guarded the floor. Emelia and Laylee both charged at them. Before they could draw their weapons, Laylee snapped the neck of her target while Emelia removed her target's head with one swift and powerful swing of her katana-like sword.

Once they were all on board, Emelia piloted the shuttle out from the ship. Lieutenant Mont instructed her to stay on a specific vector until they were out of sensor range. Emelia checked the charts of their current location to find a destination. She plotted in a course to Crenerek. Lieutenant Mont suggested the planet of Chabreel. Emelia stated Crenerek was much closer and had a large Black Guard base. Chabreel was further and only hosted a Black Guard medical facility. Lieutenant Mont admitted that Emelia was correct, but they could not be sure that Mortigan had not corrupted the base on Crenerek. Emelia asked him what made him so sure that Chabreel was safe. He pointed out that it was a more out-of-the-way outpost and, as she said, only a medical facility. Mortigan was only looking for weaponry and power. Chabreel could easily be overlooked for the two factors he listed. Emelia remained impressed and adjusted the course.

* * *

The crashed Honsho freighter repairs had been completed. Gold, Vally, and the other Honshos had boarded. Gold took the pilot controls and the shuttle lifted off. Strong turbulence was experienced as the Honsho freighter attempted ascension through the atmosphere and into space. Honshos were fixing stations as they shorted out because of system stress. Pieces on the outside of the ship had fallen off in the process, including two minor wind flaps for atmospheric stabilization. Once in orbit, Gold did an assessment of the damage. He figured the freighter could dock easily at a station or other ship, but as far as planetary landing was concerned, until they fixed it further, the freighter would only survive through one more atmospheric flight.

* * *

The Luth Bik shuttle entered the near orbit of Aklowda as the Luth Bik Resistance warship reentered far orbit with the Albejen shell ship in tow by means of tractor beam. Josh answered their hail, and the Luth Bik commander explained what had happened. The whereabouts of Cody were still unknown.

* * *

Mortigan was channeling with the darkness power inside of him in an attempt to locate Epitaph's location in the universe. The Darkness was aware of his survival and that he was a threat. Mortigan was interrupted and informed by one of his Darkest that Emelia and Laylee had escaped. Mortigan was furious. He was easily calmed though by the fact that they had tracked the shuttle that was taken. Before the signal was lost, it appeared that the shuttle was on course to Chabreel. Emelia was the bride of Epitaph and another threat to Mortigan's command. Mortigan ordered the fleet to redirect to Chabreel.

* * *

The Honsho freighter had returned to the sight of the space battle and begun to survey the debris. There were no life signs detected. A small group of other mixed ships of various races had also entered the area including a Luth Bik science ship and warship as well as two other Honsho freighters from the Gatling Legion. Gold hailed the two Honsho freighters and was surprised that the hail was answered by Luth Biks. Gold agreed to dock with the Luth Bik warship.

* * *

Epitaph had traversed the dark and desolate planet he was stranded on. He had come across a downed orbital station. The damage from its crash had left many areas of it open for access. Epitaph had entered it and found many stations with minimum but fading power. He was able to assess that the power supply core was leaking and everything that still functioned would not be doing so much longer. He also accessed the logs and discovered that the station had lost orbit stabilizers as the reason for its crash on this planet called Gelemar. He also learned that the race that had operated the station was Lashar. Epitaph accessed the star charts and attempted to locate Gelemar as the power faded in and out. Through all the blinking information, he had determined that he was stranded in Ubide and Derth space.

* * *

Emelia and Laylee had arrived with Lieutenant Mont on Chabreel at the Black Guard Medical Facility. Emelia had requested a meeting with the highest-ranked officer at the facility. The human male officer General Born Falitte introduced himself and ushered

Emelia into a closed meeting. Emelia was seated at a table with other generals, colonels, majors, and captains as well. General Falitte informed Emelia that the current command of the Black Guard was in chaos. Some supported Mortigan's faction, while some supported Epitaph despite rumors of his demise. He put forth that all here at this facility were very aware of her attempt to take command. In response to that, he added that they have all decided to pledge allegiance to Emelia until the condition of Epitaph's life or death was confirmed. He promised that if Epitaph had perished, all in this room and those under their command would then still stand with Emelia.

General Falitte then cleared the room of the other officers. As they cleared out, a Black Guard scientist entered from another doorway and engaged the holographic table display. General Falitte introduced Doctor Nalton Eviss. Doctor Eviss was a gray-haired and gray-bearded older human that, for his age, appeared to move well. He took charge of the conversation. He started by stating that they believed Epitaph was still alive and asked if she would be willing to help locate him. Emelia agreed but was confused where to start looking. She asked if they had received any transmission from him.

Doctor Eviss utilized the holographic display to reveal an implant that Epitaph had installed into her brain at her resurrection cycles ago. It was classified secret even from her until its activation. He continued to explain that it would activate the one implanted in his brain as well if he ever fell from power and lost all control of the Black Guard. Doctor Eviss stated that the implants were linked, and as a result, he would be able to electronically adjust her implant without any surgery to act as a tracker that would lead her to his location. He added that it would only work if Epitaph was still alive.

Emelia immediately granted permission to perform the task. Even Emelia knew that with the chaos that had torn the Black Guard apart, her task of taking command would be more difficult. Emelia's and the Black Guard's best chance of survival and continued reign now depended on the fate of Epitaph being known. The situation would be best if he was found alive. If he was found dead, it would eliminate any question of her rule as she would try to take command again. Doctor Eviss waved a small hand-held box device around Emelia's head until the device lit up with a green light. He proclaimed the implant tracking engagement was successful. Emelia could instantly sense that Epitaph was alive and there was guidance pulling at her to follow.

* * *

Laylee had found a room of solitude. She had been experiencing a feeling of independence, fighting her new programming. She had been trying to keep an image up around Emelia that she was functioning perfectly. Now where she was alone, she could allow herself a chance to, in essence, meditate and perhaps understand.

Chapter Thirty

Scripting a Union

THE NEXT MORNING on Aklowda, Josh had landed the Luth Bik shuttle and retrieved Slade and the two Luth Biks that had stayed with him. During their flight back to Aklowda's near orbit, Josh explained what they knew about what had happened to Cody. Both Josh and Slade knew they must locate Epitaph and kill him, but they were unsure where to look. They both were willing to put the Epitaph mission aside to search for Cody, but again they were clueless where to look. They had to see which mission the Luth Bik ship could find information on first.

* * *

The five Black Guard ships under Mortigan's command had arrived and entered near orbit of Chabreel. All five warships on Mortigan's order had commenced planetary bombing on the planet below.

There was no warning to the planet except for the detection of the warships. The heaviest of the bombing was all around the Black Guard medical facility. General Falitte had, upon the warship detection in orbit, already ushered Emelia and Laylee through a secret exit of the medical facility. They had traveled from there through an underground tunnel that was experiencing falling debris as the surface above it was pounded without mercy from the bombing. The sheer number of bombs seemed more like heavy rain as they fell from orbit and hit the surface. Emelia and Laylee were doing their best to stay ahead of the falling debris.

The bombings slowly drizzled to a halt. Mortigan then released a video hail to all the planet but specifically directed to the Black Guard medical facility that he had assumed would have been her destination. There was no doubt that the video hail was chosen to install fear as people saw a man with patchwork skin of various races and shadow that poured from his eyes. Mortigan agreed to cease the bombing on the one demand that Emelia and Laylee be turned over to him. He announced that he would commence the bombing again in ten moks if he had not received word that they were being delivered to his ship.

* * *

The docking had been successful, and Gold Gatling stepped onto the Luth Bik warship in the fleet of mixed ships. Vally and the other Honshos followed his lead. Gold Gatling introduced himself in his usual state of arrogance.

Gold was informed by the ranking Luth Bik officer that everyone in this fleet had vowed to serve the Luth Bik Resistance, even the Honshos and Wobmats on the two Honsho freighters stated as former ships to the Gatling Legion. He said that they had been separated from the main fleet of Luth Bik warships. He also stated that the last assigned rendezvous point had been decimated by a Black Guard attack before the fleet could fully assemble there. Gold was further briefed on the current Black Guard chaos including Epitaph's unknown status and Mortigan's rise to leadership.

Intel had just been gained from a comm of two other Luth Bik warships that they had been tracking seven Black Guard warships loyal to Epitaph. They had responded to a distress call from the

Black Guard medical facility on Chabreel where there were already five Black Guard warships loyal to Mortigan bombing the planet.

Gold asked if Mortigan's presence could be verified at Chabreel. The intelligence they had suggested that he was on one of the five Black Guard warships already there. It was the one that he had renamed the *Dark Wish 2*. Gold wanted to go there to find his daughter that Mortigan was holding in custody. He was willing to take his freighter alone if he had to but hoped they would join him. The Luth Bik officer stated that they would be slaughtered. Gold appealed to the Luth Bik code of honor, and by not helping him, they did not display honor. The Luth Bik officer admitted that he wanted to help, but it would be a suicide mission. All the Black Guard warships in the report would be there before them.

Gold clasped his palms together and said that it was not a bad thing. He explained that the twelve Black Guard warships in question would be in the middle of a civil war and they could use that to their advantage. Gold asked if the other two Luth Bik warships that were tracking the Black Guard ship movements would meet them there. The Luth Bik officer believed they would but pointed out that there would be twelve Black Guard warships there that they knew about and there could be more that they did not know about. He added that in the assumption the other two Luth Bik warships met them at Chabreel, they would only add their fleet of mixed ships. That fleet consisted of the Luth Bik warship that they were on, one Luth Bik science ship, three Honsho freighters if they included the one Gold had brought, one Canian battleship which was much smaller than a warship, two freighter-sized Kemyyon attack ships, and one confiscated Jaskan pleasure cruiser with extremely minimal weaponry for the task. Gold displayed excitement that they would have eleven ships against the twelve Black Guard warships and those Black Guard warships would be fighting each other. Much damage would be done before the Luth Bik Resistance even arrived.

Gold flashed a smile and jumped up in excitement that he liked those odds. He yelled out, "The Battle at Chabreel, where the Luth Bik Resistance turned the tide of war!" Gold could read people very well, and he looked around at the Luth Biks that surrounded him.

He knew that he almost had them convinced. The Luth Bik officer admitted that he was the highest officer on the ship and he was only a lieutenant. He added that they had no strong leader. Gold said that they did now and offered to take command. The Luth Biks looked around at each other and nodded hesitantly. The Luth Bik lieutenant clarified that it would be a temporary command until a proper Luth Bik command officer arrived. Gold agreed then jumped up again in excitement and told them to spread the word.

* * *

Cody had stepped onto the God Planet with the translucent humanoid form that claimed to be a god itself. Cody had asked what he should call it. The being said that it was a god to all the races that did not believe in a god, like the Canians. It said that Cody could call it Avia Tor if it would be easier for him. Avia Tor then ushered Cody along as they walked among all the gods worshiped by the other races.

The gods had begun a telepathic discussion amongst each other. Avia Tor informed Cody that they had learned that Mortigan, corrupted and possessed by an Incurro, a banished dark god, had taken the Books of Prophecy from their library. Avia Tor admitted that they were prohibited to directly interfere but asked if Cody could help stop Mortigan and possibly retrieve the books. Cody had been humbled by the experience and agreed to help.

* * *

General Falitte had commed Emelia and informed her that she had to hurry. There was little time before the bombing resumed. She replied that she was running up the boarding ramp of the Black Guard shuttle he had stashed for her as they spoke. Emelia made preparations and lifted the shuttle off the ground. She told Laylee to take the gunnery station. As Laylee did, she felt even more of a conflict toward her programming. She then started having flash memories of Josh Broody and her being happy and smiling and even making love. She uttered out loud accidentally that she loved him. Emelia was preoccupied with ascending through the atmosphere but heard Laylee say something.

She asked Laylee what she had said. Laylee was unsure of what was happening and also unsure of allowing Emelia to know. The fact that she was unsure of anything was odd. She was an android and should not be having such issues. As she thought about the word "android," she again spoke aloud without realizing. She said, "I am a Simulent." Emelia seemed shocked at the claim and asked again what Laylee had said.

Before Laylee could answer, the bombings resumed just as Emelia broke the shuttle from atmosphere into space. Once in near orbit, the shuttle was detected, and Mortigan was notified that a Jaskan was detected on the shuttle. Mortigan was told by the darkness that they had to stop her. It was Emelia, and she could not be allowed to find Epitaph. Mortigan ordered the shuttle fired upon, but it was already moving away. Mortigan was asked if he wanted to cease the bombing. He ordered the bombing continued and a squadron of schisms deployed in pursuit of that shuttle. He was then informed that the Black Guard shuttle was a prototype and had the capability of hyperspace travel. Mortigan sneered at the report and stated that it had better be destroyed before it could jump then.

* * *

Slade, Josh, and Tana had retaken control of the Albejen shell ship and were following the Luth Bik warship to the area in space where the spherical light had taken Cody. Suddenly the Luth Bik warship had received a hail from Cody. The Luth Bik officer informed Slade and opened the hail on both ships. Josh had jumped in and asked Cody where he was at.

Cody told Josh that he was in the spherical light with Avia Tor. "What?!" was the collected response from both Slade and Josh. He admitted that he was involved in matters of prophecy and gods and did not know how to begin an explanation. He told them to send the Luth Bik Resistance warship to join him at Chabreel. Josh said that they would be there also. Cody insisted that Slade and Josh had to stop Epitaph now. Slade stated that they had no idea where to find him. Cody told them that they were brothers united and had to start acting as such and terminated his hail. Slade sent the Luth Bik warship to Chabreel. They admitted that they would need prophet guidance to locate Epitaph.

* * *

Emelia tried evasive maneuvers to escape the squadron of eight schisms that had overtaken her, but the shuttle was not designed for combat flight. The schisms opened laser fire on the shuttle. The damage was minimal, but Emelia knew any more would be fatal. Laylee announced that there was a hyperspace portal opening ahead of them. The schisms broke off their attack as seven Black Guard warships exited hyperspace. They prepared engagement maneuvers against Mortigan's Black Guard warships. Schisms were launched from both sides. Emelia hailed the warship in the rear of the formation. They declared that they were loyal to Epitaph and asked her intentions. Emelia said her intentions were to find Epitaph and put him back in charge. She admitted that in order to do that she would need a lift. She was given permission to dock. Laylee mentioned that this shuttle seemed to have something similar to a hyperspace drive. Files on board referred to it as a morph drive with hyperspace access. Emelia claimed she was more comfortable with traditional and proven forms of hyperspace travel for the moment.

After landing in the docking bay, the commander of the warship approached her and stated the fleet had been informed of their departure from the battle and the reason for it. He asked Emelia where they could take her. Emelia felt the link increase in strength and said they needed to get to Gelemar. The commander seemed to be a bit confused and told Emelia that he believed that Gelemar was near the border of Ubide and Derth space. Emelia responded by stating it was a little further in Ubide and Derth space. She ordered the course plotted and assumed command of the ship.

Chapter Thirty-One

A Sealed Fate

ON THE ALBEJEN shell ship, Slade had suggested they find a place to hide while they figured out how they were going to find Epitaph or a prophet to assist them. They were not far from Aklowda, and that had put them in the outer region of Ubide and Derth space. The Albejen had greatly detailed data on much of the universe. Slade brought up a map on screen of Ubide and Derth space. An appealing choice was a planet in a remote region with only two moons. It was classified as desolate and former homeworld to the Lashar race. Lashars were humanoid in form with dark shiny skin almost slippery to the touch and could morph into black slime. Reports from the Albejen section on Gelemar claimed that most of the Lashars had been removed from the planet by Ubides or by necessity. It also appeared that the Ubides had abandoned a great number of sectors around Gelemar. A dark, desolate, and remote planet was a good place to hide. Slade set course.

* * *

Gold Gatling's command of the Luth Bik Resistance aligned ships had just entered the Chabreel system and witnessed, like Gold had said, Black Guard ships in a civil war with each other. He was still on the Luth Bik warship and instructed the Luth Bik lieutenant to identify ship allegiance. He claimed only six of the seven expected that were loyal to Epitaph. There were five loyal to Mortigan, and he highlighted them on screen.

Gold asked, "Which one was Mortigan on?" Call signs were not being used in this battle, so they could not locate the *Dark Wish 2* in that manner. It was tough in the battle to determine the command ship. Mortigan would not be using standard Black Guard ship formation.

Gold said, "Well, let us get to know our enemy." He sent out a general hail stating that they were the Luth Bik Resistance first wave and ordered surrender.

The Luth Bik lieutenant reminded him that they were the only wave. Gold threw his hands up and into the air. He asked with disbelief if they had never heard of bluffing. The Luth Bik lieutenant replied that Luth Biks did not bluff in combat. Gold, in response, lowered his head into his hands. He rose his head up again and told the Luth Bik lieutenant to pay attention in his class of bluffing. He added that they might just win a war.

Gold's original intent paid off as they were receiving a hail from Mortigan. He told the Luth Bik comm officer to open and track it. It was a visual hail, and Mortigan stood hunched behind a crying and severely bruised ten-cycle-old Honsho girl with blood in her long and straggled blond hair. It was clear to Gold that she had been beaten. He demanded Mortigan released her at once. Mortigan claimed he was not done with her yet. Mortigan's gruesome image had seared itself into Gold's mind.

Gold stressed his demand again: "You will stop beating her and release her to me."

Mortigan grew scarier as he laughed with an increase of dark shadow flowing from his eyes, and the Honsho girl increased her crying state. Mortigan then offered a trade of Gold himself for the girl. Gold agreed instantly. Mortigan continued to laugh and said that he would send a shuttle.

He then added that the girl was strong. He had beaten her and removed her four thumbs. The image of her butchered hands was now driving rage in Gold. Gold swore that he would kill him. Mortigan continued and said that even with the removal of her thumbs, she would not break. He said he had to do more before the girl would admit that Gold was her father. Gold had a deep fear that rose from his gut and rested just below his anger. He asked Mortigan what he had done. Mortigan pulled back on the girl's long blond hair, and she screamed in fear and pain. Mortigan yelled at her to tell her daddy what he had done. She continued to cry and scream. He pulled harder on her hair as Gold could only watch in terror.

Mortigan then screamed again, "Tell your daddy what I did!"

The girl through her crying voice screamed out that he had raped her. Gold wanted to jump through the viewscreen. Mortigan continued to laugh. He said he had indeed raped her over and over and over again. He threw the girl off to the side of view and said he might just get inside her one more time before he sent that shuttle. Gold replied that Mortigan might not be so pleased once he was standing face to face with him. Mortigan terminated the transmission.

* * *

Emelia had entered Laylee's provided quarters on the Black Guard warship and asked her if she had run diagnostics on her programming. Laylee said that she had done so and all was well. Emelia claimed she did not believe her at all. Laylee stated that she was an android and would not be able to lie. Emelia agreed with the statement but added that Laylee was indeed programmed to lie to infiltrate and to survive perceived threats. Emelia then followed by asking why Laylee was seeing her as a perceived threat.

Laylee admitted that she was conflicted by memory flashes of being with Josh Broody. Emelia ignored the part about being with Josh and stated that her memory had been wiped and as a result she should not be experiencing any memory flashes of anything before reactivation. She added that memories could not flash uncontrollably anyway; she would have to intently recall them. Emelia then asked Laylee to recite her primary directive. Laylee struggled and could only get out Josh's name.

Emelia followed by asking, "Are you an android or a—what did you call yourself in the shuttle—oh yes, a Simulent?"

Laylee paused. Emelia gave a yelling tone command to answer the question.

Laylee seemed to have trouble saying the word but eventually answered with "Android."

Emelia smiled and admitted she was pleased. She was departing and then turned back and asked what Simulent actually meant. Laylee said that Simulent was a token term for androids. Emelia continued to smile. Emelia claimed that she had looked into the databanks they had retrieved from Xotosia. At Laylee's point of initial construction, there was an interesting report of androids believing they were alive and those that had rerouted programming to believe that, had actually taken the term Simulent as a state of being. Emelia asked if Laylee was conflicted between the two terms. Laylee remained silent. Emelia then commanded her to shut herself down. Laylee seemed hesitant. Emelia then pointed out that androids upon command would shut themselves down, where Simulents would not do it except by their own choice. Emelia's smile had disappeared. She told Laylee to shut herself down by command or choice. Emelia then revealed an ion pistol that she had taken from concealment under her jacket and set it to stun. She then told Laylee that one way or another, she would be shutting down. Laylee paused before lunging forward at Emelia but was shut down with a single shot from the Ion pulse. Her charging motion stiffened, and she lowered her head as her power shut down, and doing so in mid lunge had also caused her to drop to the floor.

* * *

Cody and Avia Tor had arrived in the spherical light at Chabreel and observed the situation. Two Black Guard fleets were firing upon each other, while a fleet of various ships assembled around a Luth Bik warship with their shields up and weapons readied according to scans. The mixed ships seemed to be holding position just off from the Black Guard warship battle, perhaps waiting for one faction to fall before engaging the other.

Avia Tor could not take the chance and flew the spherical light into the main battle. Cody assumed firing controls and fired heavy solid blasts of light energy at both factions of Black Guard warships and schisms, while Avia Tor maneuvered rapidly and evasively around them.

The commanders on warships of both factions had evaluated the spherical light as a threat and agreed to temporarily call a truce and fire against it and the Luth Bik Resistance. The Black Guard warships adjusted position. The Luth Bik warship and its allied ships did the same. Just as they did, another Luth Bik warship entered the system from a hyperspace portal and joined the Luth Bik Resistance formation.

* * *

Epitaph had sensed that the implant in his brain had been activated and that Emelia was on her way. He had also heard rumblings in the overhead levels of the downed orbital station. Before the final power drained, he was able to locate a weapons locker and opened it. He walked in and armed himself with a blaster rifle and four grenades. He also placed a blaster pistol in a concealed holster at the backside of his armor and concealed it further with his cape. He then heard something outside the weapons locker and stepped out with his blaster rifle charged and ready.

His dark vision saw four humanoid bodies of movement in an attempt to surround him. They were the planet's main race of Lashars. Their shiny black skin aided them to hide in the pitch-black darkness, but just as they could see Epitaph with their dark vision, he could see them with his. There was plenty of equipment and stations to maneuver around. Epitaph fired his blaster rifle and hit one as it ran between cover. The Lashar fell to the ground. Epitaph quickly reacted and turned to blast another one from its leaping attack toward him. That one also fell. There were two more out there as Epitaph crouched down and began to use the equipment and stations as his cover as well. He slowly walked through the area and carefully looked around each corner. He turned to another noise and stepped into a puddle of black slime. As he tried to move, the black slime crawled up his leg and onto his back before morphing into the Lashar that now grappled him around the throat. Another puddle of black slime across from him morphed into another Lashar form and jumped forward at him, struggling to disarm the blaster rifle from his grip.

Between the two Lashars and their strength and holds, Epitaph was taken to the ground as they tried to pin him. His forked tongue flicked wildly as the first Lashar continued to tighten the choking grip around his throat and prevented him from use of his dark chanting powers. Epitaph's blaster rifle was now on the floor in front of him.

Suddenly, the lights from the Albejen shell ship that was flying overhead and surveying the land had pierced through the many shattered openings in the fallen station. The light was bright and forced the Lashars to release their grips on Epitaph as they scattered away into the darkened areas. Epitaph was able to recover and get back to his feet with the blaster rifle before the bright lights vanished as the ship moved away.

Epitaph ran to the outside darkness and looked for the ship that had passed by, believing it could have been Emelia. He saw it land just beyond the dead trees. As he looked down, he also saw a pool of black slime crawling toward him. He shot the slime with multiple energy bolts from his blaster rifle. He then saw more movement within the fallen station. About three forms were jumping around as they moved toward his position. Before they could get outside, he threw one of his grenades inside. The concussion grenade exploded with a blast radius within the fallen station area where Epitaph had first encountered the Lashars. He threw a second one in as well for good measure and at the other end of the section.

A barrage of blaster bolts now hit Epitaph and the ground around him. He dropped the blaster rifle as a result. His armor was absorbing much of the shots, but not all. He dodged for cover of the outer terrain and spotted two Lashars on top of the fallen station, both armed with blaster rifles of their own. Epitaph released a hail of his own blaster bolts from the blaster pistol that he had concealed under his cape. He ran again toward the fallen station and pressed his back up against the outer walls. He could hear the two forms above him moving but unable to get a shot on him as long as he was pressed up against the wall. As he further sidestepped his way along the wall and aimed upward, he stepped into what he thought was one of the many puddles of water across the dark planet terrain. It, in fact, was not water but another puddle of slime that again morphed into a Lashar as it crawled up Epitaph's leg. The Lashar again pulled Epitaph to the ground and away from the wall that he had been using as cover. The two Lashars fired down another barrage of blaster bolts on and around him as the Lashar that had taken him down again morphed into the form of black slime and scurried away. Epitaph, with a weakened armor and in a hurried defense against the blaster fire on him, had thrown his third grenade upward. The concussion grenade again exploded, and the two Lashars were caught in the explosion. One fell back as the other fell to the ground, morphing into black slime as it did so.

The sounds of gunfire and explosions had drawn attention. Epitaph noticed three figures cautiously approaching through the dead trees. The Matrasus moved with a stalking hunt pattern, often crouching down and crawling. The other was a human he did not immediately recognize and seemingly shining a light from a device on his lower left arm. Epitaph was more alarmed as he saw Josh Broody cross the path of light with a blaster pistol drawn and advancing with them. Epitaph moved silently back inside the fallen orbital station.

* * *

A shuttle landed on one of the Black Guard warships and an unarmed Gold Gatling was escorted off without his jumpband by two of the Darkest in Black Guard armor but armed with the solid shadow staffs. Two other male Honshos were with him. Mortigan then walked forward and was dragging Gold's little daughter along with him. Mortigan threw her in front of his own feet. Her garments were shredded, she was covered with blood and bruises, and she was still bound at the wrists and ankles with energy cuffs. Gold lunged forward again, threatening to kill him, but was held back and restrained by the Darkest and could only watch Dyam cry out, "Daddy!".

Mortigan tossed a pair of energy binds to one of the Darkest and instructed him to bind Gold's wrists. Once that was done, Gold demanded the trade of himself for his daughter. Mortigan's evil smile accessorized his shadow-dripping eyes. He reached down and caressed the side of the little girl's neck. He said that he was going to miss little Dyam, but she would forever remember him. Evil laughter followed his remarks as he licked the side of her face and then kicked her forward. She was still bound but able to crawl forward as the Darkest brought Gold closer to Mortigan. The two other Honshos rushed forward and picked Dyam up from the floor. They rushed her into the Black Guard shuttle. Mortigan then motioned to the docking bay control to allow the shuttle to launch. Mortigan walked away with the two Darkest forcing Gold along. They stopped at an observation deck, and Gold continued to watch as the shuttle departed the docking bay and headed back toward one of the Honsho freighters away from the battle. Suddenly, Mortigan's laugh grew louder just before the shuttle exploded.

Gold screamed out, "Noooooo!"

Mortigan then ordered Gold taken to a hatch and spaced.

* * *

Emelia had a naked Laylee on a table with her head opened. Emelia finished reprogramming her again with electronic waves and other tools. She severed the wire from Laylee and the computer. As Emelia closed up Laylee's head, she was informed by a Black Guard officer that they had arrived at Gelemar, but the unknown shell ship was already on planet. They had detected many life signs clustered together. They were still trying to differentiate the lifeforms. Emelia said that Epitaph was one of them and she sensed through their link that he was in trouble. Emelia ordered her shuttle prepared at once and the warship to remain at far orbit. Emelia then activated Laylee.

Laylee's eyes opened and she sat up on the table. Emelia asked Laylee to recite her prime directive.

Laylee said still with her exotic accent but in a calm and cold tone, "Kill Josh Broody."

Emelia threw Laylee a Black Guard gray prisoner jumpsuit. She told her to get dressed and follow her to the shuttle.

Chapter Thirty-Two

Resolutions

THE SPACE BATTLE at the Chabreel system raged on. The schisms had drawn the spherical light away from the warships and swarmed around it, but the spherical light displayed maneuverability unmatched to any known starfighter. As it moved so evasively, it continued to hit them with its beams of solid light energy, taking many of them out. Another wave of schisms had engaged the two Kemyyon freighter-sized attack ships and the Jaskan pleasure cruiser that had already taken severe damage and was acting more now as a rescue ship for escape pods and ejected pilots and gunners from the Luth Bik shards. A wave of Luth Bik shards flew in attacking the schisms and drawing them off the Jaskan pleasure cruiser.

The Black Guard warships had decimated the Luth Bik science ship, and it was under evacuation. The remaining ships continued to battle. The third Honsho freighter that had positioned away from the battle moved back into position after the Black Guard shuttle it was waiting for exploded. The three Honsho freighters united together and displayed the ferocity of the Honsho Piracy as they engaged one of the Black Guard warships and forced it from formation. More Black Guard warships were entering from hyperspace portals away from the battle but were engaged by more Luth Bik aligned warships that entered there as well.

The biggest blow was delivered as the severely damaged and failing Canian battleship plowed through three of the Black Guard warships that had been the most damaged before the Black Guard factions had joined together. The collision path was massive and sent out explosions all around it. Battling shards and schisms from both sides were taken out as well. The Canian ship had been destroyed but had taken out three Black Guard warships with it, and very few escape pods had been released from either side.

Mortigan was informed that his Black Guard warship had taken severe damage and was attempting to withdraw, but increasing Luth Bik firepower from shard starfighters was hampering its movements. Mortigan refused to evacuate despite the pleas of his Darkest.

Elsewhere on the ship, two of the Darkest had removed the energy binds and prepared to open an airlock and throw Gold out of it. The hull suddenly breached in front of them, and all three started to be sucked out. All three of them had clung onto internal fixtures as debris and other Darkest were sucked passed them and into space. Gold had locked his arm tightly around a thick ship conduit and was able to tear away his pant leg and reveal the jumpband that he normally wore on his upper shoulder, now worn on his lower leg. He watched as the two male Darkest lost their grip and were sucked into space. The section of conduit that Gold had braced himself to exploded as the ship was hit from the outside. Gold started to be pulled into space but was able to activate his jumpband.

Gold fell through the teleport portal of light established in the sucking path toward exposed space and tumbled out from another one to another section of the ship and witnessed the Darkest there fleeing for escape pods and docking bays. They were paying no interest to him. Most of them despite their solid shadow staffs, still wore the Black Guard armor and weapons. Gold was able to trip one and get on top of him. Two others did help their companion by swinging their solid shadow staffs at Gold. Gold, though, had seen their attack, and as they swung, Gold had again teleported away through a portal of light and they struck each other. They were stunned and fell onto their comrade.

Gold had teleported onto another ship level by diving out of a portal of light. He tumbled up to his feet. He had managed to take a Black Guard axe with him that he had pulled from the soldier he had tripped. Again, the ship was taking heavy damage and the Darkest were more interested in their own evacuation than that of Gold Gatling. Gold accessed a computer panel in the corridor and detected Mortigan's location.

Gold had retuned the jumpband to his upper arm and rushed through the corridors and reached a walkway above the war room that Mortigan was monitoring the battle from. The darkness inside Mortigan warned him that Gold was close. As he turned to look around, Gold had leapt over the railing and jumped down onto him, driving the Black Guard axe into his back and rolling away as Mortigan dropped to his knees. Gold saw Darkest troopers rushing toward him and scrambled for the control panel on the nearest wall. He brought up a forcefield barrier around the center section of the war room. The Darkest that were not fleeing had been blocked by an energy forcefield dome. They could only watch as Gold circled around Mortigan, who had struggled back to his feet with the axe still stuck in his back. They were alone inside the forcefield dome.

Mortigan laughed in defiance. He then began to walk in a circle, matching Gold's movement. As he did so, he pulled the Black Guard axe from his back with great agony and threw it at the center of the floor between them. Mortigan claimed that the darkness was with him and would not let him die. Gold ran toward the axe, and Mortigan rushed toward him. Gold tumbled by Mortigan and picked the axe up as he did. Gold returned to his feet and smiled. He stated that if Mortigan could not die because of the darkness inside of him, then he would not have moved for the axe. Mortigan again laughed in response. He moved toward Gold as Gold circled around him again to make his way to the central command console. Mortigan continued to walk around Gold's location and, with each lap, drew closer. Gold waited until he was close enough and threw the axe at his head. Mortigan used the darkness to catch the axe. He then threw it back at Gold. Gold had leapt through the air and toward the axe thrown at him. He managed to grab onto it just as he activated the jumpband again, but this time he did not vanish through a portal completely. The portal of light was not stable as usual and shimmered as it extended beyond Mortigan as well. Gold was in a ghostly transparent state and passed through Mortigan with the still solid axe in hand. He landed on his feet and stepped out from the extended portal and Mortigan's body, as he transformed back to a tangible state. Gold stood behind him covered in Mortigan's own blood. Mortigan hunched forward and staggered about before regaining his stability. He was bleeding from the chest as well as his back. Gold admitted that he was unsure if adjusting the materialization mid jump would work. Gold then charged Mortigan while he was still disoriented and drove the axe straight into the top of Mortigan's head. Mortigan collapsed to the floor, and a humanoid-shaped shadow stepped out from him. It moved toward Gold, as it transformed to a wide floating shadow form. Gold stood ready with his fingers again activating his jumpband and stepped into another standard teleport portal of light that closed just before the shadow slammed against the forcefield dome. Gold stepped out from another opened portal just outside the forcefield. The shadow hit the forcefield but could not pass through. The shadow took a spiral formation and tried desperately to exit the forcefield dome from other points. Gold revealed that he had also taken a remote-control device from the central command station and activated the self-destruct. The self-destruct countdown started. The shadow moved back into Mortigan's body. Gold now laughed. The shadow was what was keeping Mortigan alive; once it left, Mortigan's body died. The shadow could control the living but could not reanimate the dead. The shadow spiral form again desperately tried to escape the forcefield with no success. Gold took off running down the corridor.

* * *

The two Luth Bik warships over Chabreel had taken down two more Black Guard warships. The Black Guard warship that had been attacked by the three Honsho freighters had destroyed one of them before it too exploded. The Luth Bik shards had herded the schisms back against the remaining Black Guard warships. The spherical light ship was still chased by another squadron of schisms, and they were all hit by the explosion of the self-destructing Black Guard warship, the *Dark Wish 2*. The spherical light ship survived with much damage as its light flickered out and it crashed into one of the minimal hull breaches of a Luth Bik warship.

Cody crawled out from the spherical ship, now lightless. The translucent pilot was also gone, but Cody felt different as his brown fur began to glow. He could feel another presence joined with him. It was that of the being he had called Avia Tor. Another being, though, was crawling from the spherical ship wreckage. It was Gold Gatling. He had fried his jumpband on his last teleport attempt to get off the Black Guard warship. The closest jumping point was the passing spherical ship.

Reports were coming in from the other battle set aside from Chabreel as well. Black Guard ships that had not been destroyed were surrendering. The Luth Bik Resistance was sending comms out reporting the victory at Chabreel. They were also receiving comms from other systems that Black Guard ships and bases were falling or surrendering to other forces aligned with the Luth Bik Resistance.

* * *

Emelia had landed her Black Guard shuttle on the surface of Gelemar and near the wreckage of the downed orbital station where she was detecting Epitaph. Emelia and Laylee disembarked and approached the fallen orbital station. They increased to a running speed when they heard blaster fire.

Inside the fallen station, Josh had shot a Lashar that had gotten a surprise attack on Tana. He helped her back to her feet. He then saw Emelia and Laylee running toward the structure from the outside. The sight of Laylee pleased him, but Emelia running alongside her was confusing. He looked back at Tana. The three women he had loved were converging together.

As they entered, Josh hollered out to Emelia. Both Emelia and Laylee looked toward him. Josh slowly approached with his blaster holstered and his arms outstretched to his sides. He tried to reach the Emelia he had known before Epitaph had claimed her as his own. Tana stood behind him, ready to pounce. Both Josh and Tana sensed something was wrong. Laylee had remained silent, and her approach matched that of Emelia's. Emelia continued to move to the side with her blaster pistols drawn but lowered to her side. As they drew closer, Laylee ran forward and directly toward Josh. She stopped suddenly before him. Josh and Tana were both happy to see her but uncertain of the situation.

Laylee stared at Josh and Tana without saying a word. Josh spoke her name first. Suddenly without warning and with lightning speed, Laylee clutched Josh's throat. Tana tried to stop her but found herself being shot with blaster fire by Emelia. Tana ran for cover, and Emelia ran after her, never ceasing the barrage of blaster fire.

Laylee had one hand clutching tightly at Josh's throat. She was repeating her command to kill Josh Broody. He was trying to pull her hand free with both of his hands, but her strength was too great. He had already been taken to his knees. He gasped for what air he could get. Several pulsating energy blasts then hit Laylee from the rear. Slade had engaged his war arm. Laylee picked Josh up with her one hand still clutching Josh's throat. She turned to place Josh's nearly limp body in the line of Slade's pulsating energy blasts. Slade stopped shooting. Laylee was still repeating her command to kill Josh Broody as she threw him at Slade's direction.

Josh's limp body fell near Slade. Slade checked Josh over, and he was still alive, just unconscious. Laylee walked toward Slade and looked down at Josh's body. She said, "Kill Josh Broody!" She then stepped on his chest and continued to apply pressure. Slade engaged the blade on his war arm and stabbed Laylee through the neck. Electricity shot from all around her neck as well from her mouth, nose, ears, and eyes. Slade pushed her back off Josh and finally retracted the blade. Laylee fell motionless with all her internal circuitry fried. Slade went to again check on Josh. He was then shot at from an above level. The blaster bolt dropped him next to Josh. Two more blaster bolts hit him as he tried to locate sight on his attacker.

Further back in the fallen station structure, Emelia had lost track of Tana. She was slowly stalking through the darkness. She had holstered her blaster pistols and drawn her katana-like sword. Emelia was blinded by the dark but had honed all of her senses. One hand held the katana, while the other felt ahead of her for obstacles or beings. Her footsteps were slow and deliberate as each small step registered the terrain ahead of her. Emelia was drawing heavily on smell, touch, and sound.

Emelia turned quickly to a sound of movement. As she did, she was grabbed around the throat from behind and tossed to the floor. Tana had better hearing and scent to hunt with. She also had dark vision. Tana had used her foot claws to attack Emelia's wrist and forced the katana-like sword to fall from her hand. Tana's two hand claws slashed into Emelia's face and chest. Tana leapt away. Emelia rolled over and started to stand. She drew both her blaster pistols and shot into the dark ahead of her. She heard something that was hit ahead of her. She holstered one pistol and knelt down. She kept her main pistol raised and reached out to feel what she had shot. She felt the burns on the body. She had hit it with both shots but seemed questioned by what she felt as a slippery humanoid form. It was not the Matrasus she had been stalking. She tensed up as she heard something, but Tana had already leapt forward and taken Emelia down on her back. Emelia had fired one shot off from her blaster before it was knocked from her hand. Emelia had heard the savage scream and now felt a panting breath above her. Tana was on top of her, but from the growling and breathing, Emelia could tell that she had hit her with that blast. Two deep, puncturing claws then pierced her midsection and she felt Tana's claws ripping inside of her. Emelia's scream was silenced as Tana's sharp teeth cut across her throat.

* * *

Slade was wounded by the three energy bolts. His armor was what had saved him. He was on the ground and next to Josh's still unconscious body. He heard something above him from where he had been shot. He still could not see through the darkness, but someone was trying to chant, "Ssaiyai lissith ffleess copssnaith!" Each word seemed as if it was hard to get out. Slade suddenly felt his armor beginning to burn away.

The chant stopped, and Epitaph's head flung forward just as his wide opened mouth returned to normal. He was too weak to continue the chant and use his dark powers. The shots and bruises he had suffered from the Lashars had taken a great toll. Epitaph was struggling to breathe but still pulled himself back up to the railing where he had braced a blaster rifle that he had taken from a fallen Lashar. He regained his composure and his forked tongue flicked rapidly as he smiled with his wide reptilian grin. Epitaph had lost sight of his opponents even with his dark vision, but he knew they had dropped behind the rubble. He threw his last concussion grenade, and it exploded. The radius burst threw everything around.

Epitaph smiled wider. He said, "Ssso muchch for dessstinysss, brothersss." He leaned back against the backside railing and tried to strengthen his breathing.

The dual moonlight had shifted and now had broken through the cracks of the fallen station wreckage. Epitaph had managed to climb down and approached the debris where he had thrown the grenade. He still held the blaster rifle in his lowered hand. He stepped through the debris and pulled Slade's battered body from atop of Josh's. As Slade's body was pulled away, Josh raised his blaster and shot Epitaph through the head. Epitaph dropped dead next to Slade's body. The armor on Slade was shredded and his body cut. His internal cyborg parts showed damage; even his tissue and metal bonded cyborg brain was damaged but intact. Slade was still alive, barely but alive. Slade had thrown himself over Josh's body to protect Josh from the blast. The prophecy had completed. As the prophecy stated, "One brother will lay over the other, and the dark lord will perish before them." Epitaph had been taken down by the two brothers. True—only one brother had killed him, but the other brother had kept him safe to do so.

Tana had staggered out with a blaster burn at her left side. She had Emelia bleeding and draped over her shoulder. Emelia was not dead but severely wounded. Josh was slowly crawling over toward Slade to check on him, still shocked at how much of Slade was cybernetic and how little was flesh. It was his soul that still made him human. Luth Bik soldiers had landed and moved inside the structure with medical aid. One Luth Bik officer said that the Black Guard warship in orbit had left upon the arrival of their fleet. He reported that they learned of Emelia's destination through the Black Guard files they had obtained. They informed Josh and Tana that the Black Guard had fallen. Emelia's badly wounded body was taken into custody. She would stand trial for her crimes. Laylee's fried android body was also taken away.

* * *

Rotations passed as Slade, Josh and Tana healed. There had been great strides of improvement in the cybernetic field, and Slade's parts were replaced. They were able to reboot his own cybernetic brain components, and he seemed to have all of his memories. Josh and Tana had reunited with a glowing lighted and almost shimmering crystal fur version of Cody. Cody revealed everything about the god he called Avia Tor and then prepared them for the shock. Avia Tor had merged with Cody and now granted him extraordinary powers. Cody was charged with the duty of protecting the universe. He informed Josh that he would be setting out on his own because of the great responsibility he had of being a walking god through the stars. They shared in their grief of departure but knew they would always be friends. One thing he could not do was bring Laylee back, and they were saddened by that.

Gold Gatling had come to Slade after his recovery and introduced himself. He told Slade about the switch and about his time on Slade's world. He had seen how much Slade was loved, and it saddened him that he had no way to send Slade back. They were interrupted by Josh and Tana. Slade apologized for killing Laylee. Josh and Slade hugged. Josh had accepted that what Emelia had done to

Laylee's programming had stripped away the Laylee he knew. Slade excused himself.

Tana hung on Josh's arm as Josh admitted to Gold that he was still unsure that he was in reality. Gold asked what he had meant. Josh continued his point. First, there was the fact that he had heard Gold was sorry that he could not return Slade to the planet called Home. Then there was the rumor that Gold Gatling had a daughter. On top of all that, Gold Gatling had pushed for an ambassador-ship role in the new government being constructed under Luth Bik guidance. Gold had requested the ambassadorship be granted to a Honsho woman named Vally Wait, who he claimed to love.

Gold responded that it was all true. His daughter had survived the shuttle explosion with the aid of two loyal Honshos and their jumpbands. His daughter had a lot of physical and even more men-tal and emotional healing to go through after all that Mortigan had done, but she still wished to be a pirate. The Honsho charter listed that she would have to work her way up through another legion. To keep her safe from being used against the most famous and legendary pirate, she would take an assumed name of Dyam Wailing. Gold had already made plans and called in favors to keep an eye on her from afar.

Gold then asked if Josh and Tana were going to take a role in the new government. Josh looked at Tana and claimed that they were better suited to explore the wilds of space. Josh then turned it around quickly and asked Gold Gatling for his plans. Gold admitted that he had an important role with all his clout to find a way that the Honsho Piracy and the legions under it, as well as his own, could survive under the new government's rules. They parted with a palm on each other's shoulders.

Slade had been walking through the halls of the medical facility, saddened by the fact that he could not return home. Cody called him into an isolated wing of the facility. He said that he could return Slade home. He could only risk opening a portal once, but Slade deserved to be with those he loved and that loved him.

Cody held out his open palm, and his hand began to glow a bright and intense light. From the light, a portal opened. Slade thanked Cody and wished them all luck with their new futures. Slade stepped through the portal, and it closed behind him. A sphere of light then erected around the crystal and light version of Cody. It lifted with Cody inside it and darted away.

Slade stepped out from another portal by a large tree on his world called Home. Erikai and Eva both rushed into his arms.

Elsewhere in the Universe

A CRASHED ESCAPE pod on a barren and rogue asteroid was overshadowed. Captain Krissondra Gwen had been waiting for her distress call to be answered. The pod was lifted by tractor beam and pulled into a Black Guard warship. She stepped onto a docking bay and was greeted by a female Imu, which was a humanoid being but looked like a rotting and walking corpse, a male Dovol that looked exactly like a red devil, a male Canian with dark-black shaggy fur, and former Fright Agent Maddo. Maddo welcomed her aboard the renamed warship, the *Horro*. He said they needed her to help rescue Emelia. She agreed, and he welcomed her to the Fright Agency.

The End

The Fright Agency—as well as Josh, Tana, and Cody—will return in book four. Be a witness in book three to the future of Home. The children of Slade—Eva, Erikai, and Rayk—will experience their first adventure.

Coming Soon
Book Three
Shadowed Stars: The Children of Home

About the Author

STEVEN KOUTZ IS originally from St. Paul, Minnesota, USA. He has been writing stories for as long as he can remember. Although he writes many different genres, his favorite is science fiction. He was inspired by watching many different shows and movies old and new. He likes to write his science fiction with continuity and serialization of characters and events. He enjoys characters that are always growing. He will also add small hints of old black-and-white classic auras hidden in tales of more modern and graphic flavor. He also likes to work in elements of other genres that he can fit in a science fiction tale, such as western, horror, and romance. His hobbies are collecting comic books, action figures, busts, and trading cards. He also plays many trading and customizable card games as well as many various role-playing games, miniature games, and elaborate board games. His passion is storytelling in the science fiction genre. He is a fan of many of the sci-fi franchises and has always wanted to write his own series, and that is the book you hold now, *Shadowed Stars: The Reign of the Black Guard,* which is book two of at least an eight-book series. There are many other titles planned beyond the eight numbered ones. Steven has assigned one set of characters for even-numbered books and another set of characters for the odd-numbered ones. They are structured that way for the reader and Steven to avoid tire and overuse of the same characters. Steven also feels it keeps his writing fresh and wets an appetite for characters loved by the reader as they wait for their favorite character's return. Steven also likes to let the story flow and write itself with just moderate control.

CPSIA information can be obtained
at www.ICGtesting.com
Printed in the USA
BVHW080600220721
612425BV00001B/49